MONICA DICKENS

The Follyfoot Collection

FOLLYFOOT
DORA AT FOLLYFOOT
THE HORSES OF FOLLYFOOT
STRANGER AT FOLLYFOOT

DEAN

Dean in association with
Heinemann Young Books

Follyfoot first published in 1971.
Dora at Follyfoot first published in 1972.
The Horses of Follyfoot first published in 1975.
Stranger at Follyfoot first published in 1976.
This edition published in 1991 by Dean
an imprint of Reed Consumer Books Limited
Michelin House, 81 Fulham Road, London SW3 6RB
and Auckland, Melbourne, Singapore and Toronto
Reprinted in 1992, 1993

ISBN 0 603 55030 4

Printed in Great Britain by The Bath Press

CONTENTS

FOLLYFOOT 7
DORA AT FOLLYFOOT 147
THE HORSES OF FOLLYFOOT 283
STRANGER AT FOLLYFOOT 425

Follyfoot

I

On these early spring Sundays, there were usually a few visitors who came to the farm at the top of the hill.

Some of them were regulars, horse-lovers and children with carrots and apples and sugar for all the horses, and special snacks for their favourites. Peppermints for Cobbler's Dream. Soft stale biscuits for Lancelot, who was too old to have much use of his teeth.

Some of the people who came into the yard under the stone archway were strangers who had been driving by, saw the sign, 'Home of Rest for Horses', and stopped to see what it was all about.

'What's it all about then?' The two boys who had roared up on a motorbike were not the sort of people who usually came to the farm. Nothing much doing here. Daft really, the whole outfit. 'What's it all about?' The taller boy swaggered across the yard as if he had come to buy the place: cracked leather jacket with half the studs fallen out, cheap shiny boots, long seaweed hair, a scrubby fringe of beard that wouldn't grow.

'Saving lives,' Steve muttered, not loud enough for them to understand. They wouldn't understand anyway, that kind. Steve went on sweeping the cobbles, his head down, dark hair falling into his eyes.

'Huh?' The shorter, thicker boy looked as if his mother should have had his adenoids out long ago.

'Horses that are too old to work, or too badly treated – we give them a good life.'

'Daft, innit?' The boys went jeering towards the loose boxes that lined three sides of the yard.

9

'Willy. Spot. Ranger. Wonderboy.' The younger boy, about sixteen, with a stupid hanging lip, spelled out the names above the stable doors, to show he could read. 'Cobles Dram. Whoever heard of a name like that?'

'Cobbler's Dream.' Callie came out of the stable, where she had been brushing the mud off the chestnut pony, whose favourite rolling places would delight a hippopotamus. 'And everybody's heard of him. He was on television. He was in all the newspapers for catching a horse thief.'

'Thrills.' When the boy hung his big cropped head and looked up at her with his slow eyes, she thought for a moment she knew him. Where had she seen that broad earthy face with the thick lips hanging open, because he could not breathe through his pudgy nose?

One of the boys threw up a hand and the pony flicked back his ears and jerked his head away.

'That's not the way to go up to a horse,' Callie said. 'Especially Cobby. He's half blind.'

'Don't tell me about horses,' the boy grunted. 'We've got dozens of 'em at home.'

'Bad luck on *them*.' Usually Callie was polite to the visitors. Her mother was married to the Colonel, who ran this farm, and Callie loved to take people round the stables or down the muddy track to the fields, and tell them the history of each of the twenty horses, or as much as they would listen to.

But these boys would not listen to any of it. When she started to tell them about Wonderboy, who had been her father's famous steeplechaser before he died, and Ranger with the ruined mouth, and Spot, the circus rosinback with the rump as broad as a table, the taller boy said, 'Oh shut up, you silly kid,' and the younger one stuck out a boot and tripped Callie up as she turned to go on to the mule's box.

'What the hell are you playing at?' Steve was there in

10

seconds, holding the broom like a weapon, his clear blue eyes hard with anger.

'Don't touch me,' the boy whined, 'or I'll call the coppers.'

'I'll call them myself if you don't get out of here.'

'Can't wait,' the older boy said. ' "Visitors Welcome", it says on the sign. Some welcome. Come on, Lewis.'

Willy the mule stared sadly over his door, a pocket of air in his lower lip, lop ears sagging. Callie, inspecting her grazed hands for blood and disappointed to find none, yelled after them as they ran under the arch, 'Don't bother to come back!'

'Don't worry!' Lewis yelled back over his shoulder. Yes . . . there was something familiar about him. Where on earth – ?

'Lewis.' She wiped off her hands on the seat of her patched jeans, as if she were wiping off the disgustingness of Lewis.

'Louse,' Steve said.

The motorbike snarled, spat foul smoke and roared away.

2

Dora, the girl who worked with Steve in the stables, had been home for the weekend, but she came back on an early bus, to help with the feeds. She would rather be here than at home anyway. The Colonel had to force her to take an occasional weekend at her parents' flat in the industrial town which sprawled along the valley, to keep her mother from storming up the hill to complain.

Steve's mother did not come, and he had no father. This was his home, and his family. Cobbler's Dream, the pony he had rescued from a spoiled and vicious child, was the horse he loved best.

It was going to be a wet night, so Dora brought the rest of the old horses in from the fields. She was coming round the corner of the barn with the two Shetlands, a handful of shaggy mane in each hand, when a car stopped in the road and a man walked into the yard. A worn-looking horsey type of man, with bow legs and a lean brown face.

'I'm sorry, we're closed to visitors.' Dora shoved one Shetland into its stable with a slap on its bustling bottom, and made a grab for the long tangled tail of the other, as it ducked under her arm and headed for the feed shed. 'Shut that door!'

The man moved quickly and shut the door in Jock's square face. Dora got her arms round his neck and practically carried him back to the loose box he shared with Jamie and the tiny donkey. They had tubs on the floor because the manger was too high, and they nipped each other round and round the box, going from tub to tub like a buffet lunch.

'I've come to see the manager,' the bow-legged man said.

'The Colonel?' You were supposed to say he was not at home on Sunday afternoons, but Dora always stated facts, even when they were ruder. 'He's in the house, but he can't see you.'

'Why not?'

'He's probably asleep.'

The man bit his lip, which was cracked and dry, like badly kept leather. 'Could you possibly. . . . It's an emergency. About a horse.'

'Another customer?' Callie came up. The stables at the farm were full, but she always wanted more.

'It's a hard case.' The man looked sad. He looked defeated, as if he had known a lot of disappointments and could not stand any more. 'The mare is in bad trouble.'

'I'll get the Colonel,' Dora said, but Callie said, 'Let me. He hates being woken up, but at least I do it gently.'

The last time a horse was down at night and thrashing in its box, and Dora had shouted in the Colonel's ear, he had sat up and yelled, 'Messerschmitts – take cover!'

The Colonel came out of the back door with his yellow mongrel dog, pulling his worn tweed cap over sleepy eyes. He was a tall thin man with a slight limp from the war, and a scar by his eye where a kick from one of his horses had left him able to move the right side of his face more than the left, so that you could not always tell if he were serious or joking. He limped down the cinder path in his socks because he couldn't find a pair of shoes, walking on his heels with his toes turned up, because the ground was damp.

He and the bow-legged man leaned against posts with their hands in their pockets and talked quietly. Callie put a wheelbarrow in a doorway and pretended to be cleaning out Lancelot's clean stable, so that she could hear.

'. . . but I can't do any more,' the man was saying, 'because I lost my job.'

13

'I'm sorry.' The Colonel waited. He was a good listener.
'Down at the Pinecrest.'

The Pinecrest was an unattractive shabby hotel outside the town, with no pine trees in sight and not on the crest of a hill, but in a swampy valley where a polluted stream ran sluggishly through, gathering more pollution from the garbage that the Pinecrest cook threw out of the back door.

'I was in the stables there. They hire out riding hacks, you know.'

'Yes, I know.' The Colonel made a face as if he would rather not know.

'It's been on my mind,' the groom said. 'I done my best for my horses, but they want to get the last scrap of work out of them, and they're not fit for it.' The Colonel waited. 'Well, you can't feed more than the owner will buy, can you? The pasture is all grazed out and the hay he bought – you wouldn't use it for bedding.'

'They got a licence to run a riding stable?'

'Must do, or they couldn't be in business. I don't know how they got it though, unless they bribed the authorities, *which* I wouldn't put it past them, the kind of people they are.'

'Why did you stay with them?'

'Work's not easy to find.' The groom shrugged. 'I kept my mouth shut, because I needed the job, and my horses needed me. But then I couldn't hold myself in any longer. When I hit that boy of theirs – he was lucky I didn't kill him – they said, "Pack your bags and keep walking." '

'What happened?'

'They've got this old mare, see? A good one once. They got her off the track because she wouldn't race, and they've always kept her down and very poor, so she'd be quiet enough to ride. Quiet! The poor thing can hardly raise a canter. She gets a saddle sore, of course, with that thin thoroughbred skin and no flesh on her. Well, then it's my day

14

off, and this fat lady comes to the hotel. "I want to ride Beauty Queen," she says. Beauty Queen, that's what they call her, though she'd win no prizes anywhere. I come back early with a bag of cracked corn I'd managed to scrounge from a friend of mine who has some poultry, and someone yells, "Hey you! Saddle up Beauty for this lady." "Her back's not healed," I says, shutting the door of my car quick, so they wouldn't see the bag of corn and grab it to make porridge for the guests. "Saddle her up, I told you!" That was their eldest son, name of Todd, very ugly customer. When I refused, he gets the saddle himself and thumps it on that poor old mare's back' – the groom winced, as if he could feel the pain of it himself – 'and leads her out. I grab the rein and start to lead her back inside, and when the boy gets in the doorway to stop me, I knock him sideways.'

'Into the manure heap, I do hope.' Callie was frankly listening now, standing in Lancelot's doorway with a foot on the barrow handle and her chin on the fork.

'Right.' The groom smiled for the first time, then turned back to the Colonel with a long face. 'So I lost my job, and the horses lost me, and Beauty – well, God knows what will happen to her.'

'What about the RSPCA?'

'The Inspector is away. I can't wait, because I'm leaving for Scotland first thing tomorrow. I've a pal up there might have a job for me. So I came to you, because I'd heard what you do here for horses. Will you help?'

'Oh Lord,' the Colonel said. 'I'll try.' He hated trouble and this looked like trouble, but for a horse, he would get into trouble with both feet. Last year, he had got himself knocked out at Westerham Fair, taking on a giant of a man who was dragging off a mare in foal tied to the tail gate of a lorry.

3

'Remember when you pulled that chap out of the driver's cab and found out how big he was?' Steve laughed, remembering, as they drove next day down the long winding hill and headed towards the Pinecrest Hotel.

The Colonel grinned with the agile side of his face. 'I wouldn't have tackled him if I'd known.'

'You would.' Steve drove fast and cheerfully. He liked to drive the little sports car, which the Colonel wasted by driving too cautiously, and he loved to go on rescue missions like this. It made his nerves hum and his body feel light and strong at the same time. If he had lived in olden days, he would have gone off hacking at dragons with a two-bladed sword.

'Don't drive so fast,' the Colonel said. 'I've got to think out how I'm going to handle this.'

'Why can't we just march in, demand to see the horses, and if the mare's condition is as bad as the groom said, take her away? I could start leading her home while you go back for the horse box.'

'And get charged with – let's see: forcing an entry,' the Colonel ticked it off on his fingers, 'breach of the peace – that's if you get into a fight – trespassing, horse stealing. No, Steve, we've got to be very careful to stay on the right side of the law.'

'Oh that.' Steve shifted impatiently. When he was younger, he had got into a lot of trouble for not caring which side was which. 'The mare is in a bad way. That's what counts.'

'We've got to do it right.' The Colonel bit at the skin

16

round his nails, a habit that Callie's mother Anna had been trying to get rid of since she married him. He remembered, and put the hand down into his jacket pocket. 'I've got twenty other horses and ponies to think of. No help to them if I get my stable closed down.'

'No one would do that. Everyone's proud of the farm.'

'You'd be surprised, Steve. There are people round here who'd be glad to see us go out of business. They think the farm is a waste of money and a waste of land. Unproductive. Plough it under and raise wheat for the starving millions.'

'Couldn't grow much wheat in our chalky soil.'

'Face it, Steve,' the Colonel said gloomily, biting his nails again. 'There are people who don't like horses. Incredible, but true. Horses smell. They bring flies. They give you asthma. One end kicks and the other end bites. They get through gaps in hedges and go across people's land.'

'Old Beckett.'

'If a brewery Clydesdale with feet the size of Stroller's went over *your* lettuce seedlings, you wouldn't be so keen on horses either. These people at the Pinecrest sound very tricky. I can't risk any trouble. So back me up, Steve. Try and look like the assistant to the Agricultural and Domestic Animals County Surveyor.'

'Who's he?'

'I've just invented him.'

'Good morning to you!' The Colonel was always at his most polite when he was nervous. 'Am I speaking to the lady of the house?'

The elderly woman who was crouched over a weedy flower-bed outside the hotel looked up, brushing back wild grey hair.

17

'If you mean Mrs H.,' she said, 'I think she's in the kitchen discussing menus with the cook. Listen – you'll hear plates and saucepan lids flying. I merely live here. But there's nothing to do and the garden is so run down, I thought I'd give myself some bending exercise, at least.'

She began to get up, clutching her back and groaning, and the Colonel gallantly helped her to her feet.

'If you've come about taking rooms—' she looked suspiciously at the Colonel and Steve.

'No, we – er, we've come to see—'

'"—my advice to you is forget it.'

She paddled off in grey gym shoes with her toes turned out. The hotel door had opened, and an anxious little woman with nervous hands and a twitching mouth had come out.

'Dear Mrs Ogilvie.' She tried a laugh. 'Quite a joker. No need to take any notice of what she says. She's a bit – *you* know.' She tapped her head, which was done up in pink rollers.

'Too true.' Mrs Ogilvie spun round in the gym shoes. 'Anyone must be to stay in this dump.'

'She's been here for five years,' Mrs Hammond whispered. 'We can't get her out of the bridal suite. But come in, do. Mustn't keep you standing. It looks like rain.' She put out a hand and squinted suspiciously up at an innocently blue sky. 'Come into the office and let's see what we can do for you.'

She was all smiles and pleasantries, and so was her husband when he came into the office, summoned by a maid who opened a door and yelled down an echoing stone passage, 'Mr H! You're wanted up front!'

After what the groom had told them, Steve and the Colonel were surprised to find him quite an agreeable man, a bit soapy and smiling too much, with an oiled wave in his hair and small pointed teeth like a saw, but not the mean and brutish tyrant they had expected.

18

The Colonel was thrown out of gear. They chatted politely about nothing much, and although he kept trying to start his piece about the Agricultural and Domestic Animals County Surveyor, he could never quite get it out. Instead of being put at his ease by the smiling Hammonds, he was even more nervous. He shifted his feet. He blew his nose. He bit round his nails – what a giveaway. Steve wanted to slap at his hand as Anna would have done.

When Mr Hammond finally stopped vapourizing about the weather and taxes and asked him, 'And what can I do for you, sir?' the Colonel lost his nerve completely and blurted out, 'Well, it's like this. I'm from the Home of Rest for Horses, up at Follyfoot Farm.'

That did it. Steve had told him at least twice. 'Keep quiet about the farm, till we see the mare.' But Mr Hammond said without relaxing his smile, 'I know that, of course.'

'You know the Colonel?' Steve asked, surprised.

'Oh yes, I've heard a lot about the Brigadier.' Mr Hammond deliberately upgraded him. 'It's wonderful work you're doing up there.'

'Yes indeed, very wonderful. The poor dumb beasts.' Mrs Hammond's anxious eyes misted over slightly under the rollers.

'Of course,' said the Colonel, trying to get the talk round his way, 'most of my horses are past working, but in a stable like yours, they have to earn their keep.'

'You've hit it on the nail, Brigadier,' Mr Hammond complimented him as if he had said something clever. 'I'm not a rich man, but I feed the best. Hard food, hard grooming, hard work, and what do you get?'

The Colonel's eyes were glazing over. They were all sitting down, too comfortable, and Mrs Hammond had sent the noisy maid for coffee. Would they ever get out to the stables?

'What do you get? I'll tell you what you get.' Mr Hammond, with his long glossy sideburns and his smiling sharp teeth, was an unstoppable tap of horse hokum. 'You get a fit horse, as you and I, sir, very well know, eh? Eh, lad?' He winked at Steve, as if this was a chummy secret.

The Colonel cleared his throat desperately. 'How about stable help? Hard to get these days.'

'You've hit the nail again, Brigadier. I'm not a rich man, but I pay the best. But they don't want to work, that's where it is. Had to get rid of a chap just the other day. Lazy! You've no idea. And when my son had to speak to him about neglecting the horses, he went for the boy. Like a madman, Brigadier. He had to go. I'm running the stable now with my boys, though one's still at school. Too much for me, with the hotel as well, but the horses come first.'

'I'd love to see them.' The Colonel stood up quickly and moved towards the passage door, but Mr Hammond was quicker.

'Flattered, Brigadier, flattered.' He moved casually but swiftly in front of the door. 'A man of your experience, interested in our modest—'

'I am,' said the Colonel firmly. 'Let's have a look at 'em.'

Still smiling, still soapy, Mr Hammond managed to say No without saying it. 'Feeding time . . . highly sensitive animals . . . nervous when they're disturbed. . . .' The coffee arrived right on cue, and the Colonel and Steve had to sit down again and drink it. It was as soapy as its owner, with scummy milk and bitter grounds. Steve's cup had lipstick on it.

They left in a flurry of smiles and compliments. 'So kind of you to drop in . . . always nice to swap horse yarns. . . .' and a shout from the grey-haired lady who was back in the flower-bed, cutting everything down with a pair of rusty sheep shears, 'I didn't think you'd stay!'

Steve drove out by the back gate, past the stables, a patched

20

together, rickety line of uneven sheds with a couple of thin horses in a yard outside, nosing sadly about in the trodden mud. Bales of mouldy hay were piled in an open shed. A boy was leaning against them, a cigarette smoking on his hanging lip.

It was the boy Lewis, who had tripped Callie up in the yard at the farm.

4

'He bluffed me out,' the Colonel said.

'That wasn't difficult,' Steve said glumly.

'Don't talk to the Colonel like that,' Anna said, and the Colonel said, 'He's right. I was a flop.'

They were all sitting round the kitchen table at the farm-house, trying to work out the next move. Anna, the Colonel's wife and Callie's mother, with her long pale hair pinned on top of her head. Callie in her school uniform, trying to do homework and be part of the talk at the same time. Steve disgusted, but eating slice after slice of home-made bread as Anna cut it. Dora with her untidy hair and brown blunt face, two puppies snoring in her lap. Little Slugger Jones, ex-jockey, ex-boxer, who worked with Steve and Dora in the stables.

'He wants to keep his nose out of trouble,' Slugger said. 'That's what he wants to do.' He had been punched about so much in his boxing days that he could no longer talk directly to anybody, only to himself.

'That's no help to that poor mare,' Dora said.

'There she goes again.' Slugger munched cake with his gums. He was losing his teeth and hair at an equal rate. 'All excited over hearsay talk.'

'Slugger might be right, you know,' the Colonel said. 'Sometimes he is. How do we know that groom was telling the truth?'

'Of course he was. You heard him.' Callie drew beautiful lines under her Earth Science heading, but could write nothing more.

'Suppose he was trying to get back at them for sacking him?'

'But *suppose*—' Callie was having an idea – 'suppose those boys came up on the bike yesterday because they thought the groom might be here?'

'Good grief, she's brilliant,' Dora said.

Steve said, 'She's almost human.'

'That boy Steve saw at the Pinecrest. Lewis. Louse. I've seen him too, but I can't think where. He's no good. Oh, Colonel.' She still called him that, although he was her step-father. 'Please – you must go back!'

'When the Cruelty to Animals man gets home—'

'It can't *wait*!'

'That wretched mare—'

'An infected sore on a thoroughbred—'

They rounded on him, Dora, Steve, Callie, even Anna, who was quickly moved to pity.

'I can't get in. He'll bar the way with those teeth.'

'Pretend you want to hire a horse.'

'I can't. They know me.'

'But they don't know *me*.' Dora stood up, spilling sleepy puppies. 'I wasn't here when the boys came. "Good morning, Mr Hammond, I want to hire a hack" (anyone got any money?) "Certainly, madam." "Let me see all your horses, and I'll choose." '

'They'll rumble you,' Steve said. 'One look at your hands, and they'll know you work in a stable.'

'No they won't. I'll go disguised as one of those silly women who say they can ride and then don't even know how to hold the reins. Anna – lend me those pink flowered pants.'

'Yes, and that nylon top with the frills.'

'What on my feet?'

'Those plastic sandals Corinne left.'

23

'Long dangly earrings.'

'Lots of makeup.'

'Nail varnish.'

'Scent. My "Passion Flowers".'

'Love beads.'

'A hair ribbon.'

'You're putting me off my tea.' Dora pushed away her plate. 'But I'll do it. For poor old Beauty Queen, I'll do it.'

Steve drove her in the farm truck to a crossroads half a mile from the Pinecrest Hotel, and got her bicycle out of the back.

'Be sure and wait for me,' she told him. 'I'm not going to ride this thing ten miles home and up that hill. Especially in this outfit.'

Dora never wore anything but jeans and sweaters and old shirts of Steve's that had shrunk in the wash. She had one skirt for going home to her mother. She felt ridiculous in the flowered pants and the earrings, with the garish eye make-up and the pale shiny lipstick and silver nail varnish with which Anna and Callie had prepared her as carefully as if she were a film star going on the set. The 'Passion Flowers' scent made her slightly sick. Horses were her natural perfume.

She approached the Pinecrest stables doubtfully, but the man who came out greeted her without surprise.

'Looking for someone, dear?'

'I want to hire a horse to go for a horseback ride,' said Dora in the kind of voice someone would have who would go riding dressed like this.

'All right, dear,' said the man, still unsurprised. First bad mark to him. If he ran a decent riding stable, he would have said, Go home and get a proper outfit.

24

'My friend told me you had beautiful animals here.' Girls who looked like this always had 'my friend' who told them this or that fantasy. The man was grinning as if he liked girls who looked like this, so Dora risked a seductive smile and a bit of a hip swing through the muddy yard. 'Might I see them all?'

'Come along in, my dear.'

Steve had said, 'Yuch!' when Dora got into the truck with him, but Mr Hammond ('Call me Sidney') seemed to find her divine.

The stables were what you would expect of a second-rate riding school just managing to sneak in under the law. Outside, a scrubby paddock with a trodden ring and a few flimsy jumps made of oil drums and old doors. Inside, jerry-built loose boxes with no windows, and narrow standing stalls, with a clay floor stamped into holes and hillocks. Woodwork chewed from boredom – or hunger. Scanty, dirty bedding. Flies. Thin horses with dusty coats, many of them with tell-tale patches of white where the hair had grown in over an old sore. As far as Dora could see, most of them needed shoeing.

'What a pretty horse. Oh, I like that spotted one. Why is he waving his head like that? What's he trying to say? Ah, the wee pony. Got the moth a bit, hasn't he?'

As Sidney Hammond showed her round the stable, she made stupid remarks to disguise what she thought. Some of the horses were fat enough, the chunky, cobby kind who wouldn't lose weight if you fed them diet pills; but many of them were ribby and hippy, gone over at the knee, and you could tell by their eyes that they had lost hope. Dora wanted to untie all their broken and knotted rope halters, let them all out, and herd them slowly back to the farm, wobbling behind them on her bicycle.

But, as the Colonel said, 'Face it, everyone isn't like us. If

25

we took away every horse that wasn't kept by our standards, we'd have half the horses in the county up here.'

And she was here to look at Beauty Queen. That was her job.

And Sidney Hammond, although ignorant and probably miserly, was quite nice to his horses. He slapped them on their bony rumps and thin ewe necks, and told tall tales about their breeding and performance.

'This little grey. Irish bred. What a goer across country! Now here's a bay mare. Perfect lady's hack. Suit you all the way, she would. Todd!' He shouted towards the tack room, where a transistor radio was blasting.

A tall weedy boy with a feeble growth of beard appeared in the doorway. 'What do you want?' he shouted back. He inspected Dora from head to foot and back up again, and favoured her with a breathy wolf whistle.

'Get the tack for Penny.'

'Oh, just a moment, there's one horse I didn't give a sugar lump to.' In a dark corner box, Dora had spotted an unmistakable thoroughbred head beyond the cobwebby bars. She ran down the littered aisle, stumbling in the loose sandals. Before Sidney could reach her, she slid back the bolt and went into the box, where a thin chestnut mare rested a back leg in the dirty straw, wearing a torn rug.

'Why is she wearing pyjamas?' Dora looked innocently up at Sidney. Anna had put so much black stuff on her lashes that she could hardly see.

'Keep her warm, love.'

'But she's sweating. Let me—'

'Best not touch her,' Sidney said quickly. 'She's nervous.'

'Oh, I'm not afraid of her.' She reached up and quickly but carefully folded the rug back on to the neck of the mare, who jumped away in pain.

26

No wonder. The saddle sore on her high withers was two or three inches wide, oozing and raw.

'Oh God!' Dora said in her normal voice, but Sidney Hammond was too busy explaining to notice.

'Looks worse than it is. All my groom's fault. I sacked him for letting it get so bad. It's clearing up with this new ointment.'

'Have you had the vet?'

'Of course, love.' When he was telling a full scale lie, his mouth went on smiling, but his eyes did not.

'He can't be much good. I know someone who could help.'

'I'm not a rich man, you know. I can't afford these huge fees.'

'No, I mean at Follyfoot Farm. The place where they have the old horses.'

'But Beauty Queen isn't old.' If Mr Hammond guessed at a connection between Dora and the Colonel, his soft-soaping smile didn't show it.

'They might take her though. I know a boy—' Dora lowered the heavy lashes coyly – 'a boy who works there. Shall I ask?'

Mr Hammond sighed, and surrendered. 'If it's best for Beauty. I'm up to my neck here, short-handed, all these animals and a hotel full of guests. . . .'

He started to cover the mare's back, but Dora said, 'Let's take off the rug and put ointment on, and a clean rag or something.'

'You're a great girl.' Sidney squeezed her hand. 'A real little Samaritan.'

When they left the box, the bay mare was drooping between pillar reins, with a long-cheeked curb bridle and an ugly old saddle that made Beauty's back understandable.

'You pay in advance,' said smiling Sidney.

'How much?'

27

'Seventy-five pence to you, my dear.'

'Oh, I'm afraid that's too much.'

Some other people had come to ride, three women in tight jodhpurs who looked as if they were housewives hoping to lose weight, and other horses were being saddled.

Sidney lowered his voice. 'Fifty pence then, but keep it dark.'

'Oh *no*,' said Dora, glad to find a way out of riding poor Penny, although she would only have taken her round the nearest corner and let her graze for an hour. 'That wouldn't be fair on you. I'll come back when I'm not so broke. I'll ring up the farm about Beauty. Don't worry.'

She ducked under Penny's pillar rein and got herself out to the yard, where one of the housewives already had her stout thighs across a hairy cob with its eyes half shut. Dora paused briefly to let out a couple of links in its curb chain, and ran – slop, slop in the plastic sandals – to her bicycle.

'Don't forget to come back, my dear!' Sidney Hammond was in the stable doorway, smiling and waving.

5

'And perhaps I will,' Dora said. 'Don't laugh, but I quite liked him. He was nice to me.'

Beauty Queen had been brought up to the farm, Sidney Hammond profuse with thanks, blessings, promises to pay whatever he could ('though I'm not a rich man'), and make endowments in his will.

'I've got to laugh,' Steve said. 'You had him cornered and he knew it. He had to be nice.'

'He fancied me.'

'Hah!' said Steve. 'Listen to that, Callie. Get her all dressed up, and look what happens.'

'It was the Passion Flowers.' Callie was standing on a box, very tenderly smoothing the ointment the vet had prescribed on to the chestnut mare's back. 'It went to her head.'

Callie had inherited from her mother a natural gift for caring for sick or injured animals. Beauty Queen, rechristened Miss America, was in the foaling stable behind the barn, and since Steve and Dora and Slugger were busy enough, it was Callie's job to clean the wound with warm water and hydrogen peroxide, and put on ointment and antiseptic powder.

She got up earlier to take care of Miss before she went to school, and rushed straight back to the mare as soon as she got home on the bus, so that her uniform was always smeared with ointment and powder and her school shoes full of bedding.

29

When Anna complained, Callie said, 'Then don't make me go to school.'

She had never liked the big rough school on the outskirts of the manufacturing town which lay farther along the valley; but it was the only one, unless she went to boarding school, and Callie would not hear of leaving the farm.

This year, school was worse than ever. There was a rotten gang of older boys who were always in trouble, except with those teachers who were afraid of them, and who got themselves through the boredom of the day by terrorizing some of the younger children. The sneaky kids sneaked, and got beaten up. The fighting kids fought back, and got left alone. The others simply tried to keep clear of the bullies. Callie was one of the others.

But one day when she was sitting on the playground wall reading, because she got all the exercise she needed at the farm, and she hated games with balls because she was short-sighted, a foot suddenly came up underneath the open book and sent it flying.

Three big brutish boys scrummed for it, knocking each other down, and when they got up, howling like inane hyenas, the book and cover were in shreds.

It was a library book and she would have to pay for it, but Callie walked away in silence, stretching her eyes to keep tears back.

'Hey!' A hand took her arm and spun her round. 'I know you, stupid cry-baby!'

'Let me go. I'll scream.'

'Try it.' The boy guffawed. 'We'll give you something to scream about.' He had a broad stupid face, with a pudgy nose and thick hanging lips. It was Lewis the Louse. This was where she had seen him before. Hanging about with the bad crowd. This school was so big that you couldn't know all the names, nor even all the faces.

'Yeah.' He dropped her arm, staring. 'I do know you. You live up the hill, doncher?'

Callie nodded, sick with fear. The three large boys stood round her. With such a shrieking mob in the playground, no one would see or hear whatever they did to her.

'You belong to that chap with the gimpy leg – haw haw, jolly good show and all that sort of rot.' The Louse did a rotten imitation of what he thought would be the voice of someone like the Colonel.

'My mother is married to him.'

'Oh girls! It's too romantic.' Lewis snuffled in his horrible blocked-up nose. Then he leaned forward and put his face so close to Callie's that she could see all the pimples and open pores. 'You know who I am, doncher?'

She nodded, staring at him like a rabbit.

'Your lot tried to make trouble for us. Remember that, you guys.' He jerked his head at his friends, who were even uglier and stupider (if possible) than him. 'We don't like this person.'

'But I'm taking care of your horse!' Callie was bolder, thinking of poor Miss America, who was her life's purpose at the moment.

'Quite right,' said Lewis, 'quite right. And we'll take care of you. Don't forget it.'

He snapped his thick grubby finger in Callie's face and sauntered off, his friends behind him, singing a crude song, whose key words they changed briefly while they passed a teacher, and then took up again.

When Callie was really upset, she couldn't talk about it. All she could do was to say she had a bad headache the next day, and all this got her was that Anna made her stay in bed and would not let her go out to the stable to take care of Miss America.

She knew that Callie had not got a headache. That was why she did that. And because she knew she hadn't got a headache, she sat on Callie's bed in the dark that night and asked her what was wrong.

'Oh – nothing. It's just school.' Callie tossed about, and the kitten who was on the bottom of the bed made a pounce at her toes.

'Was there trouble? Work, or what?'

Usually Callie did not like to have her hair touched, but when her mother stroked it at night, it was all right.

She shook her head under the stroking hand. How was it you could manage not to cry until someone gave you sympathy? It ought to be lack of sympathy that made you cry.

'What then?'

Callie sniffed. 'It's just – oh, I hate the kids.'

'Aren't there any friends?'

'I'm not the type that makes friends, you know that. All my friends are here. Most of them have got four legs.'

'You ought to have friends your own age.' All mothers worry once in a while that their child is 'different', though they wouldn't really like it if they weren't. 'Perhaps we should think about boarding school.'

'Mother, you promised.'

'Let's see how things go then.'

6

But things did not go any better. They went worse. Wherever Callie went, Lewis and his gang seemed to be there, jeering at her, tripping her up, jumping out from behind lockers, tweaking a pigtail as they ran by.

One day she was changing classrooms, going upstairs as Lewis was coming down, and he bumped into her so hard that he knocked her back down the stairs. She caught the rail and steadied herself against the wall. The rest of her class went on up the stairs. In this school, if you saw trouble brewing, you got out of the way.

'What do you want?' Callie stood against the wall with her hands spread out as if she was going to be shot. When she was afraid, it went to her stomach. She thought she was going to bring up her lunch all over the Louse's elastic-sided boots.

'Don't be afraid, little girl.' He put on a kind of leer which he thought was a smile. 'I got a present for you.'

Callie managed to say, 'Oh?' and swallowed her lunch back down.

'Knowing how much you love our four-footed friends—' from behind his back he held out a parcel wrapped in news-paper – 'I brought this for you.'

Callie took it, watching him.

'Go on. Open it. You'll like it, really.'

It smelled peculiar, but Callie gingerly unwrapped the newspaper and saw that she was holding the hoof of a dead horse. Where it had been cut off, it was congealed with black blood and dirt.

She wrapped it up again quickly and handed it back to Lewis. She could not speak.

'Don't you recognize it?' he jeered. 'You should do. I thought you was so fond of poor old Beauty Queen.'

'You couldn't—' she whispered.

'It's still our horse, ain't it? Too bad you didn't take better care of her, for we had to have her destroyed this morning. Very 'umane. A merciful release.' He shoved the newspaper bundle back into Callie's hands and ran away.

She could not believe him. Yet she had to believe him. It was a narrow, well-bred hoof, the pale colour that goes with a chestnut's white leg. She must telephone her mother. Yet she could not telephone her mother. As long as she didn't hear the truth, it still could be not true.

After she had been sick in the cloakroom, she went down to the basement furnace and got a shovel, and buried the hoof in the newspaper under the bushes behind the goal posts. Then she went back to her classroom.

'Where on earth—' Miss Golding began, then saw Callie's face.

'I was sick.'

Immediately there was a clamour from the class of, 'I knew that sausage was off', 'It was the spuds, they boil 'em in the dish-water', 'You won't catch me eating their treacle roll.'

'Do you want to lie down? Shall I ring up your home?'

'I'm all right.' Callie sat down.

At the end of the day, she went to the bus like a sleep-walker, and sat at the back, staring straight ahead, not looking out of the window all the way to ride a cross-country course alongside the road, as she usually did. The bus climbed the hill and stopped by the gate of the farm.

'Give my love to the old horses,' the driver said, as he always did.

'Thank you,' Callie said, as she always did. She went under the stone arch and walked across the yard going towards the house. Her mother would be starting supper. She would turn from the stove and Callie would know at once from her face whether it was true.

Several horses called to her. Cobbler's Dream in the corner box banged on his door and swung his head with the flashy white blaze up and down to get her attention. She was almost to the corner of the yard where the path came in from the house when Steve backed out of the Weaver's stable, dragging a loaded barrow.

'Hi!' he shouted. 'Aren't you going to see your patient?'

Callie turned slowly round.

'Her back looks much better today. You're doing a good job.'

Callie ran. It was not until she was in the loose box with her head against Miss America's thin thoroughbred neck that she began to cry.

After the Easter holidays started, Callie told her mother that she could not stay at that school.

'I'd better start finding out about boarding schools.'

'We can't afford it.'

'No.' Anna laughed. 'But you could try for a scholarship.'

'I'm not clever enough.'

'We'll see.'

They did not discuss it any more. Why spoil the holidays? The days were roofed with blue sky and whipped cream clouds. The old horses luxuriated in the sun on their dozing backs. Callie rode Cobbler's Dream, and the mule, and Hero the circus horse, and anyone else who was rideable, and she and Steve and Dora jogged up to the higher hills where the turf was patched with rings of white and yellow flowers, like fried eggs.

Miss America's back was healed and they could ride her too. Fleshed out and well fed, she was a pleasant ride, although her thoroughbred stride had been stiffened by pounding on roads, and from the way she chucked up her head, you could guess at the kind of hands that had tugged at her reins.

They rode her in a snaffle, bareback to make sure of not hurting her, and the mare flourished in the warm spring.

'But there's always a fly in the ointment,' Dora said.

The fly was Sidney Hammond, arriving with a lopsided trailer with the tailboard tied with rope, to take back his mare.

'Don't let her go.' Steve and Dora cornered the Colonel in the tack room when he went to get a halter.

'It's his horse. We've done what we set out to do. He's very busy, he says. He's getting a lot of people from town, secretaries and things wanting to go pony trekking at weekends. He needs the mare.'

'She isn't a pony.'

'Dora. Don't *try* to annoy me.' The Colonel did not want Miss America to go either.

Mr Hammond was as smiley and ingratiating as ever, as well he might be, since he hadn't paid a penny for the mare's keep, in spite of all his blessings and promises.

Dora kept out of his sight, in case she might need to put on the pink pants and 'Passion Flowers' disguise again to go and check on Miss America when she was back at the Pinecrest as Beauty Queen. Steve helped Mr Hammond load the mare, making a big fuss about spreading straw on the rotting tailboard in case of splinters.

As the trailer pulled away, he said, 'What a hunk of junk,' loud enough for Mr Hammond to hear, but smiling Sidney merely waved and grinned, and leaned out of the car window to call once again, 'I can never thank you enough, Brigadier!'

'I'll send you a bill!' the Colonel called after him, not loud enough to hear.

'You know he won't,' Slugger grumbled, sweeping up the old manure that Steve had kicked out of the van before he would lead Miss America in. 'You know he's too soft with these folk who could well pay to help out them as can't.'

'Shut up, Slugger,' the Colonel said. 'You know we only ask people to pay what they can afford.'

'And that one could well afford.'

'I said I'd send him a bill.'

'Oh yes, just like he sent in a bill to that old clothes and firewood chap as brought the pony in here for two weeks rest and we had the beggar all winter. Have us all in Queer Street, that lot will. Oh yes, he says. Send in a bill, he says. . . .' Slugger grumbled away, sweeping the gravel before him with short testy jabs.

7

It was Dora's birthday. She had wanted to spend it at the farm, but her mother wanted her at home, so she had to put on her skirt and go down into the town.

Her mother, who was still hoping that she would grow out of horses, although there was no evidence, at seventeen, that she ever would, had assembled a group of 'interesting' people to try to show her the kind of life she was missing.

A girl from an art school, starved and pale, with round glasses like wheel rims and a long dusty dress with a trodden hem. Two serious boys with bushy beards who were teaching problem children to get rid of their problems by screaming and hitting each other. A few grown-ups whose mouths kept on opening and shutting long after Dora had stopped listening.

She was so bored that she ate too much to pass the time, fell asleep on the bus going home, and was carried past the village where she was supposed to change buses.

'Where are we?' She woke with a start as the driver braked round a sharp corner.

He stopped at the next cross-roads and showed her a lane which led to the main road, where she might get another bus back.

It was late afternoon, with twilight settling on the budding hedges in the valley, and damp beginning to rise from the ground through the new spring grass. Dora walked by the side of the road, getting her feet wet. She was not sure where she was, but when she went over a bridge, she thought she might be crossing the sluggish brown river that ran by the

38

Pinecrest Hotel. If there were no buses on the main road, she would get a lift from the first car that would stop.

'Come back with her throat cut one day, she will,' Slugger Jones always grumbled when Dora turned up from town in a strange car or on the back of a motor-bike.

'There are some weird people about these days,' Anna warned, but Dora said, 'No weirder than me,' and went on hitch-hiking.

She had promised to be back for supper. After that lunch, she could never eat again. But Anna had made a cake. And there would be no 'interesting' people with 'stimulating' talk. Just people who knew each other well, and were sure of being liked.

Behind her in the lane, she heard the clop-clop of a trotting horse, that always stirring sound that brings people to their windows or out to the gate, even if they have their own horses to clop-clop with.

Dora turned and stood still to watch it come by. As the man and horse came into view out of the dusk, she saw that it was Miss America. Dora stepped out into the road and held up her hand like a school crossing patrol man.

The mare stopped of her own accord. She was not so much being ridden, as carrying an unsteady rider, who nearly pitched over her head when she stopped.

'Whoops.' He clung round Miss America's neck and smiled foolishly at Dora, who saw that he was drunk. She also saw that the saddle with which he had so little contact was a heavy broken thing, well down on the mare's bony withers.

Dora saw red. She grabbed the man's arm and pulled him off the horse. He was half-way off anyway.

'Thanks.' He landed on his feet, with the luck of a drunk. 'I was wondering whether to get on the ground or back in the saddle.'

'You shouldn't be *in* that saddle.' Furiously, Dora

39

unbuckled the girth and lifted off the saddle. The sore back had broken open again, raw and bleeding.

Dora swore. 'Here – just a minute—' The man lurched at her, but she went to the side of the road and pitched the dreadful old saddle over a thick hedge into the bushes.

'Now look what you've done!' The man's red face was woeful. 'How am I going to ride this thing home?'

'You're not,' Dora said.

'Have to walk then.' Strengthening himself with a swig from a flask in his breeches pocket, he looped the reins over his arm and started off down the road. The mare was slightly lame.

Dora followed a short distance behind. The man weaved down the lane in the failing light, staggering now and then and propping himself up with a hand on the mare's neck. When he came to the main road, he stood for a while watching the cars go past, turning his head from side to side as if he were at a tennis match.

Dora watched him. Finally he seemed to make up his mind. He took the reins over Miss America's head and tied them very carefully round a signpost. Then he stepped into the road with his arm raised, outlined unsteadily in the lights of a car. The luck of a drunk still held. The car stopped, and he got in and was driven away.

Dora untied the mare and they walked along the grass at the side of the road until they came to the Dog & Whistle, where Dora could telephone for Steve to bring the horse box.

In the farmhouse, Callie greeted her. 'I got you a present. Want to see?'

'Thanks. I got you one too. Want to see?'

'Where?'

'In the foaling stable.'

'A new customer!' Callie ran out.

Dora asked Anna, 'Is – er, is the Colonel in a good mood?'

'He was,' Anna said. 'What have you brought home?'

'Miss America,' Dora said. 'Her back has broken down again.'

The Colonel did not say much. He waited to see what would happen. When nothing happened, he telephoned the Pinecrest Hotel.

'Good morning, Brigadier. Nice to hear your voice.'

'I've got your mare.'

'That's good of you.'

'Her back is almost as bad as it was before.'

'That fellow – that stupid drunk – it's all his fault. I tell you, Brigadier, this riding school game is one long headache.'

'What happened?'

'I wish I knew. He came back here with a hangover and a cockeyed story about losing the saddle and tying the horse to a signpost. He'd been back to all the signposts on all the side turnings along the main road, and when the mare wasn't there and wasn't here in the stable, he thought he'd imagined the whole thing, and swore to go on the wagon.'

'Good.' The Colonel waited.

Mr Hammond waited too. Finally he said, 'I thought the mare might have run to you, seeing she was so well kept there before. I'm grateful, Brigadier.'

'You want me to keep her?'

'You know I'm short-handed here.'

'So am I.'

'But your staff is reliable. I work my fingers to the bone, but I have to leave a lot to my boys, and – well, you know what they are these days. You can't trust them with anything. Especially a valuable horse like Beauty.' He would not even stick up for his own family. 'So if you could do me a favour, Brigadier, I'll pay anything you want.'

'You didn't pay the last bill,' the Colonel murmured without moving his lips. He hated talking about money.

'The cheque is in the post.'

Mr Hammond rang off cheerfully, with best wishes to all for the Easter season. The man was incredible. He had no shame at all.

'He's not going to get the mare back though,' the Colonel said. 'But somehow I don't think he'll ask.'

'I worry about his other horses.' Dora frowned. 'I don't see how he ever got a stable licence.'

'Perhaps he didn't,' Steve said. 'Why don't you ask the County Council, Colonel?'

'They'll think I'm suspicious.'

'Well, you are.'

At the County Council, they told him that the Pinecrest's application for a riding-stable licence was on the files, awaiting an inspection.

'Our regular man is off sick. I wonder, Colonel – I know you're a busy man, but you're fully qualified, and I'm sure the hotel wants to get it cleared up before the summer.'

So the Colonel and Steve went back to the Pinecrest Hotel. He refused to take Dora in the sandals and earrings, but he did take Steve in case of trouble.

There was no trouble. He had written authority to inspect the stable. He spent half a day there, with Sidney Hammond

42

following him affably round and thanking him at the end for his time and trouble with a smile like the jaws of a gin trap.

The Colonel turned in an honest and detailed report. It was not his decision whether or not to grant the licence.

8

Since last year, when Cobbler's Dream had captured a thief and saved his own life by clearing the impossible spiked park fence, Steve had begun to jump him again.

The Cobbler had once been a famous juvenile show jumper. When the girl who trained him grew too big, he was bought by a hard-handed child who wanted a vehicle for winning championships, rather than a pony to love. Steve worked for her father. He had to see the marvellous pony making mistakes because of the child. Finally he had to see him blinded in one eye by a blow from a whip. He had taken him away then, and brought him to the farm, and they had both stayed here.

The other eye became half blind, but Cobby had adapted so well that he was almost as surefooted as before, and his fantastic leap over the Manor park fence had proved that he had acquired some kind of sixth sense to judge a jump. He would jump almost anything if you took him slow and let him get the feel of it.

Steve put up some sheep hurdles in one of the fields, and he and Dora made a brush jump with gorse stuck through a ladder. Most of the other horses were too old and stiff to jump, so Dora was teaching the mule Willy, who had no mouth at all, and either rushed his jumps flat out or stopped dead and let Dora jump without him.

Steve and Dora had the afternoon off, so they took the Cobbler and Willy through the woods on the other side of their hill, where there were fallen tree trunks across the rides.

Cobby jumped them all without checking his canter, bunching his muscles, arching his back, smoothly away on his landing stride with his ears pricked for the next jump. Willy jumped the smaller trees. If they did not reach right across the path, he whipped round them with his mouth open, yawing at the bit. If they were too big, he dug in his toes, and Dora had to get off and lead him over. He would jump his front end, stand and stare with the tree trunk under his middle, and then heave his rear end over with a grunt like an old man getting out of the bath.

Near the far edge of the wood, Cobby shortened his stride, trotting with his head high, and turned to the side, listening.

'What does he hear?'

There were people who came to the woods with guns and shot at rabbits and foxes and anything that moved. Sometimes they shot each other.

Steve and Dora both stopped and listened. Only the continual sigh of the breeze moving through the tops of the tall trees.

'I don't hear anything.'

'Cobb does. His hearing is sharper now that he can't see much. So is his nose.'

The chestnut pony had his nostrils squared, as if he were getting a message.

Steve pushed him on, over two more jumps, but he slowed down again, listening.

'There is something. Let's go the way he wants to.'

They rode out of the wood and along the edge of a cornfield. In a grassy lane beyond the hedge, a grey horse was grazing in a patch of clover.

It was a calm horse. It stood still and exchanged blown breaths with Cobby, and then the ritual squeal and striking out. The mule laid back his long ears like a rabbit and said nothing. He distrusted strange horses. When he was turned

45

out with a new one, he would communicate for the first two weeks only with his heels.

The grey horse wore a head collar. It let Steve slip his belt through the noseband, and trotted quietly beside Cobby back to the farm.

The Colonel did not recognize the horse. 'Someone will be worried though,' he said. 'It's a nice-looking horse and well kept.' The grey looked like a hunter, coat clean and silky, whiskers and heels neatly trimmed, tail and mane properly pulled. 'Better ring the police, Steve.'

Sergeant Oddie said at once, 'Oh no! Not that grey again. Look here, I've got the big wedding to worry about, two men off on a drug raid, a three-car crash on the Marston road and some nippers have set fire to the bus shelter. That horse is the last thing I need.'

'It's been out before?'

'Time and again. The neighbours are on my neck about it day and night. Regular wasps' nest, it's stirred up. Here, I'll give you Mrs Jordan's number, and I wish you'd tell her how to build a fence to keep a horse in.'

'But we have,' Mrs Jordan said. 'It's not our fault, or the horse's. Oh dear. I'll come and get him.'

'I'll ride him home, if you could bring me back,' Steve said.

The grey horse looked like a lovely ride, and he was, well schooled, a beautiful mover, quickly responsive, but you could stop him by flexing your wrist.

Steve was surprised when he saw where he came from. The Jordans' house on the edge of a small town had obviously once stood in fields, but new houses had been built close all round, and the fenced paddock was not much bigger than a

46

tennis court. The fence was strong and high enough. The gate looked sound.

'It's they who are doing it,' Mrs Jordan told Steve. 'They used to do it at night, but they're getting bolder now, and they've begun to do it in the daytime if I go out.'

'Who do what?'

'The neighbours. The people in that pink house with gnomes in the garden and plastic flowers in the window-boxes. They open the gate and let David out, then they quickly ring the Police and complain that the horse is loose and trampling on people's gardens.'

'How do you know?'

'Oh, I know all right.' Mrs Jordan was a faded, once beautiful woman, with lines of work and worry round her big sad eyes and her full, drooping mouth. 'When the police were here last time – they were nice enough at first, but now they're getting fed up – I saw that front curtain move, and another time, the woman was standing in the window, blatantly watching and laughing.'

'Why don't you padlock the gate?'

'We have. But she somehow pried the rails loose at night, and then got them back up after she'd chased David out. It's her, not her husband. He's not so bad, but she's a fanatic. She hates horses, because she thinks they're something that rich people have. Rich! She's much better off than us. Her husband is a plumber. But she's the kind of person who can't stand anybody having something she hasn't got, even if she doesn't want it. She wants to buy that piece of land where David's paddock is, and breed chinchillas.

'Chinchillas!' She looked at Steve with her tragic eyes. 'On what was once our back lawn, where the girls used to have their summer house and swings.'

After they had put the grey horse away in the open shed in the corner of the paddock, Mrs Jordan made Steve go into the

47

house for something to eat before she would drive him home. She seemed lonely, glad of someone to talk to. He sat in a comfortable shabby armchair and listened. He had learned from the Colonel that if you will only shut up and listen, people will tell you things they won't tell to someone who is trying to keep up their end of the conversation.

It was a tragic story. Her husband had been a trainer and show judge. A car crash had killed their younger daughter and left him unable to work for a long time. They had to borrow money on their house and land. Their other daughter Nancy left college and went to work, and Mrs Jordan got a job in an old people's nursing home, but they could not pay the interest on the mortgage. Four acres of their land had been seized, and sold to the builder who had put up all these ugly little houses where the pastures and stables had been.

All the horses had gone, of course, except David, who had belonged to the dead girl.

'How could we part with him? Nancy rides him occasionally, but she has so little time, and she's always so tired. We're all tired, Steve. My husband has a part-time job now, but it doesn't pay much, and he's not well enough even for that. I lie awake night after night wondering what will happen when they take our house in the end and that horrible woman gets David's paddock – our last bit of land – and keeps her wretched chinchillas in prison cages.'

'Death row.' Steve nodded. 'Only one way out.'

'I hate her.'

'So do I,' Steve said with feeling, although he had never seen the woman with the plaster gnomes in her garden.

'Sergeant Oddie rang me up after he talked to you, and said if the horse got out again, we'd have to get rid of him.'

'I thought the sergeant was so busy,' Steve said.

'Not too busy to tell me *that*. And that's what that woman wants.'

48

'Why don't you turn her in?'

'I can't prove it. She's cunning. I've never been able to catch her.'

'Mind if I try?'

'It's not much use.'

'You all go out some night. Make a big noise about driving off in the car, so she knows. But I'll be here. I'll be in the shed with David.'

No need to tell the Colonel. Not that he would mind, but . . . no need to worry him.

'I can't risk any trouble,' he had said. He had his own problems with neighbours. 'We've got to stay on the right side of the law.'

Well, this was the right side, but . . . no need to tell him.

Steve did not tell Dora either, or anyone at the farm.

9

The next evening, after the horses had been bedded down and fed and watered, Steve asked if he could use the truck.

'All right,' the Colonel said. 'What for?'

'I'm going out.'

'Who with?' Dora's rumpled head came over the top of a stable door, where she was rubbing liniment on Dolly's chronic foreleg.

'A girl I know.'

'You don't know any girls.'

'How do you know?'

'You'd tell me.'

Dora rested her chin on the door. Old Doll put her head out beside her and laid back her ears at Steve. She had once been so badly abused by a man that she still only liked women. It was Dolly who had kicked the Colonel in the head.

'You'd be the last person I'd tell.' Steve laughed. 'You'd want to come too, and sit between us and talk all through the film.'

'Are you going to a film?'

'Yes.'

'I want to come too.'

'No.'

'What's her name?'

'Nancy.'

'I don't believe you're going out with a girl,' Dora said, but more doubtfully.

When he drove off, Dora was sitting on the wall by the gate, polishing a snaffle bit and kicking her heels against the bricks. Her face looked closed and sulky, her lower lip stuck out. Steve waved. She did not wave back or look up.

Mr Jordan was a grey, stooped man, with a mouth stiffened by pain of body and heart. Nancy was a bright-cheeked girl with thick bouncing hair and good legs, the kind of girl Steve would have gone to the cinema with if he had been going to the cinema with a girl.

They made the necessary noise about leaving. Racing the engine, slamming the doors, going back for a coat, calling out that they would be late.

'The film starts at eight!' Mrs Jordan called from behind the wheel, to let her neighbours know that they would be away at least two hours.

In the pink house with the window-boxes full of impossible flowers that never bloomed in the spring, nor even in England at all, a shadow moved behind the curtain.

Steve sat in the straw of the open shed and talked to the grey horse and thought about things long gone. Other nights of adventure when you waited, with your nerves on edge and your hair pricking on your scalp. The night when he had stolen Cobby away to safety with sacking wrapped round his hooves.

About nine-thirty, with the family still in the cinema, David raised his head from his hay and swung his small ears forward. Steve listened, holding his breath.

Were there footsteps on the soft ground? Did the night breeze shiver that bush, or was someone behind it? Steve watched, motionless in the dark corner.

David, who liked people, walked out of the shed in a rustle of straw and into the paddock. A thick woman in tight pants was climbing through the fence. She held out her hand as the horse went up to her and gave him something. In the still night, Steve heard his teeth on the sugar. He followed the woman as she moved quickly across the small paddock to the gate.

Steve waited. It was too dark to see much. She had her back to him, but he heard the clink of the chain on the gate. He got up quickly, went silently up behind her and said in her ear, 'Can I help you?'

'Oh my God!' The woman jumped round with a hand on the ample shelf over her heart. As she moved, Steve was almost sure that he saw her fist clench over a piece of metal that could be a key.

'What do you want?' She was breathing fast, and he could see behind her dark fringe tomorrow's imagined headlines chasing each other through her head.

WOMAN FOUND STRANGLED. HOUSEWIFE KILLED IN NEIGHBOUR'S GARDEN. SUBURBAN SLAYING, MYSTERY GROWS.

'What you – what are you doing here?' The woman must be bold to have done as much as she had, but her mouth was twitching now with nerves, because Steve was looming over her threateningly.

'I'm a friend of the family,' he said. 'The horse looked as if he might be headed for colic, so I was watching he didn't lie down. Someone might have slipped him something. People round here have been making trouble, you wouldn't believe it.'

'Oh, I know.' The woman relaxed. 'The poor Jordans, it's dreadful for them, on top of all their bad luck. I try to keep an eye on things for them, when they're not here. That's why I came out, to check on the gate fastening.'

'Oh, I see,' said Steve. 'To check the gate.'

'That's right.' The woman started to move towards her house. 'To check the gate.'

'You keep an eye on things. That's nice.'

'Well,' she said, 'one does what one can. We were all put in this world to help each other, that's what I say.'

'Oh so do I.' With a hand on the neck of the grey horse, Steve watched the woman climb through the paddock fence and go back into her own house, waggling her bottom righteously, like a good neighbour who has done her duty.

'So that's what you ought to do,' Steve told the Jordans.

They looked at each other. 'I'm no hand with electricity.' The father looked baffled.

'I'll do it.'

'She'll see you.' Mrs Jordan glanced towards the pink house. 'She sees everything.'

'I'll do it after dark. There's no moon. She won't try anything on tomorrow after the scare she got tonight. If I use a rubber hammer, I can get the insulators on without making any noise, and I'll put the battery behind the shed so she won't hear it ticking.'

Next day, Steve offered to do Anna's shopping, and bought the battery and thin wire and the insulators while he was in town.

In the evening, when he asked casually for the truck, Dora did not ask him where he was going. She had not allowed herself to ask him about the film last night, which was a good thing because he had forgotten to find out what was on.

At the Jordans he rigged up two strands of electric wire close to the paddock rails where it could not be seen. Then he turned on the battery and waited at the side of the shed.

He chirruped softly. The horse came up to the rail, put out his nose, then jumped back and snorted.

'Sorry, David.' The grey horse stood in the middle of the paddock, looking very offended. 'I had to test it.'

Two nights Steve waited in the straw, with the battery ticking softly on the other side of the shed. He dozed and woke and dozed, but he was sleepy in the daytime, and Dora made embittered remarks about people who stayed out so late with girls that they couldn't do their jobs properly.

Why not tell her and let her watch with him in the shed and share the adventure? Because she kept saying things like, 'When are we going to see this famous Nancy? Not that I care. Or is she too hideous to bring here?' Talking herself out of the adventure.

'She's gorgeous, as a matter of fact,' Steve said, irritated. 'Marvellous legs.' He winked at Slugger.

'Can't go far wrong with that.' Slugger winked at the horse he was grooming. ' "When judgin' a woman *or* a horse, you gotta look at the legs, of course." That's what me grandad used to say.'

'Anyone can have good legs.' Dora's, which were rather muscular and boyish, were covered in torn faded blue jeans, which she refused to let Anna patch, or hem at the bottom.

On the third night, Steve went to bed early – 'What's the matter? She sick of you already?' – and got up again at midnight after everyone was asleep. He stopped the truck before he got to the Jordans', and walked quietly through what was left of their garden and round the side of the house to the shed.

When he whispered, to show the horse he was there, a voice answered him.

'Nancy?'

'I couldn't sleep.' She was lying covered with straw, only her face and hair showing.

'I wanted to do this alone.' Steve came in and sat beside her. 'Why?'

'It was my idea.'

'It's my horse.'

They lay side by side in the straw and talked softly. Nancy told him about the man at work she thought she was in love with. Girls always started to tell you about other men just when you were getting interested.

Steve wriggled his fingers through the straw to find her hand.

'But he's almost old enough to be my father,' Nancy said.

Steve took her hand, and at that moment there was a blood-curdling scream from the other side of the paddock.

David jumped. Steve and Nancy scrambled up. The plump woman in the tight pants was sitting on the ground with her arms wrapped round herself like a straitjacket, rocking backwards and forwards and moaning.

'It can't have been that bad.' Steve and Nancy slid carefully under the fence and went across to her.

'Oh, I'm killed,' the woman moaned. 'Oh, my heart—'

'Just going to check up on the gate, eh?'

She looked up at Steve, her hair, disordered from bed, standing wildly up as if the electricity had gone right through it.

'Yes,' she croaked. 'One does what one can. But there are some people—' she glowered up at Nancy, still rocking and holding herself as if she might fall apart – 'some people who don't know the meaning of the word gratitude.'

After this, Steve did take Nancy to the farm at the weekend, to show her the horses.

The Colonel was delighted with her. He conducted her round himself, hands behind his back, cap over his eyes, very military. Callie was pleased with her because she asked the right questions and said, 'How lucky for Miss to have Callie to look after her,' when they visited Miss America, queening it in the orchard so that the other horses would not disturb the healing wound.

Dora was rather gruff. She took a long look at Nancy's legs, then went off to greet a family of visitors and became very busy giving them a conducted tour of all the horses.

The family, who had only come to see the donkey which had once belonged to their Uncle Fred, kept saying, 'Well, better be getting along,' but Dora dragged them on from horse to horse, so as not to have to talk to Nancy.

Soon after this, Steve got a letter from Mrs Jordan. Their telephone had been cut off because they couldn't pay the bill.

The plump woman and the plumber had put the pink house up for sale and gone away. Two days later – '*If she'd only waited two days, she could have had her revenge in chinchillas*' – Mr Jordan was asked by a friend in Australia to go out and join him on the ranch where he was breeding horses.

'*So we're all going, Steve. A new life. Free passage out if we stay two years, and they can have this poor house and make it into a pub or a Bingo hall or whatever they want. No regrets. Except about David. We sail next week. Please find him a good home and use the sale money for the farm. The best home only. I trust you.*'

David could stay out at night, so the Colonel let Steve bring him to the farm.

'What's *that*?' Dora made a face at the grey as he backed neatly out of the horse box and stood with his fine head up and his mane and tail blowing like an Arab, staring at some of the old horses, who were drawn up in the field, all pointing the same way like sheep, observing him.

'It's the horse we found on the other side of the wood. You know.'

'Nancy's horse.'

'Yes,' Steve said. 'They're—'

'It's too long in the back,' Dora said, 'and I don't like the look of that near hock.'

'They're going to Australia. With Nancy.'

'But other than that, it's the best-looking horse we've ever had here.' Dora grinned. 'Can we ride him?'

'Till we can find the right home.'

'Let's not start looking yet.'

'We've got to work with him a bit,' they told the Colonel. 'He hasn't worked for so long, we'll have to school him before we can show him to anyone.'

And every day when the Colonel, during his morning rounds, asked, 'You got a prospect for that grey?', they said, 'He's still a bit tricky. We want him perfect.'

David already was perfect. They had never had such a marvellous horse to ride. They were not going to let him go in a hurry.

'Got to work with him a bit longer.'

10

Callie had dreaded going back to school, but when the summer term started, Lewis seemed to have been converted by the glories of Easter, because he left Callie alone and did not bully her.

She watched him from a distance. He was strangely quiet. He did not make a dead set for the new, younger ones, as he usually did, twisting their arms to see if they would cry, knocking into them in the cafeteria to make them drop their food.

'School isn't so bad,' Callie told Anna. 'Perhaps I will stay.'

'Take the scholarship exam anyway.' Anna was used to Callie's frequent changes of mind. Tomorrow school might be no good again.

But tomorrow, Callie actually had a conversation with Lewis the Louse.

They were in the library, where you were not supposed to talk, but they were behind a stack of shelves and Mrs Dooley was busy at the far desk.

Lewis had taken down a book and opened it, but he did not seem able to read. Callie was searching for something in an index. She was aware that Lewis was watching her, so she looked up and smiled nervously.

To her amazement, he smiled back, his lower lip hanging on his face like a hammock, his teeth as pointed as his father's, but with gaps from fighting.

'What you do in the holidays then?' he asked.

Callie was so surprised and flummoxed that she could not think of anything.

'Oh – nothing much. I rode. I worked most of the time in the stables. I helped Steve build a gate.'

'Who's Steve?'

'The boy who works at the farm.'

'*Oh*, yeah.' Lewis nodded, remembering.

'He did a marvellous thing.' Callie babbled on, making the most of the chance to get on the right side of the Louse. 'He foiled a woman.'

'Foiled?' Lewis's mouth hung. His vocabulary was not very large.

Callie told him about the woman letting out David and then ringing the police. He listened, his slow dull eyes following the movement of her face, breathing through his mouth like a patient under anaesthetic.

'Who's talking there?' Mrs Dooley came round the end of the bookshelves. Lewis had disappeared. There was only Callie there to take a discipline mark.

Two nights later, the door of the Mongolian horse's loose box was open, and Trotsky wandered across a field of young wheat, eating it as he went and occasionally lying down for a crushing roll.

'Good thing he didn't have shoes on,' the Colonel said nervously to the farmer.

'Good thing I wasn't out there with a gun,' the farmer said grimly.

Trotsky was wily enough to undo a latch if the bolts were not fastened.

'But I know I bolted Trot's door,' Dora said. 'And the bottom bolt too, because he bit me while I was bending down.'

'Someone opened it then,' Steve said. 'Like the Jordans' neighbour.'

Callie kept her mouth shut, which was how she should have kept it behind the library shelves. Was it possible that she had put this idea for new trouble into the Louse's thick head?

He left her alone. She told her mother that she was definitely not going to take the exam. But when Lewis saw she was off her guard, he invited her one day to go with him and buy a chocolate cornet before it was time for her bus.

She went. They never got to the ice-cream van. As soon as they were round the corner from the school, Lewis pulled her into the overgrown garden of an empty house and knocked her backwards into the bushes. She picked herself up and was going to run away, but he grabbed her.

'That's just the beginning.' He stared at her with his horrid revolting slab of face.

'What for?'

'Stopping us getting a licence.'

'What do you mean?'

'Your stepfather. The Sergeant, the Bosun, whatever his daft name is. He done it.'

'It was nothing to do with the Colonel. He only sent the County Council a report on your stable.'

'He wouldn't know one end of a stable from the other.' Lewis was gripping her arm so hard that she would scream if it went on. 'Much less a horse.'

'Let me go!'

'He's got it in for us. Trying to keep an honest man from earning a crust of bread, my Dad says. We've lost a lot of bookings, you know.' His gorilla brow came down threateningly. 'People come to us for the riding.'

'Why don't you clean the place up and apply for another licence?' Callie bit her lip. Her arm was going numb. She would not scream.

'There's nothing wrong with our place,' Lewis growled.

'It's your stepfather, that's who there's something wrong with. We'd ought to put him out of business too. Perhaps we will. Yeah.' He dropped her arm, frowning under the weight of what passed for thoughts. 'Perhaps we will. My Dad says it's a crime to keep them poor old horses alive against their will.'

'It's not against their will!' Callie could have run now, but she stayed to argue, rubbing her arm. 'They're all fit enough to enjoy life. The Colonel says it's wrong to take life from an animal while he can still use it.'

'A crime against Nature.' The Louse was obviously echoing his father. 'Shouldn't be allowed.'

'We save horses! We saved your horse because you were all too cruel and stupid—'

Lewis pulled back his arm and took an open-handed swipe at her, and she ran, ducking through the bushes until she was out on the road where there were people.

When she got home, she kept her sleeve down over her bruised arm and explained her scratches by telling her mother that she had got off the bus half-way up the hill for exercise, and taken a short cut through the brambles.

She told the Colonel that the Pinecrest Hotel had been refused a licence to run a riding stable.

'Thank God,' the Colonel said. 'There is some sense to the Town Hall after all.'

'I'll bet they wish they could put you out of business too.' Callie watched his face to see how he would take that.

'Oh, I don't think so.' In spite of all the cruelty and ignorance he had seen in his work for horses, the Colonel still believed the best of people, right up to the time when he discovered the worst.

'And I've decided,' Callie told Anna and the Colonel – the pain of her arm kept reminding her – 'that I do want to go away to that school.'

61

'Your name's still on the exam list,' Anna said. 'I didn't keep asking Miss Crombie to take it off every time you changed your mind.'

'Suppose I don't get the scholarship?'

'Miss Crombie thinks you have a very good chance.'

I I

One of the disastrous things that people did was to give their small children day-old chicks for Easter. Dear little fluffy yellow Easter chicks. You could buy them in cut-price stores.

Some of them fell out of the paper bags and were stepped on or run over in the crowded street. Some of them were crushed to death by hot little hands soon after they got home. Some died of cold. Some died of the wrong food. Some died of not bothering to live.

The few who survived were either given away when they grew into chickens, or kept in a cellar or a cupboard, or even the bath, until the people got sick of it and gave them away or killed them, or the chickens got sick of it and died. It was a total disaster for all concerned.

This Easter, a town family had staged an even bigger disaster.

Their little daughter was 'mad about' horses, and so when she woke up on Easter morning, the car was standing in the road and there was a horse in the garage.

It was not much of a horse. The family had bought it quite cheaply at a sale. It had a big coffin head, lumps on its legs, a scrubby mane and tail and large flat feet that had not seen a blacksmith for a long time.

'My horsie!' They had bought an old bridle with the horse, and they put it on back to front with the brow band where the throat latch should be and the reins crossed under its neck, and the little girl climbed on, rode away down the middle of the road and fell off before she got to the corner.

63

She hit her head and was in bed for two weeks, and the horse went back into the garage in disgrace.

Now and then when someone remembered, they fed it a soup can of oats, which it could not chew properly, because it had a long loose tooth hanging at the side of its mouth. It had no hay, because they thought that hay was only for the winter, and no bedding, because they did not know about bedding. There was a small patch of grass behind the garage, and the horse ate that bare, and then licked the ground.

When the little girl was better, she got on the horse again with her friend and the two of them rode round and round on a patch of waste land, clutching the mane and each other and shrieking with joy. Finally, the horse stumbled and fell down, and the children tumbled off, which seemed the easiest way to get down, and a great joke too.

The floor of the garage was concrete and the walls were concrete blocks, sweating a chill damp. When the horse lay down, which it did more often as it grew weaker, it rubbed sores on its elbows and hocks.

If it was lying down when she came home from school, the little girl would get it up by holding the soup can of oats a little way off. When it stood up, she would take the oats away and put on the bridle.

'Work before food, Rusty dear,' she would tell it, and she and her friend would take Rusty to play circus on the piece of waste ground.

She was devoted to the horse. She sang to it. She made daisy chains to hang on its ear. She brushed it with her old hairbrush, but she could not get it very clean, because she did not like the smell of manure, and so she did not clean out the garage, although she told her father she did.

Her father hardly ever went to look at the horse, but he was very proud about it, and told everyone at work how his little girl thought the world of Rusty and it would do your heart good.

The mother did not look at the horse very much, because she was afraid of horses, and said she was allergic to them, which she thought was quite a grand thing to be, and she also did not like the smell that was accumulating in the garage.

But her little girl was happy, and she thought it was a lovely thing for a kiddie to have a faithful pet.

The faithful horse was willing enough to keep going somehow, although he was very thin and lumps of his hair fell out, and he was becoming dehydrated from only having small amounts of water, which the little girl brought him in a seaside toy bucket.

One day when she and her friend were riding him proudly down the road to the pillar box, slapping his ribs to keep him moving, he stopped and lay down in the road with his nose resting on the kerb. All the shrieks and wails and kisses and smacks of the children and the shouts of some masons who were building a wall and the advice of housewives who came out of their houses and flapped their aprons could not get him up.

It happened that the Colonel and Anna were taking a detour across the end of this road to avoid rush hour traffic. They saw the excitement, and turned the car up the street to see what it was.

The Colonel walked through the small crowd and stood for a moment with his hands in his pockets, watching the little girls swarming round the horse like distressed bees, patting it and kissing it and begging it, Rusty dear, to get up. The Colonel looked at the horse and the horse looked at the Colonel, and a message passed between them like old friends.

When the Colonel had got authority to take the horse, he telephoned for Steve to come with the horse box.

'But I don't understand.' The mother had taken the little

girl home and the father was back from work and standing nonplussed in the road, where street lamps were coming on and the masons had knocked off for the day and the house-wives and the other children had gone indoors. 'She loved that horse like her own brother. Thought the world of him, it would do your heart good.'

'I'm sorry.' The Colonel was sitting on the kerb in his best suit with the horse's head in his lap. 'But a small child can't be left alone to take care of a horse.'

'But we didn't know!'

'Famous last words,' the Colonel muttered. 'People who don't know anything about horses should stick to goldfish.'

'That's a good idea.' The man began to cheer up. He was glad he was going to be able to garage his car again, anyway. 'I'll get her a bowl of nice fish tomorrow. Take her mind off it. They soon forget, the kiddies.'

He went back to tell his wife and daughter the new idea. The Colonel took off the jacket of his best suit and laid it over the rump of the horse, who lay like a heap of roadmenders' sand in the shadows between the street lamps.

At the Farm, the Colonel pulled out Rusty's loose tooth by rubbing the opposite gum to make that side more sensitive, and then quickly tapping out the tooth with a small hammer.

'Bran mashes now?' Steve let go the bluish tongue, which he had been holding out to the side to keep the horse's mouth open.

'Give him anything he'll eat, if he'll eat.' The Colonel got up from the straw where Rusty was lying. 'He hasn't got much longer.'

'Will he die?' From the doorway, Callie saw the horse through a glittery haze of tears.

The Colonel nodded. That was the message that had passed between him and the horse in the road.

I am dying.

You shall die in peace.

12

Lewis went back to bullying the younger ones, and Callie kept clear of him. If she could keep out of his way until the end of term, she would be safe and free.

The week before she was to take the scholarship exam, she went early to school for some extra study with Miss Crombie. 'Not that I want to lose you next year, Callie, but I shall be thrilled if you do well.' Miss Crombie flushed and scratched her head with the pencil she wore through her hair like Madam Butterfly. She had a pretty boring life and not much to be thrilled about.

When Callie was in the cloakroom, she heard shouting in the yard outside, and running feet. The bigger boys never came so early, but there was a pack of them, galloping across the empty yard like hounds after a fox. She could not see what they were chasing, but whatever it was had dashed into the bicycle shed and bolted the door.

Whooping and shrieking, the boys attacked the shed with feet and stones and bits of wood. One of them broke a window. It was Lewis, of course, climbing on the bicycle rack and putting in the boot with a crash of glass.

Callie watched, paralysed. She had heard about a girl in New York being stabbed in the street while people hurried past or watched from their windows, and would not do anything to help. Now here she was, just as cowardly herself. *Don't get mixed up. Keep clear.*

Lewis was too big to climb through the window. He and the others went round to attack the shed from the back. As Callie heard the glass of the back window break, the door of the shed burst open and a little spindly boy, legs going like the spokes of a wheel, ran for his life across the yard. The boys were already round the shed and gaining on him as he wrenched open a door and got inside the school.

Help him, Callie. But she could not move. The boys were at the outside door as the little boy rushed into the cloakroom, gasping and wild-eyed.

'They're after me!' He could hardly speak.

Don't get mixed up. Keep clear. 'I can't – this is the girls'—' she began, but the child stammered, 'Save me!' and without thought, she pushed him into her open locker and shut the door.

It locked automatically. It was a tiny space, but the child was tiny, and there were air holes at the top to let out the smell of hockey boots and gym shoes.

Feet clattered on the stone stairs, and Lewis was in the cloakroom with three or four grinning cannibals behind him.

'Well, look who's here.' Lewis began to throw coats and scarves about, looking for the little boy.

'Get out of here.' Callie held herself tense so that the trembling of her body would not reach her voice. 'You're not allowed in here.'

'Who cares?' Lewis began to try the doors of the lockers, pulling out stuff from the open ones, while his mob tore clothes off the hooks and threw shoes and tennis rackets about, just for the mess of it.

'Where's that mucky kid?' Lewis was looking through the air holes of the lockers. What would happen when a pair of terrified eyes met his? What would happen when he saw it was Callie's locker and went at her for the key? It was round her neck on a string. He would probably strangle her.

'What's he done?' If she could just keep them talking, someone would come.

'Croaked to a teacher. Got us in trouble.' A gym shoe, a

purse, a stuffed bear flew out of a locker over his shoulder.

'Why?'

For answer, he tore the photograph of a boy from the back of a door, crumpled it up and threw it in her face.

He was getting near her locker. Her hand went up to the key string at her neck. 'There's no—' she said, 'there's no one—'

'Shut up.' Lewis took hold of Callie's long pigtails, wrapped them round her throat and pulled the ends.

Choking, Callie looked desperately out of the window. Then she saw a miracle, right before her anguished eyes. Big bold Betty Rundle, goal for the hockey team, was rolling in early across the yard. The boys saw her too. Lewis let go of Callie's hair, and they ran. Coughing, Callie pulled the child out of her locker, and dragged him – he could hardly walk from cramp – down the corridor and round a corner before Betty Rundle kicked open the outside door and came whistling down the stairs.

Miss Crombie was angry, puffed in the face. 'What's the point of me getting here early if you can't bother to come early too?' She was never at her best in the morning.

'The bus was late,' Callie said faintly. Her throat still hurt.

'It's for your sake, not mine', Miss Crombie went on without listening. 'Now hurry up and let's go through that French translation before the pagan hordes arrive.'

While she read aloud, misreading some of her own words so that they sounded like mistakes, Callie thought about the little boy as she had left him sitting alone in his empty classroom, sheltering behind an oversize desk as if it was a fortress. After he had told the teacher about his books being thrown in the pond, Lewis had lain in wait for him one morning last week and bent back his fingers behind a bus shelter. That was why the boy came to school early.

'But not early enough for *him*,' he told Callie.

His name was Toby. He was about ten – no one at home remembered his birthday – but undersized, with weak, skinny legs and a large shaggy head on which his ears stuck out like the handles on a porridge bowl. He was a weird-looking child, like a goblin changeling. Callie hoped she would not get mixed up with him again.

'Don't leave me,' he had said, when she put him into his classroom.

'Oh, look. I only hid you to save my own skin.'

'You live up the hill, don't you?' His pointed, big-eyed face was like a marmoset. 'So do I. What bus do you get home?'

When she told him, he said, 'I'll wait after my last class and go with you.'

'Oh, look.' She did not want to get *mixed up* with this child.

'I'd be safe with you, see?' Sitting at the desk that was too big for him, he had nodded confidently, as if Callie was as big as Betty Rundle, and as bold.

He was waiting for her. He waited every day and chattered by her side on the bus. In the morning, he was on the early bus, with his face unwashed and his socks in holes on his dangling legs, his books on the seat to keep a place for her.

He chattered while she was trying to read, telling her things about his home and his cats and his brothers and sisters who were bigger than he was – even the younger one – because he had been ill.

'They gave me up for dead,' he said cheerfully. 'I heard them say so in the hospital.'

The exam was only two days away. Callie swotted all the time.

71

'Why are you always reading?' Toby asked her when she only grunted at his twentieth question about the horses at the Farm, which fascinated him.

She told him about the scholarship. 'If I get it, I'll be out of this rotten school next term.'

Toby said nothing. This was so unusual that Callie looked at him. Tears stood in his big eyes, and his mouth drooped at the corners.

Why should she feel guilty? It was her life, not his. But she did. Before they got to the top of the hill, she told him he could get off the bus with her and see the horses.

Steve was very nice to Toby. He picked him up so he could see over the half doors. He took him on his shoulder out to the fields and let him open gates and hold them for horses coming through. When Cobbler's Dream came in, he put a saddle and bridle on him and let Toby ride in the jump field.

On the ground, the child was topheavy and misshapen, but on the pony, he did not look odd at all. He sat well by instinct, held the reins the way he was told, and learned the rhythm of rising after Cobby had trotted carefully round a few times on the lunge rein.

'Never seen anyone get it so quick.'

Toby grinned with his mouthful of bad teeth. When Steve lifted him down, he clung to the chestnut pony's neck, went into the stable with him, pressed his big head to his strong chest while he was eating, and had to be prised away by force for Steve to take him home.

Callie went with them. Toby lived in a tumbledown sort of cottage with thin prowling cats and decrepit vegetables and a collection of rubbish and old cooking pots and broken furniture outside, as if there had been a fire.

His mother came out, holding a baby which was dribbling at the mouth and nose. 'Where the hell have you been?' Her

72

voice began to lash at Toby before he had opened the gate, lifting it creaking on its one hinge.

Steve explained. The mother still looked grim, partly because she had not got her teeth in.

'He can come back any time,' Steve said.

'We'll see,' the mother said ungraciously.

Next morning on the bus, Callie was reading history.

'I hope you get bottom marks in everything,' Toby said. 'I'll die if I do.'

'I'll die if you go away,' he said, not in sorrowing self pity; just as a statement of fact.

When the examination came, it was like preparing a horse for a show. There was a special supper the night before. Callie washed her hair and cut her toenails and went to bed with hot milk. Her mother was up early to cook her a big brain-building breakfast, and everyone came from the stables to say good-bye – 'As if I was going to my execution.'

Toby behaved as if she was. 'This is my worst day,' he kept saying. 'This is the worst bloody day I ever had in my whole life.'

When Callie left him at his classroom, where she always had to take him because of Lewis, she said, 'Wish me luck,' but Toby only looked at her as if she were a traitor.

'Good luck!' Miss Crombie patted her on the back outside the examination room. 'I know you can do well.'

And when Callie saw the first paper, she knew she could too.

Waiting to see exam questions is one of the worst times in life, doomed, sick, your brain empty of everything you ever learned. The papers are passed out. You turn them over. Your eye scans quickly down and you see, yes, yes, one after the other, things you know, things you have revised, favour-ite things – two you never heard of, but there's enough choice without them – and then it is your day.

73

It was Callie's day. She picked up her pen, squared her elbows, smiled at the invigilator, who did not smile back for fear of cheating, and wrote her name beautifully at the top of the beautiful clean paper. *Question No. 1: Name the 6 wives of Henry VIII and say what you know of each.*

Easy, easy. Katherine of Aragon, Anne Boleyn, Jane Seymour, Anne of Cleves, Katherine Howard, Katherine Parr. She knew them backwards in her sleep.

She began to write: '*Katherine of Aragon, Anne Boleyn, Jane Seymour . . .*'

The image of Toby's face, pinched, pale, grubby, the big marmoset eyes and the pointed chin, lay on the white sheet of paper.

'*I'll die if you go away.*'

Callie sighed, crossed out her first words, and began to write again:

'*Katherine Taragon, Ann Seymour, Marie Antoinette, Katherine the Great, Bloody Mary, Katherine Dubarry.*'

No one could understand it. They called it bad luck, an off day, stage fright. Miss Crombie was upset enough even to call her stupid.

'You *knew* most of those questions. They were tailor-made for you.'

'I lost my head.'

'And lost the scholarship.' Miss Crombie was bitterly disappointed.

'I don't really mind. I never did want to go to boarding school.'

'*I* mind,' Miss Crombie said. 'And I mind for your mother.'

'She didn't really want me to go away.'

Toby said, 'I knew you wouldn't get it. But I'm glad you didn't.'

Callie did not know whether to be glad or sorry. She had thrown away her chance – but was it worth it? At school, there was not much she could do to help Toby. It was actually worse for him to be the friend of someone whom Lewis hated as much as he hated Callie.

Once when he tripped Toby up in the corridor, Toby managed to bite him as he scrambled up. The Louse had teeth marks on his hand.

Callie saw them, and jeered. 'He's got rabies, didn't you know? Ooh look – you're foaming!' and ran into the crowd.

Toby came quite often to the Farm to ride. Cobby could be a bouncing, jet-propelled handful when Steve got him on his toes to jump, but he was clever enough to know when to take quiet care of a rider. He had once worked for a paralysed girl, walking by himself into a pit so that she could heave herself from her wheel-chair on to his back.

Riding David, Steve took Toby along the top of the hills, through woods and fields and ferny lanes where he had never been before, because his legs would not carry him far. Colour came to his cheeks and his muscles grew stronger. Even his mother, who never admitted optimism, was forced to say that it might be doing him good.

One evening when Callie brought him back to the Farm, he said he could not ride.

'I hurt my hand.' He had it in the pocket of his droopy shorts which were handed down from someone bigger.

'Let's see.' Steve took out the hand.

'Nothing much.'

Steve gently unwound a blood-soaked handkerchief. The nail of one finger was torn off down to the quick.

'Why didn't you go to the nurse?' Anna asked, when she was cleaning the finger and bandaging it.

'I dunno.' He kept his eyes down.

'Did Lewis do that?' Callie asked.

'Who's Lewis?' asked her mother.

'That boy from Pinecrest. You know. The one who is our enemy because of Miss America, and the stable licence. He's Toby's enemy too.'

'Surely he wouldn't do a thing like that to a little boy?' Like her husband, Anna had an enduring faith in human nature, sometimes ill-founded.

The day when he was chased like a small animal, running for his life into the bicycle shed, had taught Toby not to tell tales to grown-ups. But he told Steve how Lewis had caught him on one of the swings and twisted it, jamming his finger between the chains.

Next day, when Steve had finished the morning work in the stables, he went down the hill to the school.

Callie had told him that some of the big boys went down to the end of the playing fields for a smoke after lunch. Steve hid in the bushes, rubbing his knuckles.

Half a dozen boys came down and lounged about for a while, talking in grunts and guffaws, making grubby jokes about the teachers. Steve recognized the Louse's voice, oozing thick and stupid through his adenoids.

Steve crouched, then suddenly leaped out and grappled with him. Surprised, Lewis went down, and they rolled over and over, punching and kicking and scratching and hurting each other in any way they could.

As Steve had expected, the other boys were too yellow to

76

join in. They watched for a while, circling the desperate fight like dogs. Then when Lewis began to scream as Steve was on top of him rubbing his face into the ground, they ran off.

Cursing, his face smeared with earth and blood, Lewis somehow scrambled up. Before he could get away, Steve caught him with a fist on the side of the jaw and the Louse went down like a felled tree.

Steve wiped his face on his sleeve, rubbed off his hands on the grass and ran them over his curly hair. He found a piece of paper in his pocket, and left a scribbled note tucked behind the ear of the snoring boy.

'You want more of the same? Try starting anything else with the little kids.'

14

Nothing happened for a while. The Louse was away from school for the rest of the week. Steve had a scratched face and a lot of bruises and Callie got up very early, did all his stables for him and brought him a mug of tea in bed.

The grey stable cat had three kittens. They were keeping the prettiest one with the Elizabethan ruff of white fur round its face, and a home had been found for the other two at a village grocery whose storeroom needed the protection of this famous family of mousers.

On Sunday evening, Steve put the kittens in a canvas shoulder bag and rode Cobby to the village, trotting along the side of the road in the gathering dusk.

The grocery people insisted on giving him a snack – he was the kind of boy whom women instinctively fed, not to fatten him, but to mother him – and it was almost dark by the time he started for home.

Dark, light, sunlight, grey shadows, it didn't make much difference to the Cobbler with his half sight, especially on a road he knew so well.

He trotted steadily, ears constantly moving, alertly forward, swivelling back, one forward and one back, because he depended so much on his hearing.

Steve rode half dreaming, the empty bag swinging at his hip. He knew the feel of the pony so well that it was almost like the movement of his own body. He sat relaxed, with a loose rein, not bothering to rise to the smooth trot, fancying himself a cowhand, legs stuck out in chaps, shoulders slack, single-footing through the desert sagebrush behind a herd of lowing cattle, going leisurely to the water-hole.

The motor-bike came out of nowhere, with no light. It threw itself at them round a corner and roared by so close that Steve saw the rider's face in the instant before Cobby reared, slipped on the road and came down hard, with Steve underneath.

His leg was pinned under the saddle. The pony struggled, and at last the weight of him lifted and he was up. Steve did not even try to get up. He did not try to move his leg. He was cold and sweating at the same time, with lead in his stomach and a sick spinning head, and he knew that something was badly broken.

He raised his head to try and look at his leg, lying with the foot at a strange angle, then quickly dropped his head on the ground and kept it there until the blood came singing back into his ears and he knew that he would not faint.

In books when a rider lies hurt on the ground, his faithful horse lowers its head, nosing him gently, and he whispers into its ear, 'Go home!'

In life, things don't work out like that. Cobbler's Dream was a few yards away at the side of the road, his foot through the reins, tearing at the long grass as if he had not had a decent meal for weeks.

Steve whistled to him. He moved on, contentedly grazing. It was almost dark now. Steve could barely see the rounded outline of his quarters, moving steadily away.

No cars came by. Steve's leg had been shocked numb at first, but now feeling was coming back, and with it pain. If a car did not stop soon, he would have to start screaming. If the Louse's big brother came back on the motor-bike to see how much damage he had done, he would have to shout to him for help.

Someone must help. Anyone. Help me. 'Cobby!' he shouted, his face in the long grass.

'Who's there?' A high, nervous voice, some way down the road.

'Help!'

A small dog yapped. Feet on the road. Then they stopped – 'Help!' – came on again. Then a hysterical tongue was licking at his face and Steve grabbed the little dog tightly, in a sweat of panic that it would touch his leg.

'What's happened?' A woman walked round and stood in front of him, staring down, her hand in her mouth. She looked in a panic too.

'I've broken my leg.'

The woman gasped and knelt down.

'Don't touch it!' Steve shrieked. She pulled back her hands and got up.

'I'll run back and get help. I live quite near. You stay there,' she added unnecessarily and ran, feet fading down the road, the dog yapping and yipping as if something marvellous had happened.

Steve closed his eyes and began to groan.

He was in a small hospital in the town where the Jordans had lived among the harassing new neighbours. His leg was in plaster to the thigh. It was very uncomfortable, and 'Yes, it does hurt,' he answered to the question that everybody asked.

The Colonel was furious. He was usually easygoing, a peace-maker; but after what Steve told him, he wanted to steam right down to the Pinecrest Hotel and tell soapy Sidney Hammond what he thought of his rotten, vicious, ugly son Todd.

'No, don't.' Steve closed his eyes. It still made his head ache if anyone raised their voice. 'It was an accident.'

'That's not what you told me when you came out of the anaesthetic. You said it was deliberate. He came at you without lights and practically knocked the pony over. He probably did knock him over.'

'He slipped.'

'What difference?' The Colonel picked up his cap and stick. 'I'm going to tell that two-faced swine—'

'Then he'll tell you what I – what I – oh hell. What I did.'

'What did you do?' The Colonel's voice dropped with a sigh from indignation to resigned patience.

'It was a revenge thing. I'd beaten up his younger brother. You know,' he added hopefully, as if he could persuade the Colonel that he had already heard about the fight, and had not minded.

'I thought you weren't going to get into any more fights, Steve.'

'I can't now.' Steve closed his eyes again and lay like a corpse in a coffin. The Colonel put a hand on his forehead and went away.

15

Steve came back from the hospital with his leg still cocooned in the long heavy plaster, scrawled over with messages from the nurses.

'Behave yourself – Cathy.'

'Good luck from Rosalita.'

'Mary Ellen – don't come back.'

'Love always Susie' and a heart with an arrow.

He could move about slowly with crutches. He spent one day sitting in the garden with his radio and various dogs and cats who were glad to find someone sitting still, and Anna bringing him things to eat and drink.

'This is the life,' he told her, but the next day he was out at the stables, trying to do his work again.

'Here, let me.' Dora ran up when she saw him at the outside tap.

'Go away. I am going to be the only man on crutches ever to carry a full bucket of water.'

He settled the crutches under his arms, bent down with difficulty, tried to pick up the bucket and grab the bar of the crutch with the same hand, and lurched forward in a flood of spilled water as Dora caught him just in time.

'Careful.' She propped him up against Ginger's stable. Her face was grave with anxiety, so she quickly smiled. 'That's expensive plaster, you know.'

Gradually Steve found out what he could do. He could carry a feed bucket, hung round his neck on a piece of bailing wire. Then he had to get into a loose box, move the horse out of his way with his shoulder or his voice, prop a crutch against the wall by the manger, unhook the bucket from his neck without the horse getting its nose in and strangling him, and tip the feed into the manger before the greedy horse knocked the bottom of the bucket and scattered the whole lot into its bedding.

He could sweep a bit, and do some grooming, leaning against a quiet horse. He cleaned all the tack, which there hardly ever was time for, and blacked the harness that Cobby wore to pull the blue cart out to the fields. But there was not much more he could do except sit on the old mounting block made out of a milestone (CLXVI miles to Tyburn) and play the guitar to Dora and Callie.

The Shetlands and the donkey had gone back to the children's camp for the summer, and one of the very old horses had died, but five skeletons had come in from the stable of a man who had skipped the country to avoid arrest, and abandoned them. Dora and the Colonel and Slugger had more than they could do.

Steve's plaster would not come off for at least a month, the doctor had said after the last X-ray. So the Colonel rang up the Employment Office and asked for a temporary stable hand.

'I mean a real one. I'd rather have nobody than a damfool girl who gets her big toenail trodden off, or a long-haired layabout who shouts at the horses and goes to sleep in the hay with a lighted cigarette.'

After a few days, Mac turned up. He came in a fairly decent car, but terrible old clothes, a burly man with shaggy hair and a grizzle of growing beard, some age past forty.

'I'm looking for work.' He came rather shyly into the yard. 'They told me to come here.'

'Know anything about horses?'

83

'Not much.'

'Like 'em?'

'I guess so.' He was American.

'Worked with them before?'

A pause. '*Uh*-huh. But I can learn.'

'References?'

The man smiled and shrugged his shoulders. Under the hair, he had a weathered face, craggy, with the kind of thoughtful, clear-sighted eyes made for scanning far horizons, or searching a face. The Colonel liked the look of him and took him on.

In his dirty old trousers and his yellow-grey sweater that had once been white, pulled out of shape, with loops of thick wool hanging, Mac went straight to work helping with the evening feeds.

There was a storm coming up. You could see it far down the valley, rolling blackly towards the hills, so all the horses were brought in.

Mac pitched hay and carried water buckets, doing what he was told, not asking any questions, not answering any about himself, quiet with the horses, though he seemed to know nothing about them. When Dora said, 'Two on that side need water – the grey and the roan. Know what a roan is?' he thought for a moment, then smiled. 'Sorry.'

When he smiled, his broad tanned cheekbones lifted and his eyes narrowed to a grey glint.

'It's a sort of reddish speckled—' Dora looked at him sharply. 'I've seen you somewhere before.'

Mac shook his head. He had hay seeds in his hair and beard. 'Only in your dreams.'

'What do you think of him?' Dora asked Slugger Jones, as he was leaving for his cottage across the road.

'What do I think? she asks. I seen 'em come, I seen 'em go. Mostly I seen 'em go.'

'I hope Mac stays.'

'Call me Mac, he says, coming out of nowhere. I seen 'em come, I seen 'em go,' Slugger grumbled to no one in particular, clicked his knotted fingers for his terrier and ambled through the archway.

When the work was done, Dora took Mac round to all the loose boxes and told him the names and stories of the horses.

'Cobbler's Dream.' Everyone started with Cobbler's Dream in the corner box. He was so striking, with his bright white blaze, his head always over the door, watching, demanding attention, chewing his hay now, and dribbling it into the yard. Mac picked up the bunch of hay and gave it back to him. Cobby turned his head to observe him with his good eye.

'He was hit in the head,' Dora said. 'Spoiled, stinking brat with a whip. He used to be a champion show jumper. Still could be, even though he can't see much. But we don't go to shows.'

'Why not?'

'We're not good enough. We couldn't afford the clothes anyway. And – oh, I don't know. A horse doesn't mind showing off, but having to perform perfectly, dead to order, our idea not his . . .'

'Maybe he likes it.'

'How do we know?' Dora looked up at him. 'We say a horse loves to jump because he gets all excited, but perhaps he's only nervous. Look at this one – Wonderboy. He belonged to Callie's father, who died. He loved to race, they said, but how do we *know*?'

Mac went 'Hm' into his beard. Dora wondered if she was being a bore.

'I'd love to know what Spot thought about the circus.' She showed Mac the broad-backed apaloosa. 'Three fat ladies in silver wigs and spangled tights danced on him at once, the

Colonel says, though I don't know how he knows, because he won't go to the circus. Anna, his wife, took Callie once and they saw Hero.' She took him across the yard to the brown, ewe-necked horse that Callie had saved. 'His rider was forcing him to lie down, and pulling his head so far round that he couldn't, and then beating him when he didn't. So Callie stole him.'

'How did she get away with that?'

Mac seemed interested. Perhaps he – perhaps he was a thief too? He would tell nothing about himself. On the run? Incognito? The beard looked fairly new and the car was too good for the clothes. If he had stolen that, he'd better get it away from the road.

She showed him the four newcomers – the fifth had had to be destroyed yesterday – the pitiful thin horses which had been abandoned, tied by the head and helplessly starving.

'The owner was some sort of underworld gambling type, who had bought this big house and the horses to make himself look respectable in the neighbourhood. He left in a hurry, he—'

She stopped dead, staring at Mac. What if he—? The thought was into her head and out again in a fraction of a second. She laughed.

'What's so funny?' Mac was frowning at the black horse with the wound on its bony head, shoulders hunched in the awful sweater.

'Fantastic things one thinks.'

'Such as?'

Dora always said what she was thinking. 'I thought for a second, what if you were that man?'

'What would you do?'

'Kill you, I suppose. The halter on this horse was so tight that it was embedded in the flesh. The vet had to cut it out under anaesthetic. Even if it heals, he'll have a dent in his head for ever, like a fossil. All the horses had halter sores. They had nothing to eat. They had chewed all the wood within reach. The one we put down yesterday had started to bite at her own chest.'

'It's unbelievable,' Mac said.

'It's true.'

Dora showed him Fanny, with an empty socket where a drunken gipsy had knocked out her eye, and Ranger and Prince, whose mouths had been cut to bits by the gangs of 'Night Riders', with wire for a bridle. She showed him Pussycat, who had broken down on her way from Scotland to London with a petition for the Queen, the brewery horse and the old police horse and ugly Ginger, who used to have a milk round before the dairy went motorized.

'They were going to put him down, but all the ladies in one street clubbed together and bought him. They call him Peregrine. They think he's beautiful. Do you?'

'I wouldn't know one horse from another,' Mac said.

Heavy drops began to fall out of the sky like lead pellets. The sky blacked over at great speed, like the end of the world. Dora shook back her short hair and stuck out for her underlip to catch the rain. Mac pulled up the collar of his bulky sweater and lowered his beard into it.

Anna ran out, with a coat over her head. 'Come on in!' she called. 'Come in and have some supper,' she told Mac.

'Thanks,' he said. 'I'll get something. I have to go find a room.'

'You can stay here.'

'Thanks.' He backed away. 'I'll be O.K..'

The rain suddenly came down like a waterfall. He ran, splashing to his car.

Anna ran with Dora back to the house.

'What's he afraid of?'

'I don't know,' Dora said. 'I don't think we'll see him again.'

16

He was back in the morning.

He worked steadily and well. He came on time. He left late if there were extra things to do. He became part of the Farm.

After a while, he gave up his lodgings and came to live in the little room behind the tack room.

There was room for him at the farmhouse, or across the road with Slugger Jones and his wife, but he preferred the stuffy little room, which was built into one side of the stone arch, and smelled of leather and horse nuts and his pipe tobacco, and the soups and stews and beans he cooked up on a small stove.

Anna would gladly have fed him, but he wanted to be alone. He was nervous among a lot of people. When visitors came, he got busy in the barn or out in the fields. Sometimes he talked to Steve or Dora or Callie, telling very little about himself, and that little different each time.

He said he had been in gaol, been in the Army, been at sea, been to Australia, lost everything in a flood, lived under the ice in the Antarctic for two years. He threw out bizarre bits of information as if he did not expect to be believed, and nobody believed him.

He still said he knew nothing about horses, but he was naturally good with them, and seemed to like being with them better than people. The Colonel thought he might have been a ranch hand once. There were days when he walked like a cowboy, and when it rained he wore an old hat he found in the barn, tipped over his eyes like a ten-gallon Stetson.

Besides the car, he did not seem to own much. He had very few clothes, a few paperback books, but no photographs. No pictures at all of anybody who belonged to him.

'Haven't you ever been married?' Callie asked him. She and Toby were the only ones who were allowed to come into his room. When the evenings were cool, he sometimes lit a fire in the smoky fireplace and cooked something marvellous in a black iron pot – beans and sausages and molasses and onions and hot pepper ketchup with beer poured in on top. It was much better than supper at the house. They sat on the floor and ate out of the pot.

'Like in the Wild West,' Toby said. 'Was you ever out West, Mac?'

'Listen kid, I been everywhere.' He always said something like that, to stop a question.

'What was it like?'

'Like everything else – loused up.' He always said something like that too.

While they were eating the marvellous beans, he would drink whisky out of a tin mug, and afterwards he would lie down on the low sagging bed and go to sleep. He slept for hours. They had never known a man sleep so much.

Lancelot, an ancient rickety skewbald who had been saved from the fate of being shipped abroad for slaughter, was the oldest horse in the stable. The Colonel judged him about thirty. When Dora or Steve showed him to visitors, they always added a few years to make the people gasp and give him extra sugar. 'Ah, the poor old thing!'

'What's poor about him?' This always disgusted Slugger. 'Life of Riley, he's got. Nothing to do but eat and sleep and make a big mess in his manger.'

You always had to look in Lancelot's corner manger before you tipped in his feed. His front end was fairly strong, but like most old horses, he was getting weak in the loins, so he sat on his wooden manger.

One night the manger went.

Steve, lying stiffly in bed in his uncomfortable plaster cast, heard a splintering crash from the stable. It sounded as if a tree had fallen through the roof.

By the time he had lifted his heavy leg to the floor and groped for his crutches under the bed, the upstairs corridor of the farmhouse was full of running feet. When he got out to the stables they were all there – the Colonel, Anna, Dora and Callie, pulling and pushing at Lancelot who was sitting on the floor like a dog, with his brown and white tail fanned out among the wreckage of his manger.

They finally got him to his feet, where he stood trembling like an old man with ague.

'Once more down like that, and he won't get up,' the Colonel said. 'I'll get Mac to fix a bar across the corner. He can sit on that.'

'Where is Mac?' Steve was leaning on his crutches in the doorway, hating to be only a spectator.

'Fast asleep.' Callie had looked through his cobwebby window. 'The whole place could burn down before he'd know it.'

The surgeon at the local hospital was worried about Steve's last X-rays. The leg did not seem to be mending properly, and he wanted Steve to go to London for a specialist's advice about another operation.

'Over my dead body,' Steve said. 'I'm not going through *that* again.'

'You want to limp for the rest of your life, like me?' the Colonel asked.

'Doesn't seem to bother you.'

'And stiffen up and have to stop riding?' The Colonel had been marvellous in his military days, riding for the Army in international shows, working one year with an Olympic team.

'That damn Toad.' When Steve thought about Todd Hammond and what he had done, he burned with rage, and the palms of his hands sweated with the desire to take him by his stringy throat. 'I should have crippled his lousy little brother. I will too when I get my leg back.'

'I'll drive you to London,' the Colonel said.

Anna went with them, and Callie begged to miss two days of school, so that she could go too.

School was a farce anyway. She had studied so hard for the scholarship exam that the muscles of her mind could not cope with revising for end-of-term exams.

Miss Crombie was very disappointed in her. 'You've gone off,' she said, as if Callie were sour milk.

'What'll I do for two days without you?' Toby put on his pathetic face, eyes very large, mouth drooping, those big bat ears sticking out at right angles.

'Dora is going to take you for a ride.'

Dora was going to ride with him over to the park of the deserted Manor house to show him the famous spiked iron fence which Cobbler's Dream had once so heroically jumped. They started off that evening as the others were leaving for London.

Steve hugged Cobby round his strong arched neck and said good-bye to him, as he always did before he went anywhere. He got into the back of the car with Callie, stowing his clumsy leg away with difficulty, wincing.

Dora and Toby rode out through the archway, Toby with

91

his head up and his back straight, short legs very correct, his small triangular face split by the smile that would not leave it until he scrambled down at the end of the ride.

'Take care of the Cobbler, Tobe!' Steve leaned out of the car window.

'He's supposed to take care of Toby,' Dora said. 'You care more about that horse than anyone.'

'Why not? He cares more about *me* than anyone else does.'

'Fishing.' Callie pulled Steve back inside, the Colonel crunched his gears in a way almost impossible to do with this car, and they drove away.

Mac was going to drive his car to the park of the Manor house.

'If you'd only learn to ride,' Dora said, 'you could come with us.'

'I'd be too scared.'

'You could ride Willy. Anyone can ride a mule.'

'Except me.'

He followed them slowly in the car along the switchback road at the top of the hill, past the racecourse where some men were staking out enclosures for the point-to-point meeting, and then he went ahead to open the cattle hurdles across the Manor drive so that they could ride in the park.

Because he was watching, Dora showed off a bit with David: slow canters and figure-of-eights with a flying change of lead, turns on the forehand and what she thought was a turn on the quarters. David was well schooled, but he needed a lot of leg and a lot of flexible collection. His figure-of-eights were fast and wide and he was not always on the right lead, but Mac would not know that.

'You see?' Dora pulled the grey horse up in front of Mac. 'It's easy. Isn't he a great horse?'

'Except that he don't always change leads in back as well as in front.'

'How do you know?' He wasn't supposed to have seen that. 'I thought you didn't know anything about riding.'

'Oh, I don't.' Mac had his head under Toby's saddle flap, tightening the girth. 'I guess I read it in a book. I read where it said you should use a lot more outside leg.'

'Well, you read it *wrong*.' Dora pulled David round. Steve was always telling her she did not use enough leg, but she was not going to hear it from Mac, who didn't know what he was talking about.

She took Toby down to the bottom slope of the park where the terrible fence stuck out above the brambled undergrowth, a ditch on the take off, a drop on the other side into the road.

The leader of the Night Riders, trying to escape capture, had ridden Cobby at this impossible jump, not caring if he impaled the pony on the rusty spikes.

Toby and Mac looked at the wicked fence with reverence.

'I could jump that, I bet,' Toby swaggered, but without conviction.

Mac said, 'You'd be crazy to try.'

They went back through the gate to the other side of the fence, where Cobby's rider had fallen and been caught unconscious, with the side of his face split open.

'On that very patch of stones,' Dora said. 'If you look, you can probably still find some teeth.'

Toby got off immediately to look. They let him search for a few minutes, scrabbling among the stones like a miniature grave robber, but it was getting late, so Mac lifted him on to the pony and they went home.

After seeing the jump, which had become a famous legend and was known among local people as Cobbler's Leap, Toby was prouder of the pony than ever. Dora let him unsaddle him and feed him by himself, and he stayed in the loose box, brushing and fussing and trying to whistle through his teeth like Slugger, while Dora and Mac finished the other horses.

When Dora looked over the door, Cobby was still eating.

'How much did you give him? He should be done by now.'

'Just a tiny bit extra.' Toby measured a small gap with the thumb and finger of his birdlike hand. 'Because he was so good.' At home, Toby did not get enough to eat, so to him, feeding was loving.

'Not too much, I hope.' Dora did not go in to check. Toby raised his arms and she lifted him easily over the half-door and carried him out to the car because he was tired.

Cobby went on eating.

17

When they came back from the cottage, Dora felt she had to ask Mac, 'Do you want to come up to the house?' It seemed odd for her to be alone there with all the food, and Mac alone in his little room with perhaps bread and cheese, which was sometimes all he had.

'*Uh*-huh,' he said, and she wished she hadn't asked him. 'I'm going to have a drink and go to bed. I'm bushed. You want a shot of Scotch?'

Dora said, 'No, I hate it,' and felt childish. It would have been more sophisticated to try and drink it.

Her mother had always insisted, 'Have a glass of wine. Learn to drink at home.' Last time Dora went home, her father gave her a glass of water that turned out to be vodka. Dora had been sick.

She went to bed early too, and saw Mac's light go out as she passed the staircase window.

She was woken out of her first deep sleep by a noise from the stables. Banging and thumping, hooves against wood. She sat up. Better go out. What was the good of Mac sleeping out there if he never heard the horses? Poor old Lancelot would have sat all night in the ruins of his manger before Mac woke.

Dora pulled a sweater over her pyjamas and trod into her frayed gym shoes. When she ran out of the back door and down the path, she saw that the lights were on in one block of the stables.

Mac was in Cobby's corner box. The pony was down and groaning, swinging his head about, kicking out at the wall.

'Colic.' Dora went quickly inside.

'Yeah. We've got to get him up.' Mac had a halter on the pony and was tugging at his head. 'Come on, boy – hup, hup! Come on – get up there! Here Dora, you pull this end, I'll try and heave behind.'

They struggled, pushing and pulling, but the distressed pony was as heavy as the great brewery horse.

'I thought you never woke,' Dora panted.

'Couldn't sleep. My past catching up on me. Good thing. If this jughead don't get up, he'll twist his gut and we'll lose him. Try the broom.'

Without questioning why Mac seemed all of a sudden to know what to do, Dora ran for a broom and poked Cobby in the side with the bristle end, trying to shift him. The pony groaned and swung his head round, bumping his nose against his distended stomach.

'Yes, *I know*,' Dora gasped. 'I know what's wrong.' She jabbed hard and the pony snapped at the broom, drawing back his nose from his bared teeth. 'If anything happens to you, Steve will – oh Cobby, get *up*!'

'Move over.' Mac pulled back his foot to kick the pony in the ribs.

'No!' Dora kicked Mac herself. 'Don't you know his stomach is full of gas? Don't you know *anything*?'

'Not much,' Mac said mildly. He went out of the box.

All right, she had kicked him. He wasn't much use anyway. She went on tugging at the rope in a hopeless kind of frenzy. Cobby would die. Steve would come back and Dora would tell him about Toby and the feed. Her fault, her fault. She began to scream at the pony, half sobbing.

'Here, let's try something else in his ear besides yelling.'

Mac was in the box, crouching in the straw beside Cobby's head, which was held out rigid, his jaw set against the tug of the halter rope.

96

'Hold him like that – tight.' Mac had a tin mug in his hand. He caught hold of Cobby's ear and quickly poured something into it. In a moment, Cobby was up, struggling and staggering, tossing his head and agitating his ear, furious, distressed, distended – but standing up.

'Warm coffee.' Mac emptied the mug into the bedding. 'Learned that from an old horse thief out in Nevada.'

For the rest of the night, they took turns walking Cobby in the yard. He was no better. They had to keep him moving. When Dora telephoned the vet, his wife said he was out with a foaling mare. He would come as soon as he could. No idea how long.

They had tried everything. Colic drench. Liquid paraffin. Huge dose of aspirin in Coca Cola, most of which went down Dora's sleeves as she held up the pony's head. When he would not walk, she went behind him with a broom. He was still in pain, nipping, cow kicking, swinging his head about like a club. He would lie down if they let him.

'Will he die?' Dora had accepted that Mac really did know what he was doing.

'Maybe.'

'We can't – oh Mac, *do* something!'

'Try one more thing.' He gave her the rope and ran across the yard to his room. When he came out, he had one of his flat pint bottles of whisky wrapped round with sticking plaster.

'Hang on to him. Don't want to lose any of this.' They backed Cobby into a corner, Dora got hold of his tongue, and Mac poured all the whisky down his throat.

18

When Steve came back, Cobby was his old self. The whisky had begun to shift the painful blockage in his intestines almost at once.

'Mac saved his life.' Dora said. 'Why did he pretend to know nothing about horses?'

'Perhaps he was a groom, and got sacked for drinking.'

After the heroic night, Dora tried to get the lonely man to talk to her.

'If you can talk about things, they aren't half so bad,' she said.

'They aren't bad,' Mac said. 'Go away Dora, there's a good kid, and leave me alone.'

'At least come for a ride. Do you good. I don't believe any more that you can't ride.'

'I don't want good done to me. I want to be let alone.'

'I came to see if you wanted to go to the cinema.'

'You joking?'

'Why?'

'I already told you. I hate the movies.'

'There's an old Cosmo Spence film on. He's good.'

'Big deal.'

Dora went to the cinema with Callie and they sat through a rather dated film made several years ago, about a Centurion of ancient Rome who rode thousands of miles bareback, looking for his girl friend who was carried off by barbarian hordes. As usual in a Cosmo Spence film, the horse part was the best. He rode a big creamy Arab and performed incredible feats of horsemanship.

'He does all the riding,' Callie whispered to Dora in the dark. 'No stunt man.'

'How do you know?'

'I read it in a magazine. That's how he got famous. After all, he's not that good at acting. You don't need to be if you look like that, the magazine said.'

'You don't need to be if you can ride like that.' Dora watched the screen enviously.

The last point-to-point of the season was late this year, because there had been epidemics of coughing in several stables.

Part of the course was over Mr Beckett's land. He went wild if one of the Colonel's horses was on his property, but the races were different. He got paid, and they didn't go over his vegetables or his seedling fir trees.

At one point, the course ran past the Farm's bottom pasture. You could sit on the fence and get a grandstand view of the horses coming over the brushwood jump at the top of the hill, galloping down to make the turn at the flag, then slowing through the plough to the stone wall, and on to the turf again and out of sight behind the wood. After the second time round, you could run up the hill, through the hedges where the first two jumps were, and into the crowd along the main part of the course to see the finish.

It rained all day. It always did. This course was known as The Bog. But everyone at the Farm went to the races, except Mac, who had begun to drive off somewhere in his free time instead of staying in his room and sleeping.

He had been gone every afternoon last week. They thought he had a girl friend, but no one knew who or where, and no one asked him.

After the second race, Callie and the Colonel stayed at the top of the hill to see the next lot of horses come into the paddock. None of them were special, except a big bay who walked with his groom as if he owned the ring of turf, catching at his snaffle, tail swinging, splendid muscles moving under his shining hide.

'That horse of Dixon's looks well,' the Colonel said. 'I think I'll put something on him.'

'Don't waste your money, Brigadier.'

He turned and saw smiling Sidney Hammond at his elbow, all his teeth on show, a sporty black and white check cap pulled over one eye to make him look like a shrewd judge of horse-flesh.

'That liver chestnut there. That's the one.'

'That weed? It couldn't run water.'

'Make no mistake, Brigadier.' Mr Hammond winked with the eye that was not covered by the check cap. 'You've got to know the inside story on these nags.'

'I do, with a lot of them,' the Colonel started to say, but Mr Hammond had taken his race card and was marking horses in other races that 'couldn't lose'.

To get away from him, they left before the jockeys came into the paddock. As they went towards the line of bookies under their dripping coloured umbrellas, Callie said, 'If he did know anything, he'd give you all the duds.'

'He seems friendly enough.'

'Make no mistake, Brigadier.' Callie looked up at him and winked. 'He'd put you out of business, if he could. The Louse said so, and I believe it.'

They went back to the pasture fence and watched the big field of horses come over the thick brush fence in a bunch, riders leaning back for the drop on the slope of the hill.

Blue with white cross, red and yellow spots, orange with green sleeves and cap. The colourful thunder of them was gone too quickly, crowding round the flag and spattering away through the sticky plough.

'Dixon's horse is going well.' The Colonel had his field glasses up. 'Anyone else have anything on him?'

No one answered. They were all staring after the horses.

'I said, "Anyone—".' The horses disappeared over the wall and behind the wood. The Colonel lowered his glasses and looked round. 'What's the matter?'

'Didn't you see?' Callie spoke at last. 'That man on the weedy liver chestnut, with the gold jacket and blue cap?'

'It fell back there, through the plough. I knew in the paddock, it—'

'But didn't you see? It was Mac.'

When the field came round the second time, Mac was far behind, the liver chestnut black with sweat, nostrils wide and scarlet. It heaved itself through the brush rather than jumped, landed with its head low, and was held together cleverly by Mac's hands and balance.

When he got to the plough, he pulled up and turned the horse. He rode slowly back, reins loose, slumped in the tiny racing saddle in the gold jacket that was too tight for him, the blue silk-covered helmet clamping down his thick hair, the chin strap round his beard. He looked more like a trick motor-cyclist than a jockey.

'Hi there,' he said, as he came nearer.

'Good race,' the Colonel said politely, 'as far as it went.'

'He's not half fit, but this friend of mine had a good sale for him if he ran well. Broke his collar bone last week and couldn't ride, so he asked me to help out. Some help.'

'He's not a stayer,' the Colonel said, 'but you got him farther than most people could.'

Mac laughed. 'I was practically carrying him.'

They were having an ordinary horsey conversation as if nothing strange had happened.

101

With his tacky old raincoat over his muddy borrowed silks and boots, Mac came up to the house for a long hot bath. He stayed for supper, but left before the end of the meal. He did not say any more about the race, and no one asked him, although they were bursting with the need to ask him many things.

When he had gone, the Colonel said, 'You know, he does look slightly familiar, under all that face foliage. He rides like an old hand. Perhaps he's a trainer, who got ruled off for dope or something.'

'I think he's had some tragedy.' Anna said, 'and has come here to forget.'

'Perhaps he's a murderer,' Dora suggested.

'A spy,' said Steve, and Callie said, 'Perhaps he fell out of a train and lost his memory.'

Mac did his work. What difference did it make?

Except that now that they knew he could ride, he started to ride David. He worked with him every day, schooling him in the jump field, while Dora and Callie and Steve watched and marvelled at what he could do with the grey horse.

'It will add a hundred pounds to his price.' The Colonel was delighted. 'I'm glad I waited to sell him.' Though he would have sold David long ago if Steve and Dora had let him. 'I'm going to start talking about him to some of the dressage people. We should get a really good price for him.'

'Couldn't we possibly . . .' Mac was giving Dora some lessons and David was beginning to go well for her too.

'I need the money,' the Colonel said, 'for these other horses who need us.'

'. . . just for the summer?'

'The barn roof has got to be repaired. I can't afford to keep him.'

19

The Colonel was always hard up. The Home of Rest for Horses was run mostly on gifts of money. Even the people who paid something to keep their old horses here did not pay enough. Sidney Hammond had not paid a penny for Miss America, who was still at the Farm and growing quite fat and leisurely on a life of good grass and no work, a big welt of scar tissue still disfiguring her back.

The price of feed and hay and bedding went up every year. Repairs were expensive. All the gutters needed replacing; they dripped rivulets down hairy old heads stuck out into the rain. The new barn roof would cost far more than the sale of David would bring.

The Colonel would soon have to talk to the Finance Committee. He hated to do that as much as they hated having to hear him.

And so when the continuity girl walked into the yard one day and asked the Colonel if he would ride in the Battle of Marston Moor for a historical film they were shooting locally, the Colonel could have cried, because of the money she offered.

He laughed instead. 'Me? Ride down the side of a gravel pit and jump a stream with a wounded man across my saddle? Good God, no. It would kill me.'

'But I heard you were the finest rider round here. Olympic team and all that.'

'Oh, I could ride a bit in my day.' The Colonel screwed up the side of his face, as he did when he was embarrassed into modesty. 'But that's long gone. Damn knee's too stiff. Look

103

at it.' He bent his lame leg as far as it would go. 'Not much more movement in it than that boy.' He nodded at Steve on his crutches, playing hopscotch in the yard with Callie.

The plaster cast was slightly bent at the knee, so that he could sit. He had found that he could sit on Cobbler's Dream, with the plaster leg stuck out with no stirrup. Since the London specialist had said that he thought it would mend without another operation, Steve was taking more chances with it.

'Oh hell.' The continuity girl was small and dark, with a lively manner and bright black eyes. She looked Italian, but her name was Joan Jones. 'I'm sorry.'

'So am I,' said the Colonel. 'I could have paid half my next winter's hay bill.'

'And we could have finished our outdoor shooting this week. We've been on location too long already. We've got to get the battle scenes done before the weather breaks.'

'Marston Moor?'

'Sixteen forty-four.' Callie had hopped over to listen.

'First defeat of the Royalists,' Joan Jones said, to show she also knew a thing or two. 'Michael Fox, who plays Prince Rupert of the Rhine, he's in command of King Charles' men, and when they're routed by Cromwell and that lot, there's no one to rescue this wounded Cavalier, so Rupert does this great bit on the horse to save him.'

'And breaks his own neck,' the Colonel said.

'No.' Callie had studied the Civil War for the scholarship exam. 'Rupert lived for years after they cut off Charles the First's head.'

'You should have told the stunt man that,' Joan Jones said. 'The first time we tried it, he fell off and cracked two ribs and dropped the Cavalier into the water.'

'You didn't tell me you'd tried it,' the Colonel said.

'I wasn't going to until you said you'd do it. We've got just

104

the right place, over the other side of the valley, that marvellous stretch of bleak moorland, and the sudden sheer drop into the quarry. It looks twice as high and steep from where we've got the camera.'

Mac had been working with David in the field behind the stables. He came round the side of the barn, the horse walking relaxed and limber, the man moving easily to David's long swinging stride.

As he came into the yard, one of the puppies ran at him from nowhere, yapping under his feet. David shied violently, and whipped round to bolt off with his head up.

Mac hardly moved in the saddle, just shifted his weight slightly back and somehow controlled the horse and turned him quietly round without appearing to do anything.

'My God.' The continuity girl was standing in the yard, staring at him with her mouth open and her black eyes astonished. 'Cosmo Spence.'

'What? That's one of my staff,' the Colonel said. 'Mac – bring the horse over here.'

'He's the living spit of Cosmo Spence. Same build. The eyes. The lazy, insolent way he sits a horse. Take off the hair and beard and I'd have sworn . . .'

'I've doubled for him,' Mac said, 'in my movie days. I was supposed to look like him, but I think that's an insult to me.'

'He did all his own stunts,' Joan Jones said.

'Says who? He had a good publicity man.' Mac grinned, his teeth very white through the grizzled beard. 'I done a lot of riding for him, back in the States.'

'Was it *you*,' Callie said, 'in *Angel on Horseback*, where the Centurion jumped right over that cart with the oxen and through the tent and out the other side?'

'Yup.'

'And in *Calgary Stampede*, where he was the only one who

105

could ride the black horse? And in *Blue Ribbon*, where he's jumping against the clock and the flashbulb goes off and the horse crashes through the barrier?' Callie had seen nearly all the Cosmo Spence films.

'Uh-huh. I cracked my ankle doing that, and they had to lift me on and off.'

'Listen,' the continuity girl said excitedly, 'you want to make some big money?'

Mac shook his head. He was not interested in money. He would not even let the Colonel pay him overtime when he worked in the evening, painting doors.

'Pity.' She turned away. 'The Colonel could have used that money, even if you couldn't.'

'What would I have to do?'

'One day's work.' She whipped round at once. 'Ride for Michael Fox. Prince Rupert of the Rhine at the Battle of Marston Moor. Long curly hair and a suit of armour and those floppy boots. The Mad Cavalier, they called him.'

'Michael Fox, that jerk.' Sitting on David, Mac spat on the ground, a bad habit he had picked up in his Western days. 'He couldn't play a Cavalier, sane *or* crazy. Why give a part like that to a guy who can't ride a bicycle, let alone a horse? Why didn't you get Cosmo?'

'Didn't you hear? He had a breakdown. Very bad. His wife walked out on him, and he was drinking. He's washed up, I'm afraid.'

'You are Cosmo Spence, aren't you?' Steve and Dora and Callie had forced their way into Mac's room with a bowl of Anna's chicken soup – rice and celery and onions and big chunks of chicken. You could almost eat it with a fork. They came in quickly before he could stop them, and stood with

106

their backs to the door so that he could not open it and throw them out.

'What do you think?'

'I knew all along,' Callie tried, then shook her head. 'No, I didn't. But when we saw that film, it bothered me all the time. He looked familiar, Cosmo did. I mean, more than just from other films.'

'If I was Cosmo Spence,' Dora said, 'I'd want everyone to know it.'

'That's just it.' He – Mac – Cosmo – sat on the edge of his bed and ate the soup out of the bowl, with the spoon handle sticking up into the side of his beard. 'Too many people *did* know. And they get sick of you.'

' "All these new kids coming up." My agent used to call me every day, long distance, collect, Hollywood to New York – wherever I was. "You got to get a new image. You've got to get another big part or you'll be finished." '

He put the bowl down on the floor, wiped his mouth on a dirty towel and threw it into a corner. 'Television. That stupid Western series with the fat guy and the little black kid, and I'd done three movies in a row that were all stinkers. I was so goddam tired. My wife stayed in New York. She never came on location with me. I rang her every day. I was lonely. I had all those phoney friends, but no one really but Elsa, after our – well, we had a little girl, but she died.'

No one said anything. He had never talked before. Now it seemed as if he could not stop.

'It wasn't the babysitter's fault.' He ran his strong hands through his beard and his thick hair, and dropped them, slapping the edge of the bed. 'We went to a party. She suffocated in her crib. I never went to any more parties after that. I'd never liked them anyway. Horses were the only thing. I had ten one time when I lived in Wyoming. That was – oh,

I don't know – one time when Elsa left me. She always came back after a bit, and we'd start over.

'Then I came over here to talk about a part my agent wanted me to do – lousy part, jolly coaching days, in capes and beaver hats, I'd have looked like hell – and Elsa wrote she'd gone to Mexico for a divorce. I cracked up. All shot to pieces. Nervous breakdown, you know?'

He looked up at them. Standing by the door, they nodded, although they did not know what it must be like to have the very fibres of your being snap, so that you could not cope with yourself, or anyone else.

'Every time I had to talk to anyone, I cried. Hotel clerk, taxi driver – God damnedst thing you ever saw. They were going to put me in a clinic. I ducked off, got on a train to somewhere, got me – room – I didn't even know what town I was in – hid from everybody and let my hair and beard grow, and didn't surface until I was flat broke.'

'Was that when you came here?' Dora asked.

'Yeah. I'd gone to the Employment Office to get work as a builder's labourer, or something, but someone said "Horses", so I scooted straight up here. Glad I did.' He grinned at them.

'Has it – I mean – has it helped?'

'You bet. I think I'm beginning to be real again. I think I'm beginning to be real for the first time in years.'

'Mr Spence, would you mind,' Callie asked politely, 'if we went on calling you Mac?'

He laughed. 'Finest thing I ever heard.'

20

When Mac saw the gravel quarry that the film director wanted him to ride down, carrying a limp man, and when he saw the common grey horse he was to ride, he said, 'Nothing doing. Not on that clumsy screw.'

'The stunt man took him down O.K.'

'And fell off into the stream, man. They told me.'

'It's the best horse we've got. It's trained.'

'I got one back home is better trained. I got one will go anywhere with me, *and* stay up on four feet.'

'Bring it over tomorrow, and we'll retake the close-ups with Michael.'

The Colonel said No. 'Not David. It sounds too tricky. Never mind about the money. It's not worth the risk.'

'There's no risk. I've had him down banks steeper than that. He's as surefooted as a cat. And the stream – I wouldn't have gone near it on that plug they produced, but David isn't scared of water. He'll jump big, and he'll jump clean.'

'Carrying a man across the saddle?'

'It's a little guy. I've seen him. And the armour is made of aloominum. Light as a feather.'

'I don't know.' The Colonel chewed at the skin round his nails. 'It's too far to ride over there anyway, and Steve can't drive.'

'Mac can drive the horse box,' Steve said. 'I want to take the Cobbler.'

'What for?'

'They need some more Cavaliers in retreat. Duke of New-castle's Yorkshire White-Coats.'

'With a broken leg in plaster.'

'I'll have armour and a big boot over it. They used to ride with their legs stuck out anyway. I get eleven pounds. I'll put it in the collection box.'

'Don't bribe me.'

But the Colonel eventually agreed to let Mac take David, if they wrapped his legs. They took the ankle boots that old Flame used to wear because she knocked her fetlocks with the opposite hoof, and the wardrobe people painted them grey to look like bits of armour.

David also wore an armoured breastplate, jointed armour over his mane, like the back of a shrimp, and another piece over his forehead. The bridle and reins were of wide coloured leather, studded with bright metal. When he stood on the high ground at the top of the quarry, with his head up and his long tail blowing, he did look like a seventeenth-century battle charger. Mac, in armour and boots, with a glossy wig, his moustache curled and his beard greased into a point, looked like a Cavalier.

'But he still looks like Cosmo Spence.' Joan Jones was in the group by the cameras.

'In his better days,' someone said. 'Poor old Cosmo. He's had it completely, I hear.'

'I heard he was dead,' the cameraman said.

The wounded Cavalier, a resigned young man with a chest-nut wig and a Vandyke beard, lay on the lip of the quarry, his helmet gone, his face carefully bloodied with panchromatic make-up. The cameras were placed so that as Mac galloped across them, it would not show that he was not Michael Fox, who had already climbed awkwardly on David for a close-up of the start of the heroic ride. Mac was on the horse now,

110

nudging him with his legs and holding him in lightly, to keep him on his toes.

'Action!'

Standing on the roof of the horse box in the road, Callie and Dora and Toby watched Mac wheel David, as Michael Fox had done, make him come up a bit in front, then trample, then off at a hand gallop that would look faster when they ran the film.

Behind him rode a group of Cromwell's Ironsides. The wounded boy lay like a dead doll on the edge of the quarry. The steep drop below him was the only way of escape.

Mac brought David to a stop with all four feet together at what would look like the very edge of the quarry. He vaulted off, heaved the young man on to the front of the saddle, jumped on behind him, and glancing back at his grim pursuers, he pushed David over the edge and slid him down sitting back on his quarters.

They jumped down the last part where the slope levelled out. The stream at the bottom had firm banks, and with his arm round the boy, Mac gave David three strides and he was over, just as he had said, big and clean, and galloping off over the moor to where a scattered band of White-Coats waited at the foot of the low hills.

On the crest of the hill, in silhouette, a boy on a chestnut pony waved a plumed hat to cheer him on, his leg in the plaster cast stuck out on the side away from the camera

Long afterwards, when the film was finally released, Dora and Callie saw it every day for a week.

David was superb, although you couldn't see much of Mac, because when Michael Fox found out it was Cosmo Spence, he made them cut out the bits of film that showed his face.

But on the skyline, Cobbler's Dream was unmistakable, with his head up to the wind and his long mane streaming from his crested neck. On his back, the young Cavalier stood slightly askew in one stirrup, and waved his plumed hat against the sky to cheer on Prince Rupert of the Rhine.

21

It was something to tell at school.

'Our horses are in a film,' Callie said, to anyone who would listen. She did not usually have much to say at school. It was safer to keep quiet, so that nobody could find out what your real self was like, and attack it.

'Our horses are in a film,' she told Rosa Duff, who sat next to her.

'Go on,' Rosa said.

'It's called *The Mad Cavalier*. You'll have to see it.'

'Is it a horror film?'

'No.'

'Oh.'

Toby, who had been born chattering, and had never learned to keep his mouth shut, even when he was teased, boasted to the younger ones.

'My horse was in a film.'

'Your horse. You ain't got a horse.'

'I have then. I ride it.'

'It ain't yours.'

'How do you know?'

'Because I know it ain't.'

'Well, that's all you know then, because it is.'

The arguments scuffled back and forth, as they did every day among the small boys. Toby's story of the film was submerged in a turmoil of arms and legs.

'Break it up, break it up.' Two or three big boys lounged across the playground, pushing through the smaller ones. If you did not nip out of the way, you got shoved aside or knocked down.

'Toby's a film star!' One of the small boys jumped up and down like a frog, pointing at Toby, trying to get on the right side of Lewis Hammond by jeering.

'I ain't said—'

'Better not say nothing.' Lewis pushed his face close up and wiped his horrible nose back and forth across Toby's button nose so hard it made his eyes water.

The Louse swaggered on.

The frog boy was still jumping up and down inanely, jabbing a finger at Toby.

'Toby is a li-ar,' he sang. 'Where is Toby's fa-ther?'

Toby's father was in prison, but he did not think they knew that.

'Shut up!' he screamed, his eyes still watering, from rage as well as pain. 'You think you're so big, but we got a famous film star at our place, so stuff *that*.'

He was at the Farm so much that it was 'our place', just as the horses were 'our horses'.

'Go on.' The boy stood still.

'Who is it then?' The others, who had been running after the Louse and Co., throwing gravel as near as they dared, turned and came back.

'Cosmo Spence.'

'Who's he?'

'Never heard of him.'

'Been dead for years.'

'I'm sorry, I forgot.' Toby told Mac about letting the secret out at school.

'I told you not to tell anyone.'

114

'Oh, it's all right,' Toby said cheerfully. 'Most of them had never heard of you and the others thought you were dead.'

Instead of cheering him, this upset Mac more than the letting out of his secret.

'You see,' he said. 'I am finished. They don't know me any more, the kids.'

'I thought you didn't want to be known.'

'Only if *I* choose. Not if they choose.'

He was gloomy for the rest of the afternoon, muttering about being all washed up, and giving the best years of his life, and nobody caring.

But towards evening, there was a tremendous noise in the road outside. Three cars pulled up together, and a crowd of screaming women rushed into the yard. 'Where is he? Where is he?'

The schoolchildren had told their mothers, and they had all come looking for Cosmo Spence, idol of their youth.

'Cosmo!' They rushed at him like a pack of yapping beagles.

Dora looked at Mac, and saw that he was terrified. He was pale and shaking, unable to move. She pushed him into a stable and bolted the door.

His fans were streaming through the archway. Dora had been washing down the yard. The hose was still running. She grabbed it, twisted the nozzle to a full jet and turned it on the women.

Their giggling shrilled to screams. They ran, skittering over the cobbles, while Dora stood in front of the stable door where Mac crouched, holding the hose like a fireman, flushing out one woman who had ducked behind a wheelbarrow, and chasing her out after the others, through the arch and into the cars.

'Thanks, pal.' Mac stood up and peered cautiously over the door.

'You still want to be known?'

'No, sir. It brought it all back. The shakes. Geez, I'd be a nervous wreck if I ever had to go to a première again. They tear your guts out. It's terrifying. They eat you alive.'

'Like vampires,' Dora said.

'Yeah. They suck your blood.'

Next morning, they found him in his room, packing the few clothes and possessions that he owned.

'I hate to let you down,' he told the Colonel, 'but after yesterday, I can't stay here.'

'Where are you going?'

'Back to the States, I guess.'

'To Hollywood?'

'No, sir. Being here at the Farm has taught me a hell of a lot. It's shown me the way I want to live. I'm going to get me a ranch somewhere and start a place like this for old horses in the States. Get a couple of good kids to work with me—'

'I'll come,' Callie said.

'Maybe later.' He smiled at her with his very white teeth which had been straightened and capped in his film star days. 'I'll be there a long time, honey. Just another old horse put out to grass.'

22

In the summer holidays, Callie worked harder than she ever did at school, but it did not seem like work. It seemed like the real purpose of living.

With the horses mostly in the fields, there was not so much stable work to do, but summer was a time for repairs and painting and mending fences and trimming hedges and restoring the land. With the money Mac gave him from the film, the Colonel was able to buy a small tractor to plough up part of the pasture, and harrow and re-seed.

In the long evenings, Steve and Dora and Callie rode on the fine springy turf along the top of the hills, or went down to the river, bare-back, and barefoot in shorts. They rode the horses into the water, then tied them up to graze in the lush meadow, while they had supper on the midge-misted bank.

One evening, the Colonel came into the kitchen, where Dora was starting to make sandwiches.

'If you're going riding,' he said, 'don't take David. A chap is coming over to try him.'

'Are you really going to sell him?'

'Dora, I must. I can't have a fit young horse taking up room here. We'll be crowded for the winter as it is, with more coming in.' He went on through into the office.

Dora put down the knife in disgust, threw the bread back into the bin and gave the end of the ham to the dog that was sitting behind her, as a dog or cat always did when anyone worked at the counter.

She and Steve and Callie stayed at home to view this interloper, whom they were prepared to hate.

He was a quiet young man in well-cut breeches and decent boots, with a country face and not much to say. He stood at the door of the loose box and looked at David for a long time without making any comment.

The Colonel did the same. They both chewed a piece of hay. Then the young man went up to David and patted him casually on the neck and murmured to him. He ran his hand down his legs, and picked up a foot, then came back to stand by the Colonel, and they both looked at the horse again.

Horse-trading is a strange, slow, closed-mouthed business. As an old sportsman once wrote:

The way of a man with a maid be strange,
But nothing compared
To the way of a man with a horse
When buying or selling the same.

'Throw a saddle on him?' the young man said at last.

'If you like,' the Colonel said, as if the young man had not come especially to ride David. 'Steve?'

Steve took his time. He went slowly on his crutches, although he was by now quite nippy on them, and carried the saddle back on his head. He brought the worst saddle, and had to be sent back for another. He took a long time tacking up, moving the buckles of the cheekstraps up and down and ending in the same hole, since it was David's bridle and already fitted him. The young man watched. Another unwritten law of horse trading is that you don't help to get the horse ready, even when the groom has a broken leg.

'Go easy with him,' Steve said, as he held the grey horse for him to mount. 'He's very jumpy.'

'Shies a bit, does he?' The young man sat sideways, adjusting a stirrup leather.

118

'No,' said the Colonel, and Steve said, 'Yes, he shies a lot. He's a very nervous horse.'

He showed him where he could try David, and disappeared. He could not bear to watch.

The young man rode quietly for a while in the schooling ring, hopped over a few jumps, then trotted down the lane alongside the hedge to the big field where he could gallop.

When he was nearly at the gate, Steve suddenly started up the tractor with an explosive roar behind the hedge. David shied violently – any horse would – shot off with his head up, jumped the high gate with feet to spare and galloped off before the young man could collect him.

'That's the end of *him*,' Steve said to Dora behind the hedge.

They worked with the tractor for a while, and when they came back to the house, the Colonel said, 'Chap's coming back for David tomorrow. He's very pleased. He thinks he can make him into an Event horse, when he's worked up his dressage and his jumping.'

They stared. 'Can he handle him?'

The Colonel smiled. 'He should. He was runner-up in the Pony Club Combined Training Finals two years ago. Bad luck, Steve.'

Bad luck because the horse was sold, or because the trick didn't work, or both? With the Colonel, you were never quite sure how much he knew.

At the beginning of August, two girls in a red Mini were driving by and saw the sign on the gate and came in to visit the horses. They were secretaries from London, and they were on their holiday.

'At least, we *were*,' they told Anna, who greeted them, as

119

everyone else was in the hay field. 'But it's all been ruined this year.'

In answer to an advertisement in a magazine, they had booked rooms at the Pinecrest Hotel.

'*Ride every day,*' they had been promised. '*Fine mounts. Beautiful countryside.*'

'When we got there,' the fair plump one was round all over, with round eyes and round pink cheeks like polished apples, 'the stable was almost empty. Just two skinny old horses, but Jane and I wouldn't ride those poor things.'

'The people were quite nice, but we wouldn't stay. It was the horses we'd come for. They wouldn't give us our money back.' Jane was the dark one with glasses. 'We tried to protest, though Lily and I are no good at doing that, but they showed us a piece in small print at the bottom of their letter.'

She fished in her shoulder bag and showed Anna the letter, which warned in a fine print whisper, '*Deposit not refundable under any circumstances.*'

'Anyway,' Lily said. 'It's too late to get in anywhere else where there's horses. On the way home, we saw your sign and thought we'd just come in. It's the nearest we'll ever get to a horse this summer.'

When Anna had showed them the horses in the orchard and the top field, Lily and Jane helped her to carry cold tea and buns down to the far hay field. Cobbler's Dream was in the shade of a hedge with the cart, and they fell on him with affectionate cries and gentle caresses. They were frustrated horse lovers, who had always lived in the city and could only pat police horses and watch the Lifeguards. While the workers drank tea and rested, they seized hay forks and began to turn the windrows, with more energy than skill.

Anna talked to the Colonel, and then she said to Lily and Jane, 'Why don't you spend your two weeks here? You can have a room with Mrs Jones across the road. Steve won't have

120

his plaster off for another week or two, so you can help us in return for a free holiday. If you'd like to.'

'If we'd like to!' They dropped their forks, prongs up, the way amateurs did, and rushed at her.

23

They were not much use, because they did not know much, but they were sweet and amiable girls, and kept saying that it was the happiest holiday they ever had.

They were never out of bed in time to do the morning feeds. They overturned wheelbarrows full of manure in the middle of the yard. They put horses into the wrong stables. They went barefoot and got their toes trodden on. They ran the lawn mower without oil. They left potatoes on the stove to boil dry. Lily dropped the wire cutters down behind bales of hay. Jane dropped her glasses into the pond and could hardly see. They left a gate unchained, and the Weaver, who was always chewing on things, flipped up the fastener and let himself and Stroller out into Mr Beckett's clover.

Fortunately, Lily and Jane were out for a late moonlight walk with Slugger's terrier. They could never bear to go to bed before midnight. That was why they could never get up.

The little fox terrier squeezed through a hedge and set up a frenzy of barking, which began to be answered by dogs from all round and far away, until it seemed that the whole hillside was awake.

When the terrier would not shut up or come back through the hedge, Lily and Jane ran down the road to the gate and found the Weaver and his friend gorging themselves on the ripe clover.

The girls sat on the gate in the moonlight and thought how nice it was to see the dear old horses enjoying such a succulent meal.

The terrier was still barking, and so were all the other dogs.

An upstairs light went on in Beckett's farmhouse, and then a downstairs light.

'I say,' Lily said to Jane, 'if this field doesn't belong to the Colonel, perhaps we'd better try and move the horses.'

Jane had a belt. They tried to get it round the Weaver's neck, but he always moved just a few steps away. They got it round Stroller, and tugged and entreated and slapped him gently on his broad rump, but his huge feet were planted firmly in the clover and he would not budge.

The belt broke. While Lily and Jane stood and watched the horses and talked about what they should do, they heard Slugger call to his dog from the other end of the field. The dog went to him, and when he saw the horses, he came wheezing up through the field.

'What's this, what's this. Come up, you old fool. Get out of it.'

Although the girls had not been able to get a hand on the Weaver, Slugger went easily up to him, grabbed a handful of his mane and yanked him off towards the gate.

'If them fool women would get behind that dray horse and throw a sod at him, he'd follow,' he grumbled.

'It seems a shame when he's having such a good feed,' Lily said.

'Good feed? They never heard of grass staggers?' Slugger asked the moon disgustedly.

He got the horses back into their own field before Mr Beckett came down the lane in his Land Rover, with his two big dogs in the back, still barking. He saw the trampled clover and the hoof marks and started walking towards the Farm.

'It was our fault,' the girls told Slugger. 'We'll talk to him.'

'Good luck to *them*.' Slugger whistled his dog and hobbled off towards his cottage.

'We're so sorry.' They ran panting up to Mr Beckett.

123

'It was dreadful of us.'

'We forgot to chain the gate, you see.'

'It won't happen again.'

'Wasn't it lucky they didn't get grass stumbles?'

'Grass staggers, Lily.'

'They did love your clover though. It's a beautiful crop,' Lily said, as graciously as the Queen Mother congratulating a cottager on his tomatoes.

Mr Beckett, with Wellingtons and a raincoat over his pyjamas, stood scratching his bristly grey head as they bombarded him with friendly apologies. He did not know what to say. Even his dogs had stopped barking.

'So please don't be angry, because we're dreadfully sorry we woke you up, but everything is all right now and there's nothing to worry about.'

'I told the Colonel, if his horses got on my land again—'

'Oh, but look. They haven't done any harm. The clover will all spring up again.'

'—I'd shoot 'em.'

'Oh, you can't have meant that, surely.' Lily beamed at him with her polished cheeks, and Jane asked him to come back to the cottage for a cup of tea.

'I've not seen you two before, have I?' Mr Beckett looked at them suspiciously. 'Are you related to the people here, or what?'

'Oh no, we work at the stables. Grooms, we are.'

'We take care of the horses.'

'Oh my,' Mr Beckett said. 'The Colonel must be hard up for labour.'

He went back to his Land Rover, cursed at the sleeping dogs and drove off.

Lily and Jane passionately wanted to ride, but when Dora let them try with the mule, Lily got on facing backwards, and then Willy headed Jane straight back into his stable and almost knocked her brains out on the doorway.

'Oh Willy, that wasn't very nice.' Lily led him out again.

'How could you have ridden every day at Pinecrest if you didn't know how?' Dora asked.

'That was why we wanted to ride every day, silly. We were going to learn. Turn him, Jane! Don't let him run back again. Pull the left strap, same as a bicycle.'

Dora let them fool about for a while with Willy. The long-suffering mule either stood like a rock with one girl on his back and the other dancing backwards in front of him, holding out a lump of sugar, or made sharp rushes for his closed stable door, the feed shed, the hay barn, and finally out through the archway.

Jane shrieked like a train whistle. A man and a boy coming in from the road grabbed the reins and brought the mule back into the yard.

'Going to a fire?' The man laughed at Jane, showing all his teeth.

The lanky boy, with pimples and long greasy hair, stared insolently, sucking his teeth and looking Jane up and down.

'I was going out for a ride, thank you.' Jane dismounted with what would have been dignity if her knees had not buckled at contact with the ground, so that she had to clutch at the man's arm.

'Whoa there, Missy,' he said.

She peered at him shortsightedly. 'I know you, don't I?'

'Should do.' It was Sidney Hammond, proprietor of the Pinecrest Hotel.

'Well, er – excuse me. I've got to go.' Lily had run to the house. Jane left Todd Hammond holding the mule and followed her. Dora had disappeared too when she saw who

125

it was, in case they recognized her as the girl with the pink slacks and Passion Flowers.

She sent the Colonel out to them.

'A pleasure, Brigadier,' Sidney said, pleasantly enough, though his teeth were gritted, rather than grinning. 'I see you've got two of my young ladies up here. I didn't know you'd gone into the hotel business.'

'Who—? Oh them. They're working for me. They had a bit of bad luck, they – oh yes.' The Colonel remembered.

'Two rooms for two weeks.' Mr Hammond said. 'Plus all meals, not to mention what that kind will spend at the bar once they're in holiday mood. That's quite a little loss to me, you will agree.'

'They wanted horses,' the Colonel said. 'It's not my fault.'

'And yet my memory tells me – correct me if I'm wrong – that not too long ago, you gave yourself a little tour of my stables.'

'Oh, that.'

'Yes, that.'

'It was nothing to do with me,' the Colonel protested, but Sidney Hammond held up his hand.

'Please, my dear Brigadier, we'll let bygones be bygones. I'll not hear another word.'

Which was a good thing, since the Colonel was quite embarrassed, and did not have another word to say.

Willy relieved the tension by snapping at Todd, who hit him on the muzzle. The mule spun round and kicked out, as the Toad jumped out of the way.

'You've got to be careful with mules.' The Colonel took hold of Willy.

'Is that why you let those silly girls ride him?' Sidney Hammond asked. 'I hope you've got good Third Party Insurance, Brigadier, ha, ha.'

Miss America was in her stable because of midday flies, and

when the Colonel had unsaddled Willy, he found Mr Hammond and Todd looking at her.

'My mare looks a treat.' He was smiling Sidney again. 'I must say you've done a fine job with her.'

'Thank you.'

'I came to tell you I'll be bringing my trailer up for her tomorrow.'

'I thought you – I thought you'd given up your stable.'

'In a business way, yes. With the money we spent on those horses, we couldn't make it pay,' said slippery Sidney, as if they had never had the conversation about the riding stable licence only five minutes ago. 'But we still keep a few favourites for our own use. My boys are great riders. Beauty Queen will get plenty of work, don't worry about that.'

'That back of hers won't stand any work at all,' the Colonel said, 'the way the scar tissue has lumped up. You put a saddle on it, it will break down again.'

'Oh, I *know*. We just want her as a pet, and I'm going to lead my little grand-daughter about on her. "Grandpa," she says. "Take me for a wide." Of course, she thinks it's riding, though all she does is sit there while I lead her round the path and her Granny snaps her picture.'

It was a beautiful image, except that the Colonel was almost sure he had not got a grand-daughter.

'It came to me what he was going to do,' he said later at supper. 'He was planning to get some horses in again, and get round the licence difficulty by raising the price of rooms to include riding, so that he wouldn't actually be charging for the hire of a horse.'

'Very clever,' Steve said.

'He is cunning. I wish he wasn't so affable with it. I always find myself quite liking him, although I know he's a rat.'

'Rat, Toad, Louse. You should call the exterminators.'

'I told him he could have the mare—'

127

'Oh *no*!'

'—when he paid the bill. She's been here quite a time. If I charge full boarding fees, he can't possibly pay.'

Everyone applauded him, and Lily said, 'Colonel dear, you *are* clever!' as if there might have been some doubt.

24

Towards the end of their holiday at the Farm, Lily and Jane got restless, and wanted to go into town to dance.

'Dora, you come. Do you good.'

'I can't dance.'

'You can stand in the crowd and twitch,' Jane said. 'That's all there's room for.'

'It's not my style.'

'Perhaps it ought to be,' Anna said. 'Sometimes I worry about whether this kind of life is right for a young girl.'

'You sound like my mother,' Dora said.

'Thank you. Is that a compliment?'

'No.'

The three girls went off on the bus, but they never got to the dance place, or even into town. On the way, they passed a fairground, and it looked so inviting, with coloured lights and blaring music, that they spent the evening there instead.

Dora went on the big roundabout three or four times. It was strange. She could ride a real horse at the Farm almost any day, and yet she could not resist the fascination of sitting astride the cool wooden painted horse, up and down and round and round, all four legs impossibly prancing, nostrils flared, teeth bared, the twisted barley sugar brass pole to lay your cheek against, the crowd and the trodden grass and the upturned faces spinning faster and faster into a blur, the blare and tootle and thump and clash of the pipe organ, swelling and fading and swelling again as you came round past the bosomy figurehead ladies, the painted signs: 'Longest Ride at the Fair', 'Oh Boy!', 'Yes! It's the Galloping Horses!'

When Dora got off, Jane, shooting at random without her glasses, had won a large yellow rabbit at the rifle booth. 'Something for our money at last.'

'What can you do with it?'

'What can you *do* with it?'

What did you have to do with an enormous yellow nylon fur rabbit except keep it on your bed until you got sick of it and stuck it on top of the cupboard to collect dust?

There was another, much smaller roundabout at the end of the fairground, among the 'Kiddies' Rides'. Feeble cars on tracks, with steering wheels which the kiddies turned zealously and thought they were driving. Little boats that floated endlessly round a doughnut-shaped tank of dirty water, while a strong dreamy boy stood in the hole of the doughnut and turned a crank to keep them moving.

The merry-go-round was not turned by a dreamy boy. Instead of painted horses, there were four live ponies, each with a breastplate attached to a bar which turned on the hub as they pottered slowly round and round.

It was not exactly cruel, and yet it was not exactly what a pony ought to be doing.

Dora and Lily and Jane watched for a while. A big man with a simple face and a wobbly paunch lifted the children into the saddles. They rode round a small circle, the bigger ones jiggling and bouncing, or sitting tight, lost in a dream that they were galloping, the tiny ones petrified, staring at their proud mothers all the way round, begging silently to be lifted down.

The ponies were Shetlands with trailing tails, quite well kept. Although Dora and Lily and Jane watched critically, with the narrowed eyes of experts, they could find no cruelty to complain of, except possibly to small children.

But Dora said on principle, as they turned away, 'The ponies hate it.'

130

'Oh no.' The paunchy man turned round, with a wriggling child in his arms. 'They like it.'

'How do you know?'

Someone in the crowd giggled.

'When I put the harness on, each one walks to his place and stands to be hitched up. Don't you, love?' The pony hardly came up to where his waist would be if he had one. He could have bent over it, if he could have bent, and touched the ground on the other side.

He put the child gently into the saddle, whistled, and the ponies moved forward, little hoofs the size of coffee mugs pockmarking the soft ground. When he whistled again they stopped, and the children were lifted down.

'Not much of a ride for five pence,' Jane said, since there was nothing else to complain about.

The man turned his mild face round to her and said, 'Quite enough for my little ponies.'

The fair was closing when they left. They were waiting at the bus stop, when Jane suddenly cried out, 'My rabbit!' She had left it at the fair, near the pony-go-round where she had put it down to pat one of the Shetlands.

'Come back with me.' She dragged at Dora's arm.

'We'll miss the bus.'

'Anna will come for us. She said she would if we phoned.'

The bright fairground illuminations were out. There were only a few working lamps where people were cleaning up or shuttering the booths, and windows and doorways of trailers spilled patches of light on to the trampled ground.

The yellow rabbit was not where Jane had left it.

'I could have told you.'

'They probably put it back in the rifle booth for tomorrow.'

'I'm going to look. I'd know it anywhere.'

'It's all shut up.' Lily began to walk back.

'My rabbit.'

131

Going to the gate, they passed a small open-sided tent where the four Shetlands were tied in stalls with canvas partitions.

Lily ran in out of the darkness, and put her hand on a pony without speaking to it. The pony jumped, pulled back, broke its thin rope and made off, ducking and swerving in fright as the three girls tried to catch it.

It knocked over some crates, tripped over a guy rope, skittered round the ticket booth and out into the road, hard little hoofs pattering, with Dora and Lily after it. Jane had fallen over the crates and the rope too and was some way behind.

It was a fairly busy road. The cars were not going fast, but they were coming steadily in both directions. The pony ran along the side of the road, then swerved across the middle. For a moment, it was caught in headlights, outlined all round like a haloed donkey in a Christmas crèche, and then it disappeared in a scream of brakes.

The car skidded, slid into a car coming the other way, and was rammed from behind, just as the first car was hit in the back. The crashing and screeching of brakes and the tinkling of glass seemed to go on for ever.

When Dora and Lily ran up, there were five cars already involved in the crash, and one more just skidding up to bash headlights into tail lights. Screech. Crash. Pause. Tinkle. Car doors opened everywhere and the road was full of people.

'It was the pony,' the first driver kept shouting, waving his arms about.

'What pony?' No one could see a pony. Dora and Lily were on hands and knees looking for it under the car.

They thought it must be dead, but Jane, limping along with her knees grazed and her ankle bruised, met the pony going home head on. She grabbed it by the broken rope and yelled to the others, 'I've got it! I've got the pony!'

If she had not done that, the girls might have been able to slip away and let the people in the cars, none of whom was hurt, argue about hallucinations and bad lighting and blind spots in the road. As it was, the police got the whole story, and the newspaper also got the whole story, slightly wrong.

'RESCUE EFFORT ENDS IN SIX CAR CRASH'

After they explained to the police, Lily and Jane had talked to a newspaper reporter, thinking he was a detective, because he wore a belted trenchcoat with a cape on the shoulders, like old television films.

'We were sorry for the ponies,' they had said. They added, 'But then we saw that the man was good to them,' but the breakdown lorry arrived with a deafening siren as they said that, and the story that came out in the paper sounded as if they had deliberately let the pony loose.

The Colonel went to the owner of the pony and also to the newspaper, to set the story straight, but he got several letters from the kind of people who may never write so much as a Christmas card, but are always moved to write a letter when one of Our Dumb Friends is involved.

Some of the letters were cranky. Some were sentimental. One had a twenty-five pence postal order in it 'to buy the little fellow a bag of carrots.' One was a poison pen letter, unsigned.

'Why can't you people mind your own business?' it said. *'Not that your business is anything to boast of, keeping those wretched animals alive that should have been put out of their misery long ago . . . Trying to stop a man from earning an honest crust of bread . . . Should be stopped yourselves . . . We know your sort and what we know we don't like.'*

'What are they talking about – "crust of bread"?' The Colonel looked up. 'Who could have written a thing like that?'

'The man at the roundabout?' Jane suggested.

'Not with that gentle face,' Dora said. 'And the writing is too good.'

'The writing . . . Jane,' the Colonel said, 'go and get me that letter you had from the Pinecrest Hotel. The one that Sidney Hammond wrote.'

The handwriting was the same.

25

In September, when the fruit pickers came to the valley, they brought two ponies up to the Farm for their annual holiday. The Colonel would always take in working horses and ponies for a few weeks of rest. The owners paid what they could, or nothing if they couldn't.

Sometimes, about this time of year, a costermonger's pony or a gipsy horse would be brought in 'for a rest', and the owners would then disappear, so that the horse would be sure of good food and shelter for the winter. They would come back all smiles in the spring, with gifts of firewood and vegetables, and probably be back the next autumn to try the same thing again.

The Shetlands and the donkey were back from the children's camp, and Steve would soon go to fetch the nurseryman's Welsh pony who came every year. His plaster was off now, and the leg mended. He brought a piece of the cast back after they took it off at the hospital, and they buried it at the spot where the motor-bike had ditched him, and Callie drove in a stake, as if it was through the Toad's heart.

An old man wandered vaguely into the yard one day, clutching the newspaper story about Dora and Lily and Jane and the fairground pony.

'I seen about this place in the papers,' he said. 'Touched my heart. I wish I could give you people something for the wonderful work you do, but I'm not a rich man.'

'Who is?' The Colonel had Ranger's foot in his lap, trimming the hoof.

'Got my pension, that's about all it is, and my chickens and goats, just about keeps me going.'

He had watery blue eyes and wispy grey hair over a pink scalp. 'I got an old mare. Hard-working old girl. I'd give anything to give her a bit of a reward for all the years she's given me.' He sighed and shook his head at his turned-up boots, then raised his eyes to see how the Colonel was taking it.

'I'm sure you would.' The Colonel put down Ranger's hind foot and moved round to the other side.

'I seen in the paper that they can come here for a rest.' The old man followed him round, shaky but determined. 'So I came up to ask whether my old girl—'

'I'm awfully sorry.' The Colonel kept his head down, because he hated having to refuse anyone. 'I'm full up at the moment.'

'She can stay out in all weathers. She'd be no trouble to you. I just thought, if I could get her on to some good grass for a month or so, it would mean the world to her.' He paused, and watched the Colonel working skilfully on Ranger's hoof. 'She's earned her rest, mister.'

'Oh, all right.' The Colonel put down the hoof and stood up, slipping the curved knife into the pocket of his leather apron. 'But only for a month. We've got too many for the winter already. Just a month, all right?'

'God bless you, sir.' The old man's eyes swam with emotion. 'And all who work with you.'

But in spite of his shaky hands and his moist, emotional eyes, he turned out to be a pretty shrewd old man. In a neighbour's truck, he brought the mare, and also her treasured companion, a nanny goat in milk, so that the Colonel should have some return for his kindness.

136

'Who's going to milk it?'

'Not me.'

'Count me out.'

'I'm too busy.'

'I don't know how.'

It turned out that the only person who would milk the goat was Toby, and he managed it very well, sitting on a stool with the three legs cut down to make it the right height, and the goat working on her cud like chewing gum. She was crabby with everyone else but him. He milked her twice a day before and after school.

'Who wants to drink goat's milk?'

'Not me.'

'I hate it.'

'Anna can make cheese with it.'

'I don't know how.'

So Toby took the milk home to his mother, and she gave it to her sickly new baby, who began to thrive.

The goat was out in the fields all day with the mare, making rushes if the other horses came close. The dusty black mare was getting on in years, with battered legs and a long bony head with flecks of white round the eyes like spectacles. Her name was Specs. She had been in the old man's yard for years. She was reasonably fat, but she tore into the meadow grass like a fanatic. After two weeks, someone discovered that she was in foal.

'The old game,' the Colonel said. 'Sneak them in here to have it. But he's not going to get away with it.'

When the old man did not turn up at the end of the month, the Colonel went to the town where he lived and drove round for two hours looking for the address the old man had given him. There was no such address. No one had ever heard of the old man, or his mare, or his goats and chickens, or even his neighbour with the truck.

137

'He'll be back in the spring,' the Colonel said when he came home, 'for his mare and foal. The old devil.'

But Callie and Toby were thrilled, and so were Steve and Dora. They had not had a foal at the Farm since the Colonel had rescued the mare at Westerham Fair.

Callie took extra care of Specs. The vet said it was a first foal, and she was a bit old for it, so Callie brought her in every night and gave her extra food and vitamins, and came out in her nightdress long after she had gone to bed to shut the top door of the stable if the night turned cold.

They kept her in the separate foaling stable behind the barn, since she seemed to be getting pretty near her time.

'Will you wake me?' She made the Colonel promise to call her if the foal was being born. She had a private fantasy that the old man would never come back, and they would be able to keep the foal. She would call it Folly. Follyfoot, after the Farm. She would handle it and play with it right from the start, so that it would always like people.

'Don't worry,' she murmured into the mare's long furry ear. 'Callie's here.'

The old lady rested on her scarred and weary legs, with her grizzled head low and her bottom lip hanging, ratty eyelashes down over her spectacled eyes. She was not beautiful, but she was content. Her sides bulged like a cow. The Colonel thought it would be any time now, and Callie would hardly risk going to sleep.

On the bus to and from school, Callie and Toby talked endlessly about the foal, planning its future like doting parents. New babies in Toby's family had always been more of a burden than an excitement, but this one was different. He and

Callie could hardly exist through the school day until they could rush back to the farm.

Callie started to ring her mother up half-way through the morning to ask, 'Any news?' Once, at break, she was in the call box at the end of the staff corridor, and she turned and saw a squashed white triangle of nose flattened outside the glass, where the Louse was staring at her. When he took his face away, it left a wet smear.

Callie held the receiver and kept on pretending to talk long after her mother had rung off. But the buzzer went for class, and she had to hang up and come out of the box. Lewis fell into step beside her, quickening his pace as she quickened hers.

'Talk to your boy friend?' he asked.

'It was my mother.'

A teacher was passing. Lewis put his hands in his pockets, to look like two friends strolling. 'Everything all right at home?'

'Yes.' Callie did not dare to say, Mind your own business. 'We're expecting a foal,' she said nervously, because they were turning into an empty corridor and it was safer to keep him talking. 'At least, Specs is. That's what we call her, because she's got white hair round her eyes, like spectacles.' She laughed uneasily.

Lewis did not say anything. When they reached a corner, he suddenly peeled off like a fighter plane and was gone. He did not seem so vicious this term. Perhaps he was growing out of it at last. Perhaps it was going to be a lucky year.

26

Two nights later, the telephone rang. Everyone in the house woke and sat up. It was two o'clock in the morning. The ringing in the hall sounded loudly through the still house, like disaster.

It was Mr Beckett.

'This is it, Colonel.' He was sputtering with rage. 'The horse was all over one corner of my winter wheat, and then right through my seedling fir trees, galloping as if the devil himself was behind. I took a pot shot at it. Said I would, didn't I? No, I didn't hit it, but I tell you, Colonel, I almost wish I had.'

It was Specs. The door of the foaling stable was wide open. Her hoofmarks led through the orchard and the open gateway, across the lane and on to Beckett's land.

The Colonel got into the car to go round to the other side of Beckett's farm. Steve and Dora and Callie were starting out on foot through the orchard when Steve stopped.

'Let's ride,' he said. 'If they chased her, she may be miles away.'

When they came out of the house, they had all heard the motorbike, screeching along the road into the downhill curve. They did not see the riders, but they were all sure who it was.

They took Cobby and Hero, and Dora rode the mule. It was a dark night. No moon, and a damp mist hanging over the ground, and on the trees like veils. They could not follow the mare's tracks.

They rode round the edges of Beckett's arable land, and

along a cart track between his cow pastures. Ahead of them, they saw the Colonel's lights on the road and went to join him.

'Better go home,' he said. 'We'll try in the morning.'

They went back into the fields, but they did not go home. They kept riding about in circles, farther afield, covering the land. If Specs heard or smelled the horses, she might come to them.

When the first line of light began to creep along the edge of the far hills, they were all exhausted, and the mule was falling into every rut and over every stone, even those that were not there. Callie was cold and Hero was bored. Every time they made a turn away from home, he would fight to turn back. Steve and the Cobbler rode ahead, picking their way between the low bushes scattered over a fallow field. They were a long way from home. Callie was not even sure where they were.

Halfway across the field, Cobby suddenly raised his head, his small pointed ears tightly forward. He stopped. Steve pushed him on, but he stopped again, head up, all his senses alert.

'He's heard something,' said Steve, 'or got a scent.'

'Probably a field of oats,' Dora said.

'Let's see where he'll go.'

Steve dropped the reins and sent him forward. Cobby broke into a jog. They went through a gap in the hedge and over a stubble field. At the far end, a plank bridge took them over a deep dry ditch. The mule hesitated, distrusting the bridge. Dora slapped him with the flat of her hand, and he was just scrambling across when Cobby stopped again and backed, almost knocking Willy into the ditch.

He switched off to the side, and as they followed the edge of the ditch, they saw the dark shape of the mare.

Callie held the horses, while Steve and Dora jumped down

to Specs. The foal had been born. It had been born still wrapped in the thin sac of membrane which had protected it for so long, floating inside its mother. Jammed in the ditch, weak and exhausted, the mare could not turn and rip the sac with her teeth, and the foal was suffocating, drowning in the fluid.

'Just in time.'

Steve freed the small wet head. They could not tell if it was alive or dead. Dora had once seen a man fished out of the river and saved by mouth-to-mouth breathing. She took the foal's head and breathed steadily into its nose, until its lungs moved and the foal began to breathe life of its own.

When they showed her her wet black colt, poor old Specs was too weak to lick it. She bumped it with her grey whiskery nose, and then dropped back her head.

Her eyes were glazed and dull. She looked as if she would die.

Steve rode across the field, and followed the road to the nearest house, where he astonished a sleeping family with a demand for blankets for a dying mare and her new-born foal.

When it was light, the Colonel came with a break-down lorry and a canvas sling. Somehow they got Specs out of the ditch and on to her feet. The Colonel and Steve and the two men from the garage pulled and pushed and half carried her up the ramp into the horse box. Callie sat on the floor in front with her arms round the struggling, long-legged foal.

As soon as he was in the stable with his mother, he pushed his face against the exhausted mare and tried to suck, but there was no milk for him.

The vet came three times that day, and gave Specs injections, but she had been infected from the difficult birth, and in the evening, he said, 'She hasn't got much chance. You'd better try and find a foster mother.'

142

'We're going to raise him by hand.' Callie pulled the colt away from his mother and pushed the bottle of milk into his soft mouth.

Slugger's wife had found a feeding bottle that had been used for one of her grandchildren, and they fed the colt with milk from the old man's goat. It had to be fed little and often, the way a mare feeds her foal, wandering away from it before it can take too much.

'Never rear it,' Slugger droned. 'You know what they say: Lose a mare, lose a foal.'

'What about cows? They take the calf away at once and feed it by hand, don't they?'

The Colonel borrowed a special calf feeding pail from Mr Beckett, who had calmed down when they explained that last night was not their fault, but the colt much preferred Slugger's grandchild's bottle.

He was always hungry. It seemed to be always time to feed him. At almost any hour of the day or night, you could find the Colonel or Anna or Steve or Dora or Callie or Toby tipping the bottle of goat's milk down to the soft, demanding nose, the long legs braced, tail quivering, blue eyes bulging with greed. They took it in turn to set their alarm clocks and go down in the night to the stable where Specs lay in the straw, licking anxiously at her foal, her white-rimmed eyes full of the trouble she could not understand. The fever had gone into her feet, and she would not stand.

But the colt would not give up. He was full of life and bounce, and he gave his mother no peace.

'Shouldn't we take him away from her?' Dora was trying to get Specs to eat, holding the food in her hand. The mare would nibble a bit, then turn her head away. 'She isn't getting any better.'

'But she's alive.' The Colonel would never give up his stubborn hope of life for his animals. 'She's alive because she's

143

got a colt. Take him away, and you take away her will to hang on.'

The colt was called Folly, as Callie had planned. Cobbler's Folly, Steve called him, since it was Cobbler's Dream who had found him.

Callie hated being away from him at school.

'Had your foal yet?' Lewis asked quite affably.

'Yes. A colt.'

He raised his thick eyebrows, which met in the middle of his nose, so that his whole brow furrowed when he moved them.

'Mother and child doing well?'

He lowered the brows. With those dull eyes and that hanging mouth, you could not tell how much he was hiding. It *must* have been him and the Toad who chased our poor Specs. But there was no way to prove it.

'The colt is lovely,' Callie said. 'But the poor old mother nearly died.'

'Oh well,' said the Louse. 'We all come to it.'

Callie did not tell him that because the lovely colt had kept bothering Specs to get up and feed him, the milk had begun to come at last, and the fever left her. She did not tell him about the miracle. He would not understand things like that.

Some time after that, Lewis stopped coming to school.

Steve had to go back to the hospital for a final X-ray. While he was there, one of the nurses, the one who had written, 'Love always Susie' on his plaster cast, gave him some interesting news.

144

Two patients had come in with food poisoning, which was traced to a tin of contaminated meat found on the rubbish heap at the Pinecrest Hotel, where they were staying.

The hotel had been closed down and the owners had gone away.

The old man came back in the spring. When they told him about Specs, he nodded and sucked his loose false teeth and did not say anything.

Specs and her colt belonged to him, of course. Callie went sadly out to the field. Folly left the other horses and came to her at once. He still liked people best, because they had first cared for him.

He put his inquiring nose into her hand. She let him lick the salt of her skin, and then flung her arms round his neck and wept into his growing mane. The colt put his head down to graze, to get rid of her, and moved away.

When Steve came to the gate, Callie was sitting in the grass, tearing daisies to pieces.

'Stop sulking,' he said. 'He's gone.'

Callie looked up and saw Steve through a mist of sun and tears.

'The old man has moved into his daughter's flat. We're keeping Specs and Folly.'

Dora at Follyfoot

I

When Dora went into the stable yard after lunch, Slugger was sweeping.

'What's wrong, Slugger?'

Slugger Jones, a man of habit indoors or outdoors, always slept after Sunday lunch, and never swept the yard until after the evening feeds. Especially on a Sunday when visitors might come and scatter toffee papers, and cigarettes hastily stamped out when they saw Steve's notice:

'EVERYTHING AT FOLLYFOOT BURNS,
INCLUDING MY TEMPER.'

He had originally written, 'The Colonel's temper,' but had blacked that out and put 'my'.

'What's wrong, she wants to know.' Slugger swept towards Dora's feet, and over them. 'Man doing a bit of honest work and she wants to know what's wrong.'

Dora looked over Willy's half-door and made a face at the mule, who dozed with head down and ears lopped out from wall to wall. She felt like riding, but there was nothing much here that wasn't lame, stiff, blind, ancient, or pensioned off from work for the rest of its life. That was the only snag about a Home of Rest for Horses. Dora and Steve were always trying to sneak in a horse that was fit enough to ride.

Dora put a bridle on Willy and the old Army saddle that was the only one that fitted him, since his back had been permanently moulded by his days as an Army mule. When she brought him out, Slugger was leaning into the water trough to pull out the stopper.

149

'Where are you going?' His voice was a muffled echo inside the trough.

'Into the woods. I'm still trying to teach Willy to jump logs.'

'I wouldn't go there. Not in the woods I wouldn't, no.'

'Why?' What did he expect? Murderers? Madmen? The shadowed rides through the beechwoods were calm and safe as a cathedral.

'Ask a silly question, you get a silly answer.' Slugger was scrubbing a brush round the sides of the trough. 'You might miss someone.

'What do you – oh Slugger, was that what the telephone was? The Colonel?'

The Colonel, who owned Follyfoot Farm, had been in hospital for nearly two months. He was coming home at last.

Dora climbed on to the mule, slapped him down the shoulder with the reins because his armoured sides were impervious to legs, and rode out of the yard and down the road to be the first to greet the car.

At the crossroads, she stopped and let Willy eat grass while she lolled in the uncomfortable saddle and drifted into her fantasy world where she was brave in adventures and always knew the right things to say.

She heard the sports car on the hill. Even with Anna driving, the gearbox still made that unmistakable racket from losing battles with the Colonel. When the car stopped and he looked out with his lopsided smile, Dora hardly knew him. His face was thin and pale, his eyes and teeth too big. His hand on the edge of the car door was bony and white. He was still biting round his nails, but they were clean. At Follyfoot, nobody's nails were ever competely clean, finger or toe.

'Hullo, Dora.'

'Hullo.' She pulled up Willy's head, not knowing what to

say. 'Are you all right?' Well, he must be, or he wouldn't come home. 'Did it hurt?' Operations always hurt. 'I'm glad you—' Willy suddenly dropped his head and pulled her forward on to his bristly mane.

The Colonel laughed his old laugh that ended in a cough. Anna moved the car forward. Dora kicked Willy into his awkward canter and followed them home on the grass at the side of the road.

Callie, the Colonel's stepdaughter, was at the gate to open it, with his yellow mongrel dog in ecstasies, tail beating its sides. Slugger was in Wonderboy's loose box, pretending not to be excited. He came out with his terrible old woollen cap tipped over his faded blue eyes, and the Colonel laid an arm across his shoulders.

'Good to be back, Slugger.'

'How's it gone then?'

'No picnic.'

'Teach you to stay away from that foul pipe.'

'It was the old war wound. The doctors say it was nothing to do with smoking.'

'That's what *they* say. I burned that old pipe.'

Anna wanted the Colonel to rest in the house, but he had to go all round the stables first, leaning on his stick, lamer than usual, and then out to the fields where some of the horses were grazing in the sweet spring day.

Fanny the one-eyed gipsy horse trotted up to him. The Weaver lifted his head with his cracked trumpet call, and then went back to chewing the fence rail, weaving hypnotically from foot to foot. Lancelot, the oldest horse at the Farm, perhaps in the world, mumbled at the grass with his long yellow teeth and looked at the Colonel through his rickety

151

back legs. Stoller the brewery horse plodded up and nosed into his jacket for sugar.

'He remembers which pocket.'

The Colonel had gone into and out of hospital wearing the patched tweed jacket with the poacher's pockets wide enough for a horses' nose.

In the jump field, Callie was lungeing the yearling colt, Folly.

'Shaping up quite nicely.' The Colonel watched with his horsy look, eyes narrowed, a piece of hay in his mouth. Horses are always chewing grass or hay, and people who live with them catch the habit.

'What do you mean?' Callie bent as if she were going to pick up and throw a piece of earth, to make the colt trot out, head up, long legs straight, tail sailing. 'He's perfect!'

The Colonel laughed. 'Nothing changes, thank God. Where's Steve?'

'I think he's out with the horse box,' Dora said casually.

'What for?'

'Oh—' She stuck a piece of hay into her mouth too. 'To bring in a horse.'

'I thought the stable was full.'

'Well it is,' Dora said. 'But we found this horse, you see. The junk man died, and the old lady, she tried to keep it in the back garden, tied to the clothes line, and it's all thin and mangy like a worn old carpet, and so we . . .'

'And so they thought it was just what we needed to keep us busy in our spare time,' Slugger grumbled, leaning on the gate.

The Colonel laughed. 'Nothing changes.'

2

A few days after he came home from the hospital, the Colonel took Steve into his study for a long talk, and later he called in Dora.

He was sitting in the leather armchair with his feet on the fender in front of a bright fire. It was a good day, but he felt the cold more than he used to.

No one had used this room while he was away. It was so unnaturally tidy and clean that Dora stopped in the doorway to take off her boots.

'Come in, come in, there's a hell of a draught.'

She padded in her socks over the carpet that was as thin and worn as the old horse they had just rescued from the widow's clothes line. Its name was Flypaper, because it attracted flies. Dora was treating its motheaten patches with Slugger's salad oil.

'Sit down, Dora.'

She sat on the stool at the other side of the fireplace. The Colonel's hand wandered to the desk where his chewed pipe used to be, groped for a moment, then came back to his pocket and took out a paper bag.

'Have a peppermint.' He held the bag out to Dora and took one himself. 'Poor substitute for tobacco.' He stuck it in his lined cheek. 'But I'm trying.'

'Are you really all right?' The others pretended that he was the picture of health, but Dora always said what she thought. 'You look terrible.'

'Thanks.' He shifted the peppermint to the other cheek. 'I'd rather hear that than people telling me I look wonderful when I feel like death. It's going to be a long pull, I'm afraid. I've got to go abroad for a bit, Dora. Down to the South where it's warm and dry and there's nothing to do.' He made a face. 'I'd much rather be slogging round here in the rain and mud with the horses.'

'Don't worry about them,' Dora said quickly. 'We can manage.'

'Can you? I've been wondering if I ought to get someone in to run this place.'

'Oh no!' Dora stood up, her face stubborn. 'I couldn't work for anyone else.'

'What about Steve?'

'He's only a boy. I wouldn't let him boss me about.'

'All right,' the Colonel said. 'Give it a try as your own boss. I think you can cope, between you. If you get into a muddle with bills, my accountant will help you. Just be careful with money. Don't buy any horses. If you get a really needy case, of course take it in. Slugger will gripe, but fit it in somewhere. But no buying. Remember that Shire horse – the one you and Steve found at the Fair, and you sold the bicycle to get it?'

'And then found he was stolen anyway, and I had to give him back to the farmer.' Dora smiled, remembering the fat, sloppy horse with the curly moustache. 'Yes, I remember. It wasn't Steve. It was that boy Ron Stryker, and *he'd* stolen the bicycle.'

'That was when I fired him. Useless layabout. I never should have hired him. But you take what you can get these days. If you need any help—'

'We won't.'

'There's this chap I know. Bernard Fox. The one who has the big stable over the other side of the racecourse.'

'Where you can eat your dinner off the yard?' Dora had once sneaked a look round the grand Fox stables. 'It doesn't even smell of horse.'

'Well, we can't all manage that, Dora.'

As she stood with her arm on the mantelpiece among the Colonel's photographs and trophies and the silver model of his famous grey jumper, the fire brought out the stable essence of Dora's clothes.

'But Bernard says he'll be glad to help any time you need him.'

'We won't.'

'He may look in at the Farm some time. Be reasonably polite, will you?'

'I always am.'

'You do try.' The Colonel reached out and took her hand and squeezed it. 'Go ahead with the work then, Dora. It's all yours.'

When she went out, Steve was grooming a horse in the corner box. His head came over the door when he heard her feet on the cinder path.

'What did he say?' He had been waiting for her to come out of the house.

'He's got to go away.'

'I know.'

'He said about being careful with money. Not buying horses, and all that. What did he say to you?'

'That too, and – well, I'm more or less in charge.'

'Funny,' Dora said. 'That's what he said to me.'

'Who is in charge here?'

The woman who stormed into the yard was red in the face under a plastic rain bonnet. 'One of your ponies was out last night and walked all over my pansy bed.'

155

'The black and white beggar?' Slugger knew that Jock the Shetland was a magician pony who could squeeze through hedges and between fence rails, and undo bolts with his teeth.

'I didn't see the beastly thing.' She glared at Slugger from under the rain bonnet. 'Only its nasty little hoof marks, all over my pansy bed.'

'Spoil many plants?' Slugger asked.

'I haven't put any in yet. But that's not the point. I want something done.'

'I could send the boy up to rake over the bed,' Slugger said, and the red-faced woman pounced.

'Are you in charge?'

'Oh dear me, no. In charge, she says. Oh no, lady.' Slugger faded.

'Who *is* in charge here?'

'Not me.' Steve put on a dopey face.

'Not me.' Dora backed away.

But that evening when some visitors with children were going round the loose boxes, exclaiming and sighing and mooning over the old horses, the father asked Dora, 'Where's the boss then?' and she heard herself answering, 'Here. It's me.'

Then when she was with the children in the donkey's stable, lifting them on to his back, she heard the father say Steve, 'Bit young, that girl, to run this place.'

And heard Steve laugh. 'She doesn't, actually. I do.'

3

Callie had refused to go abroad with her mother and the Colonel. She made the excuse of school.

'But there's only a few more weeks,' Anna said. 'You could join us at the villa then. You can swim down there, and sail and play tennis, and there are lots of young people your age.'

'I don't need young people my age. I need horses. And they need me.'

It was true. Callie was needed at Follyfoot. Steve and Dora and Slugger all worked extra hours, but the stable was full, and this was the time of year to mend fences and gates, to lime some of the fields, and prune dead branches out of trees and touch up peeling paint. Soon it would be time to get in the first crop of hay.

Dora sat up late at the Colonel's desk, falling asleep over bills and letters. Steve had taken over all the hoof care and the treatments for the unsound horses that the Colonel used to do. Slugger, who did the cooking as well as a thousand outside jobs, had not had a day off for weeks.

His sister came up to the Farm in her husband's dry cleaning van to see if he was dead.

'Sorry to disappoint you, Ada.' Slugger set down a loaded wheelbarrow.

'An old man like you.' His sister clicked her loose teeth. 'You'll collapse on this job.'

'Then I'll be at the right place, won't I? They can put me out to grass with the old horses.'

Callie got up early to help in the stables before she caught the bus to school, and did mucking out instead of homework in the evenings.

Her teacher sent a note home. Dora answered it, signing herself 'Guardian', but the teacher threatened trouble if things did not improve, so Callie stayed away from school, to avoid the trouble.

An extremely polite man came to the Farm one afternoon and found Callie in the feed shed with a brush and a big pail of whitewash. She gave him an overall and another brush, and they worked together for the rest of the afternoon, and Slugger made tea for him before he left.

'Nice of him to help.' Steve came up from the bottom field with Dolly and the cart full of planks and saws and hammers. 'Friend of yours, Callie?'

'He was the attendance officer.'

Callie had to go back to school for the rest of the term, and she had to do her homework, to stop them writing to her mother and the Colonel.

There were two reasons why no one must write that sort of letter to Anna and the Colonel. *One:* Not to worry them. *Two*: If he thought Steve and Dora couldn't cope, the Colonel might bring in a manager to run Follyfoot. Or write to his friend Bernard Fox.

The Farm was sloppier than usual. The horses were content, but there was no time to do everything. The manure pile had not been spread, and was growing out alarmingly from the side of the barn. Straw was not stacked away in the Dutch barn. The horse box was still covered in mud from its last trip across a field. They did not want the grand stable keeper coming round with burnished boots and foxy face to match his name.

He did come. He came one morning when Steve and Dora were doing what Ron Stryker used to call 'taking five minutes'.

They were stretched out in the sun on two bales of straw, with Steve's radio going, and the brown mare Pussycat, who was wandering loose in the yard to pick up dropped hay, thoughtfully licking the sole of his shoe.

'Good morning, good morning.' He strode briskly into the yard, burnished Bernie Fox in tall polished boots and sharply cut breeches, cap over his eyes, crisp ginger moustache at the ready. 'I hope I'm not interrupting your work.'

Steve jumped up and banged off the radio on a supersonic howl. Dora scrambled upright, pulling straw out of her hair. Old Puss leered with her lower lip hanging, and shambled stiffly away.

'Fox is the name. Bernard Fox. Good friend of the Colonel's. He asked me to keep an eye on things, so I thought I'd just look in as I was passing by.'

'How – how nice of you.' Steve said nothing. Boys never did, in a pinch. So Dora produced a few cracked words. 'Would you like to see round?'

Bernard Fox had already seen quite a lot in the few moments he had been in the yard. Straw bales in the corner instead of stacked away. A fork left in a loaded wheelbarrow. Muddy heads looking over doors, with burrs in their forelocks. Pussycat licking the door of the feed shed, the nearest she could get to oats.

'Better shut the yard gate while she's loose,' Mr Fox said.

'She never wanders away,' Dora told him.

'You can't assume anything with horses. They're unpredictable.'

'She knows when she's well off. She's gone far enough in her old life. A man was riding her from Scotland to London with a petition for the Queen. After a week, Puss lay down by the side of the road and wouldn't go any farther, so the man had to go on by train, and when he got to London, the Queen was in Australia.'

Dora thought Bernard Fox would be interested, but he only said, 'I'd still like to see you shut the gate.'

He did not exactly order (he'd better not). He just stood there in the superb boots, with his foxy head cocked, confident of being obeyed.

Dora stamped off, muttering and growling. The gate had dropped, because the hinge was loose. With her back to Bernard Fox, she tried to latch it without him noticing that she had to lift it.

'Need some longer screws in that hinge, don't you?' he called out breezily.

He had several other breezy suggestions.

'Better get that muck pile shifted.' He looked round the side of the barn. 'Danger of spontaneous combustion. It's hot enough for mushrooms already, I see.'

'We're growing them to eat,' Steve invented. 'Organic gardening.'

They could not keep him out of the tack room. Cobwebs. Mildewed leather. A bridle with a grass-stained bit hanging on the cleaning hook, as if that were enough to clean it.

'Colonel forgotten his Army training?'

'Of course not.' Dora was not going to have him criticizing the Colonel. 'We've had no time to clean tack. Haven't got time to ride anyway.'

'And nothing much to sit on.' Bernard Fox's cold ginger eye took in the few dusty old saddles, which were all they had.

'Bit risky.' He looked into the loose box where Stroller was keeping company with Prince, who had been turned out of his stable for Flypaper, whose mange might be catching.

'They get on all right.'

'Start a kicking match sooner or later. Why don't you turn 'em out?'

'It's going to rain.' Steve looked up at the low sky, which

160

might let down water on Bernard's burnish at any moment. 'Stroller is rheumatic and Prince is coughing.'

'So will Stroller be, if you leave them together. Isn't there an isolation box?'

'Yes, the foaling stable. But Lancelot's in that.'

'Who's Lancelot?'

'The oldest horse in the world,' Dora said proudly.

Bernard Fox looked glumly over the door. Lancelot, with a rack full of hay, was eating his bedding. He was the only horse who could manage to have both a pot belly and sticking out ribs. His wispy tail was scratched thin at the top. He had rubbed away half his mane under his favourite oak tree branch. His long teeth stuck out beyond his slack lips and his neck curved the wrong way, like a camel.

Bernard Fox looked at him for a long time, orange eyebrows raised, mouth pursed under the trim moustache. Lancelot looked back at him, his sparse lashes dropping over his clouded eyes.

'Ought to have been put down long ago.'

'The Colonel doesn't believe in taking life.' Dora thought he couldn't know the Colonel very well, or he would be aware of that. 'Unless a horse is suffering.'

'I'm suffering just looking at him.'

'Lancelot is very content—' Dora began but he had walked off to look over the gate of the jump field, where Folly and a few other horses were grazing. The gate was tied with a halter rope. One of the jumps was wrecked from Dora's efforts with the mule.

'Nice colt.' Even Bernard Fox could not find fault with Folly. 'Who's working with him?'

'Callie is beginning with the lunge and long reins. She's the Colonel's stepdaughter.'

'You'll be sending him to a trainer though?'

'I don't see why. Callie does very well, for her age.'

161

'How old is she?'

'Twelve.'

'I see.'

He asked, 'How did the horse box get so filthy?' (Going over a ploughed field to rescue a fallen calf), and, 'When are you going to get that stand of hay cut?' (When we get time), and as he was crossing the yard to leave, 'What is *that*?'

It was Slugger, coming out of the back door in his long cooking apron and his woollen cap, waving and shouting, 'I did it! A loaf of bread – it rose! Come and get it before it falls down!'

'Would you like some home-made bread and butter?' Dora asked politely. Bernard Fox was so narrow and trim he did not look as if he got enough of things like that.

'Thanks, but I must get on. I've got an appointment. Big thoroughbred breeder from America.' (Who cared?) 'I've stayed longer than I should.' (Too true.) 'But I promised the Colonel I'd help, and I'm a man of my word.' (Too bad.) 'And help is what you youngsters need.'

Dora and Steve hated to be called youngsters. They were doing a grown-up job with grown-up responsibilities. They were paid. They were independent. They had both left home, more or less for good.

'We're all right.'

Instinctively they stood side by side, arms touching. They had fought and argued and annoyed each other many times since they were left on their own, but they were very close now, scenting the Fox as enemy.

'You need another stable hand.'

'We've got Slugger. And Callie.'

'Slugger is the one with the bread, I take it. And Callie is the twelve-year-old? I'll make some inquiries tomorrow and see if I can get hold of someone efficient. I'm sure the Colonel will agree.'

'Not to someone who treats horses like horses,' Dora said. Hard to explain what she meant – the caring, the understanding, the sharing of life between animal and man. Impossible to explain to Bernard Fox.

'Better than treating them like inmates of a cosy old folks' home,' he said. 'Good day to you, Miss Dorothy. Steven.' His hand went politely to his cap. Steve and Dora clicked heels and saluted, and Bernard turned on his burnished boots without a smile.

Dora's heels did not click very well. A puppy had eaten one of her shoes, and she was barefoot. As he passed her, Bernard Fox said out of the side of his mouth, 'You're asking for tetanus.'

4

Bernard Fox, a man of his word, as he said, cabled for the Colonel's permission, and found a new stablehand within a few days.

It was a girl who used to work for him.

'Always these mucky girls,' Slugger and Steve grumbled to each other. 'Nothing but girls. Remember those two – Lily and Jane – used to squeal all the time and get their toes trodden on? Why can't we get a man round here? Nothing but sloppy, useless girls.'

Dora went on brushing mud off the white parts of the Appaloosa horse Spot (he never got mud on his brown patches where it wouldn't show), and pretended not to hear.

'If this new one wears tight purple pants and dangly earrings and calls me Daddy-O, I'm packing it in,' Slugger said.

'I'll go with you,' said Steve, 'if she paints her eyes like dart boards and wants to darn my socks.'

'He said "efficient".' Dora hung an arm over Spot's door to bang the mud out of the curry comb. 'He didn't say insane.'

Phyllis Weatherby, the efficient stablegirl, was coming in two days' time. They pretended not to care, but they did work extra hard to spruce the place up so that she would know that this was how things were done at Follyfoot.

She was not on the afternoon bus with Callie.

'Relax, everybody.' Callie ran into the yard and spun her ugly school hat into a tree. 'Perhaps she won't come at all.'

Slugger went into the house to take off his boots and put his feet up. Steve and Dora settled down to play cards in the barn. Callie changed her hated school uniform for her

164

beloved bleached jeans and took Folly for a walk to the village, showing him the world.

She was back quite soon in a car she had flagged down for a lift.

'He got away!' She panted into the barn. 'A car backfired and I couldn't hold him. He went off down the High Street with the rope trailing, knocked over a couple of bikes, went across the main road – cars swerving and screeching, it was awful – through a hedge and off across the fields, I've no idea where he's gone!' She sat down on a bale of hay, scattering the playing cards, and burst into tears.

'I'll get the truck. Dora, you take Hero and follow the colt. You can't miss those little tracks.'

Dora put a bridle on Hero, tried to vault on to him bare-back, failed three times, and climbed on from the milestone mounting block. Steve was backing the truck out of the shed when Slugger ran shouting out of the house in his socks and his old indestructive Army vest.

'Folly's loose!'

Dora turned back. 'He's across the main road. That's where we're going.'

'He may be headed home. Mrs Ripley at the Three Horse-shoes saw him run through her yard, going like smoke, she said on the phone.'

Callie got into the truck. 'Hurry, Steve.'

'Better wait, if he's headed home.' Slugger put his hands on the door.

'How do we *know*?' Callie was anguished.

'Tearing round the roads won't help.'

'We've got to do something – let go!' She tried to pry his fingers from the edge of the door. She thumped them. She even bent down and bit the horny knuckles.

Slugger paid no more heed than if she were a fly. He had turned his head away to listen.

'Let go,' Callie pleaded. 'Oh hurry, Steve!'

But Steve had heard what Slugger had heard, and jumped out.

Specs, Folly's mother who had long ago seemed to forget the colt was hers, had heard it too. Her shaggy head was over the door, ears pricked, eyes staring out of the white circles round them. Her head swung up and she called, deep and throaty, as she had not called since Folly was a skittery foal straying too far from her in the field.

Other heads were coming out in a chorus of neighs, whinnies, grunts, and a donkey's ear-shattering bray. And then from beyond the hayfield at the bottom of the hill came the faint answer, high and shrill, unmistakably Folly.

Dora and Hero were off down the grass track, scrambling over the low bar in the gateway and down the side of the hay field to open the bottom gate for him. They came back together, Folly bounding and teasing, knocking up against Hero's stiff, steady trot, galloping off in a circle, snatching at the tall hay, running ahead with his tail up and his head down to buck and squeal.

At the bar, he stopped and sniffed. As Hero began to step carefully over, he took a flying leap and landed in front of him. Hero stumbled. Dora fell off. Hero recovered and trotted back to the yard without her.

At this moment, a car stopped in the road and a tall girl in the sort of raincoat you see in photographs of sporting events walked in.

Hero was wandering loose with one foot through his reins. Callie, with tear stains on her face, was chasing Folly round the yard, trying to grab the flying rope. Slugger was hobbling after her in his socks and khaki vest, swearing at the cobbles. Dora trailed in with mud on her behind.

'With all the practice you've had, you ought to be able to

fall off on to your feet.' Steve laughed at her, and Dora wiped a muddy hand in his hair.

'Excuse me,' said the girl in the raincoat, 'is this Follyfoot Farm?'

'Foyft Fahm,' she said. She droned in her nose without opening her mouth, as if she couldn't spare the words.

She was no girl either, when you saw her close. Dry and leathery, she would never see thirty again, nor even thirty-five, the kind of woman who has stuck with horses because she can't get a man.

'Right,' she said, when she had introduced herself as Phlis Wethby. 'Right, let's get hold of that little clod.'

'I can't—' Callie was still breathlessly playing Tag, Folly's favourite game. Phyllis Weatherby strode over, and as Callie grabbed and he flicked away, she was there to catch him on the other side.

'Get'm off guard, right?'

Most of her sentences began and ended in 'right'.

'Right,' she'd say, 'we'll get the mucking out finished and this lot turned out and these other nags groomed before we break for lunch, right? Steve, you take the end stables and Dorothy can start down that side. Right Slugger, there's all those cobwebs should have been got down from the beams years ago.'

'We keep 'em to catch flies.'

'Nonsense. Asking for coughs. Use the old birch broom, right?'

Dora followed Steve into the shed where the barrows and forks were kept.

'Right,' she droned between closed lips, 'you know what I think? She's come here to be boss, right?'

'Wrong.' Steve set his jaw.

But Phyllis Weatherby was hard to resist, because, like Bernard Fox, she expected to be obeyed, which hypnotized

167

you into obeying. Or she would tell you to do something you were just going to do anyway, so it put you under orders. She was hard to ridicule, because she had no sense of humour and couldn't tell the difference beween a joke and an insult. When Slugger was driven to mutter, 'Oh, knock it off, you silly old cow,' she slapped poor Trotsky on his bony triangular rump and said, 'Right, he does look more like a cow than a horse.'

When Dora said, 'Right Phyllis, it's your turn to load the muck cart, right?' she answered, 'Right, you can take my turn while I soak that pony's leg, right Dorothy?'

'The name is Dora, if you haven't washed your ears lately.'

'Short for Dorothy. Right.'

But she did her share of the work, you had to give her that.

Rejecting the comfortable, shabby farmhouse because there were spiders in the bath and mice in the larder, she had taken a room at the Cross Keys Hotel in the village. But she was back at the Farm before anyone was up, throwing pebbles at the bedroom windows and clashing buckets fit to wake the dead, which Slugger sometimes wished he was when he woke and found that the nightmare of Phyllis Weatherby was true.

She brought her lunch from the hotel, because she couldn't get her tight-fisted lips round Slugger's doorstep sandwiches. She ate quickly, and jostled the others out of their usual hour of lazing in the sun, gossiping, dozing, reading, swilling mugs of the strong sugary tea which Phyllis prophesied would rot all their teeth.

This annoyed Slugger so much that one day he took out his teeth in his red bandana handkerchief and opened his mouth and said, 'Look Phyll, it did.'

168

'You were right, right?' Dora grinned.

'All right, back to the mines.' Phyllis Weatherby dusted crumbs off her strong capable hands and stood up. 'Fooling about won't get the work done.'

She chivvied the old horses as much as the people who looked after them. Hero must be schooled, though he was long past it. The Weaver must wear a cribbing collar to break him of his habit of crib biting with his long yellow teeth on his manger or door (it didn't). Even Lancelot's senile dreams were disturbed. He did not care to go out in damp weather. You could open his door and he would just stand there, swinging his head like a hammer and watching the rain.

'Right, get a move on.' Phyllis pushed him towards the door with her shoulder. Though she was thin, she was sinewy and tough. 'Get out and get some exercise.'

'He's too stiff,' Dora said.

'If he's not sound, he shouldn't be kept alive.'

'That's what Bernard Fox said. Why does everyone want to put down poor old Lance?'

'If Mr Fox said it, it's right. He is a master horseman.'

'If you were the oldest horse in the world,' Dora laid her head against Lancelot's neck as he sagged at the edge of the orchard, too bored to eat grass, 'you wouldn't want a master horseman. You'd want a friend.'

'Well, he can't have it both ways,' Phyllis said offensively. 'He must either shape up or be put down.'

'That's not the point of Follyfoot,' Dora said into Lancelot's straggly mane.

'Right. I can see that.' Phyllis Weatherby began to shake up bedding, hissing to herself as if she were a horse.

How were they going to get rid of her?

169

5

Quite a lot of their time was spent discussing how this could be done without trouble. Phyllis Weatherby was in touch with Bernard Fox. He would hear from her about trouble, and report it to the Colonel.

How were they going to get rid of her?

One Sunday when Steve had gone to see his mother, and Callie and Dora wanted to try and make a dress, Phyllis insisted on taking them to a horse show to see what riding was.

'We know what riding is,' Callie objected. 'We just don't happen to have anything much to ride.'

'If some of these old horses had been kept working,' said Phyllis, to whom a horse was a vehicle, 'they wouldn't have stiffened up, right?'

The show was quite large and smart, with a lot of teenage girls on expensive horses with jockey caps tipped over their noses and a blasé air of having seen it all before. Which they had, because they had been going to shows ever since their ambitious mothers stuck them on a pedigree Shetland in the Leading Rein class before they could walk.

They all rode beautifully and their horses were perfectly trained. Phyllis Weatherby thought this should be inspiring, but Dora and Callie found it rather depressing.

'Push-button ponies,' Callie said, to cover her jealousy of the splendid well-schooled ponies trotting round the ring in the Under 12.2 Hands class. 'What's the fun of that?'

'More fun than something that either won't go or runs

away.' Phyllis stood at the rails with a know-all face, wearing jodhpurs to look like an exhibitor.

'If you're referring to the day Willie wouldn't move and Stroller took Steve into the pond—' Dora began, but Phyllis was laughing at something in the ring, high in her nose, an unusual sound. She didn't laugh much, and when she did, it was at, not with people.

'Look at that,' she jeered. 'If that's a push-button pony, someone's pushing the wrong button, right?'

Out among the show ponies and the snobby little girls with hard eyes, someone had mistakenly sent a long-legged boy, topheavy on a tiny dun Shetland. His feet were almost on the ground. When they cantered, he had to lean back to keep his balance. The little pony was slower than the others. They passed it or bumped into it, the snobby little girls swearing at it from the sides of their mouths without losing their smug, professional faces. One of them flicked at the Shetland with a whip as she went by. It swerved, the boy lost his balance, and his jockey cap, which was too big for him, tipped over his eyes.

He pushed it back vaguely and cantered on. He was a thin, dreamy-looking boy, apparently unaware that he was a spectacle.

'Somebody ought to tell him.' Dora could hardly look. 'It's not fair.'

'Let him make an ass of himself.' Phyllis Weatherby laughed in her nose again. 'Serves him right.'

'I meant not fair to the pony. He's much too big for it.'

'A Shetland can carry twelve stone.' Phyllis and Dora had got into the habit of always arguing. Either of them would say black was white to contradict the other.

The rosettes were awarded. Four smug faces rode out of the ring, and ten disgruntled ones, plus the dreamy boy who did not seem to have noticed defeat. Outside the gate, his

171

parents, plump and tweedy, received him and the pony with hugs and lumps of sugar, and the father took several pictures, getting in the way of the next class going into the ring.

'Let's go and tell them,' Callie urged Dora.

'Mind your own business,' Phyllis said. But when she was watching the next class, with comments to show she knew a thing or two: 'Snappy little roan ... pulls like a train ... overflexed, etc., etc.,' they slipped away.

Walking over to the horse box lines, Dora asked Callie, 'What shall we say?'

'He's too big for the pony. It's cruel.'

'But they look as if they were just stupid, not cruel.'

'Stupidity is cruelty.' Callie echoed the Colonel. 'People who don't know anything about horses shouldn't be allowed to keep them.'

But this was one of the most difficult things about being in the business of animal rescue. Easy to attack deliberately cruel owners who beat or starved their horses, or drove old crocks into the ground. Much harder to tell kind, sentimental fools that their 'pet' was suffering through their ignorance.

It was too late anyway to tell the plump tweed-suited people anything. Among the smartly painted horse boxes and trailers was a red minibus. As Dora and Callie came up, they saw it move away, the father driving, the mother beside him in her mauve tweed hat to match her suit, and the dreamy boy in the back with the dun pony.

They must have lifted it in, and it was small enough to stand between the seats, like a dog.

'Let's follow them.'

Phyllis had come after Dora and Callie to see what they were up to. She behaved like their keeper, in or out of the stables.

'Want a laugh?' They pointed to the minibus turning out

172

of the gates of the showground. 'Guess what's in that?'
'What?'

'Get the car and we'll show you. Let's follow them.'

They caught up with the red bus. The dun pony's head was sticking out of the back window, so Phyllis had her laugh. She passed the bus, hooted, then slowed down to let it pass her, so she could get another laugh. The boy's face was alongside the pony's, his fair hair blowing with its mane. Callie waved at him and grinned, so that he would not think they were making fun of him, and he waved back.

In a suburban road of neat houses with trimmed lawns and clipped hedges, the red bus stopped at a white stucco house called The Firs, and turned up the drive. Phyllis slowed for a last look.

'I'm going to tell them now.' Dora turned the handle of the car door.

'You can't do that.' Phyllis moved forward as the door opened. Dora and Callie fell out, and she drove away without them. Leaning back to pull the door shut, she shouted, 'All right, walk home, right?'

They picked themselves up from the drive, picked gravel out of the palms of their hands and followed the bus.

173

6

There was a sign on the side of the red minibus, 'J. R. Bunker Ltd. Builders and Decorators.'

'We saw your pony at the show,' Dora said. 'Can we have another look at it?'

'Help yourself.' Mr Bunker was headed for the house. 'Mind she doesn't bite.'

The dun pony had been put into a garden shed, which she shared with flower pots and spades and more dangerous things like scythes and empty bottles. There was no window and no half door. She stooped in the dark, and when Dora opened the door, she nipped out under her arm and off into the garden.

Callie ran to catch her.

'Don't worry,' Mrs Bunker said. 'She always does that. My little lawn mower, I call her.'

Callie was tugging at the pony's mane, but she could not move her, nor get her head up from the turf.

'She'll only come if you hold sugar in front of her,' Mrs Bunker said. 'Or an ice-cream cornet. She loves chocolate ices, anything sweet. That's why we call her Lollipop.'

'Is it good for her?' A question was more tactful than a statement.

'Good heavens, *I* don't know.' Mrs Bunker turned on Dora round amber eyes like glass beads without much behind them. 'But I'm so fond of dumb animals, you see, I can't deny them what they want.'

'That's not being kind,' Dora said bluntly, her tactfulness

used up. 'That's being foolish. Did you give your son every-thing he wanted when he was a baby?'

'Yes, of course.' The round eyes were surprised at the question. 'He's our only child, you see.'

The dreamy boy was sitting on a wall, kicking the heels of his riding boots and humming to himself. His pony had not been fed or watered. His saddle was on the ground where he had dropped it. His bridle hung upside down on the branch of a tree.

'He's too big for Lollipop.' Callie had her belt round the neck of the dun pony, whose ears did not reach her shoulder.

'I know, isn't it absurd? But all the children round here go to the shows, so Jim does too, though he never wins, because the judges are crooked. The whole thing is rigged.'

'It's because he's too big for the pony,' Callie repeated.

'Should we get another one?'

'Oh no!' Dora burst out. 'I mean, you'd have to build a proper stable, wouldn't you, and find out how to take care of it. There's a lot more to keeping a horse than sugar and chocolate cornets.'

'We didn't know.' Mrs Bunker twisted her plump ringed hands. 'Everyone seems to have a pony. We didn't know it was all that difficult. How do you girls know so much?'

'We work at Follyfoot Farm,' Dora said. 'The Home of Rest for Horses.'

Mrs Bunker's eyes misted over at once. Always a bad sign when people began to blubber at the mere idea of an old horse. 'Ah the dear patient beasts. I read a piece in the papers about the horse you rescued with the broken jaw. I couldn't do that kind of work. I'm too sensitive. I can't stand suffering.'

'You're making Lollipop suffer,' Callie said.

Mrs Bunker's hands went to her mouth. 'Oh, but we didn't know. We didn't know.'

'Famous last words,' Dora muttered.

175

'Perhaps we should get rid of her – send her to the auction sales.'

'I wouldn't. You don't know who'll buy her. Find her a good home.'

'It would break Jim's heart.'

'No, it wouldn't Mum, honest.' The boy, who had not spoken a word so far, slid down from the wall and came over. 'I don't care whether I ride or not, honest I don't.'

'Oh, but you *do*! Everybody rides. The Maxwell children ride, and the Browns, and all Sir Arthur's kiddies up at the Manor. All the children round here have ponies, and all those who don't wish they had.'

'They can have Lollipop then.' Jim kicked a stone along the path, went after it and kicked it again, scuffing the toe of his riding boot, trying to kick it into a drain.

'We could look for a home for her,' Callie said.

'But I'd be so sad. How could I face those trusting eyes?'

'We could have her at the Farm till we—'

Dora trod on Callie's toe. 'No more horses, the Colonel said,' she hissed.

'He said not to *buy* any.' Callie turned back to Mrs Bunker. 'Till we find a good home.'

Mrs Bunker went to ask her husband, who for all his proud photographing seemed glad to have Lollipop off his hands. He came out at once and put her into the bus before they could change their minds. Callie and Dora sat at the back with the pony. Jim did not come. He sat on one of the gate-posts with a magazine, waved to Lollipop and went back at once to the magazine.

Half-way up the hill, a light truck came up behind them. Dora and the pony happened to look out of the window together, and the truck swerved and nearly went into a tree. It was Steve.

He recovered and passed them, tapping his head to show

they were mad. At the gate of the Farm, he opened the door of the bus, and the pony hopped neatly down.

'What the – ?'

'Just for a short time,' Dora told him in the soothing voice she used on the Colonel.

'We agreed not to take in anything unless we both—'

'Case of desperate need,' Dora whispered. 'Extreme brutality.'

Steve scratched his head. The amiable parents in the minibus did not look like extreme brutes.

Phyllis Weatherby was waiting too, in the entrance to the stable yard.

'How *dare* you!' She was red in the face, trying to shout through closed lips. 'How dare you!'

'These nice young people are going to find a home for dear little Lollipop.' Mrs Bunker leaned out of the bus window, all smiles and beads.

'Not here, they aren't,' Phyllis Weatherby said rudely.

Mr Bunker, fearing a hitch, put the bus into gear and moved off before Phyllis could put the pony back in.

'Wait!' she called, and ran after them in her classy corduroys, knock-kneed instead of bow-legged, which she should be at her age if she was really as horsy as she said. 'Come back!'

The bus gathered speed. She stopped and shook her fist. Mrs Bunker pretended she thought she was waving, and waved back gaily out of the window.

Phyllis Weatherby was so angry, she was almost in tears, Dora was almost sorry for her.

'I *told* you not to interfere with that pony. I *told* you!'

'So what?'

'You're not the boss.' Steve had to be on Dora's side, against Phyllis.

'Mr Fox said—'

'Mr Fox, Mr Fox. He's not the boss either.'

'I'm going to tell him.'

'Tell away.' Steve laughed. If he had not been bigger than Phyllis, she would have hit him.

'Where are you going with that pony?' She picked on Callie, who was smaller. 'There's no stable room, and if you put it out, the others will kick its stupid head in.'

'I'm not going to.' Callie was walking the little pony like a dog on a lead.

'Take it back,' Phyllis Weatherby ordered. 'It's a long walk but serve you right. Take it back.'

She stormed into Flypaper's stable and began ferociously mucking out, swearing at the amiable horse to 'Move over! Get up, damn you!' Flypaper stood by the end wall and looked at her with hurt, astonished eyes.

Callie tied the pony to a stake on what had been a lawn by the house when anyone had time to keep a lawn.

Dora went to get her jacket out of Phyllis Weatherby's car. Steve called her urgently to help with Lancelot, who had sagged down to roll and couldn't get up, and she ran, leaving the car door open.

This is what they pieced together afterwards:

Callie was famous for rotten knots. Lollipop, who was a clever little pony, must have untied the rope with her teeth, wandered away and got into the car, reminded of her own minibus. When Phyllis left, still blindly furious, she banged shut the door and did not find out until she slammed on the brakes at the Cross Keys Hotel and a soft nose bumped the back of her neck, that she had a tiny pony sitting on the floor of her car.

'Carried on alarming,' the hotel manager told Dora on the telephone. 'She turns the pony loose, goes straight upstairs and packs her bags and takes off. "Send the bill to the Farm," she says.'

178

'Oh Lord.'

'It's not so much that, since I trust the Colonel. But the pony is in my wife's kitchen garden. She's holding it off her lettuce seedlings with a rake.'

Dora went on her bicycle to fetch Lollipop, and led her home, trotting by the back wheel. A car with a silver thoroughbred on the radiator slowed alongside.

'Phyllis Weatherby stopped by my place on her way home,' Bernard Fox said. 'Had some trouble?'

'Oh no, no trouble at all.' Dora wobbled. It is hard to ride a bicycle slowly and talk to someone in a car without bashing into it or falling off, especially when you are leading a pony.

'Phyllis was very upset.'

'She was tired. Working too hard.'

'Some strange story about someone putting a horse in her car . . .'

'There you are, you see. Hallucinations from overwork.'

'It will be hard to find another worker like that.'

'Don't bother.' Dora put the hand with the leading rein on the handlebar and steadied herself with her other hand on his car. 'We've got someone.'

'Have you really?'

Dora nodded. Not quite as big a lie without speech.

'I'll stop in and have a chat with them.'

'They're not there yet. They should be coming in a few days.'

'If they don't, I'll find you someone else.'

Dora let go the car as he drove on, wobbled sideways, and the Shetland pony bit her in the ankle.

7

They sat up late that evening, laughing about Lollipop in the back seat, and worrying about Bernard Fox.

'If we don't find another stablehand,' Dora was lying on the floor with the Colonel's yellow mongrel, 'burnished Bernie will.'

'And it could be worse than Phyllis.'

'Impossible.' Slugger had disliked Phyllis from the first day, when she told him to put his hands under the tap before he went to work in the stable. *'Before!'* He was still stewing over it.

' "Carrying germs of disease," she says. So I says to her, "If there's any disease round here, it's in your head".'

'You didn't,' Callie said.

'I should have. The next one we get, I'm going to tell 'em first day who's boss here.'

'Who is?'

'Me.' Slugger thumped his chest into a hacking cough.

'Who *are* we going to get? The Colonel tried all the agencies when Ron Stryker left, and there wasn't anyone who knew one end of a horse from the other.'

'Easy,' Slugger said. 'One end bites and the other kicks.'

'We'll have to try.' Steve tipped back his chair. 'Oh lord.' He let it down with a crash. *'Suppose Bernard Fox persuades Phyllis to come back?'*

'She was in love with him,' Callie said sombrely. 'The master horseman.'

180

With no Phyllis Weatherby to clash buckets and throw stones at windows, they all slept late. Callie missed the bus for school, so Steve took her down in the truck and went on into Town to go round the employment agencies.

Dora went out to start feeds. She whistled her way round the stables, glad to be on her own, although there was so much work to do. It was easier to start a day by yourself, and work your way gradually into sharing it with other people.

Horses, that was different. It was biologically impossible for a horse to get on your nerves. They were always glad to see you, each one greeting you in its own way. Wonderboy with a high neigh. Ginger with a low whinny. The Weaver with a hoof tattoo on his door. Stroller nodding his head up and down. Hero standing diagonally across his box with his nose in the manger to make sure you knew where to put the feed.

Prince, who would never trust people again, stood at the back of his box, flicking his ears. Dora spoke to him and went in quietly. He was still nervous, even with months of gentle handling, after his terrible experience at the brutal hands of the Night Riders. His mouth was permanently ruined by the crude wire bit. Dora was tipping the soft mash of bran and crushed oats and molasses into the manger when a shattering roar made the horse jump, and tread on her toe.

It is the hardest thing in the world to get a horse off your toe. Pushing her shoulder against his, Dora finally managed to get Prince off her poor big toe, which was already permanently bruised and blue, the trademark of a horse keeper.

She limped angrily out to see who was insane enough to ride a motorcycle into a farm full of horses.

She might have known. Strolling across the yard, lighting a cigarette and throwing down the burning match, his long red hair tangled on the shoulders of a fringed purple jacket—

'Ron. Ron Stryker. I might have known.'

'Missed me, eh? Knew you would. So I took pity on you and come back to work.'

'The Colonel's not here.'

'Oh, he'll be glad. Always liked me, did the Colonel.'

'Is that why he fired you?'

'Just a temporary misunderstanding, my dear.' Ron held out his hands as if to shake Dora's hand, then quickly grabbed her arm and kissed her.

Dora hated being kissed. Or did she? She was never quite sure. But she knew she hated being kissed by Ron Stryker. She wiped the back of her hand across her mouth, and Ron picked up the bucket and went into the feed shed and began to measure out oats and horse nuts, just as if he had never been away.

Dora went to tell Slugger.

'How are we going to get rid of him?'

'Why try?' Slugger had lost many battles with this cocky, tricky boy. 'If we've got to have another stablehand, you know what they say: Better the devil you know . . . Find out where he's been working, and we'll send for references.'

'Well, I'll tell you.' Ron leaned on a pitchfork, and slid his eyes sideways in the way Dora knew so well when he was thinking up a good fable. 'I been working for these blokes, name of Nicholson, see? Lovely people. Very classy. Head groom, I was.'

'Come off it, Ron.'

'Well, I mean, until we had the spot of trouble.'

'Get the sack again?'

'No dear, I resigned. We parted like gentlemen, Mr Nicholson and me.'

182

'Then he won't mind if Steve or I write for a reference?'

'Well, of course he won't *mind*.' Ron's eyes slid off in the other direction. 'But why bother? The Colonel knows me. Why waste a stamp?'

When Slugger came out and saw the shaggy red head appear over a stable door, he said, 'I thought it couldn't be worse than Phyllis Weatherby, but it is.'

'Kind of you to say so.' Ron grinned with his chin on the door like a puppet.

'Steve phoned,' Slugger told Dora. 'The truck packed up in Middlesbrough, and he's leaving it at a garage there. He never got to Town. I told him our troubles was over now that Superman was back on the job, so he said for Ron to go and fetch him home on the back of the bike.'

'There, you see.' Ron came out of the stable, wiping his hands on his tight jeans. 'You do need me. How do, General?'

He shook hands with Slugger, and Slugger yelled and pulled his hand away from the trick crusher handshake.

8

Dora wrote to the Colonel, and he wrote back, with a sigh in his handwriting:

'*All right. Keep Ron Stryker if you can stand him. At least he knows the job. Anna says lock away the silver. P.S. What happened to the girl Bernard Fox found?*'

'Better answer that bit right away,' Steve said, 'before he hears from Bernie.'

'You answer.'

'You'll make it sound better.'

Steve hated writing letters. His childhood had been a strange one, with no love and not much schooling. So Dora banged out a story on the typewriter in the study.

It began: '*There was this little tiny pony, you see . . .*' and ended up: '*I know it was bad luck on poor old Phyllis, but we laughed till we fell down and you would have too.*'

Steve offered to fetch Ron's trunk and his guitar and his stereo set and his transistor and his cowboy boots and his collection of comic papers from the Nicholsons where he had lived.

'The truck won't be ready till next week, but we can take the horse box. More room for all the loot you've probably knocked off. Come on, Ron.'

'I haven't the time to come with you.' Ron picked up a broom and started to sweep.

'Parted like gentlemen.' Dora laughed. 'Are you scared Mr Nicholson will shoot you on sight?'

'Lovely people.' Ron did not answer awkward questions. 'Salt of the earth.'

Dora went with Steve in the front of the horse box, following the directions Ron had written:

Left at the boozer, fork right past that crummy place where they make pies out of dead cats, over the cross roads where the bus crashed and they had to cut the people out with a blow torch, straight through that town where the bloke murdered his wife, right at the boozer, left at the next boozer, and down Suicide Hill, you can't miss it.

The Lovely People turned out to be horse dealers. It was a huge stable with about fifty horses in loose boxes, stalls and fenced yards, the sort of come-and-go place where horseflesh is just that – flesh, not soul – and represents only money.

Mrs Nicholson was in the large tack room, bullying two girls who were cleaning bridles. She was a beefy woman with muscles like a man and cropped grey hair round a shiny red face.

'Ronald Stryker!' She let out a bellow that set the curb chains jingling. 'I told that rotten little creep if he didn't get out of the country, I'd set the police on him.'

'What did he do?' Dora asked.

'It was what he didn't do,' Mrs Nicholson said darkly. 'Such as work. Keeping his fingers off other people's property. Following orders. Watching his mouth. Want any more?'

'We just came for his things.'

'You'll have to ask my husband.' Mrs Nicholson picked up two heavy saddles together and slung them with ease on to a high rack. 'I threw the junk out of the staff cottage and he put it somewhere. Out in the rain, I hope.'

Mr Nicholson was roughly the same shape as his wife, and

185

the same colour, and made the same kind of loud noises.

'Stryker!' His veined red face grew purple. His bull neck swelled over the collar of his ratcatcher shirt. 'You friends of his?'

Dora nodded. Ron was right. Waste of a stamp to write for a reference.

'Bad luck on you. His stuff is in the shed out there with the tractor. If he hadn't sent for it, I was going to put it on the dustcart tomorrow.'

They found the tin trunk (heavy as lead, what on earth was in it?) and the guitar and the transistor and stereo and a strange garment like a military greatcoat from the First War with holes where the buttons and badges used to be. They put it all into one side of the horse box, and were shutting up the ramp when a familiar red minibus pulled up in front of the long stable building.

Mrs Bunker waved to Steve and Dora, then dropped her hand uncertainly. 'I do know you, don't I? Oh yes, of course. Lollipop. How is the darling pony?'

'Eating,' Dora said. 'A nice family came to see her yesterday. They may take her.'

'It will break Jim's heart.'

'No, it won't, Mum,' he reminded her.

'Oh no, of course, because you'll have your new pet. We're here to look at a larger pony.' Mrs Bunker was dressed too smartly, everything matching, not quite right for the country.

'I thought you were giving up horses,' Dora said.

'We were, but people were quite surprised to hear that Jim didn't ride any more. I met Mrs Hatch who runs the Pony Club camp, and when she heard that Jim wouldn't be camping this year, she was quite disappointed. Then Mr Bunker was up to look at the roof at Broadlands. You know, that huge old place where poor Mr Wheeler lives by himself since he lost his wife. My husband does all his work. And the old gentleman asks him, "How's Lollipop?" He takes such an interest in the young people. When he heard she was too small for Jim, he supposed we'd get something larger. So when Mr Bunker went up to supervise his men who are building the squash court up at the Manor, Sir Arthur told him this would be the best place to look.'

'But you've got no stable.' Dora's heart sank. A Shetland in that cluttered shed was bad enough. A large pony would be disaster.

'Oh yes. Mr Bunker has put up one of those nice pre-fabs.'

Dora's heart sank lower. They might acquire a large pony and a nice pre-fab stable, but where were they going to get sense?

'Where's Jim?' Mr Bunker, who was also dressed rather too smartly, came out of the stables brushing hay off the trousers of his unsuitable suit.

His wife looked round. 'He's wandered off somewhere.'

'Well, you come along, Marion. They have several fine animals here, and the daughter is going to show them. Why don't you come with us?' he asked Steve and Dora, 'since you know more than we do.'

He looked down and picked another piece of hay off his suit. Mrs Bunker was easy to understand. Foolish. Mr Bunker was more complicated. Hard to tell how shrewd he was, or whether he was laughing at you.

Steve and Dora put a piece of hay in their mouths and followed him through the stables to a schooling ring on the other side, where a girl the same shape as the Nicholsons, but smaller, was leading out a nervy black pony.

She had a hard-boiled face and a tough, professional manner. She mounted, adjusted her stirrups, checked the girth, muttered to the restless pony, and looked at her father for instructions.

'Trot him out a bit, Chip.' He leaned on the rail with his cap over his eyes and his legs crossed. 'Chip off the old block, she is.' He watched her trot the black pony smoothly round the track, perfectly flexed, stepping out. 'Extend the trot!' Chip obeyed, without appearing to move her legs or hands. 'It's all there under you,' Mr Nicholson said to the Bunkers, who hadn't a clue what he meant. 'You can't fault him. Right, Chip - walk. Then canter him a figure eight. All his orders were bellowed, as if Chip were deaf or at the other end of a football field.

The showy black pony made impeccable figure-of-eights, cantering very slow and supple, performing a flying change of leads without breaking the rhythm.

'Win anywhere with that one,' Mr Nicholson said. 'Always in the money.'

Chip had stopped in front of them, as if they were judges at a horse show, the black pony standing out well, head up, ears forward. Mrs Bunker's amber eyes grew dreamy, imagining Jim in that saddle with the red rosette on his bridle.

Dora read her thoughts. 'But Jim could never ride that pony,' she said tactlessly, and realized that the thin pale boy had materialized at her side. 'Or could you, Jim?'

'I don't know.' He was a very negative boy, half in the world, half in his own dream world.

'Looks quiet enough to me,' his father said.

'That's because that girl knows how to ride it.'

'So will young Jim, He's taking lessons,' Mrs Bunker said. 'Sir Arthur suggested it, and told us the best instructor to go to.'

'But does he really want a show pony?'

On the other side of Dora, Steve nudged her and muttered, 'Shut up. It's their business.'

'That pony's hotter than it looks. The child will get killed.'

'No, I won't,' Jim said placidly.

'You like the pony, young man?' Mr Nicholson looked down at him from under his cap.

Jim shrugged his shoulders.

'He likes it,' the mother said. 'What's its name?'

'What's his name, Chip?' The dealer did not know the names of horses who passed through his hands, without looking at his records.

'Dark Song.'

'Oh, that's a lovely name.' Mrs Bunker's eyes shone. 'I think we should buy it, James.'

'How much?'

In the etiquette of horse trading, it was much too soon to mention money. Mr Nicholson cleared his throat and re-crossed his legs the other way. 'I'll make you a price.'

'How much?' repeated Mr Bunker, forging on like one of his own bulldozers.

'Five hundred to *you*.'

'Too much.'

'It's a steal.' Mr Nicholson looked outraged, trying to embarrass the Bunkers. 'He's worth far more than that, but I like to send my customers away happy. Then they come back.'

'Oh, we wouldn't come back, I don't think,' Mrs Bunker said. 'If we bought that pretty pony, we wouldn't need another.'

'It's too much.' Her husband was coming out of this more strongly than she was. 'Show us something else.'

Chip, who had been sitting impassively in the saddle, staring straight ahead, raised one sandy eyebrow and rode out of the ring.

She came back with a chunky little chestnut, white socks, white blaze, picking up his feet, very showy. She trotted and cantered him, and when her father shouted, 'Pop him over

189

some fences!' she and the pony soared over jumps of blood-curdling height without either of them turning a hair.

'Do you think Jim could learn to ride like that?' Mrs Bunker's eyes were again dreaming of her son, sailing over fences in an arena where the crowd roared.

'On that pony, he could,' said Mr Nicholson (child murderer). 'Quiet as a baby. Anyone could ride him.'

'He was pulling all the way.' Dora had to say it.

'Mouth like velvet.' Mr Nicholson shot her a look. 'You could ride him to church.' He had all the horse trading clichés. 'What do you say, young man?' He clapped a heavy hand on Jim's narrow shoulder.

Jim shifted a sweet to the other side of his mouth. 'I don't really care for jumping, thank you,' he said politely.

'O.K., Chip. Get that bay pony out here.'

A stable boy was standing by the gate of the ring, holding a pony which was probably the one they had planned to sell to the Bunkers. The other two were window dressing. It was a plain but pleasant looking bright bay. It moved rather lifelessly with Chip, who looked bored, hopped neatly enough over two small jumps, stopped, stood still.

'Perfect picture of a child's hunter,' Mr Nicholson said, though it did not look as if it had enough energy to keep up with hounds for long. 'Tailor-made for you. Willing and wise. Safe as a rock. Look at him stand. Grow barnacles, that one would, before he'd move on without command.'

'You think that's the one we should buy?' Mrs Bunker asked naïvely.

'If you ask my advice, Madam, I'll give it to you,' Mr Nicholson said, as if he did not dish out advice all day long whether anyone asked for it or not. 'You'll not find a pony of this quality, if you—'

'How much?' Mr Bunker interrupted.

The dealer named a price that was less than the black or the chestnut, but far too much for this rather ordinary pony, whose quality, if he had any, was not in his looks.

But Mrs Bunker was prodding her husband with a finger in a white glove and hissing, 'Let's!'

'You like it, son?'

'He loves it,' Jim's mother said. 'What's its name?'

'What's its name, Chip?'

The girl shrugged. She got off and led the pony away, as if she were sick of riding it.

'His name is Barney,' Jim said, more positively than usual.

'Why, dear?'

'Grow barnacles, he said.' Jim only listened to scraps of conversation. 'Barnacle Bill.'

'What do you think?' Mrs Bunker asked Steve and Dora.

'There's something not quite right about him.' Mr Nicholson had not moved away, so Dora had to say it in front of him.

'You should get him vetted,' Steve said. 'He looks a bit off.'

'The vet's just seen him,' Mr Nicholson cut in. 'Touch of shipping fever. We've only had him down from Scotland a few days. They always get a touch of that, didn't you know?'

'No,' Steve said, meaning: They don't always get shipping fever; but Mr Nicholson took it to mean that he didn't know, and said tartly, 'You kids don't know everything.'

'Will he fit in the bus?' Mrs Bunker asked.

'Hardly, Madam.' How could he sell a perfectly good pony – any pony – to people who so obviously knew nothing? 'But I'll tell you what I'll do for you. I'll get one of my men to hitch up the trailer and run him over to your place this afternoon, so your boy—'

'How much extra?'

Mr Nicholson named a figure that was roughly twice the fair price for transporting a horse that distance. Then his

191

thick hands clenched and the cords of his neck stood out as Dora told the Bunkers cheerfully, 'We've got our horse box here, and we have to go right by your place. We'll bring him.'

There *was* something a little funny about the pony. Something about the expression of his eye – what was it?'

He was very stubborn. When Chip led him up to the horse box, he stopped dead at the foot of the ramp, with his head stuck out and his jaw set against the pull of the halter rope. Mr Nicholson picked up a handful of gravel and threw it. He shouted, he hit the pony with a whip, he tried to pull it in with a long rope round the quarters. He finally hit it with a short plank of wood and called it an obstinate swine. Chip flung the halter rope over the pony's neck and went away.

Mrs Bunker began to wring her hands. Jim had wandered away. Steve, who had been standing watching with his hands in his pockets, said, 'Can I try?'

'He's all yours.' Mr Nicholson walked off, so unfortunately he didn't see Steve speak to the pony and stroke it and get it to relax. Then he held it while Dora lifted a front foot and set it on the ramp. As the pony relaxed more, she was able to put the other foot on. Barnacle Bill stayed like that for a while, with his eyes half closed, then he sighed, and walked quietly into the horse box.

9

Ron Stryker was as lazy and dodgy as ever. He had to be watched, since he did not instinctively put the horses before himself, as the others did.

Steve came in to supper one evening and found him with his face already in a bowl of Slugger's pea soup that was almost thick enough to eat with a knife and fork.

'I thought you'd done the buckets,' Steve said. 'You didn't give Ranger any water.'

Ron shrugged. 'That's his problem.'

'Get on out there and see to it.' Slugger threatened him with the carving knife.

'*I* did.' Steve sat down with a sigh.

'Don't worry, Slug,' Ron said soothingly, through soup. 'There's always some mug to do it.'

But he was an extra pair of hands, and they were getting back to their old routine, and the farm was straightening up.

'Burnished Bernie can come any time he likes.' Dora looked round the tidy yard, barrows lined up, tools hanging in place, manure heap cleared, and the clatter of Mr Beckett's mower coming up like evening insects from the hay field. 'Perhaps we should invite him before something goes wrong.'

'Never invite trouble.' Slugger shook his head.

'He's sure to come and check on Ron.'

'He'd better come on me day off,' Ron said from the roof of the donkey stable where he was plucking odd chords out of his guitar, 'for he won't like what he sees.'

'Why don't you change the image then?' Dora looked up, and he threw a piece of loose tile at her.

'Can't,' he said. 'I was borned like this.'

'With long red hair and jeans that stand up by themselves?'

'Yus.'

Callie stayed home from school and they worked all next day raking the cut hay into windrows. By the time they had done the evening stable work, everyone was exhausted. But Dora was restless. Ever since they had put Barney into the Bunkers' clean, roomy loose box, sweet with the tang of new wood, she had been worried.

'It's not your business,' Steve said when she worried aloud.

But Dora went on worrying. Every horse was her business. She hated politics, but the only reason she would like to be the first woman Prime Minister was to put through a law that people must pass a test for a licence to keep horses. Dora would make up the test.

'Is it all right if I take Hero out tomorrow?' she asked Callie. Hero, like the others, was a Follyfoot horse, belonging to nobody; but Callie had rescued him from the circus, so she was always asked.

'I couldn't even climb into a saddle.' Holding the brush gingerly in her sore hand, Callie was sitting on the back door-step brushing hay out of her long hair. Whatever she did, even raking a hay field, she always managed to get it all over her patchy jeans. 'Where are you going?'

'I thought I'd ride over to the Bunkers' and look at that pony.'

'Haven't you got enough horses here to worry about?' Steve called from inside the house.

'Let me go.' She was going anyway, but she wanted to please Steve by asking him. On friendly days like today, when they had all been close and companionable, working together in the hayfield on the side of the hill, with the early summer meadows, patched with buttercups, spreading away to the blue haze of the hills, she wanted to please everybody.

Steve laughed. 'I couldn't stop you. Somebody else's horse is always more fascinating. But for God's sake don't come back with the thing.'

Barney was out in the small paddock at the back of the pre-fab loose box, now smartly creosoted, with a white door and white trim on the window.

'But he's never been in it, the beggar,' Mr Bunker said glumly, 'since Jim turned him out to graze two days after we got him.'

'I can't catch him,' Jim said resignedly.

They stood by the gate, watching the bay pony, head down in the far corner of the paddock.

'You mean, you haven't been able to catch him for two weeks?'

'That's about the size of it,' the father said. 'We tried with oats, we tried with sugar, we tried with carrots. We tried to corner him. We got the neighbours round and tried to drive him, but he puts his head down and comes at you with his teeth, or else whips round with his heels.'

'What was he like to ride?' Dora asked.

'I don't know', Jim said. 'I couldn't get the bridle on. That's why I turned him out. But then I couldn't catch him, and I got sick of it. I don't care whether I ride or not anyway.'

'Oh yes you do.' His mother had come out of the house, looking more human in an apron, with a tea towel in her hand. 'He's longing to ride his new pony, but the animal is mad. I rang up Mr Nicholson. "Nothing wrong with it when it left here," he said. "A deal is a deal".'

195

'I'll bet I know why', Dora said grimly 'He knew what the pony was like.'

'Then why did it go so quietly with that girl?'

'Tranquillizers. It was drugged.'

'Oh no.'

'Oh yes. That's what they do. Ron Stryker, a boy who works with us, told me. He's been with second rate dealers. He knows all the tricks.'

'I'll sue Nicholson', Mr Bunker said.

'You can't prove anything. The drug has worn off long ago. That's why the pony has gone back to being hard to handle.'

Jim was looking mournful. 'I did like Barney, you know,' he told Dora. 'That first day, when he was nice and quiet, sat in the manger and told him stories about places we'd go, picnics, and wading the ford, and going up the hill to see the Roman graves. He liked it. He put his ears one back and one forward, listening with one and thinking with the other.'

'Would you like me to try and catch him?'

'Yes, please. Perhaps you can make him quiet again.'

'I can try. He must have been badly treated. Perhaps I can get back his confidence.'

Dora put Hero into the new loose box, where he began to lick the heart out of the bright galvanized manger where Barney had had his last feed. With the Bunkers perched on the gate like crows, she walked into the middle of the paddock and stood still with her hands behind her back. Most horses will eventually come up to you if you stand still. When he came closer, she would breathe at him as if she were another horse, so he could get to know her.

He had his back to her. His head was down to the grass, but he was watching her through his hind legs. She took a few steps forward. Suddenly he whipped round and came at her with his ears back.

Dora was not as brave as all that. She turned and ran.

'Join the club.' Mr Bunker moved along to make room for her on the gate. 'That's what he did with us.'

'What shall we *do*?' his wife wailed. 'We can't just leave him in that field until he dies.'

'You could ring Mr Nicholson and tell him to come and take his pony back.'

'I tried that. "A deal is a deal," he said. He was quite rude.'

'Get me some oats and a rope,' Dora told Jim. 'I'll try again.'

She put the bowl of oats on the ground and stood back. The pony was suspicious at first, but at last he moved forward and began to eat. Every time Dora moved towards him, he flung up his head and backed away. Once he spun round and kicked out.

'Be careful!' the mother called unnecessarily.

The kick had just nicked Dora's hip bone, painfully enough to rouse her fighting spirit. Shutting her ears to Mrs Bunker yelling advice and warnings from the gate, she began to move closer, foot by foot. The pony ate and watched her.

Watching him, she crouched and got her hand on the bowl of oats. He would have stayed while she held it, but Mrs Bunker shouted, 'Hooray!' and Barney jerked up his head and backed away.

Dora turned round angrily. 'You wrecked it.'

'Why don't you go in the house, Marion?' Mr Bunker said mildly, and his wife said huffily, 'All right, I will. I don't want to see her brains kicked out,' as if the whole enterprise were Dora's fault.

Dora started again. At last she was standing with the bowl and the pony was eating from it. She took the weight of it in one hand and inched the other round the rim until she—

197

Got him! She dropped the bowl and clung on to the halter as the pony pulled her all over the field, dragging her feet through the grass.

'Let go!' Mrs Bunker screamed from an upstairs window.

'Hang on!' Mr Bunker shouted from the gate.

Dora kept talking to the pony, and he was slowing and becoming quieter. At last she managed to get the rope through the halter. She pulled him to a stop and he stood, trembling and blowing. So did Dora. Her legs were like a quivering jelly. But he had given in.

She led him to the gate. The first time she put her hand on his neck, he shied away. The second time, he let it stay there. She told Jim to take out Hero, and led Barney into the loose box, stroking him under the mane and telling him how splendid he was.

'I think he's afraid, not mean,' she told Jim. 'You can tell by the eye. And the ears. A mean horse will flatten his ears back all the time, but Barney's are—'

Mrs Bunker had come running from the house, crying out how clever Dora was. Outside the stable, she flung up her hand to pat the pony, and he bit off the very tip of her finger and spat it out into the straw.

Dora stayed with Jim while Mr Bunker took his wife to hospital with a bath towel wrapped round her hand. When she came back with the finger bandaged and splinted, they were in the stable and the pony was licking salt out of Jim's hand.

'He's really all right,' Dora said, adding in thought, but not in words, *Unless you go up to him the wrong way.*

'He is not all right. He tried to kill me. We're going to ring the vet and have the pony shot.'

Jim went white. He dropped his hand and ran out of the stable and into the house.

'You can't,' Dora said. 'I mean it was awful about your finger, and I'm dreadfully sorry, but—'

She looked at Barney, with his honest bay pony head, and felt sorrier for him than for Mrs Bunker. She was in charge of her stupid life. What had happened to him was not his fault. 'Let me work with him.'

'He's got to go.' When Mr Bunker made up his mind, he was unshakable. That was why he was successful in his business. 'I'm phoning the vet. He goes tonight.'

'Then let me take him. Let me try him at the Farm. That family did take Lollipop, so there's room.'

'I don't care what you do with him,' Mr Bunker said, 'as long as he's out of here tonight. Dead or alive.'

Dora snapped the rope on to Barney's halter, mounted Hero, and led the pony down the drive at the side of the quiet old horse.

'Good riddance!' Mrs Bunker called after her hysterically. 'I never did like him anyway. Sir Arthur's boys said he was common.'

10

He was a bit common, with the rather large head and long ears, but not enough to prevent him moving well and freely. He shied at things along the road, and Hero bit him on the neck when he bumped into him. Sometimes he tried to pull away, sometimes he hung back, so that Dora had to drag him along.

It was a very tiring ride. She was glad to see the familiar white gate coming up through the twilight, and the sign: 'Home of Rest for Horses'.

'A home for you, Barnacle,' she told the pony. 'But you're not going to rest too much. You're going to work.'

'What's that then?' Slugger came out of the barn as Dora got off and opened the gate, and walked the horses through.

'I saved the pony's life.'

Slugger sat down on the edge of the water trough and put his head in his hands. 'I give up,' he moaned. 'First that motheaten rug on legs, then that nippy Shetland, and now a perfectly fit pony. As soon as the Colonel's back is turned, in they all come.'

Dora did not pay any attention to him. She was walking forward with the horses, watching Steve.

He was standing in the yard with a pitchfork held across his chest like a pikestaff.

'Oh no, you don't,' he said quietly. 'You're not getting away with that.'

'Steve, I had to.'

He was white with rage. His mouth was set. His dark eyes blazed. 'I told you not to bring him back.'

'They were going to have him shot.' It should not need more explanation than that. Steve knew what Follyfoot was for. To save suffering and to save lives.

'We said we wouldn't take in any more horses unless we both agreed.'

'You would have agreed if you'd been there. Those people were raving.'

'You could have come back and asked me.'

'You'd have said No.'

'Damn right, I would. I told you.'

'*You* told me.' Dora's anger was rising to meet his. 'Who says you can tell me what to do?'

Callie came round the corner of the barn, leading two old horses. 'What's that? What a nice pony. What is it, Dora, can we – oh.' She looked from Dora to Steve and back again, feeling the electric rage between them. 'Come on then, Ginger and Prince. This is no place for us.'

Steve did not appear for supper. Conversation was non-existent. Ron was out with a girl. Slugger was sulking. Callie read a school book. Dora couldn't eat.

She spent the rest of the evening with Barney, stroking him and talking to him to get him used to his new home. He smelled at everything – sign of a clever, inquisitive horse. He ate only snatches of his feed, going constantly to the door to look out. When the Weaver banged a hoof on the wall between them, he jumped and kicked out instinctively.

'Are you still in a mood, or can I talk to you?' Callie's face appeared, ready to disappear if Dora growled.

'I don't care.'

'Can I talk to the pony then?'

'Watch out. He's very nervous.'

201

'What of?'

'I don't know. He's been mistreated by someone. That dealer probably got him cheap.'

'He's nice.' Callie came in and stood by the door with her hands out low, to let Barney get the smell of her.

'If we work with him, he'll be a good ride for you.'

'But Steve says he's got to go.'

'Steve doesn't give the orders here.'

'Someone has to,' Callie said sensibly. 'He's trying to be like the Colonel, you see, saying we can't keep a fit horse when the old wrecks need us. Only the Colonel doesn't get into tempers and charge out of the gate in the truck and nearly kill a woman on a bicycle.'

'Where's he gone?'

'I don't know. He wouldn't speak to me.'

'Nor me either. I hope he hasn't gone to the Bunkers. Callie, we can't let them destroy Barney. Why doesn't Steve see that?'

'He does.' Callie was rather young for her age, but sometimes she was very shrewd. 'But it's got to be his idea.'

Dora could not sleep. She lay awake in the dark, her thoughts going round and round in pointless circles. Very late, she heard the noisy engine of the truck, and the headlights passed across her bedroom wall as Steve turned into the shed.

She heard him bang the door that led to the attic above the tack room where he slept, and heard his feet go up the bare wooden stairs. A horse coughed. Ranger. Another. Lancelot. Wonderboy snorted into the night. She knew the sounds of them all.

Going to the window, she saw the light go on in Steve's

room. She wanted to run downstairs and across the yard, and call up the steep stairs to him, 'I'm sorry. Let's be friends again.'

Her mind saw her imagined self doing this, but her real self stayed obstinately by the window.

She and Steve did not talk to each other for two days. It was the worst row they had ever had. Worse than the time the donkey scraped him off against a fence post, and Dora laughed at the donkey and Steve thought she was laughing at him. Even worse than the time his beloved old grey Tommy died when he was away, and he said it was Dora's fault.

They communicated through the others.

'Callie, ask Steve where he put the liniment.'

'Slugger, tell Dora I've ordered the linseed and horse nuts.'

Ron Stryker really enjoyed it. He invented messages from both of them, and carried them back and forth to annoy.

'Dora dear, Steve says your stables are a disgrace and you've to do them over.'

'Steve, old fellow, the little lady wants you to come out and see how well she rides the bay pony.'

'Dora, you and his young lordship are wanted in the house. Slugger's made boiled tripe with chocolate sauce and pickles.'

Barney had a lot of fear to overcome and a lot of bad treatment to forget, but Dora worked with him slowly and patiently.

She could see why Jim had not been able to get a bridle on him. First he walked round and round the box so that Dora could not even get the reins round his neck. When she did, he backed into a corner and threw up his head. Being taller than Jim, Dora was able to get her hand between his ears, holding the top of the bridle. Her other hand held the bit against his clenched teeth. She put her thumb into the gap between the front teeth and the tusk and pressed on the gum, but his teeth were still tightly clamped.

'Try sugar.' Callie was watching.

'If I start that, I'll never get the bit in without it. Come in and pinch his nose.'

Several times, Barney managed to jerk his head away, but at last Callie held his nose tight. He snorted, opened his mouth, and the bit went in.

'I'm sorry, Barnacle,' Dora said, as she adjusted the buckles of the bridle. 'But you're too good a pony to be left to rot.'

The first time she got on him, he bucked her off (that was the time Ron called Steve to come and watch).

She got on again, kept his head up, and sent him forward with her legs, and though he jibbed and side-stepped and did not go very straight, he did trot across the field.

Any pressure on the bit made him throw up his head, expecting a jab in the mouth. Winning him back to confidence was going to take time, but he had a comfortable, easy way of going, and Dora thought he had been well schooled once.

11

Steve, who normally would have been as enthusiastic as Dora about retraining the pony, would have no part in it. Even after the row died down and they began to talk to each other again, he still would not listen to her supper time prattle about the progress of Barnacle Bill.

'You spend too much time with that pony,' he said, 'while we do the work.'

'That's a lie!' Dora pushed back her chair and stood up. 'I do all my work first.' The chair fell into the fireplace.

'Might do that in the winter,' Ron remarked, 'when we're short of firewood.'

'Sit down and finish your supper,' Slugger said.

'I'm not hungry.'

'The pony should be turned out anyway,' Steve grumbled as she went to the door.

'But Dora might not be able to catch him,' Callie said.

As she slammed out of the door, Dora heard Steve say, 'That'll be her bad luck then, won't it?'

The row was still on.

The next day when Dora came back from shopping in the village, she got off her bicycle by the gate at the top of the hill, as she always did, to look out at the stretch of meadows where the Follyfoot horses grazed, or dozed in groups under trees like old men in clubs, stamping the ground bare, flicking idle tails.

The usually peaceful scene was broken up into movement. In the largest field, Barney was chasing round without a halter, nipping and kicking at the other horses.

Dora hurried home, dumped the shopping bags in the kitchen, and tried for more than an hour to catch the bay pony.

The field was too big and the grass was too sweet, and Barney did not want to go back to work. He was not afraid of Dora any more, but he teased her, letting her come near with the rope, even letting her slide the end half way up his neck, then jerking away and galloping off, bucking and kicking like a prairie horse.

Hopeless. Dora sat down on a tree stump and gloomily tied knots in the rope. After a while, something bumped her hunched shoulders. It was Barney. He kept his head down and let her put the rope round his neck and lead him back to the stable.

Steve was shovelling gravel from the cart into a muddy gateway. Dora had to pass him. She didn't know what to say, so she didn't say anything.

'Took you two hours to catch him.' Steve said it for her. 'Well, he's got to go out, same as the others. No one gets special treatment.'

That was a lie. All the horses got special treatment, according to their needs and natures.

But Dora said, sick of the row, hating the stupid barrier of stubborn pride that had grown up between them, 'I found out how to catch him. Turn my back. Ignore him.'

'You're very good at that, aren't you?'

'What do you mean?'

'Ignoring people.'

He drove his shovel into the gravel and threw it with a rattle and clatter that made Barney jump and pull Dora away.

206

The row was still on.

It was still stupidly smouldering when Bernard Fox strode into the Farm the next morning, bathed and shaved and laundered and pressed, looking all about him with the bright, critical air of a Lord of creation.

He had come to check on Ron Stryker.

There was a nip in the air today, and Ron had gone back into the tent-like garment which had once been a military greatcoat, years and years ago. The cloth was worn and torn. The ripped pockets flapped like spaniel ears. The buttons were gone and the coat hung open, the trailing bottom edge raking up a line of dust and hay seeds as Ron moved slowly about his work.

From the back, it was hard to see exactly what was moving. Bernard Fox had to ask. Dora looked at Steve, who turned away and whistled. He would not help her out.

'That? Oh – it's Ronald Stryker,' she said. 'The new stable hand I told you about.'

Ron turned his head at the enchanting sound of his own name. A cigarette hung on his bottom lip. His red hair was held down by a piece of baling twine.

'How do?' He set down what he was carrying and came up with what he fancied was a winning smile. 'Pleased to meet you.'

'And I you,' said Bernard Fox, whose manners were as polished as his boots. I'm keeping an eye on things here, for the Colonel. 'He is expecting my advice about employing you permanently.'

'No he ain't,' said Ron cheerfully. 'Dora's already wrote and got the reply, "*Good old Ron Stryker, best news I've heard for months*".'

'In those very words?'

'Well – in the Colonel's words. Set him up no end.'

This was a slap in the eye for Bernard Fox, and put him in the mood to find fault with everything.

Ron's coat went first.

'It's nippy today.' He clutched it round him. 'I suffer with me chest.'

'A little hard work will soon warm you up.' Bernard Fox rubbed his hands, and started in on Slugger. The old man was scouring out buckets with hot water and soda, wearing an apron made of a bran sack.

'Looks like hell,' Bernard Fox said. 'What if visitors came in and saw you like that?'

'We run this place for the horses, not the visitors,' Slugger muttered, but Bernard went on, 'Haven't you got overalls?'

There were a couple of brown work coats in the tack room which nobody ever bothered to wear. Slugger was forced into one of them, too big for him, too long in the sleeves. He went on scouring and rinsing, getting himself much wetter than when he was wearing his comfortable sack.

Bernard Fox had the morning to spare, alas, and stayed 'to give you a hand'. He found the work of the Farm grossly disorganized, and sketched out a timetable and rota of duties, which he tacked up in the feed shed. He did not exactly hammer in the tacks himself. He supervised Steve hammering.

He supervised the horses coming in from the top field. The Follyfoot way was to open the stable doors, put the feed in the mangers, open the gate of the field and let each horse walk into its own box. They never went wrong. It was a splendid sight to see them come into the yard as a herd, and split up, each with his mind set on his own manger. But Bernard Fox nearly had a fit when he saw this beautiful routine.

'Each horse must be led in and out separately. You can't have them charging about like the Calgary Stampede!'

Anything less like a stampede than the orderly disappearance of hindquarters into doorways would be hard to imagine.

Callie got into trouble for mounting Hero by her patent method of standing astride his neck when his head was down to grass, and sliding down on to his back when he lifted his head. When Bernard Fox objected, she dismounted by her other patent method of sliding down over his tail.

'You are the child who is supposed to be breaking the colt?' Bernard's marmalade moustache was stiff with disapproval.

It stiffened again when he heard about Barney. 'The Colonel has often told me this farm is only for horses in need.'

'He is in need.' Dora's heart sank. Steve was listening. Now he would side with Bernard Fox and Barney would get thrown out. 'He's in need of retraining. He's a good pony, but he's been terribly messed up.'

'That's not your job, even if you were qualified.' Bernard Fox did not like to be argued with. 'He should go to a professional.'

'We can't afford it. Anyway, he needs love too.'

'You talk like a stupid girl.'

'I am a stupid girl,' Dora said desperately, hanging on to Barney's halter as if it were her only support.

'And a rude one too,' Bernard Fox said curtly. 'I'd never employ you, and I wonder the Colonel does. Phyllis Weatherby told me a lot of things about you. I've given you every chance, but now I see that it's my duty to write to the Colonel and tell him what's going on.'

'Oh, please—' Dora could hardly speak, but suddenly Steve was there between her and Bernard Fox.

'Don't,' he said. 'Leave her alone. Dora's all right. She's the best worker we've got.'

209

He was so aggressive that Bernard's boots stepped two paces back. 'We'll see. I'm keeping an eye on all of you, and don't forget it.' He jerked his head at Barney. 'What are you going to do about that pony?'

'Keep it,' Steve said. 'Dora's right. He does need us. There's more than one way of saving a horse. A good one is happier working properly. And so will Barney be.'

As soon as Bernard Fox had driven away in his car with the silver throughbred on the radiator, they undid all his reforms.

Slugger took off the brown overall and threw it behind the rain barrel. Steve tore down the rota sheet, crumpled it up and threw it at a cat. Callie mounted Hero by sliding down his neck. Ron shrugged himself into his greatcoat again, although the sun was out in warmth. They opened the doors of the horses that had been fed and let them stampede out to graze.

'Yuh-hoo!' Ron gave a cowboy yell as they clattered round the barn and down the grassy track between the fences, stiff old legs stretching gladly, heads forward, snorting, tails up like ancient parodies of colts.

Dora and Steve watched them go.

'Thanks,' Dora said, 'for saving my neck. And Barney's.'

Steve hedged. 'I'm not going to let that Fox come in here and muck us about.'

'But thanks.' They smiled. The row was over.

12

When Dora got Barney's confidence enough to start jumping him, she saw what he really was. He jumped wide and
clean, judging his strides to the take-off, and cantered on with
his eyes and ears on the next jump.

He was a good pony hunter, a bit slow, but a miniature
horse without any pony habits. He was still nervous of new
fences, but when he knew them, and knew that Dora would
not jerk his mouth, he obviously enjoyed jumping. Callie's
summer holidays had started at last. She and Dora made a
small course of jumps round the outside of the field – gorse
stuffed between two fallen logs, sheep hurdles, a couple of old
doors for a wall, dead branches piled wide for a spread jump –
and schooled him round it with great joy. Not since the days
of the grey horse David had they had anything so good to
ride.

And then of course the Bunkers had to ring up.

They had not bothered to come over and see the pony, but
the father rang up after weeks of silence and asked if they
had sold Barney for him yet.

'That wasn't the idea.' Dora was taken aback. 'I'm working
with him.'

'We're getting another pony for Jim. His riding teacher,
Count Podgorski, tells us we should, and Nicholson says he'll
get rid of that brute for me. I want you to take him back
there right away.'

'Look, Mr Bunker.' Dora's brain did not always work fast
in emergencies, but now it whirled. 'Give me a bit longer.'

'Waste of time.'

'He's shaping into a good pony hunter. You'll get more money for him.' That argument had worked when Dora and Steve wanted to stop the Colonel selling the grey horse David.

'I'm prepared to take a loss.'

'The Nicholsons took the profit,' Dora said bitterly.

'They've been very decent about it. They're going to find us a top grade pony to make up for our bad luck with this one.'

'Very nice of them.' The sarcasm was lost on Mr Bunker.

'So you take him over there.'

'Not just yet.'

'I'll pay you.'

'Oh God, it isn't that!' The stupidity of the whole thing made Dora explode. 'I can't let the Nicholsons sell Barney to somebody else who hasn't a clue.'

'What do you mean, somebody *else*?'

'Somebody. He's doing so well. Give me a bit longer, please? Come over here, and I'll show you how he—'

'I've no more time to discuss it.' Mr Bunker had exhausted his capacity for talking about horses. 'Sometimes I wish we'd never got into this lark.'

So do I, Dora thought, but she said, 'Then you'll leave it to me?'

'Just don't bother me, girl. I'm a busy man.'

Dora and Callie had been riding Barney in one of the old junky saddles. When she heard nothing more from Mr Bunker, Dora went to the local tack shop and bought a second hand saddle on credit.

'What security?' the saddler asked.

'My wages,' Dora promised. 'I'll pay you something each

212

month.' When she got home with the saddle on her handle-bars, she found Ron Stryker fussing with his motorbike. He was wearing his purple jacket with the fringes and his cow-boy boots with the white trim. The toes were too tight, so he walked on his heels with the pointed toes turned up.

'What you got there?'

'Grand piano.' Dora lifted the saddle from her bicycle. 'What you got?'

'Three-decker bus.' Ron spat on the rear view mirror of the motorbike and polished it with his sleeve. 'Want to come?'

'Where are you going?'

'See my mates.'

'What to do?'

'Oh – hang around. Have some laughs. Nothing much. Mystery tour. Come on.'

Dora did not like Ron's mates, but she had nothing to do this afternoon, and she enjoyed riding on the back of the bike with the wind in her face and hair and the speed seeming faster than it was.

Ron wore his flashy helmet with the stars and stripes in front and a skull and crossbones on the back. Dora wore the crash helmet that Callie's father used to wear when he rode Wonderboy in steeplechases, before he died.

The mystery tour turned out to be a horse auction on the outskirts of the town in the valley, a sleazy place of broken down sheds and cattle pens patched with tin and barbed wire.

'I don't want to stop here.' Dora had heard about these second-rate auction sales to which no one would send a good horse, and no horse lover would send any horse at all.

'Suit yourself,' said Ron. 'I've got a date with one of the boys.' He got off the bike and propped it on the stand, leaving Dora sitting on the pillion in the steeplechase helmet.

Some boys stopped and whistled at her half-heartedly, but

in shirt and slacks and the helmet, they were not sure if she was a girl or a boy, so they walked on.

A man in town clothes, who did not look as if he had anything to do with country animals, was leading a skeleton that had once been a horse into a long shed. Dora took off her helmet, shook out her hair, swung her leg over the bike and followed.

Tied along each side of the shed were twenty or thirty of the most miserable horses Dora had ever seen, even in her experience at Follyfoot. Each bony rump had a Lot number on it, like a parcel. There were no partitions between most of the horses. There didn't need to be. None of them had the energy or heart to make trouble.

Dora walked sadly between the skinny hindquarters. The tails seemed to be set unusually low, because the muscle above sloped away.

'Who will buy them?' Ron was down at the end, talking to a lanky boy with pimples, whom Dora had seen at the Nicholsons when the Bunkers were buying the pony.

'Dog food makers, some of 'em.'

'I wish we could take them all back to the Farm.'

'Yeah. You would.' Although he pretended to be tough and cynical, Ron had worked long enough at the Farm to have more feeling than he admitted. But not in front of his friend.

'Some of them have been good horses. Look at that head. It could even be a thoroughbred.'

'Oh well,' Ron said, 'we all come to it.' He and his friend from the Nicholsons turned away, guffawing about something.

Dora stood at the open end of the shed and watched a man in breeches and gaiters and bowler hat lead a proper horse out of another building where the better stock was. It was a well-bred chestnut, very attractive to look at. It must have had

214

something wrong with it to be sold here, but the crowd gathered round the sales ring as it came in, and the bidding started.

Dora was going out to watch, when she had that feeling that someone was looking at her, concentrating on her from behind, almost like a spoken summons. She turned and saw a rangy cream coloured horse with an ugly freckled muzzle and enormous knees and hocks, his head turned as far as the rope would allow, looking at her.

'Hullo, friend.' She went back and pushed between him and the next horse to reach his head. It was a big scarred head, fallen in over the pale eyes and nostrils. His tangled white mane flopped on both sides of a heavy neck. The scars on his shoulders showed that he had been driven in a badly fitting collar.

Dora found crumbs of sugar in her pocket, worse than nothing, because the horse lipped and licked at her hand desperately for more.

'I would if I could, old friend.' She answered the summons the horse's eyes had sent to her back. 'Mon ami. Amigo. I'd take you home and call you Amigo.'

'You like that old skin?' Ron's lanky pal had come back into the shed. 'One of ours.'

'The Nicholsons'?' She had not seen any horses like this at the dealers' stables.

'He gets bunches in and sells 'em where he can. You can make quite a bit of money, dead *or* alive. This ugly old hay-burner has got a few pulling years left.'

'What will he sell for?'

'About sixty quid. That's the reserve Nicholson puts on all of them. If he can't get it here, he'll get it somewhere else.'

'Oh dear.' In her pocket among the sugar crumbs, Dora did not think she had sixty pence.

'Going to move along then?' Ron's friend watched her

215

suspiciously, as if she might nobble the poor old horse, already nobbled by the years, and by working for man.

She patted Amigo on his strong, hardworking shoulder, and went out to the sales ring.

13

There were several young horses up for sale, unbroken, or still very green. One of the best that came out was a strawberry roan, polo pony type, with an exquisite square-nosed head and a straight, springy action. Among the crowd, Dora spotted the Nicholsons, father, mother and Chip, watching it from the rail, sharp-eyed.

'New Forest-Arab cross,' the auctioneer described it. 'Rising four, well broke, but green. You'll never see a likelier one, ladies and gentlemen.'

'Likely to go lame,' said a grumbly man next to Dora, who had been crabbing about all the horses.

He was evidently a well-known character here. People laughed, and the auctioneer said, 'I'd back his legs before yours, Fred.'

'Back 'em to kick,' Fred grumbled.

The young roan was very nervous. He threw up his head and stared and snorted. He pulled in circles round the girl who held him. When she lunged him to show how he moved he put down his head and bucked round the ring, squealing.

'I wouldn't take a chance on him,' the grumbly man said, but the bids were going ahead. You could not always see who made them, because they did not call out. They nodded, or raised a finger without raising their hand from the rail, or coughed, or moved their catalogue slightly. When the roan pony was sold, fairly cheap for what he might become, Dora did not know who had bought him, until she saw Mrs Nicholson lead the pony away, jerking his head down hard when he threw it up in fear of her and the crowd. Dora thought of a slave sold at auction to the highest bidder, powerless over his life, his future unknown.

When she went to get a cup of tea, she found herself standing next to Chip in the line waiting at the greasy snack bar.

'That was a nice pony your parents bought,' she said.

'Mm-hm.' Chip's deadpan gaze considered where she had seen Dora before.

'Is it for you?'

'Till we sell him. I'm going to train him for the race. If he wins, he'll fetch a big price.'

'What race?'

'The Moonlight Steeplechase. At Mr Wheeler's. You know.'

Dora had heard of the Moonlight Pony Steeplechase which the rich old man at Broadlands organized every year. But it was a posh social affair, with all the Best People in the neighbourhood invited to a champagne buffet before the race, far removed from life at Follyfoot.

But now she found herself envying Chip with the lovely roan pony to train, and the excitement of racing him under the moon over the fences and fields of the pony steeplechase course at Broadlands. And she boasted, 'We may be entering too.'

'You're much too old,' Chip said, as if Dora was fifty.

'We have a rider.'

'What on?' Chip was not really interested, but the snack bar woman was pouring beer and jokes for a lot of men, and it was a long wait for tea.

'That bay pony, remember, that you sold to those people for their boy. He's jumping like a stag, you wouldn't know him.'

'That thing!' It was the first time Dora had seen Chip

smile. She overdid it. She exploded with laughter, slapping her knees, clutching her stomach.

'Well, that's one I won't have to worry about,' she said rudely.

'That's what *you* think,' Dora said, and when Chip got her tea first by pushing ahead, Dora jogged her elbow and spilled most of it into the saucer.

It had started as a boasting joke, but the idea took root. Barney in the Moonlight Steeplechase . . . Dora's mind raced ahead. Callie would have to work hard. They'd make bigger jumps, get him very fit . . . would Steve and Dora be invited to the buffet supper? She had no proper dress . . .

She was jogged out of her ambitious dream by the sight of Ron's friend bringing the big cream horse out of the shed and into the sales ring. She pushed through the crowd and stood by the rail, wondering if he would look at her again, trying to send him a thought message as he had done to her: 'Good luck, Amigo.'

The auctioneer described him as 'a big strong horse with a lot of work in him yet. Some Clydesdale about him, I'd say.'

'So's your grandmother,' grumbled Fred.

Some man bid a small amount for the awkward-looking horse. He was somewhat over at the knees. He had huge feet like clogs, turned inwards in front and out behind.

'Must be the dog meat blokes.' Ron Stryker had slid between people to stand beside Dora. 'That's about all he's good for, with that leg.'

'What leg?'

'Off fore,' Ron said out of the side of his mouth.

'He's stiff, but he walks sound.'

'Today he does.' Ron winked. 'Nerve block,' he whispered. 'Pheet!' He moved his fingers like pushing in the plunger of a syringe. 'That's why he's stiff. Tomorrow he'll be crippled again.'

The bidding was creeping up. A bent old fellow in a battered felt hat turned down all round was raising the bids just slightly ahead of the other man.

'You barmy, Norman?' Fred called across the ring to him. 'He'll pull the log cart.'

Dora remembered seeing the old man once or twice with a thin horse and a big cart piled heavy with firewood. If the cream horse was really dead lame when the injection wore off – and Ron should know after his time with the Nicholsons—

Before she knew what she was doing, she had ducked under the rail and run out with her hands up. 'Stop!' she called to the auctioneer, to the old man, to everyone. 'Please stop it. He can't work, he's lame, you can't—'

She was suddenly aware that she was in the middle of the sawdust ring with the old horse and Ron's astonished friend, surrounded by faces and voices.

She swung round. 'Please!' she said desperately. 'Can't you see he's lame?'

Someone laughed. Several people called out. 'What's the matter with her?' the old man complained.

'Go and find out, Norman,' said Fred, and a lot more people laughed.

Dora put her hand on the horse's neck, staring round in fear.

The auctioneer was professionally unruffled. 'The horse is as you see him,' he said smoothly. 'Out of the ring, young lady, and let's get on with it. The reserve is sixty, ladies and gentlemen, or the horse is withdrawn.' He looked at the old man, who shook his head.

'You pig.' It was not said loud enough for the crowd to hear, but Dora heard it, and flinched at the anger in Mr Nicholson's jowly face, scarlet over the rail. 'You pig.'

'Sixty is reserve, I said. If there are no more bids—'

'Sixty pounds.' Dora wanted to speak bravely, but her voice came out in a squeak. 'I bid sixty pounds.'

'And I wish you joy.' Fred's grumble came through the surprised, amused murmur of the crowd.

14

When Dora reached for the halter rope, Ron Stryker's friend said, 'Oh no, you don't. You pay the auctioneer's clerk first. You got the money?'

'Yes,' Dora lied. What on earth was she going to do? She looked for Ron, but he had disappeared. He had probably gone home in disgust.

She went out of the ring to the accompaniment of hoots and whistles and a few corny jokes. In the crowd, a voice said, 'Well done, good girl,' but when she turned – to ask for help, for money, what? – she could not see who had spoken.

She had bought the horse with nothing. What happened now? Would they sue her? Arrest her? The auctioneer's clerk was looking her way, so she turned her back and found herself face to face with Ron, arms folded, head nodding, mouth pursed up tight, appraising her.

'You done it now,' he said.

'Yes.' She could not even make excuses.

'What a spectacle. Christians and lions. Better than Ben Hur.'

'Ron, help me. You know these people. What shall I do?'

'Search me.'

'What will happen when they find I can't pay?'

Slowly, very slowly, Ron put his hand into the pocket of his bell-bottom denims. Slowly, very slowly, he pulled out a fistful of something that looked like money. It was money. A tight roll of five pound notes.

Sometimes Ron had nothing. Sometimes he was loaded. You didn't ask how.

222

'Ron, you wouldn't—'

Very slowly, licking his finger, he peeled off twelve five pound notes from the roll, Dora held out her hand. Slowly, licking his finger again, he counted them off into her palm. She closed her fist.

'I can't ever thank you.'

'Shut up.' He would not have it that way. 'It's only a loan, don't forget.'

'I won't.'

'I'll see you don't. You pay me in a month, with interest, or the horse is mine. Agree?'

Dora nodded. There was nothing else to do.

'All of it back in a month, or the horse is mine and I'll sell it cheap to that chap with the log cart.'

The old horse came with her, not willingly or unwillingly. He just came. His enthusiasm for life or any new scene had long ago been extinguished.

As Dora walked away over the trodden grass, she heard a lot of shouting and clatter and saw the Nicholson family shoving the strawberry roan into their trailer by brute force. The ramp banged up and they pulled out of the gate, with the pony neighing and kicking.

Dora and the horse turned into the road and began to plod along. Ron roared past them on the bike as if he did not know them. He had promised to tell Steve to come back with the horse box, but you never knew.

And she did not know if Steve would come.

Dusk came down as she and the horse walked along, and the light slipped away into lilac and green over the line of hills, and stealthily it grew dark.

They were quieter roads now, where the cars did not

223

swish by in an endless stink of noise. Going up hill, Amigo slowed, and she had to walk slower. Would they ever get home? He seemed to be favouring the off foreleg already. If he went really lame, it would take her all night to get back to the Farm. All night and all day. Would Ron tell them where she was? A normal person would, but he might think it a joke not to tell. His sense of humour wasn't normal.

Dora was walking on the right of the road. Lights came towards her and she pushed Amigo over on to the rough grass. The headlights grew and she saw the small roof lights of the horse box and its familiar bulk, slowing, stopping.

Dora stood blinking in the lights, and leaned against the horses shoulder, waiting for Steve to get out.

'All right.' He stood behind the light. 'Better make it a good one.'

'The horse is old and lame. Ron thought they'd doctored him to sell. He was being bought to pull a heavy cart. So I – so I bought him.'

'What with?'

'Ron lent me the money. For a month.'

'Then what?' Steve stepped out into the light. He looked at the horse for a long time, and then blew out his cheeks. He and Dora were perhaps the only two people in the world who would not say the cream horse was ugly. He was a horse.

'Which leg?'

'Off fore.'

He stepped round and ran his hand down the canon bone and fetlock. Amigo dropped his head and mumbled at Steve's hair with his loose freckled lip.

'Feels like a splint. And the scars, that knee could have been broken at some time. But who's going to pay? The Colonel said absolutely no buying. The Farm can't pay for him.'

'I will.'

224

'How?'

'Somehow. I'll save up my pay.'

'You already owe me most of that on the saddle.'

'I'll sell something.'

'What?'

'Oh – what does it matter?' Dora began to cry. She hid her face in the tangle of white mane that flopped on the wrong side of Amigo's neck, but Steve came round and put his hand behind her head to turn her face towards him. 'What does it matter, Steve?' A cobweb of tears glistened between her face and the lights. 'It's the horse that matters.'

'Dora—' With his back to the lights, she could not see his face.

'What?'

He suddenly put his arms round her and held her very close and tight, so that she had no breath to cry, and did not need to, because she was not afraid any more.

'It's going to be all right. We'll think of something. Come on.' He let her go and took Amigo's rope. 'Let's get this old buzzard home and fed. Get up, horse, you're going to be all right.'

15

The cream horse Amigo did go quite lame within a few days, and the vet said there was not much more that could be done. He did not seem to be in pain. They crushed aspirin with his feed to help the stiffness, and turned him out to graze with the more peaceful horses who would not bother a newcomer.

The old horse behaved as if he had not been out to a proper bit of grass for years. When Dora took him to the gate and let him go, he trotted off, dot and carry, his big feet stumbling over tufts. He even tried a canter, pushing his knobbly knees through the tall grass in the corner.

'He looks almost graceful,' Dora said to Slugger, who had come along to help her if any of the other horses were aggressive.

'Well – almost like a horse, let's put it that way.'

'Look, there he goes.'

Amigo had stopped at a muddy place much favoured for rolling. He pawed for a while, smelled the ground, sagged at all four corners, thought better of it, turned round to face the other way, pawed again, then let himself go, knees buckling with a grunt and a thump as his big bony body went over on its side.

He rolled for five minutes, teetering on his prominent spine with four massive feet in the air when he could not quite roll over. At last he sat up like a dog, lashing the ground with his tail and shaking his head. Prince nipped at him from behind, and he staggered to his feet.

'Poor old Flamingo.' Slugger and Dora turned away.

'His name's Amigo. I told you.'

'That's what I said.'

'No, Amigo. It means friend.'

'Then why don't you call him Old Pal?'

Now Dora had two special projects. Caring for Amigo, and continuing to work with Barney, who was improving every day.

One evening when Callie had jumped the pony well and was pleased with herself and him, Dora confided to her the crazy dream about the Moonlight Steeplechase.

'I'd be terrified.'

'You wouldn't, Callie.'

'The jumps are big and they go flat out for that money prize. Millie Bryant told me. She rode in it last year. She fell off at the water.'

'Barney could do it.'

'*He* might. I couldn't.'

'You could. I'd ride him myself if it wasn't fourteen and under.'

'Just because you're safely out of it,' Callie said cynically, 'don't pick on me.'

Dora put the idea back into being only a dream. Anyway, Callie was more interested in Folly than in Barney. The colt belonged to her, and she took him everywhere, like a dog, determined that they were going to grow up to have the best horse-human relationship ever achieved.

The relationship was still rather erratic. He would do things for her if he wanted, but if there was an argument, he often won.

'He still thinks he's boss,' Callie said when Folly pulled away again and again to the gate when she was trying to lunge him in a circle.' How can I explain to him that a horse is supposed to be stupider than a person?'

Sometimes when Dora and Callie were out for a ride with Barney and Hero, they let Folly run with them, if they were not going near a road or sown fields. Hero was his mate, because they shared Callie, and the colt would follow quite well.

They rode one evening down the hill and along a turfy ride at the bottom of a climbing wood. Folly trotting in and out of the trees as if he were a deer. Near the corner, Barney pricked his ears. Dora heard the faint sound of hoofs on the firm, chalky turf.

'Better get off and grab Folly,' she told Callie. 'There's another horse coming.'

Once, the colt had followed two children on ponies home. Once, he had got into the middle of a hunt. Callie did not want to remember that day. The language still burned in her ears.

A boy on a dark grey pony came trotting round the corner of the wood. Before Callie could get to him, Folly jumped out over the bank. The grey pony shied and the boy fell off.

Dora held Hero while Callie caught Folly and snapped on the leading rein. 'I'm awfully sorry.'

The boy was sitting on the ground, rather dazed, but hanging on to the reins of the grey pony, who stood with its body arched away from Folly, but its neck and head curved round to inspect.

Dora came up. 'Are you all right?'

'I think so.' He took off his riding cap and rubbed his head to see if it hurt. The boy was Jim Bunker.

With the encouragement of Count Podgorsky and Mr Nicholson (naturally), his parents had bought this pony at vast expense so that Jim could ride in the Moonlight Steeple-chase.

'Do you want to?'

'No. But my mother wants an invitation to Broadlands.'

Jim was a bit scared of the pony. Her name was Grey Lady, but he called her Maggie, which sounded less scary.

She was a lovely pony, and might give Chip and the roan some hard competition, except for her rider. His lessons with the Count had improved him enormously, but he was still rather sloppy and vague in the saddle, which was why he had fallen off when the pony shied. He had been trotting idly along with a loose rein, admiring the view, quite far from home and totally lost, but expecting eventually to come to a road or a landmark he knew.

After he found out that he had come quite near to the Farm, he often rode the grey mare over to Follyfoot. He would arrive in the morning, trotting on the hard road, or walking through growing wheat, or riding with the girths loose, or doing something else wrong, and liked to stay most of the day, working with the others, or just mooning about. Tennis lessons, swimming, Pony Club rallies, 'meeting nice new friends' – all the things his mother had planned for his holidays were abandoned, once he discovered Follyfoot.

He had always liked Barney better than Grey Maggie Lady, and he loved the old horses, especially Amigo, who was a dreamer like he was. If the cream horse was lying down in the field, resting his old bones in the sun, he would not bother with the effort to get up when Jim came near. Jim would stretch out behind him with his head against his bulky side, and the two of them would doze off together, under the song of a rising lark.

16

One day when it was too wet to ride, Jim persuaded his mother to drive him over to the Farm. She dropped him at the gate, because she did not want to risk seeing Barney. Even thinking about him made her healed fingertip throb. But when she came back for him that afternoon, Jim was in the barn helping to store bales of hay, so she had to get out of the car and look for him.

She stood in the wide doorway and watched her lanky son heave at the hay with all the strength of his thin arms, which was not as much strength as Callie, even though she was a girl.

'I wish he'd work as hard as that at home,' she told Dora.

'He's good in the stables,' Dora said.

'Not on his own. He has to be *driven* out to take care of that valuable pony. Boys. Isn't it always the way?'

'Oh yes.' Dora nodded wisely, as if she had been a mother for years.

Mrs Bunker called Jim to come down from the top of the hay. 'The Drews are coming for dinner. With their daughter.'

'That fink. Why can't I stay here?' Like every other child who became involved with Follyfoot, Jim would rather be here than anywhere.

'Come down, Jimmy,' his mother said mildly, which was how she always talked to him.

'I'll show you all the horses.' He jumped down.

'We haven't the time, and I don't—'

But Jim was already half way across the yard and waiting

230

for her by the first loose box. He gave her the grand tour, with histories of each horse, which he had learned by listening to Dora and Steve and Callie when they showed visitors round:

'This is the Weaver, who used to be with the Mounted Police until he got the habit of crib-biting. He led all the parades and once he knocked over a man who was going to shoot a politician in Trafalgar Square. This is poor old Flypaper who used to pull a junk cart. This is Hero, rescued from a fate worse than death in a circus . . .'

If Slugger was here alone when people came, they got a very skimpy tour, because he would say no more than, 'This here is an old police horse, ruddy nuisance. That's a donkey, been here as long as me – too long. Out in that field, there's a lot of lazy eating machines . . .'

When Jim had dragged her, protesting, round the stables, he insisted on riding Barney in the rain, so that his mother could see how quiet he was now.

Sheltering under a tree with a newspaper over her hairdo, she couldn't believe it. 'Is he drugged again?'

'No, he's himself. I wish I still had him, instead of Maggie.'

'No, you don't, dear. Grey Lady is worth twenty of that common pony.'

'She's got less sense.'

'She'll be the best at the races. Even Sir Arthur's boys with their fancy ponies looked a bit glum when they saw her.'

Dora was in with Amigo when Jim took his mother to see his favourite, bandaging the leg which she was treating with a new liniment.

'What a hideous horse.' Mrs Bunker recoiled as he stretched out his pink freckled nose. Since the accident with Barney, she approached a horse very cautiously, with her hands in her pockets, which meant sugar to Amigo.

'Ssh. He's got troubles enough without hearing that.' Jim

231

knew about Dora's money problems. Everyone knew. Ron Stryker teased her about it all the time, counting up the days until he would, as he said, 'foreclose the mortgage'.

Kneeling in the straw, tying the tapes of the bandage, Dora had one of her wild, impossible ideas.

There seemed to be plenty of money for buying ponies, loose boxes, recently a trailer for Grey Lady, an Italian saddle, expensive breeches and boots for Jim. The Bunkers had taken up horsiness in quite a big way. Mrs Bunker wore a Pony Club badge on one lapel, and on the other a glittery horseshoe brooch. Could Dora ever find the nerve or the words to ask her for a loan of sixty pounds?

While she was searching for them among the jumble of ideas and impulses and half-formed sentences scrambled in her head, Jim told her, dreaming with his shoulder against Amigo's wide chest, 'If Maggie and I win the steeplechase, we'll give you the prize money for Amigo.'

The prize money was a hundred pounds. Colossal largesse from colossally rich Mr Wheeler, who did not think in figures of less than two noughts.

Dora sat back on her heels. 'You wouldn't.'

'Why not? We wouldn't want the money, would we, Mum?'

'For you to win that race will be reward enough for me.'

'I don't much want to ride in it, you know,' Jim said.

'Of course you do,' his mother said firmly. 'It's the chance of a lifetime.'

For her to get into Society at Broadlands. As the parents of a competitor, she and her husband were sure of an invitation to the champagne supper. As mother of the winner, she would be the equal of anybody. If Jim and Grey Lady were first past the post, it would be the crowning triumph of her life.

Grey Lady had a chance. She was a marvellously built pony, very fast and a bold jumper, though she made mistakes sometimes with Jim, because he was nervous.

Now that Amigo's future hung on the race. Steve began to train the grey mare when Jim brought her over to Follyfoot. They had built some larger jumps and a longer course. It included jumping the stone wall on to the lawn, over the rose arbour which had fallen in the last storm, and out again by way of the trench they had dug from the drainspout so that rain and sinkwater would keep it wet and boggy, good practice for the notorious Broadlands Water jump, uneasily nicknamed Becher's Brook.

Steve was in his glory with such a good pony to ride. Jim let him do the training. He would rather ride Barney, or potter about on the donkey, or sit high on the ridge of Amigo's back as he ambled about the field.

Dora too preferred to ride Barney. Although she wanted Grey Lady to win the money for Amigo, she still wanted Barney to be in the race, for his experience and her pride.

'You still think I'm going to ride him?' Callie asked, after the ponies had completed the course, with Dora a hundred yards behind by the time she lurched over the drainwater jump and into the last stretch over the hurdles to finish at the dead tree in the orchard.

'I know he hasn't a chance, but still.'

'If he hasn't a chance,' Callie said, 'I don't mind so much.'

'What do you mean?' Dora slid off the sweating bay pony.

'It was the idea of having to try and win I couldn't face. You know I hate contests.' Callie suffered tortures in exams or on School Sports Day, or at the kind of parties where they played competitive games. 'But if it's just for fun, then I wouldn't mind so much.'

That evening, they sat at the kitchen table to make out the entry for the Moonlight Pony Steeplechase.

'Give us a bit of paper,' Ron said. 'I'm entering me old pal Amigo.'

'He's as good as mine.' Ron never lost an opportunity to make a joke about the loan that was not really a joke.

'If you're riding that Flamingo,' Slugger saw Dora's face and tried to make it into a real joke, 'I'm entering the mule.'

'Too old,' Callie said, without looking up from what she was writing.

'What do you mean, too old?'

'He must be nearly twenty.'

'Oh.' Slugger sat back. 'I thought you meant me.'

On a clean sheet of paper, Callie, whose handwriting was the best, copied out the entry:

'Barnacle Bill. Bay gelding. 14.1 hh. 7 years (he was nine, but seven looked better). Rider: Cathleen Sheppard. 12 years. Colours: Blue with gold cross' (her father's racing silks, much too big, but Dora would take in the seams).

Callie read it out.

'Disqualified already.' Ron was picking his teeth with a chicken bone. 'Warned off the course.'

Callie and Dora stared at him.

'Barnacle still belongs to the Bunkers. Ponies must be ridden by owner. Chip told me when I was down at their place last week to see how she's going with that roan.'

'How is she going?'

'Lovely.' Ron made a circle of his thumb and forefinger, and kissed it into the vague direction of the Nicholson's stable. 'Makes Grey Maggie whatsername look like a plough horse.'

'We'll see,' Steve said.

'But if I'm not going to win,' Callie was working carefully

234

on the flourishes of her signature under the entry form, 'it won't matter cheating. It's just for fun, isn't it, Dora?'

'Yes.' But secretly, crazily, Dora had never stopped dreaming that the bay pony might win the race. 'Just for fun.'

17

He was too slow. Dora gave him plenty of oats and plenty of galloping, and also walked him endlessly uphill to develop his muscles, but he was not built for speed, and he did not have the speed.

She thought he was galloping faster, until she went with Steve and Ron to a meeting at the race course near Bernard Fox's stables and saw the thoroughbreds run. That was really galloping.

It was a flat racing course a mile oval of beautiful turf, with the double line of rails newly painted, and the red brick stands and buildings bright with white paint and window boxes. There were flowers everywhere, and neat trimmed evergreens. Even the bookies, on a lawn by the grandstand, looked more colourful than usual, with gay umbrellas up not for the rain today, but the sun in a dazzling sky.

Ron Stryker went to every race meeting and came back a plutocrat or a pauper, usually a pauper. Steve and Dora did not go often, because they had no money to lose, and if you followed Ron's tips, you lost, even when he mysteriously won. But on a fine day this course was attractive and the races were exciting, and easy to see all the way round without buying a grandstand ticket.

Dora stood by the rail of the paddock all the time the horses were being led round before the race. She could never get enough of watching that marvellous swinging thoroughbred walk, the arch of the fine-skinned neck as the horse caught impatiently at the snaffle, the muscles moving under the shining skin, the whole bloom of a perfectly fit horse from

236

the tip of the slender curved ears to the brushed tail swinging like a bell.

Dora envied the stable lads and girls who led the horses, but they looked quite unexcited. So did the owners and trainers as they chatted in a sophisticated way in the centre of the paddock. Only the jockeys, when they came out, gave a hint in the eyes and mouth of being tense and excited, although some of them who had been riding for years joked casually, as if riding a race at thirty miles an hour were no more than going to the cinema.

When the horses went out to canter down to the start, Dora pushed through the crowd to get a place on the slope of grass at the side of the stands. From here you could see the whole race streaming round the course like a train, turning the bend, and head on into the straight, pounding, thudding, the leading jockey glancing back, each horse's head going like a piston, its hoofs reaching for the turf and flinging it behind, a galloping marvel.

They were made for speed, and made for a course like this where they could gallop flat out. The pony course at Follyfoot was full of odd quirks and corners, rough ruts and soft patches, muddy wallows through gateways, short stretches of grass where you could let your pony go if you were sure of stopping him in time for the bend round the tree and the tricky hop onto the bank, with a drop into the lane. If Barney could only gallop here, he might learn to stretch and reach and gallop out, as the thoroughbreds did.

Dora was standing among the cheering and clapping people round the unsaddling enclosure, watching the pretty woman owner in a white dress and sandals who was holding her horse's bridle, when the idea came to her.

'Good race, Jessica!' someone called, and the owner waved to them in the crowd. She patted her horse's dark

237

soaked neck and smiled for a man with a camera, wrinkling her eyes against the sun.

When the Pony Steeplechase was run and won, it would be moonlight, not sunlight, in which the winner would stand, with the cheers of praise all round.

Mr Wheeler always picked a date when the moon would be full. If it was cloudy, the race was put off to a clear night. The course was lit by the moon, with floodlights in the trees at the start and finish, and the headlamps of cars positioned to light jumps without dazzling.

This was the great risk and venture of the race, which some people (not invited to the supper) said would need to have a huge prize to get anyone to enter. No one, they grumbled, but an old fool like Mr Wheeler, who had been a daredevil rider in his day and was said to have broken every bone in his body, would dream up a night-time race. Although horses, like all animals, can see better than people in the dark, ponies who galloped and jumped well out hunting or in training would be much more uncertain and nervous under the moon.

But if Barney could gallop here on the race course, if he could learn to gallop by moonlight, flat out with confidence on the smooth turf . . .

18

Dora did not tell anyone her plan. She could not even tell Callie, because if she knew how serious Dora was about training Barney, she might refuse to ride in the race.

'Just for fun,' she had insisted. But there was nothing funny about sneaking Barney out of the small field at night, and riding him down the moonlit lanes into the valley and up the other side to the race course.

This was serious. Dora had turned him out tonight, so that Steve would not hear him come out of his box and across the cobbles. She had taken his saddle and bridle from the tack room where Steve slept above, and hidden it in the woodshed. She had gone upstairs with Slugger and Callie, and then dropped silently from her window into the tomato bed, using a branch of lilac to swing herself down.

Barney was easy to catch these days, as long as you pretended you did not want him. If you stood still in the field, not looking at him, he would come up and drop his mealy nose into your hand and practically beg you to take hold of the halter.

The moon was three quarters full, bright and pearly. A fairly strong breeze blew small clouds across it, but they were quickly gone. Barney trotted quite happily in the half dark, his big ears alert to the unfamiliar black and white landscape, but without shying or stumbling Dora would be able to let him gallop flat out. Neither of them would be afraid.

The main entrance to the race course would be shut and locked, but Dora knew that she could go round to the far side, where there was a gate used by the man who grazed a

239

couple of horses on the grass in the middle of the course. They lifted their heads as Barney came in, and one of them called, but as he trotted down the side of the course to the stands, they dropped their heads again, well used to seeing horses gallop here.

Dora went through a gap in the rail, dismounted, and took Barney into the paddock. Walking casually with a blade of grass in her mouth like one of the stable girls, she led him round and imagined that thoroughbreds walked in front and behind her, and that the knowledgeable crowd were standing round with astute comments, and people like Ron were giving people like Steve unreliable tips about what and what not to back.

Her other self was there too, at the rail, watching herself with envy.

She was also there in the middle of the paddock as an owner, chatting easily with the woman in the white dress, and with her trainer, who bore a resemblance to Bernard Fox, except that he was polite to Dora, and with her jockey, who nodded briefly as she wished him Good Luck.

Then she was the jockey, coming out a bit bow-legged. She mounted, touched her cap to her invisible self as owner, nodded at a last minute instruction from Bernard Fox, rode out and cantered down to the start.

Barney trampled as she collected him, and closed her legs against his sides.

They're off! He bounded ahead, and settled down to drum the turf in a steady gallop that seemed, that was, faster than he had gone before.

He galloped so fast that the wind roared in Dora's ears as if she were flying in an open plane. He galloped half way round the course before he slowed to a canter, and finished with his head down, blowing, the streaks of foam on his dark wet neck white in the moonlight.

The crowd went delirious. They cheered and shouted in the stands. They threw caps in the air, and crowded round Dora as she came off the course, reaching out to touch Barney.

Well done! Good race! The winner, the winner!

Dora got off Barney, and invisible hands slapped her on the back. She led him into the small unsaddling enclosure with the little room where the jockeys weighed in after a race.

She stood there with Barney, his neck steaming under her hand, his nose squared, in and out, to get his breath back, and peopled the rail with admiring faces, and imagined the applause and the excited voices and the click of cameras.

'Oh, my God. Oh, good God, I can't believe it. I absolutely and finally will not believe it.'

The vision fled. The cheers of the crowd faded. Dora and Barney stood alone in the empty unsaddling enclosure. Behind them at the gate were three men. One was Bernard Fox.

'Get that animal out of there.'

Dora led Barney out, feeling more foolish than ever in her life, which had already included many foolish moments.

'I dread the answer,' Bernard Fox said, 'but I'll have to ask you to explain.'

'I didn't think anyone would be here.'

'We happened to have a late committee meeting, and that's a better explanation than yours. A thief climbs a drainpipe and gets in through a bedroom window. He's at the jewel box when the woman pops up in bed. "A burglar!"'

Bernie was showing off for the other men.

'The thief shoots her dead and takes the diamonds. When they catch him, he explains, "I didn't think anyone would be there."'

241

The other men, one tall, one small, laughed. Dora did not crack a smile. Barney put his head down and cropped the short clovery turf.

'You'll have to think up a better excuse than that, Dorothy.'

'You know the girl?' The tall man looked at Dora down his long nose.

'She works for the Colonel at Follyfoot Farm. Mad as hatters, the whole lot of them. And the Colonel's the maddest to leave them on their own. I'll have to write to him again,' he told Dora, 'so let's hear your reason for trespassing.'

Dora shook her head, 'There isn't any.'

She could not say, 'I'm training the pony for the race.' They would say, 'What race?' and laugh when they heard. She thought of the marvellous big horses streaming round at thirty miles an hour. They would laugh at poor little Barney with his burst of speed that ended in a canter.

'I don't make sense of it,' the small man said.

'These young people,' the tall man said, 'they just want to barge in to other people's property as an act of rebellion.' He put on the voice with which grown-ups who can't remember what it was like to be young tell each other what the young are like.

'A revolutionary, eh?' The small man was quite twinkly and nice.

'Nothing so dashing.' Bernard Fox would not let it improve to a joke. 'She's a trespasser, and should be prosecuted. I shall write to the Colonel and warn him, in case the committee decide to tell the police.'

'Please don't.'

He did not answer, so Dora got on Barney and walked away. Before she turned out of sight behind a clipped hedge, Bernard Fox, delivered his parting shot.

'And you're too big for that pony.'

242

19

As the night of the race approached, excitement grew. Stories kept coming in about the other competitors, mostly exaggerated for good or bad.

Mrs Bunker reported that Mr Bunker had been up at the squash court at the Manor and had seen one of Sir Arthur's ponies jump almost five feet. The carpenter had measured it.

Jim reported some highfaluting claims that Count Podgorsky had made for one of his other pupils.

But Jim had also seen the pupil fall off. 'For nothing. She rides worse than me, if you can imagine it.'

Steve had heard from the feed merchant that Mrs Hatch from the Pony Club was buying cough medicine for her daughter's pony.

Ron was still hanging about with his pal at the dealers, keeping out of sight of the Nicholsons, but watching the roan pony, now fancifully named Strawberry Sunday.

'That's your competition,' he told Jim. 'The Nicholsons have made up what they like to call their minds that they're going to win. When they go after something, that lot, they get it. It's not only the money and the sale of the pony, see. But people round here don't think so much of them. They gotta win, see, and show who's best.'

'That's that, then.' Jim was sickeningly defeatist. 'If they're the best, they'll win.'

'*You've* got to win.' Steve made a fist and held it under Jim's pointed chin. 'Think of Amigo. Get out of here, Ron. You're bad news.'

'I'm only saying what I see. Just thought you'd like to know, that's all. I seen that strawberry roan last Saturday gallop alongside their big thoroughbred, and she was right there with him all the way.'

Steve groaned.

'Just thought you'd like to know.' Ron went across the yard, chucking a pebble at a swallow swooping under the barn roof, and out to his motorbike.

'I thought you were going to help me hang that gate,' Dora called. 'Where are you going?'

'Down the Nicholsons. I got everybody here all sweated up about the roan. May as well get Chip into a lather by telling her how good our grey is.'

The excitement began to build up in the neighbourhood. Among people involved with the race, who talked of little else, it became clear that Strawberry Sunday and Grey Lady would be the favourites.

Poor Barnacle Bill. If he could not even gallop a mile on the flat, he would be lucky if he finished the steeplechase course at Broadlands. But he needed to work, so Dora went on training him and Callie, if only to keep herself from worrying about what Bernard Fox and the committee were going to do to her.

What had he written to the Colonel? What would the Colonel write to Dora? She still had not told anyone about the moonlight gallop. One morning, she almost told Steve, but when she opened her mouth, the words sounded foolish before she ever got them out.

'Steve.'

'What?'

'Nothing.'

244

'Get a move on then. Maggie's all tacked up. I'm going to race you and Barney across the big stubble field.'

'Let Callie ride him.'

'Why not you?'

'I think I'm too big for him.'

'Since when?'

'I just think so.'

Why care what Bernard Fox had said? But when someone you don't like tells you something you don't want to hear, you do care. You even begin to believe it.

After Steve and Callie had ridden off, Dora heard his bossy voice.

'Anyone about?' He was calling out of his car window, as if he expected a reception committee.

Dora ducked into the tack room. She heard the car door slam and his boots in the yard. No escape. Bernard would be sure to snoop in here to see if they had cleaned the tack, so she nipped up the stairs and hid in Steve's room.

Crouching by the window, she heard him talking to Slugger.

'Where is everyone? The place is deserted.'

'No, it aint. I'm here.'

'Where are those lazy kids at this time in the morning, with all the work to be done? Look at the bedding. Hasn't been mucked out for days, by the look of it.'

'Well, you see, it's like this.' Dora heard Slugger go into the slow, maundering voice he put on to annoy people who annoyed him. 'That there is the Weaver's stable, that is.'

'It's a dirty stable. I don't care whose it is.'

'Ah, but if you knew the Weaver. Very messy, he is. I knew a horse like him once, long ago, before the war, it must have been. Big brown horse with sickle hocks. Name of – name of – what was that beggar's name?'

'Where's Dorothy?' Bernard interrupted.

'In the tack room,' Slugger said. 'Cleaning tack.'

'I'm glad to hear it.' Dora heard him open the door and shut it. 'If she was, she isn't now, and from the look of the tack, she ought to be. I can't stop any longer. I came to tell her I'd heard from the Colonel.'

'Oh yes?' Slugger was interested. Dora's heart fell into her stomach like a stone.

'He said he'd written to the Farm and settled the matter. I wanted to know what he wrote.'

The stone leaped out of Dora's stomach, suffocatingly into her throat.

The Colonel had settled it. How? The sack? When the letter came, she would not be able to read it.

But after she heard Bernard's car leave, and turned to go down, and saw the letter with the familiar writing and the foreign stamp on Steve's table, she had to pick it up. It was addressed to Steve, but she had to read it.

'*Dear Steve,*

I owe you a letter, so I'll send this one to you.'

Sitting on the unmade bed, Dora glanced through the first pages, which were about the villa and his health and some people they had met who used to breed hunters, and some details about the Follyfoot horses, and the forms from the Ministry of Agriculture.

On the next page, her name stood out from the Colonel's scrawly handwriting as if it were up in neon lights.

'*So Dora has been having some fun. Never a dull moment, eh? I've calmed Bernard Fox down, but tell her to watch her step, like a good girl. We don't want any trouble at the Farm. The old horses come first.*'

When Steve and Callie came back, with Barney very blown, Grey Lady still on her toes, Dora said, before Steve had even got off, 'I read the Colonel's letter.'

'In my room?'

'I was making your bed.' It was still unmade. 'No, I wasn't. I was hiding from Bernie.'

'Oh God, is he—'

'It's all right. He's gone. He wanted to find out what the Colonel wrote. So did I. So I looked.'

'You read other people's letters.'

'You don't give other people's messages. Why didn't you tell me what the Colonel said?'

He turned away from her to dismount. With his face to the pony, putting up the stirrup, loosening the girth, he said, 'I didn't want you to know I knew.'

'But you don't know what I did.'

'No, but I thought if you wanted me to know, you'd tell me.'

He did not ask a question with his face or voice, so Dora said nothing.

He led Grey Lady away. Dora went back to work.

Steve was the best friend Dora had ever had. He had told her once that she was the only real friend he had ever had. But sometimes they could not talk to each other.

20

Three days before the race, Mrs Bunker came over to Folly-foot, white and shaken.

She had been woken in the night by the barking of her miniature poodle, who wore a jewelled collar and slept on her bed.

'Mimsy was quite hysterical. I knew she heard something. So I put the sheet over my head and sent Mr Bunker down to investigate. He took his gun. I told him not to, because it's worse to kill someone than to be burgled, but he took his gun, and when I heard the shot, I thought my heart had stopped.'

She put her hand on it, to make sure that it was working now.

Mr Bunker had seen a figure in the shadows by the gate of Grey Lady's paddock. As he came closer, the gate swung open. He shouted, and the figure – man? boy? girl? He couldn't see – ran off. He fired a shot after it.

The shot had woken all the neighbours and, as Mrs Bunker had predicted, caused more trouble than the intruder. Mr Bunker was to pay a fine for possession of a shotgun without a licence, and Mrs Bunker had been embarrassed by stares in the supermarket, because the word had spread round like a bush fire that he had shot her.

Worst of all was the knowledge that someone was trying to sabotage Grey Lady.

'I think they were either going to kidnap her, or turn her loose to get killed on the road.' Mrs Bunker's eyes were round with horror. 'Who would do such a dreadful thing?'

Ron snickered. 'I got a good idea.'

'The Nicholsons?' Dora said. 'Oh, that's absurd.'

'I told you they were desperate to win the race.'

'And you've been scaring them about Grey Lady.'

Ron laughed. 'Shook 'em up a bit, didn't it?'

'Better put a padlock on the gate,' Dora told Mrs Bunker.

'I told Jim to keep the pony in the stable,' Steve said. 'She bangs her foot on the door in the middle of the night.'

'Hang a sack full of gorse on the door,' Steve said, 'and put a dirty great padlock on the bolt.'

'And on your oat bin,' Ron added darkly. 'There's some people will stop at nothing.'

How much did he know? The curious thing about Ron was that he could seem to be on everybody's side at once. He was mixed up in all sorts of things without ever actually taking part or getting caught. He lived on the fringes of many worlds – the Farm, the race course, horse trading, the motorcycle gangs – without belonging completely to any of them.

It was even impossible to find out whose side he was on to win the race – Strawberry Sunday or Grey Lady. He was taking bets on it, illegally. Ron would take or make a bet on anything. How many palings in a fence, or red cars passing in the next mile, or grains of maize in a handful. What time the rain would stop. What tin of soup Slugger would open for lunch. 'Two to one against tomato. What'll you bet me?'

Dora found him looking thoughtfully over Amigo's door as the rawboned old horse dozed in a shaft of sunlight, resting one back leg, his hip bone sticking up like the peak of Everest.

'What will really happen if Grey Lady doesn't win the money and I can't pay you back?' she asked.

'I told you. The old skin will be mine.'

'You don't want him.'

'He'd fetch a bit. The firewood chap still hasn't got no horse for next winter.'

'You wouldn't really—'

'You think I'm soft, don't you girl?' Ron made his tough face, jaw twisted, eyes narrowed, talking what he thought was gangster American out of the side of his mouth. 'You might get surprised one of these days.'

Ron was away from home that evening, 'checking on a few situations'. He never said exactly where he was going, or who he was going to see.

'I'm still worried about Maggie,' Steve told Slugger. 'We're going down to check the padlocks and make sure everything's all right.'

'And get a load of bird shot where it hurts,' Slugger said. He began to push aside the clutter of mugs, letters, ornaments, combs, books, pebbles, hair clips on the wide shelf above the fireplace.

'What are you doing?' Callie asked.

'They'll be needing to eat breakfast off the mantelpiece tomorrow.'

Dora and Steve left the truck down the road from the Bunkers' house, and walked barefoot up the drive. All was dark and quiet. No lights in the house. Padlocks on the loose box door and on the oat bin in the shed.

Grey Lady had been lying down, but she got up nervously, and watched them over the door as they padded about, looking in sheds and behind bushes, up into the trees and down into the non-existent depths of the ornamental well.

Often they stopped and listened to the normal noises of a suburban night. Two dogs barking back and forth. A rooster who had set his alarm clock too early. A radio. The throb of drums from some distant cafe, the beat without the music. The endless faint roar of cars on the main road beyond the hill whose edge was rimmed with brightness from the stream of lights.

Nothing to see. Nothing to hear. In the paddock, Dora stopped again. Something to smell? She raised her face like a dog and put her hand on Steve's arm.

'I smell smoke.' She gripped him tightly.

'A chimney?'

'No, nearer.'

They were by the bottom fence, looking for the footprints of the intruder at whom Mr Bunker had fired. As they ran back to the stable, the smell of smoke grew definite, grew stronger.

Steve shone the torch round the outside of the loose box. The grey pony was banging against the gorse-filled sack on the door. Dora pushed her head aside and saw, at the edge of the straw, a billow of smoke that burst, even as she looked, into a crackle of fire.

Uselessly she pulled at the padlock, bruising her fingers and yelling for Steve.

'Get her out! We've got to get her out!'

As smoke began to fill the stable, Grey Lady plunged against the door, wild-eyed. Steve wrenched at the padlock, and swore.

'Get up to the house,' he told Dora. 'Wake them. Get the key.'

Dora ran. She beat on the door of the Bunkers' house and shouted. It seemed an eternity before a window went up and a head in a sleeping net looked out.

251

'Go away. You're drunk.'

'The stable's on fire!' Dora was gasping for breath, her throat full of smoke fumes. 'Get the firemen – give me the key!'

'Oh, my God.' The head went inside and shouted, 'James – James! Where's the key?'

'Key, what key?' A sleepy rumble.

'Grey Lady's stable is on fire Oh, my God. Oh, my heart.'

'Hurry!' Dora yelled. The fire would take hold fast in the straw bedding. She might already be too late to save the pony.

When the key came sailing out of the window, she scrabbled for it in a flower bed and ran, choking with fear and the acrid fumes ahead. Gasping and sobbing, she turned the corner of the stable and saw Steve raise a huge stone in both hands and crash it down on to the bolt. Something snapped. The door splintered open, tearing away at the hinges, and fell with a noise like a cannon as the pony trampled over it and off into the night.

Running behind her, Steve and Dora heard the tattoo of her hooves on the road. They followed as far as they could in the dark, but she had run on the hard road and left no traces. They did not know where she might have turned.

'Let's go back and ring the police. Someone will stop her.'

A fire engine was in the drive, pumping water into the stable. The Bunkers stood desolately in their night clothes. The father chain-smoked nervously. The mother in her hair net clutched her shivering poodle. Jim was crying.

He ran to Dora. 'Where's Maggie?'

'She ran off, but she's all right. We'll find her.' She put her arms round him. His thin body was trembling, although it was a warm night.

Neighbours had come from all round. Raincoats over pyjamas. Mothers carrying babies. Barking dogs. Old men coughing. Children frantic with excitement. It was not until the fire was almost out, and smouldering sullenly in the wreck of the stable, that Steve and Dora saw that one of the people in the watching crowd was Ron Stryker.

'What on earth?' Steve grabbed him from behind and spun him round.

'Hands off. I didn't start it.'

'Who said you had?'

Ron always made excuses before he was accused.

'The fire engine passed me on the road. When I saw where it went, you could have knocked me down with a—'

'How did you know who lived here?'

'I didn't. I saw poor old Jim. What are you two doing here, for that matter?'

'We came to check. We were here when the fire started.'

'Oh yeah?' Ron leered.

What did he know? Was he mixed up in this himself?

Dora pulled Steve back into the shadows. 'He couldn't possibly—?'

'He may know who did.'

'If anyone *did*. It could have been an accident.'

One of the firemen, who had been looking for clues, came out of the loose box with something in his closed hand.

'People who smoke in a stable,' he said, 'shouldn't be allowed to keep horses.'

'I'm always careful.' Mr Bunker ground out his cigarette under a foot, but almost at once his hand went to his pyjama pocket and he lit another.

'But you were out here late this evening, you said.'

'To make sure the pony was all right before I went to bed.'

'Excuse me.' The fireman went up to him. 'Is that a filter?'

Mr Bunker took the cigarette out of his mouth and showed him the filter tip.

'Thank you.' The fireman opened his hand and showed

253

what he had found in the straw. The white plastic filter of a cigarette.

'It couldn't have been me.'

His wife and son were looking at him. Jim was still crying. Mr Bunker was blustery and red, as if he would cry too.

'I told you. I'm always careful.'

'Someone wasn't,' the fireman said.

Dora looked at Ron Stryker. Under the lank red hair, his face showed no expression. If he did know anything, he would never tell.

Accident or arson? To Steve and Dora it did not matter. All that mattered now was finding the terrified grey pony.

21

In the morning, the police had heard nothing. Dora and Steve spent all day until dark driving round asking people, following up false leads, getting nowhere. Grey Lady had vanished.

'She'll never come back.' Jim was heartbroken. The pony meant much more to him now that this terrible thing had happened.

'I'll get you another,' his mother said automatically, but she was desolate too, her dreams of the race and the party and the glory all shattered.

'I'll never ride again,' Jim said, with a long white face of tragedy.

His mother was too upset to tell him, 'Yes, you will.'

Next day, the day before the race, Dora rode Barney out alone all morning, following the way Jim used to ride between his house and Follyfoot, turning into farms where the grey pony might have gone looking for other horses, searching woods and thickets where she might have run blindly in and got caught up in the undergrowth.

'How do you expect that poor little beggar to run tomorrow?' Ron asked when she brought Barney back at midday, tired and sweating.

'We're not going to the race.'

'Don't be daft. I may get my money from you yet. He and Callie will have a better chance.'

'Not against the roan. They've got what they wanted.'

'You're not thinking—?' Ron looked shocked.

'I'm not thinking anything,' Dora said wearily. 'I don't know what I think any more. Come on, Barnacle, if you've finished your lunch, we're going out again.'

'Take it easy,' Ron said cheerfully.

Steve was out with the truck, looking hopelessly round the roads, while Dora rode hopelessly on the field paths. They met in the lane that ran along the bottom of the gorse common. Dora came down the bank with Barney, and found Steve sitting on the bonnet of the truck eating a sandwich and staring moodily across the broad valley, where cows and sheep and distant horses grazed, and tractors moved across ridged fields, and you could not have recognized a grey pony even if it was somewhere there.

'Any clues?' Useless to ask it.

'Only negative. I've just rung the Bunkers,' Steve said. 'The police still haven't heard anything.'

'It's hopeless, isn't it, Steve?' Dora got off Barney and let him tear grass off the bank.

'Not yet. If she'd been hit on the road, the police would know.'

'Suppose we never hear anything?'

'Then we'll never know. It will be like that poor dog Roger, who went away when he was ill.'

'I hate that. It's better to see an animal dead than not know.'

'No.' Steve shook his head. 'It's better to go on hoping.'

'I wish you had the horse box instead of the truck,' Dora said. 'Poor old Barney could get a lift home.'

'He's all right. He's so fit. It's a shame he can't do the steeplechase course.'

'I couldn't go, could you, Steve?'

'Not without Maggie. Not without at least knowing where she is.'

256

It was quite a long way home. Dora pushed on, trying to keep out of her mind the terrible visions of the beautiful grey pony smashing into a speeding car, lying out somewhere with a broken leg, stolen, abused perhaps, chased by shouting boys with stones, running into wire in her panic.

Barney was fit enough to trot steadily along, but at a cross-roads where they should have gone straight on, he stopped and tried to turn left, and would not answer the pressure of Dora's legs.

'Come *on*.' He was never like this now. He had become a calm, trusting pony who never shied or stopped or whipped round.

He stood like a mule, listening with his big ears.

'All right.' Dora heard hooves too. 'So there's another horse somewhere. There are about ten thousand horses in this country. If you stop for every one of them, we ll never get home.'

It was a grey pony. It moved from the shelter of some over-hanging trees. Barney called. The pony lifted its head and broke into a trot, its rider wobbling bareback, hanging on to a halter rope with one hand and the mane with the other, red hair flopping.

'Told you to take it easy, didn't I?' Ron grinned. 'Whoa, Maggie.' He hauled the pony in and slid off, wincing. 'I'm as sore as the old lady who rode the cow.'

'How on earth did you find her?' Dora could speak at last.

'How on earth?' Ron mimicked her. 'Not, Thanks, Ron dear, or, Oh you clever boy. Just, How on earth did *you*, a dope like you—'

'Oh, shut up.' Dora was so relieved that laughter came easily. Or was it tears that wanted to come? 'Oh Ron, I don't care. I'm just so glad she's all right. You don't have to tell me anything if you don't want to.'

'Like what? You accusing me of something?' Ron's eyes

257

were sharp. 'Just because I've got a lot of good friends who keep their eyes peeled and their ears to the ground – contortionists, they are – and know everything that goes on, I'm always getting accused. Going to have it on my tombstone. "Ronald Arbuthnot Stryker. Always Accused".'

'Where was she?'

'Man found her over Harlow way. Run herself into the ground, she had, and he got a halter on her. Seeing she was classy looking, he was going to keep her in hopes of a reward. I persuaded him different.'

'How?'

'I have my methods.' He closed one eye. With Ron, you never knew whether to believe the whole story, or part of it, or none of it.

Dora asked him no more, and he told her no more.

22

Steve was wild with joy. Everybody was. Apart from a few nicks and scratches on Grey Lady's legs, and a piece of skin torn off her shoulder, she had not suffered from her terrifying adventure.

The run across country and the long jog back with Ron had calmed her down. The Weaver was turned out, and she walked peacefully into his loose box and put her pretty head straight into the manger to lip up the chaff the finicky old horse had left.

'She'll be all right to race tomorrow.' Steve brought her a big feed. 'Ring up the Bunkers, Dora, and tell them she's here. They'll hit the ceiling.'

'Are you mad? After all I've been through to get that animal back. There's still tonight, you know. There's still *danger*.' A word Ron loved.

'He's right,' Steve said. 'Let's keep her hidden.' He came out of the loose box and shut and bolted the top door. 'Don't trust a soul.'

'I must tell Jim, and put him out of his misery. He can keep a secret.'

'It wouldn't need words to give it away. He's got to keep his misery, right up to the last moment when we tell him he can put on his new boots and his Mum can put on her new dress and meet us at Broadlands. And *then* watch some people's teeth gnashing !' Steve gnashed his own like castanets.

'You still don't think it was Mr Bunker's cigarette?'

'I'm not taking any chances. I'm going to see that pony win tomorrow if it's the last thing I do.'

Dora went to tell Amigo. 'All is not lost, old friend.'

He had never thought it would be. He hung his heavy head over Dora's shoulder and dreamed of an eternity of easy living.

'Even if Grey Lady doesn't win,' she told him. 'I'll get your money somehow.'

She heard Steve call Callie to go and clean Barney's saddle and bridle. There was that too. The saddler was getting a bit restless. She ought to be worrying, but somehow, standing in the stable with her kind old horse, sharing his content, it was hard to worry.

No time for worrying the next day. No time for anything except finishing the work of the Farm and then starting to get Grey Lady and Barnacle Bill ready for the Moonlight Steeplechase.

'Since it's going to be run in the middle of the night', Slugger grumbled, 'it hardly seems worth using all my washing up liquid on the manes and tails. "*Makes your dishes sparkle like the dewy morn*".' He picked up the empty bottle and read the label. 'Fat lot of good it's going to do Maggie and old Barn to be sparkling like the dew when there's thirty ponies kicking mud in their faces, all shoving together at Becher's Brook with the banks like a sponge.'

'They won't get mud in their faces,' Dora was plaiting Barney's wet mane, and spoke through a mouthful of rubber bands, 'because they'll be in front.'

'I don't like it.' Slugger shook his head and stuck out his lower lip. He had never liked it. 'If the Colonel was here, he'd not let you go.'

'If the Colonel was here,' Callie said from underneath Barney, where she was trimming his heels with Anna's

260

scissors, 'he'd be at the front of the crowd yelling, "Legs, dammit, legs! Where's your impulsion?" ' Memories of her jumping lessons with the Colonel.

'It's all right for them that can watch the race.' Slugger sniffed. 'But how'd you like to be left here biting your nails and wondering who's coming home on a stretcher – you or that pony?'

'Oh *thank* you for minding,' Callie said.

But Dora, realizing what was behind the grumbles, said, 'Of course you're coming, Slugger. You've got to come.'

'Didn't get no invitation, did I?'

With Callie's parents away, Dora and Steve had been sent their invitations to the supper party.

'You're the groom,' Dora said. 'We've got to have a groom. All the posh people will.'

'What about me?' Ron asked. 'If it wasn't for me, there wouldn't be no Grey Lady.'

'So you'll be her groom. Two ponies, two grooms. I told you we were going posh. You can wear Steve's jodhpurs.'

'Like hell he can,' Steve objected. 'What'll *I* wear?'

'You'll wear *the* suit.' Steve had only one set of garments that could reasonably be called a suit.

'Only if you wear *the* dress.' Dora had only one dress that could reasonably be called suitable for Mr Wheeler's party.

Two hours before it was to start, Dora rang up Mrs Bunker.

'Yes?' Jim's mother had been answering the telephone with this dead voice ever since the disaster of the fire, expecting no good news.

'Put on the red dress, Cinderella. You're going to the ball.'

'What ball? Don't play tricks with me, Dora, I've got a splitting head.'

'Take an aspirin. You're going to Mr Wheeler's champagne supper.'

'It's only for people who have a child in the race.'

'But you *have*! You *have*! Grey Lady is here and we're taking her over to Broadlands with Barney. I can't explain now.' Dora cut short a babble of excitement from the other end of the wire. 'Just get yourself and Jim dressed, and we'll see you there.'

'He's gone to bed. He's exhausted.'

'Wake him up. Give him some vitamin pills. Tell him he's going to win!'

Steve's jodhpurs were too big for Ron, who was less muscular. He reefed them in round his waist with his gaudiest tie, and put on his pointed cowboy boots and a sinister long black sweater. He added an Indian headband and a tin Peace symbol – Peace, for someone like Ron who was always making trouble! – on a thong round his neck.

Slugger looked less sensational, but more correct. He had brushed and pressed his Army breeches, and Dora had sewn a leather patch on the frayed elbow of his tweed jacket, and found him a check cap of the Colonel's. They stuffed it with newspaper to keep if off his ears.

Callie, with her hair in two tight pigtails, wore her father's blue and gold racing silks proudly. Steve borrowed Ron's orange shirt to go with *the* suit. Only Dora was still in her old bleached jeans as they loaded the ponies, rushing Grey Lady into the box as if there were spies everywhere.

Dora had the yellow dress and sandals in a paper bag under the front seat where the five of them sat crushed together, singing 'One Meat Ball' to keep their nerves calm. The moon was up and full, its mysterious face half smiling in a cloudless sky.

'I wish it was raining.' Callie shivered.

'Nervous?'

'No. Yes. No.' Callie looked at Steve. He was nervous about Grey Lady. He did not want her to be nervous about Barney. 'I'm excited, that's all.'

'He'll go well for you.' Dora squeezed with the arm that

was round Callie to make more room. 'He's a good pony. The best.'

'If everybody else dropped down dead,' Ron said. 'The waiter *roared* across the *hall*, "We don't serve bread with one meat baw-haw-hawl . . ." '

At Broadlands, Dora changed into her dress in the horse box, combed her hair and put on the sandals. Barney was being walked round by Slugger, bow-legged, very horsy, eyeing the other ponies under the peak of the Colonel's cap. Grey Lady was still in the horse box. They would not take her out until just before the race.

On the terrace in front of the big pillared house, the local socials were drinking and chattering. Coloured lamps hung in the white portico and along the windows of the great house. There were candles in glass bowls on the little supper tables. Yellow flares streamed dramatically from the balustrade.

Floodlights in the trees lit the wide sweep of parkland that was the start of the course, and its finish. Beyond, at the bottom of the slight slope, you could see the first fence, a brush jump, clear and black in the moonlight, and beyond that the post and rails, and then the corner of the copse, where they would turn across a stony road and over the bank. Headlights of cars parked to light the tricky take-off silhouetted the young trees.

Dora had walked the course twice with Callie. She knew every jump, every turn and stretch of rough going. It looked very different now, the fences bigger, the rails more solid, the grass waiting white and challenging for the charge of galloping hoofs.

Steve and Dora managed to get themselves on to the terrace by climbing over a dark corner of the balustrade, to avoid coming up the main steps in the light and the stares. They stood shyly in a corner, and a waitress brought them something on a silver tray which she said was ginger ale, but which tasted in Dora's excitement as if it might be champagne.

They saw Sir Arthur and his wife, very much at ease, talking about 'the tribe', as they called their three sons, who were indistinguishable in looks and behaviour, except that the youngest was even ruder than the others.

They saw the local Master of Foxhounds, a television personality who would rather be behind his pack than in front of the cameras. They saw Mrs Hatch of the Pony Club, with her picket fence teeth, and the famous horsemaster Count Podgorsky, slim and elegant, with shining hair and shoes apparently made from the same material.

They saw the Nicholsons, beefy and too loud in this company, talking up 'fantastic' horses they had for sale, and putting down a great deal of champagne with their little fingers crooked, to show they knew what was what.

They saw – help! – Bernard Fox's crinkly ginger hair moving through the gathering towards their corner, an amused smile lifting his marmalade moustache.

'Dorothy?'

'Hullo.' The yellow dress had felt all right, but instantly it felt all wrong, and Dora knew it was too short.

'I hardly recognized you. You look very nice.'

'Thanks.' Dora tried to move behind a small table, because he was looking at her legs.

Bernard Fox stayed, smiling at her, twirling his glass. He was obviously trying to find some slightly less insulting way of asking 'How on earth did you two get here?', so to get rid of him, Dora said, 'We brought the bay pony. The Colonel's stepdaughter is riding him.'

'Done any training gallops lately?' Burnished Bernie was mellower tonight. It must be the champagne.

'Oh yes.' Dora glanced at Steve. She still had not told him about the race course, in case he thought it was silly. 'At the Farm.'

'Good girl.' Bernie laughed at her, and then wagged his head and chuckled to himself, 'Couldn't believe my eyes,' remembering Dora in the unsaddling enclosure.

'What did he mean?' Steve whispered when he finally moved off.

'He couldn't believe seeing us here,' Dora said.

'I didn't like the way he looked at you.'

'Nor did I.' But Dora took a quick look down at her brown legs, and could not help feeling a bit pleased that Bernard Fox had admired them.

The Bunkers had still not arrived...

Suppose they never came. Suppose Jim refused to ride. Suppose Mrs Bunker refused to come to the party because it was too late to go to the hairdresser. Suppose Mr Bunker had put his foot down because he was still upset about being suspected of causing the fire.

Steve and Dora went through a dozen anxieties. Below the terrace, the young riders were having a picnic supper, on the grass, their coloured shirts and jerseys vivid in the light of the flares. They looked over the edge and saw Callie eating stolidly. Saw several girls in a group, giggling. Saw others sitting alone, too nervous to eat. Sir Arthur's boys throwing food about. A tall boy in glasses who looked too old to ride. Mrs Hatch's daughter with her teeth spaced like her mother's. No Jim.

'If they don't show up, I'm leaving,' Steve fretted. 'Ron can drive the box home. I'll hitch-hike.'

'May as well have the supper,' Dora persuaded him. But although the guests had begun to help themselves from the long buffet tables at the back of the terrace, piled with marvellous looking food, she and Steve were too shy to push through

266

the chattering crowd, who juggled plates and forks and glasses, looking for places at the tables.

'Come on, come on, you've got no supper.'

A short old man, twisted like a dune tree, limped up to them, leaning on a knobbly stick. He had thick white hair, eyebrows like fluffs of cotton wool, and a pointed white beard. His face was aged and lined, with faded blue eyes that smiled at them, a more simple, direct face than many of the others here.

'It's – you're Mr Wheeler, aren't you?' Dora asked, embarrassed because they had been too shy to speak to him when they arrived.

'Forgive me for not greeting you before,' he said, removing her embarrassment. 'You're from Follyfoot Farm, aren't you? Steve and Dora. Good. Good.' He had a way of looking at you closely, not staring insolently like Bernard Fox, but attentively, as if it mattered to him to know what you were like. 'Come on. Get some food before the savages devour it all.'

He went with them to the buffet, and even asked the butler, who looked more like a bishop, to take special care of them.

The butler carved beef paper-thin and delicate rolls of ham, and helped them to pile their plates with chicken, salad, pastry shells filled with creamy shrimp, something in aspic, pickles, olives. He invited them to come back for more, and when he had turned away to open bottles, Steve managed to sneak a plate of food and two glasses of champagne out to the far corner of the terrace, so that Slugger and Ron could reach up for them later.

267

24

After the ice cream and little coloured cakes, Mr Wheeler stood at the top step of the portico, leaning on his stick, and made a short speech about the Moonlight Steeplechase.

'I stole the idea,' he said, 'from those famous Cavalry officers of some hundred and fifty years ago, who were sitting round after dinner one night, drinking brandy and wondering what kind of lunacy they could think up to pass the time.

'They all had good horses in the stables, and as the moon was bright, they set out to race each other across country for the tall church steeple which stood up miles away in the moonlight. Using a steeple for a landmark gave us the name Steeplechase, as you know.'

He beamed down on his audience, who nodded and murmured, whether they knew or not, to show that they did. The Master of Foxhounds said, 'Jolly good luck to 'em,' and Mr Nicholson belched a champagne bubble and said, 'Hear, hear.'

'With white nightshirts over their Mess uniforms, and white nightcaps over the brandy fumes in their heads, they rode straight and reckless, taking everything in their path, over, under or through. Tonight, we have the more civilized course over my land, but the young riders will take it just as hard and straight and courageously as those first Midnight Steeplechasers.'

'For a hundred pounds, who wouldn't?' muttered Mrs Nicholson, the same shape all the way down from her square shoulders to her hips in a dress like a sack. She looked at

Steve and Dora. 'I know you, don't I?' and turned away, not caring whether she did or not.

Mr Wheeler was announcing that since the young riders were the most important guests tonight, he would introduce them all to the rest of 'this brilliant company.'

He called out the names, and they stood up in their colours, Callie blushing furiously, caught with a piece of cake in her mouth. 'Cathleen Sheppard on Barnacle Bill.'

Dora cheered, and Mrs Nicholson turned round and gave her a look.

'Betty Hatch riding My Pal' – applause. 'John Deacon,' the boy with the glasses ('How old is *he*?' from Mrs Nicholson), 'riding Challenger' – applause. 'Linda Murphy with Lassie' – applause, loud from her own family. 'Chip Nicholson, riding Stawberry Sunday' – applause, and a whistle from her father, made socially bold by champagne.

Chip stood up unsmiling, disowning him, chunky and workmanlike in good boots and white breeches and a red and white striped racing shirt.

'John So-and-so on Geronimo. Joan This-and-that on Black Velvet . . . Jim Bunker . . . Where are you, Jim?'

A slight figure idled across the grass, pale-faced under the flares, swishing a thistle with his whip, flop of hair over his narrow forehead.

'Just in time. Good boy. Jim Bunker, everybody, just in time.'

'My mother got her zip fastener stuck,' Jim said unconcernedly.

Laughter.

Poor Mrs Bunker, arriving so flustered and late in her red dress with the sequin top, the laughter met her as she came up the steps, Mr Bunker close behind, as if to stop her from turning tail and running.

But Mr Wheeler who was terribly nice to everybody,

269

came down from the portico and greeted them warmly, and took them to get food and wine. She must have broken the zip. The back of her dress was sewn up with big stitches, perhaps by her husband. Poor Mrs Bunker. Her night of glory.

But there was still Grey Lady.

All the ponies were to parade in a circle of turf marked off below the terrace. Steve got the grey pony out of the horse box, while Slugger put Dora's saddle on Barney.

Jim ran up, carrying his saddle, dropped it on the ground, and flung his arms round Maggie's neck.

'Don't make a fuss,' Steve told him. 'We don't want the Nicholsons to know she's here till the last minute.'

He saddled her up behind the box, while Slugger took Barney and walked round with the other grooms and stable girls and big sisters and mothers of the riders. Barney looked his best, mane neatly plaited, tail plaited at the top because there had been no time to pull it. Heels and head and ears trimmed. White star and hind socks washed and rubbed with chalk, gleaming in the moonlight. Slugger plodded with his head down, because that was the way he always walked, but he wore a grin of pride.

Callie stood in the middle with the other riders, riding cap jammed down tight, biting her lip, arms folded over the blue and gold silks.

'I wish the Colonel could see them.' Dora nudged Steve.

You could tell which family owned which pony. They each watched their own. Only the Nicholsons were shrewdly assessing the field.

There were twenty-eight of them. The roan had not come in yet, and Ron had been told to bring Grey Lady in last. He passed behind Steve and Dora with his mouth full and a glass in his hand.

'Where's Maggie?'

'Tied back of the box for a moment while I got the supper you left me.' He wiped a hand across his lips. 'Ta.'

'Bring her in now.'

Strawberry Sunday had joined the parade, with Ron's lanky friend leading her. Then Ron brought in Grey Lady, on her toes, jogging, reaching at the bit like a little race horse.

Dora and Steve watched the Nicholsons. If they were shocked, they did not show it. They stared at the grey as they stared at the other ponies, with a dealer's eye, shrewd, calculating, not giving away admiration or contempt.

The television M.F.H., who was in charge of the race, gave the order to mount. The riders joined their ponies among the trees at the edge of the floodlit strip of grass that swept down to the first jump.

Dora, more nervous than Callie, gave her last minute instructions to which she did not listen. 'Don't push him at the start. Take the bank turn wide, give him room to stand back. Remember there's a ditch on the other side of the cut-and-laid. Watch that little chestnut – he kicks.'

Chip was up on the roan, point-to-point saddle, stirrups very short, rubber racing reins.

'That same bay pony?' Under the pulled down peak of her cap, her face was deadpan, like her parents. The jeer was in her voice.

'Looks a lot better, doesn't he?' Callie said, naive and friendly, but Chip had moved on.

Dora saw Jim go over to Grey Lady among the people and ponies by the trees. There was a flurry of excitement. Someone shouted. She ran, and pushed through the crowd. Grey Lady's saddle had slipped round, and Jim was lying on the ground, whimpering and holding his wrist.

'Who did up the girth?'

'Don't look at *me*.' Ron, with his headband and his Peace symbol, was holding the nervous grey pony.

271

'I did. I know it was tight.' Steve was kneeling by the boy on the ground, but was pushed aside by a sobbing woman in a spangly red dress who flung herself on her son.

'My boy, my boy! I knew something like this would happen.'

Although the whole thing had been her idea: buying the pony, teaching Jim to ride, entering for the Steeplechase.

'It's all *right*, Mum.' Jim stopped whimpering and sat up.

'He put out his hand as he fell,' Steve said. 'The wrist is either broken or badly sprained. There's a doctor here. Someone's gone to fetch him.'

'It's all your fault,' Mrs Bunker said hysterically, on her knees in the tight dress, trying to get her arms round Jim, who was trying to keep her away from his hurt wrist. 'Who asked you to bring the pony here?'

This was so fantastically unfair that Steve did not answer. He got up, took Grey Lady from Ron, and went with Dora out of the crowd, as the doctor came to Jim.

'I *know* that girth was tight, Dora.'

'Ron left Maggie to get his supper.'

'And his pal was late bringing the roan in.'

'Because he was loosening the girth?'

'By God,' Steve said bitterly. 'By God, I hate to see them get away with it. This pony could have won.'

He hunched his shoulders, looped Maggie's reins over his arm, and slouched towards the horse box, swinging Jim's riding cap by the elastic.

News of the accident had spread among the riders, who were collecting for the start. Callie trotted back, her eyes dark with anxiety in a white face.

'They said it's Jim.'

Dora nodded. 'He's all right. But he can't ride the pony.'

'Oh, poor Maggie.' Callie thought of horses first. 'Poor Jim. And – oh Dora, the prize money – poor *Amigo*!'

272

'Listen, Callie.' It all came into Dora's head at once, just as if it was written down in a book and she was reading it. 'Grey Lady can win. You ride her. Jim can pretend he gives her to you before they take him to hospital. Mr Wheeler won't mind, because of the accident.'

'But you wanted me so much to ride Barney.'

'That doesn't matter now. Winning matters.'

'I can't. Maggie's too fast. I can't ride to win.'

'You can. You must. Think of Amigo, Callie, we can't let the Nicholsons get away with this.'

'They did it?'

'I think so. Are you going to let them win?'

'Steve!' Callie shouted, her voice shrill with excitement. 'Bring Maggie back!'

25

'A bad start,' the television personality called out in his voice that was familiar in the homes of almost everyone there. 'But it's going to be a good race. The moon is up. The ponies are fit. The riders are shaken, but not unstrung.' Only one girl, who was a mass of nerves anyway, had got off after what happened to Jim, and refused to get back on. 'Five minutes,. everybody, to get settled down again. Five minutes till line up.'

Callie was on Grey Lady. 'Jog her round,' Steve said. 'Get the feel of her.'

'I know her.' Callie gathered up her reins, confident now and not afraid. 'Sorry Barnacle. He would have liked to run, Dora.'

'He's going to.' Once more the book of ideas was open in her mind. 'Hold him a minute, Steve.'

She ran to the horse box, pulled on her jeans, stuffed the short yellow dress into them, kicked off her sandals and trod into her old shoes. Steve was still holding Jim's riding cap. Dora grabbed it and shoved it on her small head, tipping it down over her face.

'Who's that child in the yellow shirt?' someone asked as she joined the others, letting down her stirrups as she went. Dora did not hear the answer. But they thought she was a child. All right, Barney. You shall have your race.

The television star was holding up a flag, while he tried to get the twenty-nine ponies into some sort of line.

'Back the brown pony, bring up the little chestnut, come on, that boy in the green shirt. Look out, no barging. Yellow

274

girl on the bay, get on the end there. All right, all right everybody—'

At the end of the line of stamping, jostling ponies, Barney was wildly excited. His days of lawlessness came back to him. He trampled, grabbing at the bit. Dora shortened her reins. He reared up slightly, pulling, and just when she thought she could not hold him, the flag came down and he plunged forward in the galloping surge of ponies.

Whatever instructions had been given to anybody not to go flat out at the start of the race were forgotten, or impossible to obey. Big ones, small ones, Welsh, New Forest, cobby ones, they all went full tilt down the floodlit stretch of the park, and by some miracle were over the strong brush jump and pounding towards the post and rails.

Someone refused and swerved into someone else, who swore like a grown up – Sir Arthur's youngest. Dora had to pull Barney sideways. He got too close to the rails and had to cat jump, landing short and losing ground. Dora gathered him together and he settled down to gallop his own steady pace in the middle of the field. Grey Lady and Strawberry Sunday had pulled out ahead. Some of the smaller ponies were already falling behind.

Wide at the turn into the bank, Dora had told Callie, and she told it to herself now as they came to the corner of the copse where the lights of the parked cars illuminated the grey and the roan with haloes for a moment as they reached the top of the bank together, and dropped down with a switch of their tails.

To get up the steep bank, you had to take off from the stony road, not put in a stride on the grass. Dora swung into the light, saw people standing by the cars, a man on the roof with a film camera - one stride into the road, and then she gave Barney a kick that propelled him from his strong quarters to the top of the wide bank. He changed legs and jumped out into the drop, wide and safe.

Beside him, a pony stumbled and fell. Its rider pitched forward, and one of the people scrambled up the bank with a shout.

Don't look back. Never mind the others. It was a dangerous race, but even if they all fell, Dora and Barney must keep going, their own line and their own pace. That was how she had planned it with Callie.

As each jump came up – the cut-and-laid, the narrow brush the hedge with the guard rail, the little ditch – Dora only had time to see that Callie was over, and then it was she and Barney. He took off too soon at the cut-and-laid, dropping a leg in the ditch. He was bumped at the brush, stirrups clashing, by the tall boy, who turned his head and shouted at Dora, although it was his fault, glasses spattered with mud. He stood back beautifully from the guard rail, clearing the hedge by miles. He tried to stop at the dry ditch, because the moonlight looked like water in it, which he hated, but Dora forced him over by strength of will as well as legs, and he jumped straight into the air, much too high, and landed stiff-legged, with Dora hanging on to his mane, because she knew he would jump it like that.

Several ponies seemed to have dropped out, or else they were far behind. Dora was in a middle bunch, Grey Lady and the roan and about half a dozen others were ahead. Jumping well, Barney gained ground at the fences, but lost it in the fields between. But the pace was fast, and the others were slowing too. Dora passed the Hatch girl, floundering across a ridge and furrow, and someone else on a long-tailed black, who ran out at the low wall. Barney was still going steadily, but he was tired. Anything might happen at Becher's Brook.

It was the last fence but two of the Steeplechase course. It came after the final turn towards the home stretch, a stream with sticky banks, which ran across a corner of the park, in view of the spectators at the top of the slope.

After the brook, there was a hurdle jump, then a low rail between two trees, nothing much. But Broadlands' Becher's Brook had floored many ponies who were galloping home to win, and Dora, as she cantered across stubble, hopped a double rail into the park and saw the water gleaming, thought that it would floor her too.

Callie and Chip were still yards ahead of anyone else. Grey Lady did not mind water, and if the roan jumped badly here, as most ponies would, Callie could pull ahead and Chip might not catch her.

Headlights of cars gilded the surface of the running brook. Grey Lady went fast at it, and almost stumbled in the soft footing. Callie checked her for the take off, and she was in the air when the roan came sideways into her and they fell together on the other side, floundering in the marshy ground.

Dora saw Grey Lady struggle up. She must get to Callie. Barney stopped in a bunch of ponies, trampling the sticky ground suspiciously. Barney, you must! Dora held tight for the enormous jump that he would make over the hated water, and almost fell off when he suddenly dropped his head, and charged through the water into the mud on the other side. The dreaded brook was only a few inches deep here, and he was clever enough to know it.

And there was Callie standing up, hatless, filthy, waving to show she was all right, waving Dora on, as the other ponies splashed and floundered over the brook behind her.

Someone was alongside her at the hurdles, and hit them with a rattle. She was alone over the low rail. Barney pecked, recovered, and plodded into the floodlights, to pass the white post at the top of the slope in barely a canter between the cheering, whistling crowd.

Barney stopped of his own accord. A riderless pony crashed into him, and the rest of them pulled up in a tangle.

Slugger was running bandy-legged, his mouth open in a shout.

'Barney!' Crumpled newspaper flew out as he tore off his cap to wave it.

'Dora!' Steve jumped down from the balustrade of the terrace, and as Dora dropped off Barney, he flung his arms round her in a hug that nearly broke her ribs.

'You won.' He held her off and grinned at her before he turned and ran down the slope to Callie.

26

A lot of people were running. Callie was walking forward with Grey Lady. Chip was sitting on the muddy bank, and Strawberry Sunday stood with her head low, one foreleg dangling.

'My God, it's broken!' someone called, and Dora saw the Nicholsons' lanky boy, Ron's friend, throw down a cigarette and run towards the brook.

She left Barney in the crowd and broke away from the congratulations and the flashbulbs, and walked to where he had dropped the cigarette. It was still smouldering. Dora trod it out, then bent and picked it up, looked at the white filter, and put it in her pocket.

'Who is it? Who won?'

Mr Wheeler, fieldglasses round his neck, limped down from the terrace steps.

'Run down to the brook,' he told a boy, 'and tell me what's happened there.'

The crowd separated. As Mr Wheeler reached out to shake her hand, Dora took off her cap and shook out her short hair.

'Dora?'

'I'm sorry,' she said. 'I'm too old to be in the race, but I didn't mean to win.'

'It was a great race anyway,' Mr Wheeler began, but parents and riders were clamouring at him with protest and argument.

'She's too old.'

'She's disqualified.'

'My boy was second.'

'No, I was.

'Tortoiseshell was second.'

'Without a rider, stupid.'

'Mr Wheeler, Mr Wheeler, it isn't fair—'

'Quiet, everybody!' he bellowed with surprising volume for so old and small a man. 'Dora won, but she can't win. We know that. So whoever came second—'

'I did.'

'It was me.'

'My daughter was well ahead.'

'I saw it, I tell you, it was Bazooka.'

'I was in front of him.'

'*I* was.'

'Bazooka ... me ... my daughter ...' But since the race had no second prize, nobody had really seen, in the excitement, who was next in the bunch behind Dora and the loose pony.

Mr Wheeler took her arm and walked with her and Barney under the trees, away from the lights and the squabble.

'I can't give you the money,' the old man told her, leaning on her arm, 'so I'm going to give it where it's needed. I'm going to give it to Follyfoot. You won it, you can spend it how you like. For the old horses.'

The boy he had sent down to the brook panted back.

'The roan pony pulled a tendon. Not a break, but it's pretty bad. The Nicholsons are wild. They say the grey jumped across her.'

'*She* knocked into the grey!' Dora was furious. 'I saw it. It was delib—'

'I saw it too.' Mr Wheeler cut her short. 'But let it go. The pony's badly hurt.' He sighed. 'A sad ending to something that perhaps I never should have started. I'm not going to run any more Steeplechases, Dora. Not at night. Not for money, anyway. Money spoils everything, doesn't it?'

Dora didn't know. She never had any.

When Dora gave Ron back his sixty pounds for Amigo, he pulled a bulging wallet out of the inside of his jacket and added the money to a considerable wad of notes.

'Ta,' he said. 'And for the rest of it. Always a picnic for the bookie, when an outsider wins.'

'But the race was a washout,' Steve objected. 'Those people may want their money back.'

'They can sue me then,' Ron said smugly, 'and admit they placed illegal bets.'

'Money spoils everything.' Dora echoed Mr Wheeler.

'Speak for yourself.' Ron put the wallet back inside his jacket and swaggered off.

By the time Jim's broken wrist was healed, and the plaster cast off his wrist, Grey Lady had been sold to a hunting family who would use her well. Jim was to have Barney back.

'But don't worry,' he told Dora. 'I'll ride him over to the Farm mostly, and he can see all his friends. I'd let you keep him, but Steve says he knows you can't keep a fit pony here.'

'*I* know we can't,' Dora said. 'Steve's not the boss. We both are. We both know what Follyfoot is for.'

It was very sad when Mr Bunker rebuilt his stable, and came for Barney with the trailer behind the red minibus.

Dora watched it pull through the gate, and went out into the road to see the last of Barney, rounded bay quarters, black tail hanging over the ramp, the net up front swinging as he pulled contentedly at the hay, with a horse's trusting ignorance of parting.

281

The trailer disappeared round a corner. Dora went back into the yard and got a wheelbarrow and fork and joined the others at work.

As she backed out of Amigo's stable, a man's voice behind her said, 'Excuse me, miss.'

Dora set down the barrow.

'I've got my cattle truck outside,' the man said. 'I found this wretched horse. Belonged to a neighbour of mine, who went away for a bit. I thought he'd told somebody to look out for the horse, but when I went by his place, I saw he'd simply left him. In a little yard. No grass. No more hay. Water all gone.'

'How *can* people—' Dora started out with him towards the truck.

'They do.' The man shook his head. 'I've been abroad. Egypt, South America, India. I've seen how they treat horses. But this poor fellow . . . I can't take him, so I thought of you. When I couldn't get an answer on the phone, I pushed him into the truck and brought him over. I know there is always room here for a horse in trouble.'

'Yes.'

Dora called Steve, and they went out to the horse. He was so starved and weak, they could hardly get him out of the cattle truck. He walked with them slowly on his shaky legs into the loose box that used to be Barney's.

'Here!' Slugger was filling a bucket at the tap. 'I just cleaned that stable out.'

He brought the water over, and they watched the horse suck it in through his wrinkled lips, and then he sighed, holding the last of it in his mouth, and dribbled it slowly over Dora's hand.

'One day,' Slugger picked up the bucket and turned to fetch more water, 'one day we'll keep an empty loose box here. That'll be the day.'

The Horses of
Follyfoot

I

THE colt, Folly, son of old Specs, was two months old that year when spring first came to the farm on the hill where the old horses lived at peace.

It came late and suddenly, taking everyone by surprise. For weeks it had been raining, steely, penetrating rain that made the older, thinner horses like Lancelot and Ranger shiver and cough if Dora or Steve or Callie left them out too long.

Dora and Steve were employed at the farm to look after the twenty horses who had been rescued from cruelty or neglect, or brought here by fond owners to end their days in peace. Callie's mother Anna had married the Colonel, who owned Follyfoot Farm. Callie was unpaid, but she worked just as hard as the others whenever she was free from the hindrance of school, which interfered with the real purpose of her life: the horses.

Lancelot was twenty-nine – the oldest horse in the world. Callie was determined to keep him alive to see thirty. If it was true that you multiplied a horse's age by seven to compare it with a person, he would then be two hundred and ten years old.

Bringing him in from a short leg-stretcher one wet afternoon, she put hay on his back under a rug and made him a bran mash, spiced with salt and laced with molasses for energy. He stood steaming gently into the rug, with his ugly coffin head in the manger, his rickety legs gone over at the knees and under at the hocks, mumbling at the warm mash with his long yellow teeth.

'Pegging out at last.' Slugger Jones, the old ex-boxer who had worked for the Colonel for years, looked over the door of

285

Lancelot's stable, where Callie was brushing the mud from the old horse's legs with a wisp of twisted hay.

'Shut up,' said Callie. 'He's got years yet.'

Slugger made a jeering noise from under the wet sack that covered his balding head from the rain. 'He's older than me, the beggar.'

'Impossible.'

Callie came out of the stable. Slugger kicked out, but his boot was too caked with mud to lift far enough to catch her. Everybody's boots were permanently mud-logged at the end of that wet winter. It was not worth hosing them off. The whole farm was a sea of mud. Every gateway was a squelching morass.

Callie's hair was seaweed. Dora's short hair clung in wisps round her blunt brown face. Steve's black hair stuck out in wet spikes. Ron Stryker, who worked at the farm when the fancy took him and the Colonel could stand him, had long red hair which hung damply in his eyes. When Callie's mother gave him a rubber band to tie it back so that he could see what he was doing, he said, 'What I'm doing is mostly shovelling manure, and I'd rather not see.'

Then suddenly, from one day to the next, the rain was gone. A light fresh wind swept a curtain of last big drops over the farm and away down the hill, with the sun chasing it. You could see the rain still grey in the valley, and behind it, the broad sunlight painting the fields and hedges and the tops of the greening elm trees. Mist rose from the ponds and the river.

One of Callie's jobs was to look after the colt Folly and his mother. Old Specs had had her baby very late in life, and had almost died doing it. Callie had been keeping them in during the bad weather. When she turned them out into the first sunshine, the little bay colt went frisking and bucketing away on his silly long legs. Specs went after him in a series of feeble bucks and squeals, stopped in the middle of the field with her head up and her nostrils spread to catch the messages of the spring breeze, then collapsed to roll and wallow in her favourite substance – sticky mud.

Anna's daffodils were rioting away under the trees on the lawn. The Colonel put away the dreadful old jacket he wore in the winter, with the leather patches on the elbows and cuffs. Ron Stryker bought a fancy pair of boots, which were too good to work in, but too tight to take off. Solution obvious: don't work.

Dora washed her jeans. It was worth it now. Steve's hair lay down again. Slugger took the sack off his head and put on his woollen cap. The grey stable cat decided to have her kittens early, in the bottom of an empty bran sack. The Colonel's mongrel dog had six big yellow puppies on Steve's bed in his room over the tack room.

Cobbler's Dream, the half-blind show jumping pony, hopped through a weak spot in the hedge and went mad in Mr Beckett's clover. The vet and the blacksmith sent in their bills at the same time. Ron fell in love with the new girl at the Silver Stud Café on the London road. Dora and Steve and Callie decided to hold a horse show to celebrate this glorious late spring.

2

As soon as the school closed for the Easter holidays, Dora and Callie rode round the neighbouring villages to announce the show among the local horse and pony population.

The kind of people who came to Follyfoot shows didn't go to proper shows, because they didn't have the proper kind of ponies, or because they didn't like shows. They just liked to ride.

Dora didn't even have a proper horse. Hero was lame again – legacy of his bad days with an evil-tempered lady in the circus. Callie rode Cobby, and Steve was off in the other direction on the chestnut Miss America.

Dora rode Willy the mule in the hard military saddle that made you understand why they had to mechanise the Army. His trot was like a truck with one flat tyre. His canter loosened your teeth. To turn him away from home, you had to lean forward, grab the rein near his mouth and pull it out sideways. If that didn't work, you had to go home.

Dora dreamed of a horse of her own, finely bred and schooled, a joy to ride or watch. Meanwhile, because she lived at Follyfoot, she made do with Willy, or stiff-legged Hero, or Stroller sitting sideways, because his back was as broad as the beer barrels he used to pull in his old days at the brewery.

Callie and Dora stopped at the Three Horseshoes to tell Toby to bring his Welsh pony. They went to the forge to tell the blacksmith's daughter to come with Pogo, and through the wood to the pony farm, whose owner was infested with swarms of horsey girls, some his, some not. On the way

288

home they passed a house where a spindly roan horse was tied up in the yard, having ribbons plaited into its mane by two fat girls. The creepy Crowleys. They were famous at Callie's school for being the stupidest family ever seen in those parts.

'Don't ask them to come.' Callie jerked her head to where the girls were waving hopefully.

'They couldn't. That horse is lame.' Dora knew everything about every horse for miles round.

'That wouldn't stop them.'

The small field behind the Dutch barn had dried out enough for the show. The races would be in the middle and the jumps round the outside. Jumps at Follyfoot were not post and rails with white painted wings, or neatly clipped brush, or red block walls, the kind that Cobbler's Dream had cleared so nobly in the days when he was County champion. Follyfoot jumps were made of anything available. Fallen trees, oil drums, broken wheelbarrows, bits of old fencing. One class was called 'Back Alley Jumping' and it did indeed involve dustbins and broken chairs, a couple of old bicycle wheels which you could set spinning on the wings of a jump to test a pony's nerve, one of Anna's aprons flapping from a bar, a torn blue horse rug laid on the ground to simulate water, bales of hay and an old door. Ron dragged home some car tyres, bouncing along the road at the back of his motor bike.

'Where did you get those?' Dora and Steve walked through the yard with the mattress off the spare bed for the Refusal race.

'Down the road.'

'At the garage?'

'If you say so.' Ron never looked directly at you when he spoke.

'Didn't they want them?'

'I dunno. Didn't ask them, did I?'

The morning of the show, Anna came out to see where her washtub had gone.

'Apple bobbing.'

'Oh well.' Anna saw the mattress. 'Oh no, you've gone too far.'

Callie tried to turn her round and push her back towards the house. 'It's for the Refusal race. Don't fuss.'

Callie's narrow face was pale and fussed between the pigtails. Organising things exhausted her, and she would throw up from excitement before the show. Everyone knew that. They would not start the show until she had.

The Colonel came out to see where all the pencils had gone from his office.

'Letter race. You gallop to the end of the field, get off and sign your name, race back and post it in the bird feeder on that tree.'

'Sounds pretty dull.'

'Not when you do it bareback, on someone else's horse,' Dora said. 'You're doing it on Willy.'

The Colonel groaned.

'Oh please, you must. It gives people something to laugh at.'

'I don't think Earl Blankenheimer does laugh.'

'Who's he?'

'Friend of mine from America. He's coming to see the farm.'

'Who is?' Anna asked.

'Old Blank. You know. He was with me in the hospital last year.'

The Colonel's old war wound played him up sometimes. He would cough painfully for weeks, until Anna got desperate, and Slugger, who had once saved him from being burned alive in a tank, bullied him into getting some treatment.

'He was in the next bed to me, remember?' the Colonel said. 'Nice enough chap. He was over here looking at 'chasers. Went to the Newbury meeting. It rained for three days. He got pneumonia, more fool him, to come to England in February, and ended up in hospital. He's over here now, looking at a stallion he might buy.'

'Racehorse breeder?' Ron pricked up his ears. A racing stable was more his line than a home of rest for old horses.

'In a small way. Got a bit of money, I believe, though I don't think he knows much.'

'He don't know nothing till 'e's seen the great Follyfoot horse show.' Ron swept an arm round the field with its collection of washtubs, laundry lines and bizarre back alley jumps.

3

ABOUT twenty people came to the horse show. There was Toby, the funny little undersized boy with the goblin face and pointed ears, whose father kept the Three Horseshoes. He had a swarm of brothers and sisters. Nobody had ever been able to get them together in one place for long enough to count.

When people asked Toby's mother why she had so many children, she replied that she'd had to have a lot, hadn't she, or she wouldn't have enough older ones to take care of all the babies.

Toby's mother didn't always make much sense. His father made sense with the back of his hand. Sometimes when Callie got on the school bus, there would be a plaster on Toby's cheek, or a muffler round his neck to hide a bruise.

Toby had not had much fun in life before he met Callie and the people at the Farm, particularly the four-legged ones. Steve, who had taught him to ride, was his hero. He was in love with Dora. Callie was his best friend. Anna made doughnuts for him.

He was the only person who was not afraid of the Colonel, when something went wrong at Follyfoot. When the Colonel limped through the yard demanding to know how Stroller had got into Arthur Flagg's potato patch, or who had left a pitchfork in Ranger's stable or a saddle out on a fence all night, everybody else became very busy doing something vital. Ron Stryker, whose fault it usually was, disappeared into the pump house, but Toby stood his ground in the middle of the yard, leaning on a broom that was as tall as he was and enquired sunnily, 'You rang, Colonel?'

The Colonel liked that. In return, he revolutionised Toby's life on the day that the nurseryman said he'd gone motorised and wouldn't be coming back for his two Welsh ponies.

The grey one had laminitis, but the cream-coloured one was fat and safe, and the Colonel gave it to Toby. He kept it in a shed behind the pub. It's name was Coffee, because it coughed. It was almost wider than it was long. Toby rode with his short skinny legs sticking straight out on either side, and Coffee performed great feats for him of a slow and unambitious nature.

Some of Toby's brothers and sisters came to the horse show, fighting, screaming, whining or bellowing, according to age. His mother had two in a double pushchair and one on her back in a canvas sling. She always had a small baby at any time of year. Two last year when she had the twins.

The girls from the pony farm came through the wood and down the field track like a small army. The blacksmith's daughter, who had lost the use of her legs in a car crash, ambled down the road on her Fell pony Pogo. He was trained to stand quietly in a pit, so that she could pull herself onto his back from her wheelchair and ride him up the slope to ground level. Moll was a splendid girl with freckles and a loud laugh. When she fell off jumping the car tyres, she sat on the ground shouting with laughter until someone picked her up and put her back on Pogo.

A boy and a girl from the house at the bottom of the hill came up with their father's two elderly steeplechasers, who were retired to grass down there. Mrs Oldcastle, in old-fashioned ballooning breeches, cantered sedately across the fields from 'Rose Holme' on her large-footed cob named Harold. Two children pottered in on muddy Shetlands.

Hero was still lame, so Dora rode the mule. Steve rode Miss America, who had been rescued from a riding stable with a brutally sore back. She still could not take a saddle.

Callie, of course, rode Cobbler's Dream. He was pretty much hers now that Steve was too heavy for him. Ron refused to ride, because the girls from the pony farm laughed at him. He sat on a bale of hay at the side of the ring and did the Musical Sacks on his transistor, or squatted by jumps going, 'Kcheech!' to test the ponies' nerves.

Joe Fuller, who owned the pony farm, was the judge. To be fair, he tried not to let his ponies win too often. The show was constantly punctuated by clamouring groups of girls on New Forests and Exmoors going, 'Joe, it's not fair! But Joe, I won, you saw me! Oh please, let's run it again – come on, Joe!'

In the dog race, where your dog was supposed to follow your horse, two or three fights broke out to add to the clamour. Dora separated two dogs by flinging a bucket of water at them, bucket and all. Above the noise, she heard Callie shout at her, and saw her standing in her stirrups looking towards the road. Dora stood on a wheelbarrow and saw them coming.

One large girl riding the thin roan horse that might once have been a hunter, the other on a bicycle, fat legs in shorts revolving, the parents following in a car.

'The Crowleys.' She turned to Steve.

'They never.'

'They have.'

The Crowleys came in at the far gate, parked their car and began wiping down the horse with tea towels in an ostentatious and unnecessary way. From the back of the car, the mother unpacked an enormous amount of food and drink, which they did not offer to share with anybody.

When Dora rode down to that end of the field to practise Willy over the right-angled in-and-out jump, she saw the Crowleys trying to make the roan mare jump the brush. Marcia, the sullenest of the girls, would ride up to the jump with a great deal of arm-flapping and leg-pumping. The mare, who was dropping her left hind leg in a painful way, very sensibly stopped dead before the jump. The child beat at her with a long stick, burst into angry tears, and changed the stick to the other side.

'That horse is lame,' Dora called out. 'You can't ride her.'

'Mind your own business.' Marcia turned her anger to Dora.

'Dopey's all right.' The mother had been throwing clods of turf at the mare's bony back end. 'She's just a little stiff when she starts up.'

'She's lame in that near hind leg.'

'She's always moved a little funny.' The father came up now with a bottle of ginger beer, moon-faced, the sun glinting on his round glasses. 'That's why we got her so cheap.'

'And the girls adore Dopey. They take endless care of her. Don't you girls? Don't you girls!' The mother shouted at her sulky daughters, who scowled back at her. 'She's a darling. We wouldn't hurt her for the world.'

'You are hurting her,' Dora said, 'You can't ride her in our show.'

Dora could be pretty blunt where horses were concerned. She did not especially try to be rude. It just came naturally.

'We've come all this way,' the father said.

'Let's go home,' whined Marcia.

'You're to have your fun,' the father ordered. 'Dopey will be all right. You'll see.'

'Yeah,' said Dora. 'We'll see.' And kept an eye on them.

4

In the True Love race, pairs of riders held a strip of paper between them to represent the marriage licence. When the paper broke, they were divorced and eliminated. Callie and Toby paired off. Dora wanted to go with Steve, but there was too much competition for him from the pony farm girls.

'Will you be my partner?' Amanda Crowley rode up on the roan.

'I told you, you can't –'

'She's all right now. I need a partner.'

'I've got one.' Dora hastily grabbed at the flare of Mrs Oldcastle's breeches.

Harold cantered steadily round the outside of the ring, as if he were on rails. The mule kept veering towards the middle of the field, since the Colonel was there as ring steward, with horse nuts at the bottom of his poacher's pocket. Dora and Mrs Oldcastle were divorced after half a round. So was Amanda Crowley, since Dopey was very slow, and the girl perched on the steeplechaser couldn't hold him back.

Dora bided her time.

In the Refusal race, you had to trot up to a jump, stop the horse and sail over the jump by yourself. On to Anna's spare room mattress. Easy for Dora, since Willy naturally refused any jump. The mule trotted up to the jump with his rough, wavering gait and stopped dead with his neck out. Dora hurled herself through the air with her eyes shut, landed on her back on the mattress, and looked up into a startled face under a brand new green sporting cap, worn dead straight.

'Hullo,' said Dora. There was nothing else to say.

'Oh – hi there.' The face said uncertainly. 'I – er, I'm looking for the Colonel.'

'Over there.' Dora scrambled to her feet. She nodded to where the Colonel in shabby old clothes was lolling on Stroller's bare back, his unlit pipe in his mouth and his hat tipped over his eyes against the sun.

'Could have fooled me,' said the stranger. He must be the American from the hospital.

When Dora called, the Colonel slid off Stroller and came across with his large brown hand held out.

'Blankenheimer, my dear chap. It's good to see you.'

Mr Blankenheimer shook hands with him and stepped quickly out of the way as Willy, unpredictable as all mules, suddenly decided to jump after all. He came over in his fore and aft fashion, front end on its own, back end following a bit later, landed on the mattress, put his foot on his reins, threw up his head, broke the rein, wandered away and bit Coffee in the rump.

Mr Blankenheimer laughed nervously. 'Quite a circus you have here.'

'Great, isn't it?' The Colonel had not even stepped out of the way as the mule jumped, just bent his tall frame slightly sideways. 'It's our spring horse show.'

'Oh, pardon me.' The American was all dressed up as if he thought it was a real horse show: a bright jacket, shirt and tie with a foxhead pin, crisp trousers, jodphur boots that squeaked.

He was rather nice. He was gentle and eager to please. He smiled a lot, and cheered mildly and clapped. In the relay race, when everyone yelled for the ponies, not the riders – 'Come on, Pansy! Get going, Coffee!' – he yelled too: 'C'mawn Cawfee!'

He helped to put up jumps. He sat with Ron on a bale of hay, sucking a wisp of it and discussing the odds on the 3.30 race at Sandown. He held ponies for people who were soaking their faces in the apple bobbing. He poured cider for Anna in the nosebag race. You galloped to one end of the ring, grabbed a doughnut off a string with your teeth, and ate it before you got back to the other end, where you were handed a cup of cider, and had to trot back without spilling it. Then you drank it, if there was any left.

'More fun than a barrel of monkeys,' was the opinion of Mr Blankenheimer.

In the last jumping event, Amanda Crowley brought poor Dopey on to the course, carrying the long stick.

The Colonel put out a hand and caught the roan mare's rein as she turned her towards the first jump. 'No whip.' He took it away from her.

'She won't jump without it,' the girl protested. 'She's a pig.'

'No,' said the Colonel mildly. 'She's old and tired.'

He let Amanda have three tries, since he knew the horse would not jump. After the third refusal, he silently handed her back the stick, and she rode angrily back to get some food out of the back of her car.

'Look here.' Mr and Mrs Crowley were on the scene. 'It's not good enough.'

'To jump her, it isn't.' The Colonel was good at protecting horses from people like this. 'Dora's right. The horse is lame behind.'

'All very well for Dora,' the mother said, some spite looking out of her small black eyes above the swollen cheeks. 'She's got a stable full of horses to ride.' (Willy? Lame Hero? Spot, whose back was too broad and flat to do anything but stand on it? The shetlands?) 'My girls have only Dopey.'

'*And* spoil her to match.' The father had a manner part aggressive, part whining. 'Gone without, we have, to feed this animal. I'm not a rich man, Colonel, as you know, but I'll not have it said ... Gone without meat on the table ...'

'Horses don't eat meat.' The Colonel was easily bored. He had stopped listening.

5

At the end of the show, when Mr Blankenheimer was presenting the rosettes made by Anna out of Christmas paper, a small commotion made itself known at the far end of the field.

One of the Crowley girls, long stick in hand, had somehow beaten the roan mare into the in-and-out, and was trying to beat her out again.

Steve rode Miss America fast to the end of the field, jumped off, and into the in-and-out, grabbed the stick and whacked the Crowley girl across her fat rump.

'He hit me – ai -ai-ai!'

The father let out with his right fist and punched Steve in the face. Steve punched him back, and then they were down together, rolling about on the ground between the jumps, the roan mare nervously lifting her feet so as not to step on them.

Dora could only stand and watch from a distance. Steve had been in trouble before for fighting. When his temper was strong, he could really hurt somebody. Mr Cowley was lucky. He wriggled away, got up, shouted to the Colonel that he would sue him ('I'll be suing you,' added Ron), and left the scene.

'Will they really sue?' Mr Blankenheimer had watched the drama with his eyes popping under the green cap.

The Colonel grunted impatiently. 'It's just talk. Always looking for trouble. That's the way they live.'

'Are all English horse shows like this?' the American asked.

'Yeah, sure,' said Ron. 'You ain't seen nothing yet. Stick around, mate.'

Dora liked this small gentle man. 'Come on, I'll show you the rest of the horses.'

'Oh dear.' He looked at his watch in the fussy way of a man ruled by time. 'I can't. I have a business appointment.'

'To see the stallion?' Dora would like to go too.

'No, Miss – er.' He had been too shy to call anybody by name yet, except when he was shouting for the ponies. 'To see some – er tiling. I'm here on business too. The construction business. I'm after some of your laminated, self-adhesive, mosaic. You folks are way ahead of us, I have to tell you.'

'Thanks.' Dora was out of her depth. 'Can you come back tomorrow and see the horses?'

'Could I?' Mr Blankenheimer beamed at the favour. It was really a favour for Dora. She never got tired of showing off the horses and telling their histories. 'This is Puss, who was being ridden to London with a petition for the Queen ... this is Ginger, who used to pull a milk cart ... this is poor old Frank – see the dent in his head from the tight halter ...'

He was back the next day in his stiff, formal clothes, coming as uncertainly into the yard as if he were an unwelcome tax collector.

The Colonel was trimming feet. He greeted Mr Blankenheimer from an upside down face, without letting go of Dolly's back foot. Once you let it down, it was hard to pick up again. Mr Blankenheimer seemed a bit nervous of him. He stood and watched, and folded his arms, and put his hands in his pockets, and then behind his back, and cleared his throat, while the Colonel went on paring with his sharp curved knife, making the whistling hiss between his teeth with which all the horses were so familiar. The Colonel was shy too, and when he was with another shy person, it could be paralysing. Dora, rescuing

301

Mr Blankenheimer to begin his tour of the inmates, wondered what the two of them had talked about, trapped in that green hospital room with the high beds and sterile smells.

All the horses were out except Lancelot, who had one of his groggy spells today. He would rather be groggy indoors, than outside where the others could bother him.

Some people thought Lancelot was ugly, with his bony frame and patchy skewbald hide, but to Dora he was beautiful.

'He'd be dead if it wasn't for Follyfoot,' she said.

'Some folks would say he should be put – er, put to sleep,' Mr Blankenheimer said sadly.

'The Colonel doesn't believe in taking a horse's life if he can still enjoy it,' Dora said. 'That's half the point of this place.'

'It's splendid,' Mr Blankenheimer said. 'Very fine. A Home of Rest for Horses. How British can you get? You could never have a place like this in the States. We're too practical about horses over there. Not sentimental.'

'Not crazy, you mean.' Steve came out of Hero's stable pushing a barrow with a rickety wheel. It had been on the brink of collapse for months. A lot of the equipment at Folly-foot was old and groggy, like Lancelot. But the Colonel was plagued with bills for winter feed and bedding. When the barrow wheel let go and tipped its load almost on Mr Blankenheimer's neat feet, Steve sighed, and went off to the tool shed for some dowelling to mend the wheel again.

Dora took the American round the fields and showed him the horses and told him how each one had come here. He thrilled to the story of Callie stealing Hero from the circus, and when he heard about Ranger, whose jaw had been half torn off by a cruel wire bit, his eyes filled with ready tears.

She told him how Folly had been born in a ditch where Specs was trapped, and how Cobbler's Dream had found them.

He was fascinated. He loved the idea and the ideals of Folly-foot.

'Wouldn't it be wonderful if –'

'If what?'

'Just a dream, I guess, Miss – er –'

'Dora.'

She could not call him Earl. Nor Mr Blankenheimer. She called him Mr Blank.

Since he was a racehorse owner, she showed off Folly proudly.

'Look at that length from croup to hock.' She made the shrewd face that people make when they size up horseflesh. 'And see the muscle here already.' Dora gripped the negligible crest of Folly's young neck, and the colt struck out with his narrow hoof and ducked away. 'Look at the bone on him, look at the bone.'

'I'll say.' Mr Blank narrowed his eyes and imitated Dora's shrewd face. He did not know much, but he had a natural feeling for horses. He did not laugh at Dora, like the last visitor who had said, 'Doesn't it bother you to feed these old nags when half the world is starving?'

He wanted to go into the hay barn, to remind himself of his boyhood in Indiana.

'I love places like this.' They sat down on a bale of hay and inhaled the dusty sweet smell of outdoor preserved indoors which gave the barn its special atmosphere. The old beams were curtained with cobwebs, the floor stamped into troughs and hollows by generations of working feet.

'Where my race horses are, it's all so grand. I don't even know where they keep the hay. It's too tidy. Where I keep my daughter's horse, they don't even feed hay. Just roughage pellets. On schedule. You can't bring carrots or sugar in your pocket.' He sighed. 'You know, Dora, I'm glad it was you showed me around today. You're kinda – kinda old shoe.'

'Thanks,' Dora said. 'Thanks, Mr Blank.'

'Why do you call me that?'

'It suits you.'

'You think so?' He turned an unhappy face to her. 'You think I'm a nothing?'

'Of course not.'

'Other people do. They don't pay me too much notice.'

'Look at it this way, Mr Blank.' Dora thought quickly. 'There was a blank in my life, and you fill it.'

'Gee. Wow.' If she'd handed him a thousand pounds, he could not have been more pleased. Especially since he didn't need a thousand pounds.

They seemed to have made friends. She'd call him Blank. He'd call her Door.

'I like you, Blank.' Dora had not made a new friend for ages.

'I like you, Door.'

Blank Door. A code name. 'No Handle.'

On the way to get his car, they took a detour to see the last few horses in the top field. Magic, the black police horse was grazing peacefully with the sun on his round shining quarters and his full tail swishing rhythmically.

'He's twenty-five,' Dora said. 'Been on the streets almost all his life. Riots. Parades. Traffic. He's done his work. Now he's enjoying his rest.'

'My gosh,' Blank said. 'That old guy looks fitter than a lot of horses who are still working. Look at that roan horse there was all the trouble about yesterday. This is where that one ought to be.'

'I know,' said Dora. 'I wish we had her.'

'If she had her way,' Slugger had come to lean over the gate with them, 'half the horses in the county would be up Folly-foot Farm.'

'It's agony though,' Dora said. 'People are so stupid. I suppose they mean well, but they have all the wrong sort of sentiment, creeps like the Crowleys. I wish we could get them to see that Dopey shouldn't be ridden. Dopey – what an insult to a horse. I'm sure the Colonel would take her here.'

'Oh my Gawd.' Slugger pulled his woollen cap down over his best eye.

Dora grumbled on about the Crowleys. 'They're always carrying on about not having meat on the table and how they starve themselves to feed the 'dah-ling' horse. But one look at those fat pigs, and you know who comes first in that family.'

'If they want meat, they could shoot the horse and put him on the table then, couldn't they?' Slugger's jokes could be pretty sick.

'Shut up.'

'Now, lookit –'

Door and Blank spoke together. They exchanged a No Handle look of understanding.

'What are you planning?' Slugger lifted the edge of his cap to see.

'Nothing,' said Dora. 'I wish I was.'

'Gawd help us all,' said Slugger.

6

AFTER Blank had driven away in his hired car, turning to wave and grazing the gatepost, Dora still could not talk at supper about anything else but Dopey.

'I've still got that poor mare on my mind,' she said, sitting at the round kitchen table, picking at Anna's meat pie.

'And I've still got that man's knuckles on my face.' Steve rubbed his cheek, which had come up into a bruise of interesting colours.

'It is awful,' Dora fretted. 'That horse will never be sound, and those dopes will never give her up. I wish we could steal her.'

'You've stolen enough horses in your day,' Steve said. 'Britain's number one horse thief, you are. If you'd been sentenced for all the horses you've stolen or swindled people out of, you'd be doing hard labour for the next two hundred years.'

'That would be good.' Callie looked up. 'Then she could go down the mines and work with the ponies.'

'Women don't work in mines, stupid.' Steve kicked her under the table.

'I wish they did.' Callie made a toad face at him. 'Then I could go and work with the pit ponies.'

'They don't have ponies in mines any more, stupid.'

Callie sulked. Sometimes it was hard being the only child among grown ups. But when her mother asked her if she would like to have friends to stay, she couldn't think of anyone to ask. She didn't really have friends, except Toby. The horses were her friends. And Dora and Steve, and Ron when he wasn't being mean.

Sometimes they treated her like a silly kid. At other times they loaded a whole lot of work and responsibility on her. Her father would have understood. When your father is dead, it's easy to daydream that he would have understood everything.

She pushed back her chair into the fireplace and ran upstairs to look at the picture of him over her bed, sitting loosely on his famous steeplechaser Wonderboy, who was still at Follyfoot, idling the last of his days.

Anna followed her upstairs and sat on the bed.

'I love that picture,' she said.

'How could you marry the Colonel,' Callie said, still sulking, 'if you still loved my father?'

'You were glad when I married him,' Anna said, surprised.

'Mm-hm.'

'And you're glad now, aren't you?'

'Mm-hm.'

'Well then,' said Anna.

'Well then,' said Callie, and sighed.

When Callie came back to the kitchen, Steve reached back and picked up her chair out of the fireplace without taking his fork out of the mashed potato. Callie often pushed her chair into the fireplace and ran out of the room. No one bothered to look up. They had all been through that stage. Dora went back to it sometimes, when things went really wrong.

She was still agonising over the roan mare. 'Did you hear what he said? "I'm not a rich man, you know, Colonel."' She imitated Mr Crowley's whining voice. 'I hate it when people cry poor.'

'Well, they are poor,' Steve said.

'So are we.' There was never enough money at Follyfoot. The Colonel waged a monthly battle with the bills that silted up his office desk like river mud.

'I wish we weren't,' Dora sighed. 'I wish we could buy that mare, and take care of her here. If we made a really good offer –'

'If, if, if,' the Colonel said. 'You've got two dreams, Dora. One is about all the horses you could steal if you had the nerve. The other is about all the things you could do if you had the money.'

'I know. I'd buy this gorgeous bay thoroughbred. Two white feet. Small neat head with those sort of smiley dark blue eyes. Stepping out really free. Fit and supple. All that muscle moving like cream ... Remember David, Steve, how he moved, and how he held his head, that natural flexion ...' She went off into a dream of beautiful horses, with her elbow on the table and her cheek in her hand.

'If you're not going to eat your pudding,' Callie said, 'I'll have it.'

In the night, Dora had a revelation. She got revelations some-times in the night, and heard voices. She felt she must be psychic. Sometimes she heard horses neighing and the thunder of hoofs on hard hill turf.

Tonight she was into a dream of the open sea. She was swimming on a splendid horse, her arms round its crested neck, which was somehow part of the cresting waves. Suddenly, in her sleep or in her waking, a voice said very clearly, 'Door.'

She was wide awake in an instant, and sat upright. It had sounded just as if Blank were in the room.

That was the revelation. Blank had money. She would ask him to go to the Crowleys and buy the roan mare.

It was early, only just growing light, but Dora got up and went down to muck out. She had to do something with the energy of her excitement.

At a decent hour, she telephoned Blank at his hotel.

'Could you possibly come up here right away?'

'Well gee, honey – Door – I don't know that I can. I have this guy to see about the recycled caulking strips, and –'

'It's an emergency,' Dora said. 'A matter of life and death.'

Blank's life did not normally hold such drama. He was up at the Farm before Dora and Steve had finished the morning work. Dora had not told Steve yet. She didn't quite know why. Something about the money? Though he called her a horse thief, he had always shared in her plots and schemes of rescue. But somehow today . . .

When Blank came across the yard, she said, 'No Handle,' and pushed him into an empty loose box to tell him the plan.

He became very excited, but nervous too, his hands shaking, his eyes glancing from Dora to the door as if he expected to see a posse of sheriffs after him already.

'What'll I say?' he kept asking, even while she was telling him. 'What'll I say?'

'You can say you've seen this horse of theirs,' Dora repeated, 'and that you like his looks, and nothing will satisfy you but to buy him.'

She described the little patch of field where Dopey lived out her boring days on a bare patch of ground, with no shade.

'You can say you were driving by. You can say you're a mad American millionaire. Say you're the Mafia. Say your wife fancies the mare and won't be denied. Say anything, but *get that horse.*' She fixed him with a stern eye.

'Yes, Door, yes.' His eyes met hers at last. 'I'll do it.'

He went out of the loose box, walking with his knees slightly bent, shoulders rounded, fists clenched. Dora did not have to worry whether to tell Steve. Blank told him at once.

'I'm off on a mission of mercy, my boy.' He held out his hand. 'Wish me luck.'

'What has she got you into?' Steve took his hand and grinned at Dora.

'I got myself into it. There's no turning back. Wish me luck.' He held out his hand to Slugger, walking past with buckets. Slugger set down the buckets, wiped his hand on his baggy trousers, shook Blank's hand, picked up the buckets and walked on. Dora hoped Blank wasn't going to tell everyone he met on the way.

'Why didn't you tell me?' Steve asked Dora.

'I don't know. Something about it being money. What we've done before, it's been us doing it. We haven't used anyone's money. I thought –'

'With money,' Steve said, 'it's better not to think about it. Just either spend it or don't.'

Dora was good at creating complicated questions. Steve was good at giving simple answers.

After dropping Blank round the corner from the Crowleys, Dora and Steve took the horse box and waited in a side road some distance away. An eternity passed, during which they imagined Blank kidnapped for ransom, arrested, beaten up by Mr Crowley, poisoned by Mrs, forced to marry the oldest daughter Juliette, who was even fatter and stupider than Amanda and Marcia. At last they heard the faint sound of hoofs on the road. The hoofbeats grew louder, and Blank appeared round the corner of a hedge, leading the mare slowly, a smile of pure triumphant happiness on his innocent face.

'How did you do it?' Dora jumped down from the cab of the horse box.

He stopped, looked down, and scraped the gravel of the road with his toe.

'I charmed her,' he admitted. 'I really think I charmed her.'

'With money?' Steve jumped down and took the mare's halter rope.

'No.' Blank looked up. 'With my charm.'

'And how much money?' insisted Steve.

'More than I should have.' He looked down again. 'But it wasn't that easy. When Mrs Crowley asked me where I was taking the horse, I had to make up this story about a man delivering another horse for me, and how he would meet me on the road, and we would take the mare to this place I have, with all this good grass and so on. She wanted to know where, so I said Wales. It was the only place I could think of. "Oh," she says, "Wales, my girlhood home. Whereabouts?" "Well, I'm just moving houses." "Where to?" "Well, they've changed the name of the village because it was ugly, so I –" "No Welsh names are ugly," she says. Phew!' He mopped his beaded forehead and shook his head. 'You know how when you start with one lie, you get into more and more? I had my fingers crossed in both pockets.'

Dora put her arms round Dopey's thin neck, as she sagged in the road, resting the lame hind leg.

'Thanks, Blank,' she said.

'My pleasure.'

'Isn't it fun to be a horse thief?'

'Hey, wait a minute, Door,' Blank said. 'I paid for that horse.'

'How much then?' Steve asked. 'Tell us.'

Blank named an outrageous figure, about twenty times as

311

much as the poor old roan was worth, even for dog meat and sofa stuffing.

Steve whistled. 'With that money, you could have bought us a really super horse to ride.'

He was joking, but Blank turned on him a solemn look. 'But that's not the idea of Follyfoot, is it? I thought –'

'Of course not.' Dora patted his hand. 'You've caught on very quickly, Blank.'

7

MR Blank was in love with the whole idea of Follyfoot. He wished he didn't have to go back to America tomorrow. Instead of going to visit the manufacturer of stretchable caulking recycled from paper cups and used tea bags, he stayed to let Dora teach him how to muck out and put down clean bedding in the stable he prepared for his mare.

'So they've got you in the business, Blankenheimer.' The Colonel came and smiled over the door. 'Let's keep her in a bit till we see what we can do for that leg. What do you call her?'

'Not Dopey, that's for sure.' Blank bent down to tease straw around the mare's front feet. 'If she was a gelding, I'd call him Man-o'-War, after the most famous racehorse in the world.'

'Why not Woman-o'-War?' asked Dora.

'I like it.'

Dopey was rechristened Woman.

It was too late for Blank to keep his appointment with the tea bag man, so he decided, in his flush of happiness about Woman, to go and buy a present for his wife.

It was market day in the town in the valley. He pottered round the antique stalls, looking at silver gravy boats and tortoiseshell snuff boxes. Nothing took his eye, so he wandered on to the livestock section of the market, where the goats and chickens were.

A chocolate coloured donkey was tied to the outside of the

313

goat pen. It had a white nose and stomach and white rims to the purple pools of its eyes. Its eyelashes were longer than the ones Mrs Blankenheimer had bought to go to the golf club dance, and had to trim down because they pushed her glasses off.

A small boy was sitting on the ground near the donkey, smoking a cigarette.

When Blank stopped in front of him, he squinted suspiciously up through the cigarette smoke.

'It's all right, son,' Blank said. 'I'm not going to tell you not to smoke at your age.'

'That's O.K.,' said the boy consolingly. 'You don't have to. Want to buy a donkey?'

'Not really. I just bought a horse.'

'Go on.' The boy was not interested.

'Is it your donkey?' It was a pretty, delicate thing in its smooth summer coat, the shadow of the cross over its withers, neat shell feet, dished-in face, fat enough and well cared for. Somebody's pet.

'Nah.' The boy looked at him sideways. 'I brought it down to get it sold. Belonged to my sister, see, what died. Her greatest pet, it was.'

'Oh, how sad.' Tears welled into Blank's eyes. If Dora were here, she would have wanted to buy the donkey at once. 'Can't you keep it?'

'Can't afford to, because of the funeral bills, see.'

That did it. Blank handed over the price the boy asked and took the donkey's halter rope. Dora would be proud of him. He lifted the donkey into the back seat of his car, folded its legs neatly on the seat, and took it back to Follyfoot.

The donkey accepted these events calmly. It lay like a dog on the seat of the hired car, its white muzzle resting on its fore-leg, regarding the passing countryside with violet eyes.

It was only when Blank was half way up the winding hill to the Farm that he remembered that he had not bought a present for his wife.

'I don't believe it.' Ron Stryker opened the back seat of Blank's car. 'What makes you think we need a donkey?'

'But look at those eyes. I know Dora will be glad to have her.'

'Dora don't run this place.' Ron's eyes were sharp under the lank ginger hair. 'You'll have to take it back. The Colonel don't want another donkey.'

'But I've bought her. I can't take her back to the States. Where's Dora?'

'I dunno. She was around. Must have gone off somewhere.'

Blank left the donkey in the car and locked it, so that Ron could not play any tricks. He did not trust this sharp-tongued, red-haired boy with the wild laugh, unrecognizable as either humour or wickedness.

The day was losing its light early. The clouds were low and a damp mist had curled up from the valley to shroud the farm and fields. Blank went round the looseboxes, but there was nobody there except Woman, resting her groggy leg and too busy with her hay to greet her saviour.

He went into the tack room and called up the stairs for Steve. No answer.

'Dora!' He went down the path to the misted fields, calling for her. 'Door! Door! Door!' The rooks, swaying about in the invisible tops of the elms, gave him back, 'Door! Door!'

At last he saw her, ambling up the slope from the stream, sitting on the grey donkey, bare feet hanging, eyes half closed. Behind her, the slow movement of old horses trailed out of the mist, following the donkey, who was like a bell wether to the herd.

'I brought you a present.' Blank opened the gate.

'What is it?' Dora's eyes opened.

'That boy, the one with the red hair, he says you don't want it. It's a – it's a – well, you'll have to see.'

When each horse had turned into its own stable and dropped its head in the manger, and Dora had shut the doors on them, she went out to the car. The chocolate donkey was still meditating on the back seat.

She said at once, 'Thanks, Blank.'

'This kid's sister died, you see. It was her pet. That boy – he said you didn't want another donkey, but –'

'There's always room for one more at Follyfoot,' Dora said.

'This is such a great outfit.' Blank shook his head, smiling. 'I wish I could . . . I've got a bit of money, you know. Suppose I could start a place like this in New England, where I live. What would people think of it?'

'They'd think you were as crazy as us,' Dora laughed.

'Right now, they don't think I'm anything at all,' he said in his worst Blank nothing manner. 'But I could show 'em, couldn't I? If I did – lookit, Door – would you come out and help me get it going?'

'I couldn't, Blank. I have to work here.'

'Don't you get a vacation?'

'Well, I do, but my mother . . .' Dora had half promised her mother to go on a cultural tour of the churches of the upper Rhine.

'I'd pay your fare.'

'It's not that.' She blushed. Again money – someone else's money – was confusing things.

'You could ride my daughter's horse.' He watched her.

'Doesn't she ride it?'

'Not this year.' He looked very sad. Was the daughter dead? 'Last year she rode, but somewhere along the line, she matoored,

316

or whatever they call it. I'd bought Robin for her. Now she won't ride him.'

'I would.'

'You would?'

'In the summer, perhaps I could come, when all the horses are out. The work's easier then.'

'In the summer.' He nodded. 'Bye, Door.'

'Bye, Blank.' Smiling, she stood with the brown donkey and watched him safely past the gatepost. It was only after his car had turned the corner that she began to get scared. Go to America? Stay with a strange family, with a mysteriously 'matoor' daughter and a father who was shyer than she was? She must be mad. She would have to get out of it somehow.

The summer was weeks away. Anything might happen before then.

8

But nothing did happen. June drew near. Dora's passport photo looked like a wanted criminal. Blank sent over her ticket. The Colonel had agreed willingly. Steve and Callie were jealous.

Ron was fed up. The cheap horse auctions were coming up. The Colonel had that gleam in his eye. There'd be newcomers to the Farm and Dora gone jet-setting across the Atlantic.

'Who's to do the work?' Ron demanded. 'Who's to do her work then?'

'It won't be you, that's certain,' Steve said.

'No, because I'll be on the Costa Brava,' Ron said. 'I'm taking me holidays in Spain.'

"You can't have no holiday,' Slugger told him.

'How can Dora then?'

'She don't miss all the work days you do.'

But Slugger was dubious about Dora's trip. All he knew of America was from television. In his mind, The United States and hell were the same place.

'But it's to help start another Follyfoot there,' Dora said. 'It's a wonderful chance. Other countries might copy it. Follyfoot International. It could be the start of a whole world movement for old horses.'

'We've lost her.' Slugger sniffed his lower lip up towards his nose. 'She's gone idealistic on us.'

'No, I haven't.' Dora dropped her starry-eyed act, which was as much to convince herself as Slugger. 'I don't really want to go.'

Dora's mother was disappointed about the Rhine cathedrals, but she thought it would be a wonderful chance for Dora to

318

get away from horses. Her mother had never come to terms with the turn that Dora's life had taken the day she met the Colonel and decided that her career began, and possibly ended, among the old horses of Follyfoot.

'I'm not getting away from horses,' Dora said. 'Mr Blankenheimer has a lot of them.'

'But racehorses,' her mother said. Racehorses were all right. They lived in proper stables with proper grooms, and performed a proper function in life. 'If they have a racing stable, they must be pretty grand people. You'll have to get some proper clothes.'

'Don't they wear jeans in the United States?' Dora asked.

'You're hopeless,' her mother said, and took Dora to a department store.

They bought some shorts because it was going to be hot, and a swim suit and some bright slacks and cotton dresses and one long skirt for what Dora's mother called The Evenings.

Dora was wearing a pair of heavy ankle boots with her jeans that day. The long flowered skirt looked all right until she moved. Then it looked very odd with the boots clumping about underneath.

Dora looked at herself mournfully in the unflattering mirror of the fitting room. 'I hope the days at the Blankenheimers are going to be all right,' she said dolefully, 'because I don't think I'm going to enjoy the evenings much.'

Her mother said. 'It's the chance of a lifetime.'

'Might be the end of a lifetime.' Dora had never flown before. She was afraid.

'Don't be ridiculous,' said her mother, who flew regularly to France, Italy, Germany, and didn't let on that she had a lucky charm at the bottom of her pocket. 'People fly every day.'

'But they're not scared,' Dora said, as if that were the only thing that kept them from crashing.

319

'Let's see if we can find a nice white frilly blouse to go with that skirt,' her mother said, to cheer her up.

'I don't think I want to go.'

On her last evening, she knew she didn't want to go.

The horses were all out in the fields. The little brown donkey with the white muzzle and endless white-tipped ears, christened Dottie, was out with Don in the summer twilight, grazing the thistles and coarse grass that the horses wouldn't touch.

'Too stupid to know good grass when they see it,' Ron said. He resented the horses for the work they made, but he resented the donkeys even more.

'Donkeys are good for a pasture, fool,' Slugger said. 'That's why we have 'em.'

'The Colonel's soft in the head, that's why we have 'em.'

They were all leaning over the gate watching the horses move away towards their night-time grazing grounds on the other side of the stream. Cobby, his chestnut coat bright in the afterglow of the sunset, swishing his thick tail like a bell. Spot the circus horse, his sagging back on which ladies had once danced showing his years. Dolly with her back feet twisting outwards, sign of an animal that has been overdriven. Magic the police horse who was so fat and well this summer that dapple marks showed on his quarters.

Woman-o'-War, with that awful dropping action of her left hind leg, but filling out already, the desperate look gone from her eye. Her roan coat was less patchy, the rubbed marks grown in, the blue colour improving as she fattened up.

Dora half closed her eyes and imagined, grazing slowly forward with the herd, her horse, her bay horse, moving easily with the long thoroughbred walk that told what his gallop would be like.

320

'I don't want to go,' she said.

'This time tomorrow,' Calle said, 'you'll be miles up in the air. Maybe the window will fly out, like they do sometimes, and you'll drop down, spinning like a corkscrew, and land in Nova Scotia.'

'I don't want to go.'

The Colonel took her to the airport in his rough little sports car. It was one of the few drives with him when she had not clutched the seat convulsively, and trodden on the floorboards in a desperate attempt to brake before he did. If she were killed on the road, at least she couldn't be killed in the plane.

She was very quiet.

'Excited, eh?' The Colonel turned to look at her once, saw her tight lips and turned back to the road and left her alone.

Approaching the airport, they began to see a lot of planes overhead. Dora began to get that feeling, like trying to swallow a wet stone and having it lodge somewhere between your swallow and your stomach.

'What happens,' she asked the Colonel in a small voice, 'if I'm sick on the plane?'

'You do it in a brown paper bag.'

'I haven't got a brown paper bag.'

'There'll be one in the pocket of the seat in front of you,' he said without looking at her, 'along with instructions about what to do when the plane crashes into the sea.'

'I see,' said Dora. Her hands had begun to sweat a little into the palms.

She hardly spoke. The Colonel took care of the ticket and bags, while she stood beside him, feeling smaller than usual. When he put his hand on top of her head, she jumped. She felt extra sensitive, like a crab without its shell.

Outside the gate where she had to leave him, he started to bite his nails, because he wasn't sure whether she would want him to kiss her goodbye. She flung her arms round his neck.

'Are you sure you can manage without me?' What if they didn't notice she'd gone, and didn't care whether she ever came back?

'Of course we can't.'

'Thanks. That makes me feel much better.'

Dora walked bravely through the gate with her head up like a French aristocrat going to the guillotine.

9

'Travelling alone?' The voice made her jump. A man had come to sit beside her on the plane. Tall. A briefcase. One of those faces that have been around. 'Bob Nelson,' he said.

She nodded. Although the plane was on the ground, she was gripping the edge of the seat as if it was in the air.

'Scared?' he asked. 'Don't be. It's boring, that's all.'

The take off was so exciting that beyond a fleeting certainty that they would hit some high tension cables, Dora forgot to be afraid. She sat by the window, saw a reservoir, saw a riding school, saw the green cabbage fields of Middlesex rushing away from her, saw Windsor Castle tilting dangerously by the narrow glittering river, and then they were into a cloud, and up beyond, where it seemed no one had ever gone before. Tall stacks of piled up brilliant white cloud, cotton wool masses, the tops of clouds where before she had seen only the leaky bottom. The sky was a piercing blue and the unseen sun a dazzling presence.

The man next to her said, 'It's fun, isn't it, seeing it for the first time?'

When you could not see the ground, there was less fear of falling on to it. Dora sat back and thought she might be enjoying it.

After lunch, she went to sleep. She woke in a panic, not knowing where she was. The plane was jolting, bumping against the clouds. It felt like that sickening moment in a car when you realise you have a flat tyre on a lonely road at night, with either no jack, or no spare tyre.

'White knuckles again.' Mr Nelson saw her gripping the seat. 'Nothing to be scared of.'

But Dora was right and he was wrong. The Captain's voice came over the intercom. 'I hate to tell you this, folks.'

Dora gripped harder.

'It's O.K.,' Mr Nelson said. 'You don't have to jump yet.'

'We have developed some small oil pipe trouble. Nothing to worry about. But in view of possible bad weather ahead, we are going to take the precaution of detouring to Keflavik, Iceland, where repairs will be effected as soon as possible.'

'I'll be God damned,' Bob Nelson said.

'Do you think I'm a jinx?'

'First time this ever happened to me.'

'Last time I'm ever going to fly,' Dora said.

They dropped down through a brilliant sky and saw the coast of Iceland like a moon landscape, bare, stony, impregnable. They flew over some scattered houses and a tiny airstrip cut perilously close to a brown rocky range of hills.

They would never make it.

'You don't have to shut your eyes.' Mr Nelson took Dora's hand.

'When you go to your execution,' she said, 'they always blindfold you.'

After the anticlimax of a smooth landing, they were taken in an ordinary bus to an ordinary hotel. They were given the same kind of dinner they might have had at London Airport. Pea soup, roast chicken and coloured ice cream. Squares of stale bread. America was too far away. Dora would never get there.

In the morning when she looked out of her window, she knew she was in Iceland. On the stony land behind the hotel, a herd of thick coated, shaggy ponies, with scrubby manes and long tangled tails was nosing among the rocks, pulling at the green-grey lichen. They all looked sturdy and strong, although there didn't seem much for them to live on. At the back of the herd followed the great grandfather, grizzled nose, patchy mane, motheaten, most of his tail rubbed out at the top. He was skinny, with a combination of boniness and pot belly. A lively young pony came back to make runs and darts at him, jostling him, nipping him in the rear. The old pony stumbled and kicked out fretfully, and the young one charged him again from the other side.

Poor old fellow. In her mind, Dora put a halter on him and took him back to Follyfoot. He could be Eric the Red, after the old Icelandic adventurer.

When they took off again in the repaired plane, rising just in time over the mountains, Dora saw below them the herds of ponies dotted over the barren landscape. She leaned against the window and shut her eyes as the plane leaped upward with that powerful boost, like a good horse clearing a jump.

'I saw this old pony,' she told Bob Nelson, 'out of the hotel window.'

'You would.' She had told him about Follyfoot.

'He was old and scruffy, and the young ones were allowed to tease him because he would be dead soon. I wanted to build a crate and take him with us. He could be the first customer.'

She told him about Blank's dream of starting a Home of Rest for Horses in Elmwood, Massachusetts.

'I live near there,' he said. 'Maybe I could help.'

10

As the plane lost height and the ground became real, Dora looked down and began to ride the countryside. So many times in a train or a car, she had ridden an imaginary course alongside, taking hedges, enormous posts and rails, iron fences, clattering down roads, leaping wide streams to keep up with herself on wheels.

Now she rode the landscape from the air, covering a hundred miles in a few minutes, galloping down a straight wide path through a forest, up a hill and down and up again through what must be a fire break, through the gardens of low houses, racing her bay thoroughbred down a grassy track between two ribbons of highway where tiny coloured cars sped nowhere in both directions.

Fear returned when they landed at Boston. Dora could not remember what Blank looked like. Would he know her in the red and white suit her mother had bought her (uncreasable) to travel in?

Coming out of the customs hall, she searched the crowd. If he wasn't there, would they deport her as an undesirable alien? She saw him, and waved, but he turned away, because it wasn't him.

'See your friend?' Bob Nelson was behind her.

'No.'

But a voice was calling, 'Door!', and there he was, smaller than she remembered, struggling towards her through the embracing, laughing, crying, exclaiming crowd – 'Hey, Mom, how are ya?', 'Hi, Annie, How's my girl?', 'Oh, honey, I thought I'd never –'

'Hi, Door.'

'Hi, Blank.'

They stood and looked at each other, jostled by elbows and luggage. She had come all this way, and now there was nothing to say.

She turned to introduce Mr Nelson. 'He said he might help us with –' But before he could shake hands, Bob Nelson was pounced on by a woman and a young man, both handsome, tanned, assured, who bore him away, laughing and chattering.

'The Nelsons,' Blank said. 'They live near us.'

'You know them?'

'Everybody knows *of* them. But they wouldn't know me.'

'Oh, Blank.' Dora could talk now. 'You haven't changed a bit.'

He smiled, seeing beyond the red and white uncreasable suit and the new haircut. 'Nor have you, Door.'

'No Handle.'

Blank was proud to show Dora America. They went through an endless tunnel under the harbour, and on to a highway where four lanes of cars raced furiously. The traffic was overwhelming, but Dora was not doing the white knuckle clutch. Blank's car was so large and upholstered that it insulated you, like a tank. And she was too tired to be frightened.

'What do you think of it, huh?' Blank kept asking, but she was too tired to take much in.

At last they turned off on to a side road and drove through a lovely country of farms and fields and white wooden houses. There were quite a lot of horses. Blank showed her where the

Nelsons lived, a rambling old house with a complex of stable buildings, white railed paddocks and a riding ring.

'Wow.' Dora yawned. 'And we held hands over Iceland.'

The Blankenheimers' house was smaller, neater, the garden disciplined, chairs set formally on a stone terrace. Three cars in the shiny black drive. Were they arriving in the middle of a party? Blank stopped in front of the garage, which was a miniature replica of the house, with false upper windows and chimneys.

'Where are the horses?' Dora asked.

'My racehorses, they're at a stud in Connecticut. I've only Robin around here now. I keep him at Chuckie Fiske's stable, down the road a piece. Tremendous woman, Chuckie is. Knows it all.'

Dora had had experience with tremendous women who knew it all, and could make you feel you knew nothing, even if you knew more than they did. She was beginning to feel hopelessly tired.

Blank took her through the garage towards a door which led into the kitchen.

'Come along in,' he said. 'You're very welcome to my home.'

Dora tried to smile, but her face stretched into a tremendous yawn, like the jaw-breaking yawns of Stroller in the mornings, dribbling saliva from the vast ridged cavern of his hungry mouth. As Blank looked at her, she turned her head away to hide the yawn and yawned straight into the face of a woman coming to meet her through the kitchen.

'Hello there,' said Mrs Blankenheimer.

'Sorry,' Dora said, 'I'm terribly tired.'

'Of course you are. I know what it's like. Every time I fly the Atlantic, I just about die.'

'You only flew it once,' her husband pointed out mildly.

'And I just about died.'

She was short, like he was, a little anxious, with some bright make up that was supposed to make her look younger, but didn't.

'I'll fix you something to eat,' she said.

'I'm not really hungry.' Dora felt rather faint.

'Of course you are. I'll fix you a stack of pancakes and some bacon.'

'No, really, I –' But Mrs Blank had headed for the stove. Dora saw that this was her style of welcome, and she had better go along with it.

She sat in a kind of booth in the kitchen, which was hung with copper pans and jelly moulds and trailing plants and ornamental notices which said things like, 'BE REASONABLE. DO IT MY WAY', and, 'ABANDON HUNGER, ALL YE WHO ENTER HERE'.

Mr Blank sat beside her with a cup of coffee.

'Can we go and see Robin after the pancakes?' Dora asked.

'Sure.'

But she did not really care about that. She suddenly felt terribly homesick. As she sat at the polished table in this clean kitchen with neat Mrs Blankenheimer making a stack of pancakes, she thought of the big round table in the messy, aromatic kitchen at Follyfoot. Anna lifting the kettle off the old stove. Callie doing homework with a fistful of bread and butter. The Colonel with one of the puppies on his lap and another asleep on his foot. Steve with his dirty boots on the bar of the table and his dark hair flopped forward over the book on genetics that he was studying for his future horse breeding career. Even the noise of Ron's motorbike starting up – the whole familiar picture swam in her head like a dream. As Mrs Blankenheimer put the plate of pancakes on the table and set the maple syrup beside it, Dora fell forward fast asleep with her hair in the butter.

II

SHE slept right through that night and halfway through the next day. Mrs Blankenheimer drove her to Blank's office so that he could take her to see Robin.

In his office, surrounded by drawing boards and bits of pipe and nails and plywood and calendars from plumbers and up-hosterers, Blank seemed more at his ease. He wore stained overalls with his name Earl embroidered on the pocket, and he was called Earl by his workmen.

He took off his overalls and put on a hat – he never went anywhere without a hat – and drove Dora to Chuckie Fiske's stable. Although it was late afternoon, it was still very hot. Dora had never been so hot in her life.

The road took them between wide fields with stone walls and white fences. They stopped at an enormous barn of indoor loose boxes, with several brightly painted horse trailers in the yard. The horses were all inside. In this heat, they were kept in during the fly-pestering days. Each stall had a thick bed of clean wood shavings, an automatic watering trough, name on door, halter hanging outside.

At Follyfoot, the horses' names were on the doors, but some of them were mis-spelled, because Callie had helped to paint them two years ago when she couldn't spell. 'Lancalott'. 'Jakc and Jymmi' on the door of the box the donkey shared with the two shetlands.

Dora started writing a letter in her mind to Steve:

'When I get back, let's smarten up the stable a bit, do some painting, get the Colonel to put in automatic watering.'

Poor man, he could hardly afford new buckets.

330

They went into the tack room, where the saddles were on racks with linen covers and the bridles had not only the bits but the leather polished. Chuckie Fiske was reading a magazine, wearing cotton pants and a sleeveless shirt that showed her brawny brown arms.

'Hi,' she said without putting down the magazine.

'This is Dora,' said Blank. 'The girl I told you about, from England.'

'The one who gave you the idea about the old horses?' Chuckie lowered the magazine to inspect.

'Yes,' said Dora eagerly. 'We –'

'Economically unsound,' added the woman who knew it all, 'with the price of feed and hay hitting the roof.'

Blank cleared his throat and changed the subject. 'May we go see Robin?'

'Help yourself. He's raring' to go. He's short of work.'

'Can I ride him?' Dora asked. Mrs Blank had told her to come in jeans.

'Depends if you can ride or not.'

Chuckie reminded Dora of herself when she was bluntly rude to people without meaning it.

As they walked down the aisle between the loose boxes, a girl with cropped red hair pressed a switch and a cloud of insecticide came down over the backs of the horses.

'Are the flies very bad here?' Dora asked her.

'Mosquitoes too. They're a real pest. They carry the virus of encephalitis, you know?'

'I don't think we have that in England.'

'Lucky you. We're scared of another epidemic this year.'

'Here he is,' said Blank, as a bay head with a white star came over a door that said, "King Kong". 'Why is Robin in the wrong box?'

'That's not your horse.' The red-haired girl tried to catch

Dora's eye with a 'some people' look, but Dora wasn't having any.

Robin was in the next box. 'They are alike,' she said, although they weren't, except for being bay with a white star.

King Kong was just a horse – Robin was a dream. He was part thoroughbred, part quarter horse. He had the fineness and quality of a thoroughbred, and the short back, square chest and strong quarters of the Western cattle horse. He was, like Dora's dream horse, a bright bay with a crescent-shaped star and two white feet.

He tossed his head about and his ears moved alertly back and forth every time one of the other horses snorted or banged the side of its box. But when Dora went in to him, he examined her very gently, blowing into her hand, and going over her hair with his nose to see what kind of animal she was.

He had looked a little nervous when she was standing outside the door, but a horse's expression can visibly soften when he feels reassured. Dora saw that gentle, almost smiling look in the dark blue eye that means a horse who relates well to people.

'He likes you, Door,' Blank said.

'I like him.' Dora was enchanted. All of a sudden, she wasn't homesick any more. Before, her mind had looked forward over the next three weeks, telling herself that if she could hang on for twenty-one days, it would be time to go home. Now when her mind looked forward, the date of leaving seemed like a threat, the twenty-one days not nearly long enough.

Dora went back to the tack room to get the saddle, which had a polished brass plate under the cantle saying JODY BLANKENHEIMER. Chuckie Fiske did not lower the magazine or take her feet off the table, but as Dora went out of the door with saddle and bridle, she said, 'Watch it, kid. He's pretty fresh.'

Dora rode by nature, not by technique. She had learned from horses, and there had not been many good ones. If she knew a horse well, she could figure out how to handle him, but she was naturally nervous with a strange horse, if she felt he knew more than she did.

Blank led her out to the gate of the white-railed riding ring, as if he were leading one of his racehorses to the paddock. Two girls in shorts and pony tails who were sunning themselves in the grass, chewing gum, sat up to watch, Dora was sorry to see. She was sorrier still to see Chuckie Fiske come out of a side door of the stable and wander over to the ring.

Dora let Robin walk round the track with a loose rein. He felt edgy, very much on his toes.

'Let him walk around on a loose rein,' Chuckie ordered, as Dora came level.

'I am,' Dora muttered to Robin.

Robin's back was a bit humped. When she felt him relax, Dora let him trot on.

'Let him trot on there!' shouted Chuckie. The girls in the grass giggled.

At the far end of the ring, a riding trail went off into the wood. A woman on a big narrow chestnut came down this trail, riding 'saddle seat', with her stirrups long and her legs stuck out. The horse was artificially showy, feet and tail carriage, exaggeratedly high. They stopped at the end of the ring and watched Dora.

Robin trotted out with easy elegance, toes just slightly turned in – that was the quarter horse in him – stride long and swinging. That was the thoroughbred. His head was set just right, the neck flexed high. He had obviously been beautifully schooled.

'Canter him!' Chuckie called.

Oh God, she couldn't make him canter. She squeezed, she

333

sat down in the saddle. She chirruped. She said 'Canter', under her breath, in case Chuckie disapproved. She turned Robin in a small circle for the canter lead, but all he did was trot faster.

'Don't you know how to set him into a canter?' Chuckie called out.

'No,' said Dora to Robin.

She pulled him back to a walk, pretending she did not want to canter. When she got to where the woman sat on the showy chestnut, the woman said, 'Hey, you the girl from England?'

Dora pulled Robin up.

'I'll give you a tip,' the woman said. 'American horses only canter out of a walk. Pull him back. Get him on his toes. Just use your outside leg and you got it made.'

Robin stretched his neck towards the chestnut.

'Get going,' the woman said. 'She'll kill us if they squeal and strike.'

Dora walked, jogged a few collected steps, sat down in the saddle, squeezed with her outside leg, and Robin moved into the smoothest controlled canter she had ever felt. On a horse like this, she could be a good rider. She was not even aware of Chuckie leaning on the rail, of Blank with his arms folded, nodding happily, of the girls in the grass lying back again now that the fun was over.

Robin's canter was so creamy that Dora felt glued to the saddle, her torso moving rhythmically as he moved. She took him diagonally across the ring and off again in the other direction. He did a flying change of leads as if he had invented it. Dora had never ridden so well. She had never ridden a horse like this. Robin. She was in love.

12

THAT evening, Dora met Blank's daughter Jody.

She had gone up to her room to take a shower after her ride, and as so often happens in strange houses, when she came downstairs, there was nobody about. There was a smell of something in the oven, but Mrs Blank was not in the kitchen. Blank was not in his den. Neither of them was out on the terrace.

Dora wandered into the tidy living room and did a tour of the family pictures. The Blanks at their wedding, the bridegroom looking as if it were a funeral. A beautiful baby. A beautiful toddler. An eager small girl on a show pony, dressed to the teeth, rosettes on her bridle. The same girl, older, on Robin with his mane and tail plaited, also with rosettes.

'That was in the bad old days.'

The girl in the photograph had come into the room, older now, tattier, the eager look replaced by an air of disillusion, eyes heavily made up in a white face, long brown dress with the hem undone.

'I'm Jody.' She sat down and kicked off thong sandals. Her feet were as dirty as Dora's were at Follyfoot. They were clean in America, where she did not clean stables.

Ill at ease with the girl, her mind jetted back across the Atlantic and saw Steve and Slugger and Ron with the forks and barrows, mucking out.

No. If it was 8 p.m. here, it would be 1 a.m. in England. The only person who could conceivably be mucking out now would be Callie, who had once got up in her sleep and been found by Steve when he came home late from a party. She was pushing a wheelbarrow in pyjamas and bare feet, her eyes fixed on nothing.

She and Jody sat on opposite sides of the room and looked at each other. They were about the same age, but there was nothing to say.

'I – er, I rode your horse today,' Dora said at last.

'Oh yeah? What d'you think of him?'

'He's fantastic. Best horse I ever rode. He's beautifully schooled. Is that your doing?'

'Somewhat, I guess. I did work on him last summer. Nothing else to do then.'

'What is there to do this summer?' Dora asked.

'I go around with this group, that's what's to do. Vince and the It. They're kinda terrific.'

'Do you mind me riding Robin?' Dora asked.

'Hell, no. Why should I care?'

'Your father said – said that it would be all right.'

'No, I mean, honest,' said Jody. 'I'm glad you came.'

'Thanks.'

'Keeps Dad happy, what the hell? Keeps him out of my hair.'

The Blanks came in from the garden where they had been picking lettuce. They had steak and salad. Dora was famished. The food was marvellous. Much too much of it. She wanted to wrap up the rest of the steak and ship it back to Steve.

'You should see how well Dora rides Robin,' Blank said.

'Oh –' Dora shot a look at Jody. 'Anyone can ride him.'

'You and Jody can. He goes well for girls. They'll miss you,' he said to his bored daughter, 'at the County Fair. First year you won't have been.'

'First year I haven't been a dumb kid, let's face it.'

336

'It's a pity though. All the big exhibitors will be at the Three Day Show. Good opportunity to clean up.'

'Oh Dad, for God's *sake*.'

A horn sounded outside and Jody got up and went out with a bang of the screen door.

'Why don't you let Dora show the horse, Earl, if she's so good?' Mrs Blank suggested.

'You want to, Door?' Blank's eyes were eager.

Oh no.

'Have to get Chuckie to school you a bit, of course.'

Oh *no*.

Chuckie Fiske's schooling was pretty brutal, but Dora learned a lot. She was to ride Robin in the class for Hunters under Saddle. She learned how to keep him on the rail, not get into a bunch with other horses, keep him relaxed yet moving strongly on, trot him collected, trot him extended, stop square after a hand gallop, back him straight.

Chuckie's method was short on praise and long on anguished yells. Dora was the only person who could contrive to have the perfect horse cantering on the wrong lead.

'Dorra!' shouted Chuckie. 'You British bungler! If you have to do that, for pity's sake change leads before the judge turns around and looks at you.'

'How can I tell when he's going to?'

'How can she tell?' Chuckie clutched her short grey hair and appealed to the sky. 'Anyone who isn't a total idiot can tell.'

Chuckie took Robin to the show in an enormous van with three or four of her other horses, and the gum-chewing girls who efficiently rode them.

When Dora arrived at the County Fair showgrounds with Blank, she couldn't believe her eyes. If these were the people left over after the cream had gone to the Three Day Show, what on earth must the cream look like?

She had never seen so many beautiful, well kept horses all together in one place. Robin, who was the best looking horse she had ever had any dealings with, looked unremarkable among the splendid thoroughbreds. The proud quarter horse blood which showed in his rounded quarters and crested neck and pigeon toes might be something that, if he were a person, he would want to disguise, like a thick waist or pimples.

Robin, however, was not at all crushed by such grand company. When Chuckie said, 'Throw a leg over him and work him out a bit,' Dora took him over to the edge of the showgrounds, where some girls were doing supple, minutely controlled circles and figures of eight. Robin bucked and squealed. He tossed his head, a relic of the days when he was what they called 'Western broke' in a lethal bit that punishes a horse if he tries to take hold, which is how Western horses learn to stop dead.

Dora went back to the van to put a martingale on Robin while she got him worked down to his usual controllable self.

A girl on a grey Welsh pony, serious and determined, was jumping back and forth over a bar, held by her father and an elder brother. As the pony jumped, high and neat, they raised the light bar skilfully to rap the fetlocks and make it pick up its back feet.

Dora stopped Robin to watch. The man looked round casually, then looked again and smiled.

'Hullo, there,' he said. 'I know you, don't I?' It was Bob Nelson, from the plane, the man she had been to Iceland with.

'How nice you look.' Dora was dressed in Jody's last year's

338

breeches and jacket and boots. 'I didn't know you rode in shows.'

'I don't,' Dora said. 'It's just for fun.'

'Of course. It's no use if it isn't fun,' Mr Nelson said, his words contradicted by the fiercely determined girl, who rode up saying, 'Gee, Dad, if Colombo doesn't win, I'll kill myself.'

Her brother said to Dora, 'Nice horse that bay. Very good type.' He was a tall boy, slow and easy going, shorts and big knees and a flop of fair hair, and one of those voices that is born to have it easy. 'He certainly goes well for you.'

He grinned generously, and Dora grinned back under Jody's riding cap, flattered.

If Steve were like that, casual, assured, with one of those voices, would she like him better? On her mind's screen came a picture of her last sight of Steve, going off with Dolly in the blue cart to mend fences, hair unbrushed, clothes looking as if he'd slept in them, waving goodbye to her not with a grin, but with the kind of lost, forlorn look he used to wear when he first came to Follyfoot from a life of trouble. No, she wouldn't like him better.

Watching the classes before hers, Dora became increasingly sick and nervous. If she actually threw up, would they let her miss her class? Chuckie had talked about not making a mistake in front of the judge, but the riders Dora watched did not seem to make any mistakes at all. It was hard to see how, before the end of the class, the judge eliminated some and decided who would stay to be placed.

'Come on – hurry!' Blank, in his stylish horse show suit and straw hat called her back to the van to have Robin polished and her boots repolished, a hair net put over her protesting hair, and the number eighty-two tied round her waist. Jody's boots were too tight. Her dark blue jacket was too narrow in the shoulders. Her cap was too big, and stuffed with handkerchiefs.

339

Dora was uncomfortable and scared. She heard Chuckie Fiske's voice calling, 'Hey, Dorra!' but paid no attention. She didn't want last minute instructions.

'The last time I'll get conned into riding in a horse show,' she told Robin as they joined the line going into the ring. It was a glorious day. The fierce heat had gone from the air. A breeze pushed small firm clouds across the very blue sky of New England. A day to be out with sandwiches in one pocket and an orange in the other, riding the hills beyond Follyfoot, with no plan at all except getting back for supper.

When she was in the ring with the other horses, Dora saw that Robin could hold his own. Some of the thoroughbreds were a bit weedy. One had a very short stride. Another poked its head. Another was being clumsily ridden by a boy who let him bend in a curve at corners.

When the loudspeaker said, 'Canter', Robin slid smoothly into his creamy canter. The brown with the blaze was on the wrong lead. Hooray. Dora prayed with fleeting spite that the judge would notice, then forgot everybody else to concentrate on showing Robin off as he deserved.

'All right, all right.' Much too soon, when she was beginning to enjoy herself, although the boots were giving her hell, the ring steward called them into the middle of the ring.

The announcer's voice came over the microphone. 'The following are excused. One hundred and twenty. Nineteen. Thirty-four. Thirty-six . . .' Confident that Robin had gone well enough to be kept back among the finalists, Dora could afford to feel sorry for those who weren't. 'One thirty eight. Eighty-two.' It was like a blow to the pit of the stomach. 'The rest of you get back out on the rail, on your left circle.'

Dora rode out of the ring at the end of the string of riders who did not seem to care. She saw Blank's disappointed face and turned the other way, saw the amiable grin of the Nelson boy, about to say 'Too bad,' swerved away and almost ran over Chuckie Fiske sitting on a camp stool drinking beer.

'It wasn't fair,' Dora said childishly. 'He went beautifully.'

'Didn't toss his head one bit did he? Maybe,' Chuckie took a long swallow of beer, and fixed Dora with an eye over the can, 'maybe that's why they don't allow martingales in showing classes.'

'Is that why I was kicked out?'

'Sure was.'

Dora remembered Chuckie calling her for last minute instructions. She pulled Robin away, went back to the van to take off his saddle and bridle and walked away with him in a halter to let him eat grass and forget.

13

Dora was pretty resilient. When she was knocked down by life, she could usually find some way of bouncing herself back up again.

When she got over being angry at herself about the martingale, she bounced back with the thought that at least she could say that she could have won if she hadn't worn it, which was better than saying that she couldn't win. And she and Robin had done well, a good partnership. Only ten more days with this horse. She would ride every day and then say goodbye to him for ever and go back to Willy the mule, and tell tales about her partnership with the bay horse, which no one would quite believe.

That evening after dinner, a terrible row blazed up at the Blankenheimers' house.

Jody's boy friend Vince, of Vince and the It, was there, lounging on a terrace chair and picking skin off the soles of his feet.

Although she didn't like him, Mrs Blank was pleased that Jody and he had stayed home for dinner. She had made barbecued spare ribs and pineapple upside down cake, much too heavy and rich for this weather.

Mosquitoes were beginning to bite. 'We'll have to go indoors,' someone said, but they were too full of food to bother.

Mrs Blank got up to get the can of insecticide. She sprayed it over the remains of Jody's cake. Jody didn't want it, but she said, 'Hey, Mom, cut it out,' in her ugliest Hey Mom voice.

'You can't be too careful,' her mother fussed. 'I heard on the television that the suspected cases of encephalitis could be the start of an epidemic.'

'Scaremongering by the media,' Vince scoffed. He didn't watch television.

'What do you know about it?' Mrs Blank snapped at him.

'Don't snap at Vince,' Jody snapped at her.

'Two kids have been taken to hospital because they were bitten by mosquitoes that may have bitten infected horses. They could die, those kids.'

'Do you know 'em?' Vince asked.

'No,' Blank said. 'But they're somebody's kids, and they may be dying.'

'That's so typical of the both of you,' Jody said. 'You waste a lot of useless sentiment on a couple of strangers, and ignore what's going on with your own daughter.'

'Go on.' Vince nudged her with his big toe. 'Tell 'em.'

'It's like this, Dad,' Jody began belligerently. 'I gotta have a new car.'

'What's wrong with the V.W.?'

'It was O.K. once, when I was a kid, but look Dad, it's falling apart.'

'It's only a year old,' her father said mildly. 'If you'd taken a bit more care of it, remembered to put oil in once in a while –'

'I've seen this fantastic white Jaguar,' Jody said. 'I could get it on a really good trade-in for the Volks. Only need to add a couple of thousand dollars.'

'I'm sorry,' her father said. 'I don't know that we can afford that kind of thing this year.'

'I thought you were doing pretty well,' Vince said offensively. 'Putting up houses at the same cost, and raising the price of them to the customer.'

'Business isn't what it was.' Blank, who detested rows, didn't rise to the insult. 'People haven't the money to buy and it's harder to get bank loans.'

'You bought Mom the big Buick at Christmas,' Jody said.

'Now listen here.' Her father suddenly got angry, an unusual sight, if not very terrifying. 'If I want to buy my wife a car, who's going to stop me?'

'Not I.' Jody shrugged her shoulders. 'I merely said why shouldn't you buy your daughter one too?'

Dora sat in the middle of the row uncomfortably, her head going back and forth as if she were at a tennis match. If she had talked like this to her father at home, he'd have thrown her into the street.

'And if we're so poor,' Jody persisted, 'then how come you're spending all that money on those racehorses. And how come you're pushing this crazy idea of buying a farm and filling it with old crocks, just so people will say, "Look at that noble Earl Blankenheimer?"'

'Jody, please, honey –' her mother said nervously. 'The horses are his pleasure.'

'If he'd spend a bit more on his family and a bit less on his horses . . . Chuckie is ripping you off right and left, Dad. She's always charged you too much. But even she thinks you should sell Robin.'

'Perhaps you should.' Mrs Blank was also nervous of Chuckie, who had once nearly ridden her down on a great black horse, crying, 'Get out of the way!' 'It is an unnecessary extravagance now that Jody –'

'You could get two thousand for Robin easy,' Jody said. 'Then I could have the Jag.'

'I'll never sell that horse,' Blank said. 'He means a lot to me.' He looked at Jody. 'He means to me the time when you were a happy kid, and loved the outdoors. No bitterness. Where does that bitterness come from?'

He sounded so sad, but Jody only said childishly, 'It comes from not having a Jaguar.'

Meaning well, Mrs Blank bumbled in with, 'The Nelsons would buy him, maybe. They like his looks. Dora told me. The boy, Michael said he was a good type.'

Attacked by both his wife and daughter, Blank looked trapped. His eyes darted back and forth, seeking escape, and fastened on Dora.

'Rather than sell him,' he said, 'to the Nelsons or anyone, I'd give him away.'

'Jeez.' Vince closed his heavy-lidded eyes, and leaned back to meditate.

Dora stood up to clear plates off the table. She couldn't bear it any longer.

'People might be suspicious if you give a horse –' Mrs Blank began.

'Dora wouldn't be,' Blank said suddenly.

Dora tripped on the edge of the long skirt and dropped knives and forks on the stone terrace.

'I'll give him to Dora.'

'But what – I mean, how – I mean, I couldn't –'

'I'll fly him over to England for you. Pay his keep. I was going to make the Colonel a donation anyway.'

'Oh now, Earl –'

'But listen, Dad –'

Before Dora could answer, Blank's wife and daughter were at him. Vince woke up and said, 'Hey, lookit –'

'Yes.' Blank nodded, more confident than Dora had ever seen him. 'That's exactly what I'll do. I'll see about getting a place in a cargo plane. I'll send Robin to England for you, Door.'

•   •   •   •   •

Dora carried the plates out to the kitchen. Usually, she helped Mrs Blank load them into the dishwasher. This evening, she could only leave them in the sink and go up to her room, her face on fire, her heart thudding.

She had used her last air letter. She found a postcard – a postcard, to convey earth-shaking news – and wrote to Steve:

Back on the 15th as planned. Remember that horse I wrote to you about? Blank gave him to me. He's sending him over by air.'

Just like that, laconic, businesslike, as if she belonged to a world where horses flew the Atlantic every week.

'Love to everyone, wearing fur, hair, skin, feathers, scales (Callie's neglected fish). *Dora & Robin.'*

14

In his bedroom over the tack room at Follyfoot, Steve was writing to Dora, on a postcard which Callie's class had sold at school last year in aid of endangered insects.

On most postcards, the picture is the best side to look at. The other side says, *'Wish you were here. Los Fritos has fantastic food. Your Dad has been a bit queer ever since we came. Don't forget to water the budgie.'*

But some postcards carry world-shaking news.

'Dottie had a foal,' Steve wrote. Foal? Colt? Filly? What did you call it when it was a donkey? He crossed out foal and wrote, *'Dottie had a baby. It's name is Polka Dot. Polly for short. Love, Steve.'*

Impossible to convey on a postcard the surprise of what had happened.

Dottie, the little chocolate donkey Mr Blank had bought at the market, had always been quite plump. Nobody had guessed why. Two days ago, she had begun to behave strangely. She would lie down, get up, move away from Don to another part of the field, kick out at him if he came after her, lie down again, get up, move off.

'You know what,' the Colonel said, when Steve called him out to look at Dottie. 'I think she's going into labour.'

'Shall I bring her in?'

'No, leave her out. It's warm. Leave her alone. It's best that way.'

Steve put her in a field by herself. Early the next morning, he got up and went out through the misty freshness of the new day to see how she was. At first he couldn't find her. He walked among the bushes at the bottom of the field, and then he found her by the hedge, a tiny chocolate foal in the grass, Dottie standing over it, sheltering it with her head.

In a corner of the orchard, there was a small enclosure which they had fenced in when Miss America's back was still raw, and she couldn't be turned out with another horse. Steve and Slugger got some old planks and knocked up a shed with an open doorway, so that Dottie and Polly could go in and out as they liked.

Folly, who was in the orchard with Specs, spent most of the time with his head through the fence, trying to make contact with the new phenomenon. Folly and Specs were alone in the orchard, not because the old horses bothered Folly, but because Folly was so bold and teasing that he bothered the old horses.

Polly was everybody's new mania. Callie was out there half the day playing with her, cuddling her, holding her in her lap on the grass, taking her and Dottie into the house to lie on the rug in the Colonel's study so that Anna could make a sketch of them.

Don was an outdoors donkey, but Dottie had been coming into the house ever since Blank brought her here. She had appeared at the open side door one day, questing with her white nose and violet eyes. When invited in, she lay down in front of the fire like a dog. Donkeys are naturally clean. If you don't keep one indoors more than an hour or two, you can call it house trained.

Dottie was such a calm mother, she didn't mind how many people handled her baby. Everyone was sad that Dora wasn't there to see Polly brand new like this.

'Poor old Dora.' Steve wasn't jealous of her trip to America any more. 'It's bad luck on her, missing all the fun.'

One day the postman came when everybody but Steve was out. He saw the red van stop in the lane, and went out to get the letters. A handful of bills, advertisements for veterinary remedies and agricultural tools, a postcard with a picture of the Queen Elizabeth in Boston harbour.

He turned it over. Dora had addressed it to him, although a postcard was public property.

'. . . *Remember that horse I wrote to you about? Blank gave him to me. He's sending him over by air.*'

Steve walked slowly back into the yard and sat down on the edge of the water trough to read the postcard again. It was going to take time to adjust to this before he told everybody. Dora with a horse of her own? The Dora he knew was always scrounging a ride, arguing with Callie over her right to the Cobbler, trying to get him to let her ride Miss America, waiting for Hero to be sound, making do with Willy the mule. Dora with a quarter horse-thoroughbred of her own – that would take some getting used to.

15

THE day that Dora got Steve's postcard with the news of the birth of the donkey foal, the younger of the children who were in hospital with encephalitis died. The other one was not expected to live.

In the western part of the state, a sixteen-year-old boy was taken to hospital with a disease of the central nervous system, suspected to be due to Eastern equine encephalitis. Doctors issued statements to say this was not true, but everyone was nervous. Newspaper, radio and television stories fanned the anxiety into a widespread encephalitis scare in New England.

Two or three horses had developed the disease and died in a few days. Horses that had been exposed to infected mosquitoes might have to be put down.

This was not in the area where Robin was, but every horse along the eastern Atlantic seaboard must have two immunization shots.

'Has Robin had his?' Dora worried.

'Oh, sure,' Blank said. 'Chuckie always sees to things like worming and shots. She knows it all.'

He and Dora went to the airport outside Boston to arrange for space in a cargo plane for Robin. There might not be a place available for some time. If a vacancy came up, they would notify Blank at once.

The countryside where the Blanks lived was gradually being swallowed by building developments and creeping suburbs. Dora and Blank had looked at some possible land for a Home of Rest, but properties with grazing space cost the earth, and people whom Blank approached for contributions had regarded him with sympathy or amused tolerance, but no direct offers of help.

Blank didn't mention it to Chuckie any more. He went to see the vet. 'How many horses have been put down this month?'

'Around thirty or forty, I think. It's getting really bad.'

'I don't mean because of the encephalitis scare. I mean because they were too old or unsound to work.'

'I could get you the figures. Dozens a month, I should say.'

'What would you think of a farm where they could be well taken care of, so they could stay alive?' Blank asked.

'Look, Mr Blankenheimer.' The vet was a sharp-featured young man with thick spectacles and a businesslike manner, more like a banker than a vet. 'This country is overrun with people *and* animals. If you ever see a paper bag in the road, in the spring, drive around it. It's likely to be full of puppies or kittens no one wants. Food supplies are getting scarcer. Pretty soon, half the population will be starving. Does it make sense to you to keep alive animals that have come to the end of their lives?'

'They've only come to the end of their lives because their owners say they have,' Dora argued. 'At Follyfoot, where we keep the old horses –'

'It may be all right in Britain,' the vet said rather patronizingly, 'but I don't see it going over here.'

Because Mr Nelson had told Dora that he might be able to help, Blank approached him about the sale of a sixty acre farm that the Nelson family owned on the side of a hill. Mr Nelson was genial about it, but still vague. The land was valuable, but he might make a fair price, as his contribution to the cause.

Give him a bit of time. He'd have to talk to agents. Blank would hear from him.

'You know what *I* hear, Earl?' Mrs Blank read all the papers and listened to all the local radio stations. 'I hear that there's a housing developer after that land, and his offer is out of sight.'

'The Nelsons wouldn't do that,' Blank said. 'They're trying to preserve this countryside, not destroy it.'

'Money talks,' Mrs Blank said sagely.

'They'd never sell to anyone like that. Not without telling me.'

'Why not? They don't care, people who have it all. Why should they?'

Mrs Blank's depressing attitudes had been undermining her husband's spirit for years. He responded much better to Dora's attitude, which was that life was good and full of hope, and he could still have as much fun as he did when he was a boy in Indiana.

'Want to climb a tree?' she asked. 'I was in the wood yesterday, and there's this tall pine with branches like a ladder. From the top, you can see all over the neighbourhood. You can see the Ellsmiths' swimming pool. Their kids are washing the dogs in it.'

'Climb a tree?' Mrs Blankenheimer said. 'At your age, Earl?'

'Come on,' he said to Dora. 'Let's go!'

From the top of the tree, you could see not only the Ellsmiths' pool, which was being ruined for swimming by the addition of a great quantity of detergent and shaggy dogs, but the flat roof of the bicycle factory where the secretaries were sunbathing in their lunch hour, and Chuckie Fiske's riding ring, where Chuckie herself was out in denims, erecting large solid fences in preparation for the jumping lesson she was going to give Dora when the sun went down.

Robin had been well schooled as a jumper, starting slow and low and working up to heights. The trouble was that Dora had missed the starting slow bit, and was expected to be at the three foot six point where Robin was. She would prefer to wait till she got him home and start with him slow and easy over the pottery Follyfoot jumps, but Chuckie said she had her reputation to consider, and if the horse was going to England, Dora had got to be in shape to show him off properly.

In the Ellsmiths' pool, the children splashed and screamed and wrestled with the dogs. They had just been joined by a couple of ducks and the grandmother in a frilled black suit and floppy hat.

'Want to go for a swim?' she asked Blank, who was hanging grimly onto a branch below her.

The beach was about fifteen miles away. If they dawdled there, she might get back too late for her jumping lesson.

Mrs Blank had gone to a meeting of the Garden Club, where they taught plants and flowers to mind their place and be under control of the people who fed them with expensive fertilizers. Dora and Blank made sandwiches. Dora always felt rather guilty doing things in this spotless kitchen, which was a sacred place to Mrs Blank. She cleaned the stove after every meal, and never left dirty plates piled up. Dora had politely invited her to stay when she next came to England. She hoped that the state of the kitchen at Follyfoot, with its constant succession of meals and snacks, wouldn't spoil her visit.

Blank and Door found an uncrowded space at the end of the beach.

'Let's have lunch first and then swim.' Dora was starving.

'No, you have to swim before you eat.' Blank's mother had evidently given him the same orders as Dora's had. They had taken root in him, but not with her.

In her new red swim suit, she ran across the soft fine sand and

353

plunged ecstatically into the incoming waves. This side of the Atlantic was warmer than it ever was in England. The waves were just big enough to plunge into or dive over, or to ride on the swell with your arms out and your face to the burning sun.

She looked back to see that Blank had stayed near the edge of the sea, paddling about in the shallow water like a neat and careful dog. You almost expected to see the tip of a tail following after.

After lunch, Blank spread his beach towel out as neatly as if he were making a hospital bed, and laid himself down to sleep. He woke with a start as a large labrador jumped over his head, spattering sand in his face.

'What the –'

'Sorry!' The tall, big-jointed boy running by the water's edge looked back. 'Oh – gee, I am sorry.' He recognized Dora. It was Michael Nelson, with his sister who had ridden the grey Welsh pony at the show.

They parked their towels and snorkelling gear a little way along the beach. Dora lay down again, but she became increasingly bothered by a desire to get up and run down to the water in her new red swim suit. And she genuinely would like another swim.

'Let's go in again.' Blank was still rubbing sand out of his eyes. 'Wash yourself off with sea water.'

'Just a quick one then. We'll have to be getting back if you're to be on time for your jumping lesson.'

The tide had gone out quite a bit. After Dora had swum some way out, her feet touched bottom and she came out on a sandbank. The water was only up to her knees. She looked back and waved at Blank, splashing about between her and the shore.

'Come on!' she called, prancing about on the sandbank. 'It's quite shallow here.' She pranced down the other side of the sandbank, and out into the deeper water.

Looking round, she saw Blank paddling towards her. She stopped swimming and lay on her back to wait for him. She was floating blissfully, watching the deepening blue of the sky as the sun dropped, and listening to the desperate cries of seagulls. She became aware that there was a smaller cry under the clamour of the gulls. She let down her legs and looked back. Without knowing it, she had floated away from the sandbank. Blank, trying to reach her, had stepped off the bank into the deeper water. He was floundering out of his depth, coughing and spitting and waving his arms.

At school, Dora had passed her Life Saving certificate in the public baths. Ever since, she had hoped to meet someone who was drowning, so that she could hook her arms round their shoulders and tow them safely to shore amid the cheers of the onlookers.

She yelled at Blank, 'Hang on, I'm coming!' and swam as fast as she could towards him. It took all her energies to reach him. The current that had floated her out was very strong. When she finally reached him, he was still afloat, but gasping and panicking.

He clutched at her hair, and she went under. She came up striking out, to keep him from doing it again. He clutched at her neck. 'Stop it, Blank!' She beat at his hands, but he was petrified and could not understand.

'Come on, Blank, it's Door. I'll save you. We'll do it . . . the two of us . . . Blank! No handle!' She shouted in his ear, and he relaxed a little.

She turned him on his back and swam, towing him, kicking mightily to reach the sandbank. Blank had gone limp. Small waves washed over his face. From time to time, Dora glanced round and saw in agony that she was making no headway against the current. Her muscles were so tired that all she could do was just go on kicking automatically, without conscious effort. Blank was very still and heavy. He must have passed out.

The thought came to her that he might be dead. She was so exhausted that she could think of that calmly. How would she break the news to his wife?

Swimming half in a dream, scenes drifted in and out of her head. Herself going through the house to the terrace where Mrs Blank sat with a glass of iced tea and the evening paper and the radio news. '*This afternoon, at Belair Beach ...*' Trying to find Jody at her college. Getting Vince on the telephone. '*He's what? I can't understand you.*' Vince made a big show of not being able to understand Dora's accent. Would she have to stay for the funeral? All she wanted was to be on dry land at the top of her Follyfoot hill.

She should never have come. Never. The words matched her desperate kicks. She had known she shouldn't come. Hadn't she said so? She had thought then that it was fear of flying, but she knew now that it was a premonition of her death by drowning.

If I drown, she thought sadly, I won't be able to show Robin to Steve.

There was a splashing all round her. Arms and legs. A lot of power in the water. The Nelson boy got Blank away from her, turned him on his side with his head propped on his shoulder, and swam with a powerful stroke towards the shore. Dora, her aching arms relieved of the weight, managed to make it somehow to the sandbank. On the bank, the boy put Blank's still body on his shoulders and carried him in. Dora followed and was almost knocked down by the labrador leaping and barking at the edge of the waves.

.   .   .   .   .

They left Blank's car in the car park, and Michael Nelson took him and Dora home. She sat in the back with Blank wrapped in beach towels and a sailing jacket. He dozed and woke and apologized and dozed again and woke again, to murmur, 'Such a nuisance,' and fall asleep again.

Dora kept falling into an exhausted doze, from which she was woken by Elizabeth saying things like, 'It's weird that he can't swim,' and, 'Didn't you know about the current on the ebb tide?' and, 'Good thing Michael and I were there.'

Once she said to Dora, 'It's a blast the way you talk. Are you from Australia or something?'

'Shut up, kid,' her brother said.

16

BLANK was all right, but he had to stay in bed and rest for the last few days of Dora's time in America. He wanted to get up and go to see Mr Nelson again about the sale of the farm land, but the doctor would not allow it.

Michael came to ask how he was. He sat in the kitchen with Dora and had a Coke. When she told Michael that she was leaving in two days, he said, 'What's he going to do then with that good looking bay horse, when you're not here to ride him?'

'He's giving it away.'

'Crazy waste. Who to?'

'Me. Robin's coming to England as soon as they have space on the plane.'

'Lucky,' said Michael.

The day before she was to leave, Dora went up to tell Blank that the air cargo people were on the telephone. An unexpected vacancy had come up, and Robin could fly in two days' time.

'Chuckie will take care of everything,' Blank said. 'She knows it all.'

Dora got on the bicycle and rode down to the stables. Chuckie was out in the ring, lungeing a young horse.

'Robin can fly the day after tomorrow,' Dora said. 'Could you get him to the airport?'

'No sweat,' said Chuckie.

'All his papers are in order, aren't they?' Dora asked. 'He's had his encephalitis shots, of course.'

'Dammit,' said Chuckie. She was still lungeing the young horse. Dora rotated with her in the middle of the ring. 'I was going to have the vet come next week to give the first shot to the ones who haven't had it.'

'Can't he come today? It's an emergency.'

'The horse wouldn't get the immunization certificate. He has to have two shots at an interval of ten days.'

'But Mrs Fiske!' Dora stood wringing her hands while the colt lolloped round them. 'If he doesn't get on that plane, it may be weeks before he can get another place. I want to get him on that plane so badly.'

'You and me too, babe.' Chuckie flicked the colt with the long whip. 'I want to get him out of here. I've got a year-round boarder waiting for that stall. I can't tie up space with a horse that isn't going to stay. I'm not in this business for my health, you know. Hey, Dorra, listen.' She began to haul in the colt, hand over hand on the lunge rein. 'I tell you what we'll do. . . .'

Next day, Mrs Blankenheimer drove Dora to the airport. Robin was to follow the next day.

When Mrs Blank came out to tell Dora it was time to leave, she was sitting with Blank on the terrace in the late afternoon sun. He was wrapped in a blanket, humped and sad.

'I will miss you, Door.'

'I can never thank you enough.'

They made rather stilted conversation, like people at railway stations, not knowing how to fill in the long goodbyes.

'You'll let me know, won't you, when you hear about the farm land,' Dora said for the tenth time.

'Yes,' said Blank for the tenth time. 'I'll let you know.'

Mrs Blank came out with the local paper. She put it on the table. Dora saw the headline of a front page story.

'NELSON FARMLAND SOLD TO DEVELOPER. CONSTRUCTION TO START SHORTLY.'

Dora picked up the paper and held it behind her back.

When she said goodbye to Blank, she said, 'And look, if you don't get that land in the end, don't worry. You'll find somewhere else just as good.'

'I don't know,' he said. 'Sometimes I wonder if there'll ever be a Follyfoot over here.'

'Of course there will.'

'I'd never do it without you.'

'I'll come back some time,' Dora said.

'Bye, Door.'

'Bye, Blank.'

She dropped the newspaper on an indoor table as they went through the house to get the car. Cowardly? Yes. But his goodbye face was bad enough without having to see it slapped by the newspaper headline.

17

STEVE brought the horse box to the airport, and he and Dora spent the night with a friend of his from the reform school, who was now married and living in a caravan on the edge of a muddy field.

They stayed up half the night talking. Dora was too tired and too excited to sleep. She told everything about America, as she would have to tell it again, to the Colonel and Anna and Callie and Slugger and Ron and Toby, giving different versions according to who was the audience.

In the morning, Steve couldn't start the horse box. He had left the lights on all night and the battery had run down. By the time they got to the airport, Robin had landed and been taken to the R.S.P.C.A. hostel among all the dogs, monkeys, tropical fish and pitiful plumed birds jammed side by side in travelling cages.

A girl in a blue overall with long yellow hair took them to the stable. She was about Dora's age. Lucky girl, working with such a variety of animals. As they went through a room, Dora stopped to look into a deep box full of feathers.

'Don't,' the girl said. 'It's horrible. I was so glad when you came because I was just going to have to unpack that box.'

'What's in it?'

The girl made a face. 'Hundreds of dead turkey chicks.'

Not so lucky.

Robin was in one of the big boxes at the rear of the hostel, wearing a smart blue and white summer sheet, legs wrapped in cotton wool and a new set of blue bandages, his gentle eye intelligently curious.

Dora held her hand out to him low. He dropped his nose into it, and she moved her fingers on the silky paler hair just above his nostril, his favourite place to be caressed.

Then he smelled her hair to reassure himself, and went all over Steve.

'A horse that likes the smell of people,' the blonde girl said, 'is always an easy one to handle. I wish King Kong could stay here.'

'I thought his name was Ro –' Steve began.

Dora cut in smoothly, 'That's his pet name. Isn't he great, Steve? I can't wait for you to ride him.'

Robin went into the horse box as if he had been going in and out of it all his life. All the way home, Dora had a prickly feeling in her back, knowing that he was behind her. As they came up the last bit of winding hill before the farm, she greeted each familiar tree, each bush and heap of stones, the place where Ron had skidded, showing off, and fallen off his motor bike, the hedge where Callie found the dead owl, as if she had been away for twenty years.

Callie was sitting on the wall at the side of the gate. She jumped down at once and climbed on the mudguard to look at Robin through the slats at the top of the horse box. Ron just happened to be out polishing the metal on his bike. The Colonel just happened to be crossing the yard. Slugger just happened to be painting the gate post. As the van drove through the gateway, Dora held out her hand to him.

'So she's done it again,' he said, in his Slugger way of talking at people rather than to them. 'All the way to the U-nited States, she's been, three thousand miles she's been, to bring us back another old crock.'

'Wait till you see him, Slug.' Dora let go of his hand, and they drove into the yard.

* * * * *

Robin seemed to be all right, apart from a slight cold and loss of appetite. Dora was suffering from jet lag too. After a few days, she rode him out to get him loosened up, and used to the new landscape.

He peered a lot at stones, and white fences, and bits of paper.

'I hope he's not going to be a shyer,' Steve said.

'He's curious.' Dora would have nothing wrong with Robin. 'That's a sign of intelligence.'

They went through the wood, and decided to take the short cut home down the road, so as not to overdo Robin.

As they turned out of the narrow lane with the high hedges towards the road that ran along the top of the hills, Robin's head shot up, and a fraction of a second later, Miss America flung up her handsome narrow head. A second after that, Dora and Steve heard hoofs on the road.

They pulled in to the side. Down the hard highway, mane and stirrups flying, foam-flecked and wild-eyed, a black horse galloped frantically without a rider.

'Which way?' said Dora. 'Go to catch it, or go to see who fell off?'

'You go one way, I'll go the other.'

Steve went after the horse. Dora went on down the road. A few hundred yards farther on, she found Amanda Crowley, her doughy face distorted with tears, a painful graze reddening the side of her chin.

Dora told her to stand on a gate, and somehow got her up behind her. Robin had probably never had a doughy girl behind the saddle, but he didn't buck or fuss. Although he was so lively and responsive, he was the most unsurprised horse Dora had ever known.

Amanda had stopped bellowing and slobbering, but when Dora put her down off the horse at the back of her house, she began to weep and carry on again as she ran through the kitchen door.

Mrs Crowley came out in an apron with flour on her fore-arms.

'Can't understand it . . . gentle as a lamb, they said . . . She loves that horse like a brother . . .'

The Crowleys did not seem to have progressed much since Dopey became Woman-o'-War.

Steve trotted down the road, leading the black horse back to the Crowleys' house. Dragging it rather. It was hanging back, with its ears laid flat.

'How did you know it was theirs?' Dora went to meet him.

'It's got bits of pink ribbon tied into its mane,' he said grimly. 'Should be red. It's a tricky sort.'

'My poor baby. Poor brave little girl. Here's Rebel come back, see, safe and sound, say thank you to Steven and Doris.'

Amanda had come out again, and was snuggling and sniffling under her mother's arm.

'I didn't know you had a new horse,' Steve said. 'Where did you get him?'

'From some people Mr Crowley knows, at business. Their children have ridden him. We bought him in good faith, a real bargain and the girls have taken so much trouble over him. Can't understand . . .' The mother wiped the girl's face on her apron, rubbing the graze, and Amanda yelled and scowled and pulled away, aiming a kick at the back of her mother's solid legs.

Then she came over to the black horse and aimed a kick at him.

'Here,' said Steve. 'None of that. Was it his fault you fell off?'

'Of course it was, the pig. He pretended to be so qui-so qui-so quiet.' She started blubbering again at the memory of it. 'We were trotting along and I was singing to him, like I do, and then suddenly – he suddenly – Ow-wow-wow, it was awful, Mum!' She ran back to the apron and the floury arm.

'What then, my precious? What did that naughty horse do, and they said he was so gentle?'

'Did he shy?' Dora asked. The black horse was quiet enough now, standing with its knees slightly bent, and its large common head drooping, eyes half shut. The Crowleys certainly didn't pick horses on looks.

'Sort of, except that there was nothing to shy at.' Amanda looked out from her mother's armpit, pouting her lower lip to catch tears. 'He dropped his head suddenly and then he threw it up and hit me in the nose and sort of stood on his back legs and spun round. I didn't fall off,' she said defiantly. 'I got off. Bet you would have too.'

'Bet I would.'

Sitting on her beautiful well-behaved Robin, Dora could not help feeling sorry for the Crowleys, silly though they were, and for the bad luck they had with horses. And for the bad luck of any horse who found its way to their draughty, narrow stable in the bare paddock fenced with barbed wire.

Riding home with Steve, she was silent for a while. As they turned onto the cart track that led between the fields to the back of the farm buildings, Steve said, 'Don't bother telling me. I know what you're thinking.'

Dora sighed. 'Yes, I am. Well, why couldn't we, Steve?' She turned to him, standing sideways in her saddle. 'We've had some pretty good success with difficult horses. I know I'm not the world's greatest, but I did learn a bit about schooling from Chuckie Fiske. Rebel's not such a bad horse, in spite of that coffin head. But if he doesn't get straightened out, he'll either kill one of those girls, or they'll get rid of him and he'll be half killed by someone else who's not so soppy.'

'Now look, Dora,' Steve said. 'That's not what Follyfoot is for.

We're there to look after the horses who need us. Not to take in a rogue horse who isn't worth a day's keep.'

'There's no such thing as a rogue horse,' Dora said. 'No horse is bad by nature. People make them that way, and people can cure them.'

'Don't be daft,' Steve opened the gate and let it swing back instead of holding it for Dora. 'Horses are like people. There's some will always be no good.'

Catching the gate, Dora was going to argue that too, but Steve, whose irritation with the Crowleys seemed to have seeped over on to her, turned round on Miss America's bare back and said, 'You've got one horse here already that shouldn't be here. Don't land us with another.'

'What do you mean?'

Steve kicked Miss America and trotted into the yard without answering.

'What do you *mean*?' Dora took off Robin's tack, and went into the loose box where Steve was rubbing down Miss A with an old towel, copying the Colonel's hissing whistle.

'Are you talking about Rob?'

'About the expense of him.' Steve kept his head down against the mare's side.

'Blank's paying for his keep. He'll send more next winter. He said so.'

'He also said when he was here that he'd send the Colonel a donation for the old horses. So he's sending Robin's keep instead.'

'Oh –' Dora was horrified. She hadn't seen it this way. 'Has the Colonel said this to you?'

Steve kept his head down, and went on hissing and rubbing.

18

IGNORING Robin's impatient hoof against his door demanding to be let out to roll, Dora ran down the cinder path to the house, pushed past Ron enquiring, 'Where's the fire?' and Anna enquiring, 'Why haven't you put your sheets in the laundry?' and banged into the Colonel's study.

He was sitting on the rug with Dottie, the donkey foal curled up against her mother's rounded side.

Refusing to be sidetracked by this touching scene, Dora stopped with her legs apart and her arms folded and said brusquely, 'Have you and Steve been talking about me?'

'Dora, what on earth?' The Colonel looked up. The skin at the corner of his scarred eye twitched, and the other eyebrow went up. 'What are you so angry about?'

'I'm not angry. I'm upset.' That was a mild word for it. She was hurt, humiliated, shattered. She had thought everybody shared her joy in the gift of Robin. Now here they'd all been gossiping behind her back that she was taking Follyfoot money.

'Keep the money,' she told the Colonel. 'Use it to pay bills, and I'll find some way of paying for Robin. I'll get baby-sitting jobs.'

'I thought you didn't like babies.'

'I'll read to blind people.'

'There aren't any round here, except old Mr Corrigan and he can read Braille now that –'

'I'll sell something. I'll sell my clothes.'

'What clothes?'

Dora's suitcase with her dresses and long skirt and red swim

367

suit had been lost by the airline, and Dora had not bothered to claim for it.

'I'll work for you for nothing.'

'You are, practically, the little I pay you. Dora, what on earth are we talking about?' He stroked Dottie's endless brown ears. The Colonel was the only person she would allow to touch her ears.

'You told Steve it wasn't fair of me to have Robin here.'

'Did he say that?'

Dora shook her head. Her agitation was subsiding. You could not stay agitated long in the cool, peaceful atmosphere of the Colonel's study, with two donkeys dozing.

'Who did?'

'I did.'

'Well then,' the Colonel said. 'Shut up about it, whatever it is.' He got up without disturbing the donkeys, sleeping with their long eye lashes fanned out, and went to his desk to rummage in a drawer. 'Here.' He held out a ten pound note. 'Here's a bonus to get Robin that martingale he needs. I want him to go his best here. Gives us a good name.'

Although the Colonel had sort of made things all right by not understanding what she was talking about, he still had not solved the problem, just because he didn't understand what she was talking about.

Dora would have to solve it herself.

On Sunday, when Mr Crowley would be at home, she took Robin out by himself.

'It's too hot to ride,' Steve said when he saw her mounting. A rather wet summer had steamed up into some stifling days. Nothing moved in the hot air except biting insects. Crickets in the long grass rang in your ears all afternoon.

'I'm going down to the brook to cool his legs off.'

'Hang on, then. I'll bring Hero. Do him good.'

'I'd rather go alone. I have to think.'

'See you when you come back,' Steve said cheerfully. Dora was not really speaking to him properly yet, but he had not noticed.

Callie was coming down the road on the Cobbler, bareback in shorts.

'I've been down to the stream,' she said. 'It's great. Come on, I'll go back there with you.'

'No thanks.'

Callie stuck out her tongue. 'You've got dreadfully snotty since you went to America,' she said. 'I suppose it was bound to happen.'

Dora squeezed Robin and he moved into his long, supple, pigeon-toed trot, lightly flexed, head held just right in the martingale.

Mr Crowley had changed a bit since the day of the show when he and Steve had rolled on the ground in the middle of the in-and-out. He had struck it luckier in his business and made a bit of money. When Dora offered to take Rebel for a while for the price of his grazing and a bit extra for her schooling, he agreed, encouraged by the lamentations of his women.

'You said yourself, Dad, we'd have to get rid of the horse if something wasn't done.'

'Don't sell him Daddy, don't sell Rebel. He'll be a good boy, he says he will.'

'He wants to learn.' The horse lifted a back leg sourly. 'You want to go to school, don't you, Rebel dear?'

'I'd be glad to see what I can do with him,' Dora added.

Mr Crowley, not used to offers of help in a neighbourhood

where he had made no friends, agreed to let her take the horse, but no messing about and not letting them have it back when it was improved, because the girls would pine their hearts out until their black friend came back to them.

The Colonel agreed, because Dora needed the money, and because he didn't want another scene with her like the one in his study. Slugger said she would get herself killed, and Steve said he wouldn't touch the black horse with a bargepole.

But the horse seemed to be all right. Perhaps Amanda had invented the rearing and spinning story to cover up for having fallen off. Rebel performed quite steadily in the small field, trotting and cantering and hopping over low jumps. She ventured out with him and he didn't shy, although once he charged off with her when she bent forward as they pushed under a large tree. He was nervous after that. He jogged all the way home, driving Dora's brains up through the top of her perspiring head, laying his ears back at nothing.

Dora was pleased with what she had done with him, but he was still unpredictable. He was tricky in the stable. He had that funny way of laying back his ears, lowering his ugly head and lifting a back foot thoughtfully.

'She'd better not ask me to feed him on her day off,' Slugger said, watching as Dora groomed Rebel one sultry evening, avoiding his feet which stamped impatiently at flies.

'He's on grass, you know that.' Dora ducked her head as the horse's long black tail swished round and swatted her in the face.

'Good thing,' Slugger said. 'He'd be a maniac else.'

'Something not quite right.' The Colonel stood with him in the stable doorway, studying the black horse, as he and Slugger must have stood many times in their Army days, considering some military malefactor. 'Can't quite put my finger on it though, can you, Slugger?'

370

The old man shook his head, in the woollen hat which he still wore, even in this heat. 'It's not in me hands. It's in me head. In the eyes. In the nose.' He sniffed, scenting for trouble.

'You're always against any new horse,' Dora said. 'Rebel is all right, aren't you, sweetie?'

Sweetie swung round his head and gave her quite a hard nip. She did not allow herself to yell. As soon as Slugger and the Colonel had moved on, she pulled down her shorts and saw the bruising teeth marks on her hip.

19

ONE cooler evening, when the air was stirring at last, and free of the high whine of crickets, and the slap of hand on skin as the female mosquito stopped humming and settled to feast, Dora and Steve and Callie went out for a late ride.

Now that Steve had stopped throwing out hints about Robin, Dora was letting him ride the fine bay horse. Not because she thought it was good for Robin to be ridden by somebody else – he could happily be a one girl horse for ever – but because she wanted Steve to understand the way she felt about him. No, it wasn't that either. It was simple. She wanted Steve to enjoy what she enjoyed.

She also wanted Rebel to go well this evening, as proof of what she had accomplished. Being the perverse animal he was, he did just about everything wrong.

He kicked at Cobby while Dora was mounting, then turned and tried to brain her, going back into the stable. He struck out at one of the dogs. He pushed past Robin going through the gate. Going ahead, he humped his back and tucked in his tail and fussed about the horse behind. Following the other two, he pulled and fussed and tried to run up on their tails.

He shied. He stumbled. He yawed his head about. He jogged when the others were walking. He did all the things that make a ride no fun. Steve and Callie carefully didn't criticize, and Dora set her jaw and didn't admit that she was having no fun.

She became very frustrated. When Rebel stumbled, she

jerked his head up, which didn't help him to regain his footing. When he jogged, she pulled him back and tried to force him to walk. Robin and Cobby could both 'walk a hole in the wind' with their long easy stride. The farther ahead they got, the more impossible it was to make Rebel walk, since he had to jog to catch up.

When they came to a place where two tracks crossed, Dora said, 'I'm sick of this. You two go on ahead. I'm going off on my own.'

'Are you sure he –' Callie had her worried face on.

'He's all right.' Dora hauled Rebel's head round to go off at a right angle.

'Go easy with him,' Steve said. 'He's in a funny mood.'

'He's all *right*.'

He was better on his own, but he was still clumsy, dragging his toe and stumbling over stones. When his front end went down in a really devastating stumble over nothing, adrenalin rushed into Dora's system. She hauled up his head in the anger of fear, reached her hand forward and gave him a whack behind the ear.

He took off. Dora tried everything. She pulled and let go and pulled again. She crossed the reins, setting them against his neck. She leaned back and hauled. She leaned forward with her hand low on one rein and tried to turn him. She sawed, she swore. She contemplated hurling herself on to the first patch of soft ground.

They were headed for the road. Dora shut her eyes, opened them as they missed a car by yards and tore through a broken hurdle into a tussocky field dotted with trees. The horse stumbled, pecked with his nose on the ground, recovered with Dora's arms round his neck, and headed straight for a huge old tree.

It was unbelievable. It was hypnotizing. It was like those

films where Japanese pilots flew down the smoke stacks of battleships. The tree was upon her, enveloped her. For the fraction of a moment, she saw every ridge of its bark, every curl of lichen, then whiteness exploded.

In her room at the farmhouse, the curtains were drawn, and Dora had finally stopped being sick. Her head was banded tight by iron, but the pills that Anna had given her were detaching her from that. The pain was there, but more observed than felt.

'How's Rebel?'

'He's all right.' Anna came to the bed. 'He cut his leg, that's all. He went after Steve and Callie. They followed his tracks back and found you. Steve wants to have him put down.'

'He's not ours.'

'He's dangerous.'

'It wasn't his fault.'

'Oh my *God*,' Anna said. 'Won't you ever grow up?'

Dora slept most of the next day in the darkened room. When she woke, it was night time, a sky brilliant with stars, a three-quarter moon making black and white patterns on the corner of the stable yard she could see from her window.

She got up and opened the door of her bedroom. All the lights were out. The clock in the hall creaked the seconds. You could only hear its feeble tick when everyone was in bed.

Dora did not want to sleep any more. She put a sweater over her pyjamas and went down to see the horses.

Robin was in the long field with most of the others. At first when she went through the gate in the moonlight, it seemed like an empty field. Then here and there shapes moved, something that had been lying down got up, grunting. Dolly appeared round a gorse bush, looked at Dora sideways, then ambled off with her hips swaying, in case Dora had come to catch her for work.

Robin materialized from somewhere, blowing down his nose. His mysterious night self that slept on grass and watched the dawn come up was remote from her. He let her put her hand on his gingery nose, but his eye stared at her instead of softening, and he suddenly swerved away and cantered off, and two or three of the other horses thudded with him out of sight below the dip of the hill.

The night was theirs. Dora felt like an intruder.

Dottie and her chocolate foal were inside the shed in their enclosure. Specs and Folly were camouflaged somewhere by shadows. In the stable, only Rebel was in a loose box, resting a puffy foreleg on the toe.

He was resting his head too. The stable had a low wooden manger at one end. Rebel's clumsy head was drooped over the bar, jaw resting on the wood.

There was something strange about his head. Dora went in to him. The moon was bright enough to see that his eye was flat and dull. His lip looked slack, a dribble of saliva damp on the wood of the manger. His neck was stretched out. He looked all ribs and belly.

When she had been in the vet's office with Blank, the vet had shown Dora a picture in 'Equine Medicine and Surgery' of what a horse with Eastern Equine Encephalitis looked like.

It looked like Rebel.

But the virus of the disease had never been active in England. Only in America. Only in America, unless . . .

Dora slid to sit in the straw with her back to the wall and her throbbing head in her hands. The pain had come back. She couldn't think straight. But she must think. Robin . . . Chuckie . . . King Kong . . . The trobbing became the roar of Ron's motor bike as he skidded in from the road at his usual Wall of Death speed and shut off the engine. It coughed, hiccuped, and returned the night to silence.

Dora had left the door of Rebel's loose box open. Ron appeared in the moonlight, silhouetted like a space traveller in his leather clothes and helmet.

'Left me radio in the shed,' he said. 'Can't go to sleep without it, can I?'

Dora raised her head and stared at him, not understanding.

'Sitting up again then, are you?' Dora had sat up so many nights with sick horses. With Cobby, with Lancelot and Nigger, with poor old ruined Rusty, the night he died. 'Your pet lamb looks a bit rough.' He came nearer into the stable. 'I never seen a horse look like that,' he said.

'Nor have I. Except – except once in a book. Oh, Ron, I –' She dropped her head back into her hands and burst into tears. Rebel moved restlessly, shifting from foot to foot, grating his teeth on the edge of the manger.

'Here, what's this?' Ron was softer than he pretended to be. He knelt beside Dora and put his leather arm round her. 'Come on, girl, you're just weak that's all, after the concussion. You shouldn't be up. Come on, old Ronnie will take you into the house.'

'No, Ron.' She pushed him away and scrambled up, standing with her palms pressed against the wall, breathing heavily, staring in terror at the stricken horse. 'Something terrible has happened. Something has started. I can't tell anyone.'

But she had to tell someone, and so she told it to Ron. She told him about the terrible disease that could kill a horse in two or three days, and kill people too, if they were bitten by a mosquito whose saliva glands were infected by the virus.

376

Robin's cold and 'jet lag' when he arrived, could have been encephalitis, mild to him because of being immunized in other years. But mosquitoes, biting him, could have transmitted it to Rebel, to other horses, birds, rats, dogs, who in turn would infect other mosquitoes. The virus could be spreading in this neighbourhood, this county, the whole of England in the hot end of summer.

'You mean, it could be spreading to people?' Ron was still kneeling in the straw, gaping up at her, the hang of his jaw supported by the chinstrap of the helmet.

'Kids might die, like you said they did in America?'

'I don't know, Ron. I don't know. I have to think. Perhaps I'm wrong. It's too impossible. Rebel will get better, and it's all just a crazy idea. I don't know. I can't think straight any more.' She shook her head to try to clear it, and a whole Guy Fawkes' night of fireworks exploded among the nerves of her brain.

'Forget what I told you Ron – please?' She put one hand over her eyes and held the other out to him. He took it and pulled himself up. 'Don't say a word to anyone.'

'Like the grave. You know me.'

But Dora did know Ron. That was the trouble. He was the last person she should have shared her fears with. Thank God she had not told him the worst thing of all, that Robin had entered this country as King Kong, six-year-old bay with star and two white feet, the only official difference between them being that King Kong had a certificate of immunization against encephalitis and Robin did not.

The only clear thought that cut through the pain in her head was: *It's got to be kept secret.*

'Promise you won't tell.'

'One of us did ought, if it's true about the ensuffer – ensiffer – encephlawhatsit.'

'It's not. It couldn't be. Forget it.'

'Total blank.'

Ron saluted her, and shuffled his boots across the yard in dancing steps to get his radio.

Dora put a rug on the sick horse, and ministered to him as best she could.

20

THREE o'clock in the morning was the deadest of all the dead hours on the night desk of the *Chronicle*. It was called the night desk because whoever was on duty at night sat there; but whoever was on duty during the day sat there too and answered the telephone and made notes to be written up into news stories.

Bruce Ingersoll was on the Chronicle's night desk. He had only been with the local paper six months, and it was his first night duty ever, so three o'clock in the morning did not seem dead to him, but just as exciting as every hour of this first night of challenge and responsibility. The night reporter was on his own in the building. It was up to him whether the Chronicle missed the boat on scoops, or lived up to its local watchword of 'Always Alert'.

Bruce was like his name, a square young man with short hair, solid and eager and trustworthy. At college, he had known where he was headed. When he landed the job with the Chronicle, he had known that it was the first rung to Fleet Street and future glory.

The glory of a scoop could come any time. It could come tonight, although by three a.m. it had not yet shown itself.

The night had started promisingly with a stammering small boy calling to report a fire.

'Where is it?' Bruce pulled the notepad towards him, his voice tense.

'In the grate, stupid.' Shrieks and giggles in the background. Mr Shanker of the waterworks commission had called to render to the Chronicle some hot news that could not possibly wait till morning.

'Oh yes?' In spite of Mr Shanker's slow creaking voice, perhaps this was it.

It wasn't. The waterworks commission had held its ladies night banquet at the Dog and Fox and settled the date of its annual general meeting.

'Thanks a *lot*, Mr Shanker. We're very glad to know.'

No harm in sending the poor old guy to bed feeling chuffed.

An old lady rang to say she had let out her cat at eight o'clock and he hadn't come back yet, so unlike him, naughty Tibbs. Would the Chronicle be sure and put an appeal in the morning edition?

The small boy again. 'There's been a murder done.'

'Where?'

'On the telly, creep.'

At two o'clock, Bruce checked the police station and received some interesting news about a five car crash in a patch of fog on the London road. A concert pianist had broken his leg.

That's better. Bruce made himself a cup of tea, and before writing his story, he telephoned his favourite Fleet Street newspaper, where he dreamed of working some day.

'Night editor here. Five cars? Not really. We've had ten and twenty smash-ups coming in. The fog's nothing round your way. Concert pianist? Who? Who, laddie? Sorry, never heard of him.' Two other lines were ringing. 'Bye.'

Just before three, the small boy again and the giggling. Must be a pyjama party.

'Can you talk for a second?'

'Yes, but –'

'Ha, ha. Time's up.'

380

Bruce sighed and settled down again in the dingy room, with its long tables covered in papers and reference books, its overflowing wastepaper baskets, its grime and mess, its rusty kettle and cracked cups, which to him held the glamour of the Press.

He sat at the night desk and drank his tea and read a book called, 'How to Make it to the Top in Newspapers.'

The telephone rang. Perhaps this was it.

This was it.

'Listen.' The voice was urgent, conspiring. 'Listen, I gotta red hot story for you.' The accent was a little strange. It sounded at first like a disguised voice, hoarse and unfamiliar, but the story sounded genuine, and tremendous.

'There's going to be this epidemic, take a note of this. The public has got to be warned. Imported from America . . . one horse dying, hundreds threatened . . . the lives of thousands of 'uman beens at risk.'

'Human what?'

'Beens. People.'

'Who's this speaking?' Bruce asked for the third time.

'Doctor, er – Doctor Dillon.'

'A medical doctor?'

'Vetinery. Fully qualified vetinery doctor.'

'And where is this horse?' Bruce's pencil was racing over the notepad.

'I can't tell you where. We don't want a riot. I can tell you it's a place with a lot of horses, that's all.'

When Bruce was at school, which wasn't that long ago, he had gone on a field trip with the Natural History Class to see this place with all these old horses and some old Colonel or other who had been scared of the kids and hidden indoors. It was a ramshackle, rustic, manurey place by Bruce's neat citified standards. Just the sort of place to harbour a fell disease.

381

'Is it Follyfoot Farm?'

'Might be. Might not. Can't tell you.'

'Dr Dillon.' Bruce's mind was working like speeding machinery on how he would handle this scoop. 'We'd like an interview.'

'With me?'

'If you agree. I'm off duty at six. Could you meet me at the stable at seven – at Follyfoot?'

'Right on.'

So it was Follyfoot. Bruce Ingersoll, ace investigator. He poured himself another cup of tea, tipped in a shot of the assistant editor's rum from the bottle behind the encyclopaedias, sat down again and pulled the telephone towards him with a happy sigh.

'Night Editor.' Same voice. A bit more tired. He had probably handled sixteen dramas from all over the world since Bruce last talked to him.

'This is the *Chronicle* again.'

'What now?' The voice was bored as well as tired.

'I've really got something for you now. Something really big. A life and death thing, it could be.'

'Shoot.'

'Well – up in the hills above this town ...'

The phone call over, Bruce sat back in the broken swivel chair, breathed out, and patted his stomach as if he were already a Press magnate of international repute. The dingy *Chronicle* room with its filthy windows, scarred furniture and ravaged reporters' table was a huge modern office of stainless steel and glass. The gas popped under the rusty kettle. The old wood floor creaked. The plumbing knocked and groaned like corpses clamouring. But Bruce's head, as he sat back with a spreading smile, was filled with the roar of the presses, the clacking of typewriters, the ticking of tape bulletins, the sirens of motor-bikes screaming in with stop press news from all the trouble centres of the world.

21

VERY early in the morning, the pounding began on the door. The Colonel started awake and looked at his luminous watch. Five o'clock. He swung his feet to the floor, and searched in vain for slippers. Beside him, Anna drew the sheet up to her chin.

'Don't go down,' she murmured, still half asleep.

This old house would be easy to break into. She had always said that if thieves came, she would let them get on with it, since there was nothing worth stealing, except the Colonel's collection of horse photographs, and what thief would bother with them?

'Thieves don't knock,' the Colonel said.

The knocking was on the front door. Anyone who knew the ways of the house would come to the back door, or the side door into his study.

He went down, slid the bolt and opened the door to a small gathering of about half a dozen people waiting in the grey of dawn.

'Is this Follyfoot Farm?' The young man with crisp hair was carrying what looked like a tape recorder.

'It is, but –'

'This is where all the horses are, right? Sorry to wake you so early, sir, but this could be a big story and we want to get it into the late editions.'

'What –'

'Where's the horse?' another man asked.

'Horse? There's dozens of them.' The Colonel felt rather cross. These people, who had presumably driven here from

384

somewhere, were wide awake. He was still officially in the middle of his sleep.

'The one that's sick.'

'None of them is sick, as far as I know. There's one with a leg wound that was kept in last night.'

'The one that threw the girl?'

'Well, she was knocked off by a tree, if you call that thrown. How do you know about this horse?' He began to wake up.

'News story came through from a vet, it's understood.' The crisp young man with the tape recorder took a step nearer to getting into the house. 'Outbreak of encephalitis . . . the whole country threatened . . . dangerous to humans . . .'

'What on earth –?' For one desperate moment, the Colonel thought he was still asleep. He blinked hard, opened his eyes and accepted the fact that he was not.

'Come with me.'

He took them through the house and out by the back door to the stable yard towards Rebel's loose box.

The black horse was down, lying on his side, his forelegs, one bandaged, moving feebly in a kind of clawing motion. In the far corner of the box, somebody was curled up in the straw, asleep.

'Dora!'

She woke in a moment, jumped up and stood against the wall as the Colonel came in and the reporters crowded into the doorway. One of them took a flash picture. Dora flung her hand in front of her face.

The Colonel stood between Dora and the intruders.

'Did you telephone these people?' he asked.

She shook her head.

'Who then? Was it Steve?'

'He doesn't know.'

'Know what? Who does know it, whatever it is?'

'Well –' She bit her lip.

'Dora, don't be stupid. Who's responsible for this? Is it one of Ron's ridiculous games?'

'It isn't a game,' Dora whispered, looking down. 'Rebel is very ill. I saw – I talked to the vet in America about equine encephalitis. I saw some pictures. I think he's got it.'

'Encephalitis?' The Colonel said. 'I've never heard of it over here.'

'But if Robin could have carried the virus –'

'He'd be ill too. But he had his shots before he came.'

'Suppose he was infected before the shots?' Dora groped desperately for something to say. She could not tell him the truth yet.

'No, it's not possible ...' The Colonel dropped down and put his hand on Rebel's head. 'Poor fellow. Take it easy, old man.' The horse's eyes looked dull and lifeless. 'Robin was a bit sick when he first got here, wasn't he?'

He thought for a moment, then got to his feet, took Dora out of the loose box, and shut the top and bottom doors.

'Excuse me.' He worked his way through the newspapermen.

'Just a minute, sir.'

'Excuse me. I have to call the vet.'

Woken by the noise in the yard, Steve came out of the tack room with his hair on end and found himself instantly the target of questions and speculations.

'I'm sorry,' he kept saying. 'I've no idea what you're talking about.'

'The encephalitis epidemic.'

'What do you mean?'

'You work here, don't you?'

'Yes, but I don't know anything about it, I told you.'

'This Dr Dillon says –'

'Never heard of him.' Steve set his jaw.

From the window of his cottage across the road, Slugger had seen the cars at the entrance to the farm. He ambled over, muttering to himself.

He too was pounced on. 'You work here?'

'I hope so. Unless I've been sacked overnight.'

'What do you think of all this excitement?'

'What excitement? We've had no excitement here since the badger got into the chicken run.'

He and Steve started to do their morning work. The reporters followed them round, taking pictures. Dora came up from the fields riding Robin bareback in a halter, and they took her picture too.

'The vet's on his way.' The Colonel came out of the house with Callie. 'It wasn't he who called the newspaper.'

He got Dora into an empty loosebox.

'Listen,' he said to her tensely. 'It could be worse than we think. I've just checked Robin's papers again. He wasn't immunized.'

'But it's stamped, right on the papers.'

'Not for Robin. For King Kong. And they're not the same horse. It's described as two white feet, white star and snip. Robin hasn't got a white snip on his nose. You know what those swindling Yanks have done?'

He was very angry. Dora wanted to shout, 'Don't tell me – I know!' But she had to keep silent.

'They sent him over with another horse's papers. So he may not be immunized. This crazy story could be true.'

He looked at Dora fiercely. She looked into his blue outdoor eyes, but did not read suspicion there. So she kept silent.

When the vet arrived, the Colonel took him to Rebel's stable, and would not let the reporters talk to him, until he had examined Rebel and Robin.

'What do you think?' the reporters asked him. 'You want to make a statement about the danger?'

'I'm prepared to say ...' The vet had been a country vet for many years. He had developed a way of moving and talking slowly with sick animals. A way which pleased the sick animals, but could be irritating to impatient healthy humans. 'What I think ... I've never seen a case of, er – eastern ... equine ... encephalitis.' He measured the words. 'But from my reading ... the symptoms could suggest ... but I, er – I, er – would never think of it if it wasn't for the horse from America. However, I've a blood sample from both horses, of course. Tests on mice ... Time to develop ... There's nowhere round here equipped to do the tests. I'll be driving them up to London.'

'I'll be glad to run them up there for you.' The crisp young man had seen the vet's muddy old car, and could guess at his driving speed.

'Thank you. It's my responsibility.'

The vet chugged off in his old workhorse of a car.

'That's about it then,' the B.B.C. man said. 'Can we use your telephone, Colonel?'

'No.'

'Why not, sir?'

Callie took a look at the Colonel and saw that he was near the breaking point.

'Because I just cut the wires,' she said, took the Colonel indoors and slammed the door.

The reporters went up to the village and knocked on the door of the Three Horseshoes. The little pub had not had so many people in it since Bank Holiday. It was not opening time, but Toby's father gave everyone free beer, since fame had come to the village.

22

By the next day, the news had spread. The stories in the papers were mostly speculation, but it was enough to start wild rumours all over the country of an outbreak dangerous to humans.

Spokesmen from across the Atlantic were heard on the radio talking about the epidemic in New England. A child was admitted to a Midland hospital with a fever of unknown origin. Straightaway the cry went up that the epidemic had indeed begun.

Some people from the Royal Veterinary College drove a horse ambulance into the stable yard, somehow got a sling under poor old Rebel, hauled him into the ambulance and took him away.

His loose box was closed up, with a sign on the door saying 'Keep Out'. Callie, who had recently done the history of the Great Plague, painted a cross on the door as they did in 1665 on stricken houses. Dora just caught her in time to stop her adding, 'Lord have mercy upon us.'

Reporters came constantly to the Farm, including an eager young man from the local paper who claimed to have been the person contacted by the mysterious Dr Dillon. He was crushed to find the good Doctor not available.

'He promised me an exclusive interview.'

'Very exclusive, it would be,' the Colonel said grimly, shepherding him out of his study, 'since as far as we know, he doesn't exist.'

The reporters hung about the yard in the sun, watching rather cynically as Dora and Steve went about their work.

When Steve went into Woman's stable with a bowl of feed, and Dora followed with a wheelbarrow and shovel, one of the newspapermen was heard to sing casually:

'Will you take this advice I hand you like a brother?
Or are you not seeing things too clear?
Are you too much in love to hear?
Is it all going in one end and out the other?'

Slugger had his photograph taken in various poses. Robin, who was quarantined in the foaling stable, had a picture of his head looking over the door taken with a long range camera. It appeared in the evening papers captioned: 'UNWELCOME IMMIGRANT'.

Ron had not turned up for work. That was nothing unusual. Dora was thankful that he was out of the way. Shocked and appalled at what was happening, she could not face admitting that it was she who had broken the news.

After the brief rain, the hot weather had returned. Since there was a greater risk of a horse being bitten by a mosquito out of doors, people in the area were urged to keep their horses and ponies in at night. All the Follyfoot horses were in, of course, fretting to be out in the fields, banging on doors, calling for attention every time someone they knew came into the yard. Having them all stabled made ten times the work, and the intruders didn't help. The Colonel got his friend, a retired policeman, to sit on a stool by the gate and keep all visitors out. Being deaf and not understanding their involvement, he was rude to the Crowleys, and they went away, adding the insult to the long list they felt that life had handed them.

23

GEOFFREY Masters got pretty fed up with his parents always going out at night.

They were rather young to have a boy of ten years old, especially a very bright boy who read all the magazines they left lying about and watched television programmes meant for grownups when his parents were out.

When he said to them, 'Family life in Britain is dying and people like you are the cause of it,' they laughed good naturedly and ruffled his thatch of orange coloured hair – he hated the ruffling and the colour – and said that he should be proud to have parents who were not fuddy-duddies. When he complained about having to take off his shoes before stepping on the white carpet or not being allowed to have his cat in the house because it jumped on the dresser, his mother, who collected the kind of useless china that was too expensive to eat off, said, 'Some day you'll be proud to have been brought up in a house with such nice things.'

He was not proud yet.

His father's mother, Grandma Masters, who was quite unmasterful, lived with them in a room of her own surrounded by every present anyone had ever given her, and family pictures. Some of the old ones of his father looked like Geoffrey did now. Red hair and freckles, knock knees and long thin feet.

'Yes, my dear,' Grandma Masters was fond of saying. 'You've got your father's knees, that's for sure. And that's a funny thing,' she added. 'Considering how much time you spend on that pony of yours, a person would expect you to be bow legged.'

Geoffrey's pony was the most important thing in his life. His parents did not usually give him what he needed, since their idea of what a ten-year-old boy needed was different from his. But they had surprised him on his last birthday with Archibald.

He had not known he wanted a pony, but when he saw this one, staked out on the back lawn eating the good clover grass, his heart rushed out to it and he knew that this was what had been lacking from his life.

Archibald was a fine Dartmoor pony, glossy brown like conkers. His mane could not decide which side to lie on, so favoured both, with a parting in the middle. He had a long thick tail, which Geoffrey brushed and combed every day, and tied up in a knot when it was muddy.

This winter, when the tennis club was closed and the Sunday barbecue parties finished, his Dad was going to take some weekends off from the social round and build a little stable for Archie. Meanwhile, he stayed out in the small field behind the house and sheltered under the chestnut tree in the hot sun or the night time rain.

Geoffrey sometimes read bits of the evening paper to his grandmother after his parents had gone out. He read to her that everyone had been warned to keep their horses in at night because of the epidemic scare.

'That's all very well for those who have a stable,' he said.

'Archibald will be all right,' Grandma said. 'It's only a stupid scare.'

'That's what you said about the building that collapsed in Rochester.' Geoffrey was up with all the news. 'That's what you said about the lead in paint being dangerous to babies.'

Grandma closed her eyes. Geoffrey was about to give her a lecture.

'That's what you said when I told you they were going to make the sweetshop into a supermarket.'

'Don't you worry, dear.' She opened her eyes and turned them back to the television. He kissed her and went out. She was a decent enough grandmother, but no good for conversation.

He went out to talk to Archie in the muggy night, full of the vibrations of insects. Fireflies glinted in the hedge. Geoffrey hung his arms over Archie's back, which was just the right height for hanging your arms over and resting your chin on and thinking. A mosquito bit him on the forehead.

That did it. 'Come on, Arch,' he said. 'If I lose you, I'll lose the best friend boy ever had.'

He unclipped the halter rope and led him towards the house.

Grandma's room was at the front. At the back of the kitchen, there was a little kind of pantry cupboard where Geoffrey's mother kept flower vases and some of the china that was too expensive to eat off. The only way to get to it was through the kitchen.

Archie didn't want to come in, so Geoffrey put some sugar in the palm of his hand and walked ahead of him, holding out his hand. Archie followed, reaching out his head to lick the sweet hand.

Geoffrey managed to get him through the kitchen without too much damage. His long tail knocked down the salt and pepper shakers that were shaped like owls. Good thing it wasn't the ones that were shaped like swans, with breakable necks.

He took the pony round the table and into the pantry. Archie just fitted in there. He stood quite contentedly. It was stifling hot though, so Geoffrey squeezed past him to open the bottom of the window, squeezed back to tie his tail in a knot so that he wouldn't whisk it around the shelves, and went

393

upstairs to bed to read by the light of a torch. His mother had taken the bulb out of his lamp, so that he couldn't read.

At two o'clock in the morning, Mr and Mrs Masters were quarrelling on their way home from the party.

'I'm sick of you always imagining things,' he said.

'I didn't imagine that woman insulting me. Oh! Be careful, Roderick. There's a rabbit in the road.'

'It's a stone, you idiot. Get your eyes examined.'

As they went past the row of cottages at Upham's Corner, she said, 'I smell smoke. We should stop and ring up the fire station.'

Further on, she saw a cat up a tree and wanted Mr Masters to stop the car and climb up after it. Nearer home, seeing a man walking back from a date with his girl, she said, 'I don't recognize him. He could be a prowler. Let's ring the police.'

Roderick got pretty sick of her fancies. He did not pay much attention. As they went past the house to the gate of the drive, she gave a little scream.

'What now?'

She clutched his arm and he almost scraped the gate post.

'There's a horse's head sticking out of the window.'

'It's not your eyes that want examining. It's your head,' he grumbled. 'Get up to bed. You'll feel better in the morning.'

In the morning, when she came down in her black silk kimono with the red poppies, she didn't feel better, she felt worse.

'Archibald is in the pantry with all my good china.' She woke up Geoffrey.

'Because of the mosquitoes, you see.'

She didn't want an explanation. 'How will we get him out of there without breaking something?'

Geoffrey got up and went down. He took hold of Archie's thick knotted tail and pulled backwards. The pony came out like a cork from a bottle. He only broke one Wedgewood jug and a Rockingham saucer. Geoffrey's mother went to wake up his father.

Geoffrey's father cancelled a tennis match and a cocktail party, and spent the day beginning the work on the stable for Archibald.

24

THERE was another boy who had a pony in that neighbourhood, and he had no stable for it either. He only had it on loan for the summer, and a neighbour allowed him to graze it in his field, along with some cows.

On the local radio news, it didn't say anything about cows. It said horses and ponies. It said Grave Danger and Mosquito-borne Virus. It said (or hinted) that anyone who cared at all about their horse or pony would keep it under cover where there was less danger of getting bitten.

This boy whose name was Rubin did not actually care much about the pony. He had not been able to tell anyone that, however, since most of the children in his neighbourhood were either pony-mad or pony-hungry. They either rode all the time, or wished they could. It was a pity that the family who had lent him this pony had not lent it to one of the pony-hungry people. But Rubin had been in a lot of trouble this year, both at school and at home, and they thought that a nice wholesome summer with a fat grey pony would show him a Good Way of Life.

Rubin's idea of the good life was to hang around with his mates down by the canal. His mates were not the kind who had ponies, or wanted them. In their busy lives of knocking things off from Woolworth's and the market stalls and trading the items for cash, smashing things that annoyed them, like wind-shields, and sitting on the canal wall smoking and planning the next project, there was no time for such childish things.

Rubin had not told them about the grey pony. He had not told his parents that he was still seeing his mates. Since he rode the pony out almost every day, they thought he was getting wholesome. They did not know that he rode towards town, tied the pony up in the tumbledown shed behind Carter's coal yard, and sneaked between the buildings and down the alley to the place where his mates gathered to pass round the cigarettes nicked from a table in the caff last night and discuss new ways of destroying the plumbing in the gents at the cinema.

But when he heard the radio warning, he did confide in his best friend Arthur, who had been in so many tight places that he knew how to keep his mouth shut.

'If that pony kicks the bucket, you see,' he told Arthur, 'I'll have no cover story. They think I go riding all day. If there's no pony, they'll never let me go off on my own, and I'll miss the big thing at the warehouse.'

'You got no shed, not nothing, at your place?' Arthur asked.

'Only the garage, and that's got my father's car in it.'

Rubin and his father did not get along very well, so he spoke of him as My Father to make up for feeling sometimes that he didn't have a father.

'It's mostly nights they said was the danger time, right?'

'And that's just the time the car is always in the garage.'

'And just the time your dear old Dad will be tucked up in bed o-blivious, right?'

'Right.'

Late that night, Arthur sneaked down to Rubin's house. He waited by the garage until Rubin came out and said, 'My father's in bed and asleep.'

They opened the garage door cautiously. Rubin could not drive, so Arthur, who said he could, was the one who backed the car out.

He put it into forward gear first, and smashed the headlamps against the workbench. Because he knew how to drive, he was able to get it into reverse. He backed out fast, just missing Rubin who was holding the door, couldn't reach the footbrake, couldn't find the handbrake, and crashed through a fence with a night-shattering noise of breaking glass and splintering wood. He stopped with his back wheels against the next door garage, opened the door and ran.

When Rubin's father came out, it was obvious what Rubin had done. He tried to explain about the pony, but his father had heard enough of Rubin's stories to know a fairytale excuse when he heard one. Rubin was confined to the house and garden for the rest of the holidays. He missed the raid on the warehouse, and so missed being picked up with Arthur and the rest by the police car which was waiting for them outside the broken window.

The grey pony went back to its owners. They were very disappointed with Rubin for not having found a Good Way of Life.

There were also three girls who had a pony, which could not be brought in at night because there was no place to keep it.

Yes there was. It was a very small pony, not much bigger than a Shetland. On the day that the Royal Veterinary College sent out its warning to horse owners, there was parked outside the house where the girls lived a closed grey van of the kind used by plumbers and painters to carry their equipment. It had been there for days. On its sides was painted, 'J. E. DUGGAN. HOME REPAIRS ALL SORTS. DECORATIONS. GUTTERS. UPHOLSTERING. U NAME IT.' The van was empty. The girls knew that, because the back door was unlocked and they had looked.

So when the warning came, it was obvious where they

could store the pony out of danger. It was a lot of trouble to get it into the van, but with one of them getting her shoulders under the front end, and the other two lifting a back leg each, they finally got their beloved pet into the van, closed the door and went to bed relieved that Ponto was safe from harm for tonight at least.

Early the next morning, J. E. Duggan, who had run out of petrol and taken a bus into town, came back with a can. He put a gallon in the tank, filled up at a service station, and drove on back to Scotland with the pony.

Those were only a few of the things that happened that night of the Great Encephalitis Epidemic Scare.

25

ANOTHER thing that happened that night was that Callie found Dora crying in the tack room, wiping her eyes with a grubby rag that had last been used to polish a snaffle.

'Oh come on.' Callie quite often cried herself, but it unnerved her to see a grown-up doing it. 'Robin's all right, and if Rebel dies – well, he might never have been rideable anyway. Steve says he would have killed somebody in the end, and you'd have been lucky if it was one of the Crowleys and not you.'

'Steve says.' Dora sighed and twisted the rag in her hands. 'Steve is always saying. He knows it all. Like –' she made a sound between a laugh and a sob – 'like Chuckie Fiske.'

'Who's she? Oh, I remember. The one who said you were the only idiot in the world who could get Robin on the wrong lead.' Callie had heard the saga of America many times. 'Chuckie Fiske, she knows it all.'

'She knows nothing,' Dora said bitterly. 'It's all her fault.'

'What is?'

'Steve told me that if the disease is confirmed, all our horses here will probably have to be put down.'

All our horses here? Callie stared at Dora. She felt that the blood had dropped from her face into a pool of lead in her stomach. All our horses – Cobby? Hero? Specs and Folly? Lancelot who had survived so stubbornly?

Dora was sitting on the broken chair, staring blankly at a five-year old calendar on the wall from E. Tibbets, Grain and Hay. Callie ran out.

She went to bed early, without supper. She didn't want to see anyone. She lay upstairs and listened to voices, the phone ringing, feet running. It seemed for ever before the house finally settled down for the night.

Long after everyone was asleep, Callie was still keeping herself awake by pinching bits of skin, scratching her toenails against her ankles, reciting dates of Kings and Queens and finding towns and rivers and colours and trees and types of horse for all the letters of the alphabet.

Through her open window, she could hear the stabled horses stamping and snorting. In the winter, they mostly lay down quietly. Now they could not get used to the loss of their summer freedom. When Callie leaned out of the window and said, 'Cobby,' he heard her at once and answered.

She dressed again and went downstairs. The friendly house was still and unfamiliar, full of strange creaks and knocks and angled moonlit patches. The Colonel's dog stirred and thumped her tail. The cats sleeping on piles of laundry and newspapers took no notice as Callie let herself quietly out of the back door and went to the stables.

One by one, she led the horses out to the big field and turned them loose. Cobbler's Dream was last, and the grey donkey. Riding Cobby and leading Donald, she went down the grass track into the field and shut the gate behind her.

Dottie, watching from the orchard, brayed a strangled question.

'Shut up,' Callie told her. 'You'll have to stay and risk it.' Polly was too little to let loose with the others.

She rode among the horses, still leading the grey donkey, down the hill, across the bridge over the stream, and out to the far end of the long pasture, where the grass became harsher and the bushes thicker as the land approached the open moorland beyond the farm boundaries.

The old horses were in the habit of following Don, and they followed him now, straggling in singles and groups, pausing at the open gate, and then following Callie on through, cautiously scenting the wide spaces that were not fenced or hedged.

Callie got off, removed the donkey's halter, and threw some pebbles at him to make him run ahead. The horses followed. When they were all through the gate, she shut it behind them. With her face set as a stone and her heart numb with loss, she slipped off Cobby's halter, and without looking back at her, he trotted after the rest of the other horses over the dipping moorland.

26

RON Stryker felt deprived. Cheated of glory.

It was he who had made the historic telephone call, awakening the nation to the threat of an epidemic. Now everyone but him was getting the publicity. Everyone but poor old Dr Dillon.

He couldn't go to the farm to give newsmen the chance of a picture of the Man who Broke the News, because the Colonel would get after him with an iron rake for doing the Dr Dillon act, so he decided to go to London and let one of the big dailies have an Exclusive.

His motorbike was not licensed for this quarter. That was all right for buzzing round the local roads where the police were dozy, but a trip to London was too risky. Ron got out on the main road and started using his thumb.

Expert at the art he was, never failed to get a lift. Looks and personality, that's what did it.

Looks and personality kept him walking for about half an hour, while cars whizzed uncaring by him. Then a car going fast slowed ahead of him and pulled to the side of the road. Ron panted to catch up with it.

The driver was lighting a cigarette.

'Thanks for stopping for me.' Ron opened the door.

'I didn't,' the driver said. 'I stopped to get a packet of cigarettes out of my coat.'

'My mistake.' Ron was going to shut the door, but the man said indifferently, 'Get in anyway. It doesn't matter.'

'Going to London?' Ron asked. The man nodded and Ron hugged himself. Never failed. Always the old luck.

'I'm going to Fleet Street,' he said, 'as a matter of fact.'

Since the driver appeared unmoved, he added, 'Exclusive story on the big horse disease epidemic. They want pictures of the man who broke the news.'

'That rather suspicious sounding vet?' the driver asked. 'I'm a doctor myself, so naturally I was interested, but those first reports sounded a bit whacky.'

'Bad reporting,' Ron said. But he decided to settle for being Dr Dillon's assistant, rather than whacky Dr Dillon.

'You're a vet's assistant?' The doctor's glance took in Ron's tangled red hair, his leather jacket with the oil marks, the tattoo on the back of his right hand which said 'Rita'.

'Yerss, and so naturally I've been involved in the whole affair.' Ron had many accents available for use. This one was taken from the Colonel's friend Sir Richard Wortley, who had a strawberry nose, and pointed at old horses with his stick and said, 'Getting a bit groggy on his pins, what?'

'What is your estimate then,' the doctor enquired politely, 'of the biological factors favourable for the perpetuation of the virus through infected vertebrates?'

'Do what?'

'Next question: what's the point of trying to put me on?'

'Well –' Ron shifted uneasily. 'Just having a bit of a lark.'

'I don't like people having larks in my car.' The doctor stopped, leaned across and opened the door. Ron got out and gave a cheery wave, to show he didn't mind bad manners.

The next car that stopped was driven by a simple looking boy, with a thatch of pale yellow hair and a crop of fiery pimples. Who should Ron be this time? The boy looked impressionable. He might do his pop singer bit.

When the boy asked, 'Going to London?' Ron said, 'Yes.

Got a couple of concerts booked. I always travel this way because I like to meet my fans.'

'Who are you then?' The boy turned on him a vacant gape.

'Silk Valliant.' Ron studied his long dirty nails.

'Silk Valliant!' the boy mooed, disguising by over-enthusiasm the fact that he had never heard of him. 'Wow, wait till I tell the gang I gave a lift to Silk Valliant. I do a bit with the drums myself,' he added modestly, 'but of course, not in your class.'

'Ah well.' Silk Valliant settled back and prepared to enjoy the drive. 'We've all got to start somewhere.'

When the boy stopped to let him out at the point where he turned off the London road, Ron fished in his pocket and put two green tickets into the glove compartment.

'Tickets for my concert,' he said. 'Bring your old lady. Come round and see me after.'

'Gosh, thanks.' The boy's bumpy skin flamed. After he had driven on alone for a while, he took out the tickets. They said, 'Parish Church of Ashbury serving Little Moulsden. Summer Fayre. Grand Raffle. First Prize a 14lb Goose.'

Nobody stopped for Ron for a long time. He sat by the side of the road and rubbed his ankle, with an expression of pain that people were going too fast to notice, even if they cared. The only person who cared was a little old lady going slow enough to notice. She stopped and backed up to him fast, almost running over the leg he wasn't rubbing.

'Do you need to go to a hospital?' she asked hopefully.

'No,' said Ron. 'I've had that bullet in there so long, they reckon they'll leave it.'

He got into the car, and almost immediately regretted it.

The lady pulled across to the middle lane and drove at thirty miles an hour, with people passing her on both sides. From time to time, she wobbled off course. Drivers hooted, glared and shook their fists. Children jeered through back windows. Ron slumped in his seat, hoping not to be seen.

'Are you all right?' the old lady asked sunnily. 'You look deathly pale.'

'Please stop the car and put me out,' Ron said faintly. 'I think I'm going to be car sick.'

'Oh, we can take care of that, my dear.' She pulled out some paper bags from under the seat. 'I've got a little grandson who always throws up, so I'm prepared. Goodness, that lorry came close to me.' She had wavered almost into the path of a big lorry, who had swerved just in time, stark horror on the driver's face.

'Let me out,' Ron begged.

'I said I'd take you all the way into London. Don't thank me. I like the company.'

'I've got smallpox,' Ron said, but a car was hooting at her and she didn't hear. He prayed for a quick death, but a busy roundabout came instead. The old lady had to slow. He opened the door, jumped and ran.

He was taken on into London in a van driven by an old mate of his. Ron didn't have to put on an act for him, so he told him the story about the sick horse and his phone call and how it had started this whole hullabaloo.

The mate didn't read the newspapers, except for the sports pages, and he only listened to rock music on radio, so this was the first he'd heard of it.

'Go on,' he said. 'You must think I was born yesterday, Ronald Stryker. What a pack of lies.'

'Now it's funny you should say that,' Ron said, 'because for the first time in me life, I'm telling you the clean, unvarnished truth.'

When he got to the office of the newspaper he had picked to favour with his Exclusive Story, the doorman would not let him go up to the news room.

'Bomb scares,' he said. 'Sorry. State your business and I'll send up a message.'

'I'm the one that broke the news about the epidemic of ephalitis – elephantisis – you know. Dr Dillon. I've come to have me picture taken.'

The doorman spoke on the telephone.

'I'm sorry,' he said more firmly. 'There's no one up there able to see you.'

'But they must,' cried Ron. 'They're daft, they don't know their business.' There were people going in and out of the lifts all the time. This made him furious. 'It's hot news. Call back again.'

'I'm sorry.'

'Don't keep *saying* that.'

Ron was so frustrated that he set fire to the wastepaper basket (give 'em some hot news). The doorman smothered the fire, sighed and called upstairs for someone to come and deal with Dr Dillon.

A girl came down. They sent a mere girl, who looked as if it was her first day on the job.

'What is it that you want?'

'It's about the great epidemic, innit?'

'What great epidemic?' the girl asked. 'There never was one.'

'There was too. You don't know your job, mate. There's the

great horse epidemic. All kids in Britain threatened. Never been a story like it.'

'Never been a flop like it.' The girl laughed. 'Haven't you heard the news?'

'What news? I been on the road since morning.'

'That horse died.'

'There you are, what did I tell you?'

'They cut it open. What do you think it died of?'

'What I said – elphlacitis – elepan –'

'It died of a brain tumour. There's no epidemic.'

'But I come all the way to London!'

'Sorry about that.' She got him firmly to the door and out into the street. All right, so it wasn't her first day on the job.

Ron felt very discouraged and quite fagged out. He went to see an acquaintance of his who sold souvenirs in Oxford Street, borrowed some money, and went back by train.

His way home from the station to the cottage where he lived with his mother took him past Follyfoot. He looked across the field at the top of the hill, where lights and shadows moved across the grass in a pattern of moon and clouds. Someone was coming up the long slope. A poacher? If it was old Bob, he owed Ron five pounds.

Ron climbed the gate and stood behind a tree. It was a very small poacher. It was Callie.

'Ron!' She gasped and jumped as he stepped out in front of her.

'Been courting, dear?'

He saw that her face was streaked with tears and dust, and that her breath was coming hard, in dry sobs.

'What's up?'

'Oh Ron, it's awful.' She raised her face to his and tears

began to run again down the tracks the others had made. 'Oh
Ron –'

'Oh Ron what?'

'It's –' She took a deep breath and swallowed. 'It's one of
the puppies. The one with the bent tail. He's been missing
since morning and I can't find him anywhere.'

'Them pups is old enough to take care of themselves.' Ron
put an arm round her. 'Never you mind, love. You go on to
bed, and we'll have a good look in the morning.'

'All right,' she whispered. She was as white as a little ghost.
Ron would have liked to tell her about his horrible day, but he
hadn't the heart. He'd tell his mother and his mother would say,
'Trouble? You don't know the meaning of the word if you've
not lived with this pain I suffer in my back, night and day. . . .'

He walked with Callie to the gate that led to the stables,
boosted her over it, and watched her run like a thin scared
animal across the yard and into the house.

27

CALLIE dozed and woke and dropped into a nightmare of charging horses from which she woke with a cry and an arm flung over her face, in fear of being trampled. She had hoped to sleep most of the next day, because she did not want to face the next day, but the mercy of sleep was denied her. She lay scared and trembling, chewing on the sheet, her eyes staring into the gradually spreading light.

When she could stand it no longer, she gave a deep sigh, stepped into last night's clothes in a heap by the bed and started downstairs. Someone was frying already.

In the kitchen, Dora was scooping out of a pan three fried eggs with burned bottoms and broken yolks.

'Want me to do you some, Cal?'

Dora looked unnervingly bright and healthy compared to the way Callie felt after her night of tears and nightmare. Callie shook her head. She poured herself a mug of tea from the enormous potful that Dora had made, and sat down at the table, cradling the steaming mug moodily in her hands.

'Pig, aren't I?' Dora had started on the eggs and a hunk of bread and butter. 'I always say it should be horses first, then people, but this morning, I felt like feeding myself first before our four-legged friends out there.'

She didn't know yet.

'I was starving.' Dora sopped bread in the greasy eggs. 'Must be the relief.'

In Callie's miserable, sleep-starved brain, a thought began to register. It finally became clear.

'Relief?' She looked up.

'That's right.' Dora put down her knife and fork. 'Good

Lord, nobody's told you yet. You went to bed so early yesterday, you were asleep when the fantastic news came through.'

'What news?' No news could be fantastic at this point.

'About Rebel. He died, you know. Not that that's fantastic, but well – the poor thing was dying anyway. The thing is, what he died of. The tests on the mice still weren't confirmed, but as soon as he died, they did a post mortem, and what do you think they found?'

'Massive brain damage due to the virus,' Callie growled. She knew what encephalitis could do.

'A tumour. A brain tumour. Not that big, but in a vulnerable spot. It would account for the erratic way he behaved, if a branch knocked him, or some fool like me hit him behind the ear. So Robin's in the clear. The scare's off.'

Callie stood up and turned away from her grin. She went to stand by the window. She was going to have to speak without looking at Dora.

'We should have woken you, I suppose,' Dora went on. 'But you looked so peaceful.' Callie's faking face, that must have been, with her arms crossed over her chest like a dead maiden, lacking only a lily between her hands.

'I feel so good, I've half a mind to fry myself another egg. Are you sure you –'

'Dora,' Callie said in a hollow voice. 'Last night, in the middle of the night, I got up.'

'Why?' Dora was at the stove. She cracked one of the big brown eggs that Henrietta laid in Wonderboy's hay rack (he preferred his hay off the floor anyway) and dropped it into the pan.

'You told me that the Follyfoot horses might have to be destroyed.'

'That's what they thought then. It was unbearable. I never want to have to go through another day like that again.'

411

'This one isn't going to be too good,' Callie said in a small voice. 'I thought – you see, I thought they were going to shoot all our horses, so I took them down to the end of the long field and let them out on to the moor.'

'You *what*?' Dora was concentrating on getting the egg out of the pan, only half hearing.

'I did. I let them all out on to the moor. They followed the donkey.'

'Including Robin?' Dora turned round with the plate in one hand and the spatula in the other.

Callie nodded.

'Stupid idiot!' Callie had never seen Dora so angry. Dumb with misery, she stood and let the words of Dora's rage hit her like arrows.

'Stupid, hysterical kids –'

A cat jumped up on the table and started on the egg as Dora grabbed her jacket from the hook behind the door and slammed out.

Callie followed.

'What do you want?' Dora flung angrily over her shoulder as she ran.

'Can't I help you look for them?'

'I suppose so. I've no idea where to start. Have to follow the hoof tracks. Is there anything left we can ride?'

'All gone except Dottie and Polly.'

'Oh God.' The vision of Callie and Dora setting off to the rescue on the little brown donkey and her foal might have made her laugh, but it didn't. She strode ahead. Callie trotted after. There was nothing else to do.

They ran down the slope, crossed the stream at the bottom and began to push through the bushes that thickened the end of the field. As they came out to where they could see the gate, Dora stopped and let out a yell of laughter. Callie stopped and stared. Then all the anguish and the fear and the guilt from Dora's anger suddenly exploded into the relief of a wild, high-pitched crowing laughter. For a moment, they could only stand there, clutching each other, cackling with joy.

Outside the gate, lined up like people at a cafeteria, were all the old horses, Cobbler's Dream in the lead, the others behind him in order of rank, Robin modestly near the end as a new-comer, waiting patiently for someone to come and let them in for breakfast.

Walking back up the field with the horses, Callie said, 'What about Steve? He'll hear the horses coming in.'

'I could say that I went out late last night and turned them out after we knew there was no danger.'

In the kitchen, an hour ago, it had seemed as if Callie and Dora could never be friends again. But really nothing had changed. Dora was still the kind of friend who could under-stand when you wanted something hushed up.

'But he'd have heard them going out, if so,' Callie said. 'That's why I led them out quietly, one by one.'

'All right. I led them out quietly one by one.'

When Dora went into the kitchen after finishing the morning's work with Callie and Steve, her egg plate was still on the table, polished so clean by rough cat tongues that it appeared never to have been used.

''Lo, Dora' The Colonel, who should have been looking joyful, was looking gloomy. He had his old clacketty type-writer on the table, and was banging on it with one finger of each hand, his unlit pipe in the corner of his mouth, his giant size coffee cup that Anna had brought back from Italy beside him, just such a cosy domestic scene as Dora had imagined when she was homesick in Mrs Blank's spic and span kitchen.

413

'I'm writing to Blankenheimer,' he said. 'I've held off until I saw what was what, but now I have to write and tell him what I think of him.'

'But why?' Dora sat down and spread her hands beseechingly on the table. 'Why? Now that it doesn't matter any more?'

'Not matter?' The Colonel looked at her over the half glasses he wore for reading. 'But it's a question of principle, don't you see? There's a law been broken. There's a fishy deal been done. It's the act, not the consequences that matters. Don't you see?' he asked again.

Dora sighed and did not answer. Most of the time at Folly-foot it seemed as if age did not matter, as if everyone – Slugger, Anna and the Colonel, Steve and Dora, Callie – were the same generation, with a common purpose and a common pleasure centred on horses. But when something like this came up – forget it. If she said what she thought, the Colonel would say she was immoral.

'False papers,' the Colonel said, shaking his head glumly. 'I don't know what the immigration authorities will make of this, but it could land our friend Blankenheimer in very serious trouble.'

He had his hands raised to strike the keys again, like an arthritic pianist, but Dora got up and shouted. There was no other way to do it. It was the thought of darling Blank, innocent and kind, the most generous gift of his life shattered, just as if Robin were a precious porcelain horse shattered by careless packers. It was the vision of Blank getting out of his comfortable car at the post office, finding the letter in his mail box – 'Hey, great! A letter from the Colonel. Look, Mary, a letter from my old British buddy' – and then his face under whatever funny cap he was wearing now, stricken with the realisation of what Chuckie and Dora had done to him. That was why she had to shout.

414

'It wasn't him!' she shouted 'It was Chuckie Fiske and me. We were the only ones who knew. Yes, of course I knew.' She wouldn't let him speak, because if she stopped, she might not get started again. 'I didn't tell you because I was afraid you'd be angry. Well, you are angry and I am afraid. But Blank knew nothing, and I'm not going to let you accuse him, do you hear?'

'What's all the shouting?' Anna came in and Dora went out, on fire. She could almost see her nostrils steaming.

She had done what she had to do. She had stopped the Colonel writing to Blank, but now all his anger would be directed at her. She didn't know that she could bear the weight of it.

She tried to keep out of his way. When she did not come in for supper on the second day, Steve went to look for her. He found her in Robin's stable, her arm round his neck and her face in his fine black mane. Robin was paying more attention to his food than to her, in the comforting way horses have of showing you that the world hasn't come to an end.

'Aren't you coming in for supper?' Steve put his hand on her arm, lightly, because Dora didn't always want to be touched when she was upset.

'I can't eat.'

'Well, that's a lie,' Steve said candidly, 'since I saw you sitting on the wall this morning with a chunk of bread and butter in each fist.'

'I can't be in a room with the Colonel, if he still hates me.'

'Who says he hates you? Don't you know the difference between hate and anger? He'll get over it.'

'Never.'

'All right, love.' Steve went to the door. 'Don't believe me. Just wait and see.'

415

28

THE chalky hills rolled away on either side of Follyfoot Farm, following the lines of some ancient upheaval in the foundations of Britain. There were villages in the folds between the hills, some grazing farms and a few isolated houses in bare and windy spots, rugged, thick-walled, headed into the view.

About ten miles from Follyfoot, there was a small cottage, once painted white, now rusty where the paint had flaked and the old bricks showed through. What had once been a good vegetable garden was now sadly neglected. Only a few cabbages and lettuces gone to seed grew among the weeds and broken pea sticks.

But behind the house in the sheltering beechwood, the source of a stream bubbled up through tender bright green water plants. In front stretched the breathtaking view of gently diminishing hills, fields of all colour, farms, churches, curving roads, the willowed line of the river far away.

Mabel had fallen in love with the place as soon as she saw it. Her children hated it. That confirmed Mabel's opinion.

Mabel's husband had died a long time ago when her children were small. When her father died, her old mother moved in with her. She became more and more difficult as she grew older. The children objected to taking care of her when Mabel was out. She fell in the fire and wandered off down the road at night.

The day she almost got run over by the late bus, everybody told Mabel that her mother must go into a nursing home. The old lady was last seen being wheeled away down a corridor, calling back feebly, 'Don't leave me, Mabel!'

Mabel's children got married and had children of their own, and grew more opinionated and efficient and busy. Sometimes they seemed like strangers, who could never have been the dreamy children she had hugged. Mabel herself gradually became an old lady. She began to forget things, to stumble and lose her glasses, and repeat herself, and set fire to pans of bacon fat on the stove.

She realized that her children, particularly the girls, had begun to look at each other and mutter, and she thought that they were plotting to do the same thing to her as she had done to her mother.

But she could never go to a home, because she had dogs and cats, not to mention her old horse, who had been with her longer than anyone could remember. She had a bit of money saved, and she knew what she would do.

She sat her children down and said to them, 'I'm getting near the end of my life.'

'Oh nonsense, Mother,' Rachel said automatically. 'You've got years yet.'

'I'm going to do what I've always wanted.' Mabel ignored her. 'I'm going to take my animals and find a small cottage miles away from anywhere, and you don't have to keep coming to see me, because I don't want you to.'

'But we must. We'd feel –'

'Don't come for your sakes,' Mabel said. 'If you come at all, come for mine. If I want you, I'll send for you.'

'Will you ring us up every day? Once a week?'

'No. Because I shan't have a telephone.'

'Then how can you send for us? Letters take ages. If you were ill –'

'I'll manage. You'll know,' Mabel said mysteriously. She had become more mysterious and weird in her old age.

· · · · · · ·

417

Against her children's protest, Mabel bought the small cottage facing the marvellous view. Between the back garden and the beechwood was a good small paddock with an open shed for her old horse. This horse's name was Julian, after her lover, who had been killed in the First War. Her children considered it pretty bad taste of her not to have called him Sidney after her husband.

Julian was about twenty-two years old. He was a bit of an old crock, but could still pull the dog cart to the village when Mabel needed food. He was not a lovable horse. He had a small moustache on his top lip and hips like a cow, and a cautious way of setting his ears straight up with the insides turned sideways and showing the yellow of his eye. But he and Mabel understood each other, and his legs had served her faithfully long after her own had left her in the lurch.

One wet afternoon, Dora took Robin out for a long ride. It was the one thing that helped. Riding him was still the same pure, exhilarating pleasure that it had been in America, but more so now, because he was hers, and she could teach him things that would be for the two of them alone.

She rode along the old grassed-over Roman road just below the top of the hills, in and out of the small valleys, jumping streams, cantering tirelessly on the short turf that squelched up little fountains under Robin's hoofs. Each time she thought of turning back, she wanted to go farther. It would be a long way home, but she didn't care.

Something let go. She lurched to one side as the stirrup leather split through at the fold. Cleaning tack was not one of the strong points of Follyfoot. The dried out leather had been cracking through for a long time.

A bit of string and a sharp skewer would do it. When Dora

passed a gate half off its hinges, she turned down the lane between beech trees and found a cottage with an old horse who
gave Robin an unenthusiastic greeting, and an old lady in a dark
rain cape with a hood messing about in a neglected vegetable
plot.

'Could I possibly borrow some string?' Dora rode near to
her.

The old lady looked at Robin with pleasure, and at the
stirrup leather with tut-tuts. 'Your stuff is in almost as bad shape
as mine.' When she smiled, she didn't look so much like a
witch.

She brought out some string and a sharp skewer to poke
holes in the two ends of the leather, then took her to admire
the old horse before Dora left. It was raining quite hard. The
horse was standing in the middle of the field with his ears back
and his tail tucked in. The old lady chased him into the shed and
put up the bars.

'Do you have far to go home?' she asked Dora.

'About ten miles. I needed a long ride. Bad things have been
happening. I just had to get off on my own.'

'I know what you mean,' said the old lady. 'There were bad
things for me too. Julian and I had to get away by ourselves.'

'I like it here,' Dora said.

'Come back.' The old lady was shivering. She started towards
the house. 'My name is Mabel. I'll give you some cocoa and
some of the awful bread I bake. I'm not quite up to it today.'

After the girl with the beautiful horse had gone, Mabel went
into the house and lit the fire and fed the dogs and cats and
sat in the chair which fitted her shape like a comforting hand.
One of the cats jumped on her lap. She folded her hands across
its broad grey back, and enjoyed some memories.

419

Perhaps, she thought, I will send a message to the girls. I really don't feel up to much today. If I am going to be ill, it would be only fair to let them know. They'd feel guilty. Shut up, Mabel, she told herself. It was to get away from useless things like guilt that you came up here.

Dora thought quite a bit about Mabel and her lonely cottage, and about being old and wanting to be left alone. Mabel didn't have to worry what people thought of her, because there were no people.

Dora was still padding round, trying to keep out of the Colonel's way or trying to please him and doing everything wrong. Spilling his coffee, losing a bill for oats, leaving a rake upturned in a dark corner, where Sir Richard Wortley trod on the prongs and got konked in the forehead by the handle.

Steve found her saddling Robin.

'Where are you going?'

'Oh – for a ride.'

'When will you be back? I'm not going to start mending that roof unless you're going to help me.'

'I'm going a long way.'

'Then I'll come. Miss needs the work. We'll do the roof when we get back.'

'But –' But why not? Mabel hadn't minded Dora coming to the house. It was mostly her daughters she didn't want.

It was a glorious ride. The sun was in and out. A week of rain had drawn out all the spicy fragrance of the bushes and low clumpy plants that grew along the hills. When the horses got into the rhythm of a long canter together, it felt as if it could go on for ever.

'Remember the last ride you had with me?' Steve said as they pulled up to cross a chalky rock slide.

Dora rubbed her head. 'Almost was my last ride with anyone. Poor Rebel. I wonder what the Crowleys think about it all?'

'Just as long as they don't think about getting another bargain horse.'

'They will.'

'And you'll end up with it at Follyfoot.'

'Probably. I don't know though.' Dora thought of the Colonel. 'Have to be someone else's idea next time.'

As they rode down the lane under the roofing beeches, they heard a pandemonium of barking from the little house. Dora called Mabel, and when there was no answer, she gave Robin's reins to Steve and tried the back door. As she opened it, the dogs surged out and ran off, barking in a crazy way.

The kitchen was chaotic. Food pulled out of the cupboards, milk bottles tipped over, cat and dog mess everywhere.

Dora went out again. 'Steve. Tie the horses up and come in.'

They went through to the front room. In the doorway, Steve instinctively put his arm out and said, 'Don't look.'

'I'm not afraid.'

Mabel was sitting in a chair by the empty fireplace. She seemed to have been dead for several days.

Shut in the shed by the bars, Julian had been pawing futilely at the ground underneath them, but was now propped in a far corner, barely able to stand. He had obviously had no food or water for some time. He was terribly dehydrated.

They gave him a small amount of food and water to start with, locked the back door of the house and took the key, and went to telephone a doctor, and for the horse box to come for Julian.

421

In the lane, they met a car, full of women and children. There was only one house at the end of this road. It must be Mabel's family.

They stood their horses in the middle of the lane. The driver leaned out to tell them to move aside. Dora rode closer.

'Are you going to see Mabel?'

'Yes. Who are you? We're her family. Thought we'd stop by and see how she is.'

Dora could only stare, so Steve said, 'It's too late.'

'What do you mean?'

'She's dead.'

'Oh, my God!' The two women made fluttery movements of trying to put hands over children's ears. The children jerked away and listened solemnly.

'My God, how ghastly!'

'No,' Dora said. 'It's all right. She wanted to die like that, I think. No fuss. Off on her own.'

The hard-voiced daughter with the glistening scarlet mouth said in a shocked sort of tone, 'Last week, I was woken up by a voice quite close. It said "Rachel". I didn't pay any attention. I thought it was my conscience. She always said, "I'll send for you if I need you." I thought she meant telephone or letter. I didn't know she meant like that.'

Dora gave them the key and left them to ring the doctor, the police, the ambulance – they were arguing who it should be as Dora and Steve rode on. In the village, Dora telephoned the Colonel to send the horse box.

'Another customer, Dora?' He sounded like his old self.

'Yes. He's quite old and he's weak. He's been starved for days, but I think we can save him.'

'Good girl,' the Colonel said. 'Well done. You do seem to find just the horses that Follyfoot is here for.'

Everything was all right. Although she was still shaky from

422

the shock of Mabel, Dora came out of the telephone box feeling as if a dark cloud had lifted. Wait – there was one nagging unease. What was it? Oh yes. She had thought she was the only person who heard voices in the night. Bit disappointing to find that a girdled woman with stiff hair and lipstick like blood heard them too.

29

EVERY year as autumn approached, Callie organised a celebration for all the neighbourhood animals that had been born that summer.

Puppies, kittens, chickens, ducks, geese, fish in bowls, an abandoned fledgling Toby had found, who had refused to leave as it grew feathers and strength, and spent a lot of time in Toby's pocket.

Dottie and her foal Polka Dot, a prize exhibit. Folly, because it wasn't fair to exclude him for being born two months before spring. Three leggy young Dartmoors from the pony farm. Moll's calico cat's fifty-ninth kitten. Toby's mother's new baby. A box of young Belgian rabbits. A pair of hound pups who were being 'walked' by Mrs Oldcastle.

Everybody got a prize, because no one was better than anyone else.

Robin was allowed to enter because he had been reborn as a British citizen. Julian was celebrated because he had been born again – snatched from the jaws of death.

There was always something to celebrate at Follyfoot.

What they were really celebrating was life.

Stranger at
Follyfoot

I

'THAT horse,' Steve said, 'is leading the life of a spoiled child.'

'He is only a child.' Dora had tied the colt Folly to a ring in a post, and was going over him with one of Anna's old silk scarves. It made his brown coat shine like the burnished chestnuts on the trees which stood on either side of the gate into Follyfoot. 'He's only two. Fourteen in human counting.' She walked after him as he danced round the post.

'When I was fourteen,' Steve said, 'I was sent out to work. Folly should have been backed by now.'

'Callie's been dying to get on him, but the Colonel said not yet. He's small, Steve.'

'He's a firecracker.' Steve took hold of the rope near the halter to hold the restless colt still. 'The Colonel thought he'd be too much for Callie, but if you told her that, she'd be on him in a flash.'

'I don't know,' Dora said. 'She's a bit nervous really.'

'That's just it. Nervous people make themselves do things.'

Dora looked at him quickly. How could Steve know that? He wasn't afraid of anything.

'Callie won't be back from school till four,' Steve said. 'Come on, Dora, let's get some weight on his back. See how he takes to it. Born to work, this little devil is. He's going to love it.'

'Callie will be furious.'

'She won't know. We'll start working with him while she's at school, and when we suggest to her she gets on him, he won't give her any trouble.'

Folly had already got used to a mouthing bit, with loose

Callie can get on him. And we'll let her think she's the first.'

'Get on with it then,' Steve said, 'or she'll be home from school.'

'Not for ages yet.' Dora settled herself in the saddle as gently as an egg. 'Walk him forward, Steve.'

2

They had reckoned without the local bus drivers. They called a strike on late buses, and people like Callie who lived at the top of the hill came home on an early bus.

It dropped Callie at the farm gate just as Steve let go of the headcollar and Dora gently squeezed Folly into a trot. At the first bounce of her muscular bottom, the colt squealed, put down his head and gave a neat, but powerful buck. Dora flew through the air and landed in a patch of long grass and thistles.

Folly gave another buck, to make sure he had got rid of her, tore off round the field with the reins over his head, went down and rolled to try and get rid of the saddle, caught the headcollar on a root, broke it, got up, shook himself and stood quietly with the saddle upside down underneath him.

'What are you doing with my horse?'

Callie came dashing round the barn, pigtails flying, casting off hat, satchel and blazer as she ran.

'Nothing.' Dora limped out of the long grass, rubbing her hip. 'It's what is he doing to me?'

'You must be doing something wrong.' Callie climbed the gate, and went slowly up to Folly with her hands behind her back, so that he wouldn't know he was going to be caught. She took off the broken headcollar, undid the girths and took off the saddle. She led him over to the gate, climbed on to it and eased herself gently on to his narrow back.

'Watch it,' Steve called, running towards the colt. 'He'll buck you off.'

'No, he won't. I've been riding him bareback for days, before any of you were up. I was going to surprise you.'

429

Steve stopped. He and Dora looked at each other and spread their hands helplessly.

'I thought the Colonel told you not to back him yet,' Dora said.

'Why were you doing it then?'

Callie grinned at them and rode in a rather wavering line towards the gate that led into the long hill pasture. Dora picked up the broken headcollar and went to open the gate. She watched as Callie rode the colt down through the field where some of the Follyfoot horses were pottering about their small daily affairs at the far end by the stream. Callie steered him round trees, trotted him on the flat ground, stopped him when he got excited, then turned and trotted back up the slope, hanging on to his mane as he peered and side-stepped at familiar stones and bushes he had been grazing among all his life.

'Isn't he perfect?' Callie slid off his back, and Folly immediately dropped his nose into her hand for the horse nuts she always carried in a pocket, whether she was in school uniform or not.

One day in Social Studies class, the teacher had asked everyone to empty their pockets to see what items were necessary to human beings. Most people had money and sweets and keys and old bus tickets and filthy handkerchiefs. Callie had horse nuts, horseshoe nails, a torn newspaper picture of a show-jumper, and three inches she had cut off the end of Folly's tail to keep it out of the mud.

When she took off Folly's bridle, he galloped down the hill and across the stream to the other horses. Some of them, like Nigger and Dolly, who were irritated by the young, ignored him. Others raised their heads as he went up to them and exchanged news by nose, and a few comradely nips on the neck.

Dora went into the field to see Robin, the bay half thorough-

430

bred, half quarterhorse she had brought back from **America**. He came up to lay his nose against her cheek. He wasn't a greedy horse, like Cobbler's Dream, who was bumping his nose against the closed fists that Steve held out to tease him.

'O.K., Cobby, which hand?'

The chestnut pony smelled both hands, and then tried to pry open the fingers that held the horse nuts.

It was a beautiful autumn afternoon, warm, with the sun low in a sky that was a much deeper blue than in the summer. The green of the woodland was turning to yellows and oranges and reds before the leaves fell. The air was full of good autumn smells of fruit and bonfires. It was one of those last precious days to treasure before you wake one morning to frost on the window and the knowledge that in spite of your belief that summer will go on for ever, winter is here and you can't find last year's gloves.

Dora and Steve moved among the old horses, each of whom had a history of bad luck or cruelty which had brought them to spend their last days in peace at Follyfoot.

The spotted circus horse with a back as flat as a table from years of being danced on by ladies in spangles and rosined shoes. Hero, the other circus horse, whom Callie had rescued by stealing. Ginger from the old days of milk carts, Folly's mother Specs from the junkyard, Amigo, the pale bony horse who would have been sold to die in harness if Dora had not bought him at an auction. Dottie the donkey with her foal Polka Dot who had been born unexpectedly under a hedge in the rain. Dear old Stroller, and Ranger, and Frank, and the Weaver, all the old friends.

3

THE dong dong of the big bell outside the stables was Slugger telling them to come back and start the evening's work.

Dora and Steve and Callie walked up the hill on the cropped turf, ahead of them the low, solid farm buildings and the well known umbrella shapes of the elms that punctuated the hedge along the road.

At the top of the field, they turned, as they always did, and leaned on the gate to look back at the horses grazing peacefully in the slanted sun that turned Robin's coat to a coppery red.

'I do love this place,' Dora sighed. 'I'm going to live here for ever and ever.'

Steve shrugged his shoulders. 'Nothing's certain.'

'If I want to stay here,' Dora said, 'I'll stay here.'

'Well,' Steve said, 'you might be here, but the horses might not.'

'There'll always be horses at Follyfoot.' Dora turned and began to walk up the grassy track towards the stable yard.

'Things are getting pretty tough, you know.' Steve walked beside her with a serious face. 'The price of feed and hay and bedding goes up all the time.'

'It'll be all right.' Dora did not worry about money, because she never had any. 'It always is.'

'I suppose so,' Steve said. 'But it seems to be more of a headache. Haven't you noticed how quiet the Colonel is lately?'

'He's always quiet.'

The Colonel was a peaceful man of few words. He communicated best with horses, in a language of comfortable grunts and murmurs and low whistles.

'More so than usual.' Steve frowned. 'I said yesterday, "Colonel, if we plough up that bare corner by the wood and resow it, in two years' time, we'll have a beautiful stand of hay." Normally he'd say, "Go ahead and do it." Yesterday he just sort of patted me on the shoulder in an absent-minded way and said, "Let's not make too many long range plans."'

As they rounded the corner of the loose boxes and came into the cobbled yard, where hay seeds had lodged among the cobbles and sprouted friendly tufts of grass, the Colonel came out of Ginger's box. He was wearing the apron with the deep pockets which held hoof picks, brushes, bandages, bottles of embrocation.

'Hullo, Colonel.'

He gave Dora the jerky nod with which he acknowledged greetings.

'How's Ginger's leg?'

'So-so.' He and Dora looked over the door of the box where the old milk horse stood in a corner with his left forefoot in a poultice of hot bran in sacking tied round the leg with string.

His belly sagged behind the bony shoulder blades. His hips stuck out like a coat hanger. He had lost all the hair from the top of his tail by rubbing it against his favourite tree. Parts of his wispy mane had gone the same way. There were bare places on his coat where some of the younger horses had nipped at him. He looked like a family's well-used, moth-eaten rocking horse, abandoned in the corner of a dusty attic. He was one of more than twenty four-legged reasons why there would always have to be horses at Follyfoot.

433

4

DORA started to clean out the loose boxes on her side of the yard. The forecast was for rain tonight. They might have to bring some of the older horses in.

As she took the wheelbarrow out to the Dutch barn to get another bale of straw, a car coming down the road slowed, then stopped outside the gate with the sign, 'Home of Rest for Horses'.

It was a small dusty car, ill-cared for. A man got out and came through the gate to where Dora was heaving down a bale of straw from the stack.

'Let me help you.'

'I'm fine.' Dora thought she was probably stronger than he was. He looked like a city person, with his dark suit, black shoes and narrow tie. Close up, the suit was rumpled, the shoes worn, the tie and shirt collar frayed.

'Is this the Home of Rest for Horses?' he asked, although he must have read it on the board at the gate.

Dora nodded, brushing straw from the front of her sweater.

'I've come,' the man said, 'to ask if you could take my horse.'

'I hope so,' Dora smiled. Although she had more than twenty horses to take care of, the idea of a new one was always pleasing.

'It's like this, you see,' the man said. 'I'm going away. To South America, as a matter of fact. Got the chance of a job there with a friend of mine.'

'I've been to America,' Dora said. She had stayed with the Colonel's friend Mr Blankenheimer, who dreamed of starting a Follyfoot Farm in the United States. 'That's where I got my bay horse Robin. He's half quarter –'

The man was not listening. 'Got to make a new start, you see.' He spoke half to himself. 'Things haven't worked out for me here. It's all got to go. The factory. The house. And worst of all – Kingfisher.'

'What kind of a horse is he?'

'Well . . . I don't know. Just a horse,' the man said vaguely. 'He's sort of a mottled colour, freckled, and thick in the middle. Very gentle. I don't know much about horses and riding, but I feed him and brush him and give him sugar treats, and we have lovely trots round the roads. The King has taught me all I know.'

Which isn't much, Dora thought.

'He's been a good friend to me.' The man's face was creased with anxiety. His eyes dropped like a bloodhound. 'That's why I'd like to bring him here. I couldn't have him – you know – put away, but I can't afford to pay anyone for his keep. There's a riding stable in the suburb where I live that might buy him, but he's too old to work like that, and his legs swell up and he's a little nippy until he gets to know you.'

Dora thought, *No wonder, if you feed him sugar and pound him round suburban streets*. But she said. 'Perhaps we could take him,' her mind already switching horses about so that Kingfisher could have the loose box with the bars where he could not nip at unwary visitors. 'Come and talk to the Colonel.'

'Let me help.' The man bent to wheel the barrow. The heavy bale of straw was badly balanced. The barrow swerved, the bale fell off, Dora heaved it on again and the man let her wheel it under the brick archway into the stable yard.

The Colonel was in the tack room, looking at Folly's broken headcollar.

'How did this happen?' He hated broken tack.

'Oh, well . . . he caught it on something.'

'How?'

Dora did not want an inquisition on the headcollar, with the man in the frayed tie hovering behind her, so she said, 'This is Mr – um.'

The Colonel turned. The man said, 'Ellis Elkins,' and held out his hand. The Colonel automatically wiped his hand on the side of his corduroys and shook hands.

'He's got this old horse, you see,' Dora said eagerly. 'He can't keep him any longer, and he can't sell him because of his legs, and I thought perhaps if we moved Ranger into Fanny's box, and put Fanny into that empty –'

'Whoa,' said the Colonel, and to Ellis Elkins, 'I'm sorry. We haven't any room, except for emergencies.'

'But there's that empty –'

The Colonel was too polite to say, 'Shut up,' but he gave Dora a look which said it for him, and she shut.

'You won't take Kingfisher?' Ellis Elkins looked blank.

'I can't.'

Dora went out of the tack room. She did not want to hear any more. Elkins stayed talking to the Colonel for a while longer, and he came out and walked towards his car with his shoulders bent and his hands in his pockets, kicking a pebble.

Dora called goodbye, but he got into his dusty car without looking back, and drove away.

'Dora!' Steve called. 'I thought you were getting me some bedding.'

'Get it yourself!' She went into Ginger's stable, because he was the only horse who was not out in the fields, and she needed a horse's neck to brood on. Things were happening at Follyfoot that she did not like.

436

5

SHE was still angry when she woke next day. She grumbled at the chickens pecking hopefully round the back doorstep. When she took in Stroller's feed, she pushed the heavy horse over more roughly than usual, then swore at one of the donkeys for standing on her toe, although its little shell foot did not hurt.

At breakfast in the kitchen, Callie, who had been up long before anyone else to ride Folly, came in fresh-faced, babbling about the marvels of the brown colt.

'Give it a rest,' Dora growled. 'You'd think he was the only horse in this place.'

'What's the matter, Dora?' Callie's mother Anna turned from the stove in surprise.

'Leave me alone.' Dora buttered toast savagely.

'She's crossed in love, that's what it is,' Ron Stryker said. 'I seen her talking to that bloke by the straw stack. Very fancy car, he had. Custom made scratches, painted in dust colour, them fashionable dented bumpers.'

Dora was torn between wanting to finish her breakfast, or leaving the room. She compromised by bolting down the rest of her sausage and eggs – 'Eats like a horse,' from Ron – wiping her mouth on the back of her hand – 'Man-*ners*!' – banging her chair back into the fireplace – 'Don't take it out on the furniture!' – and slamming out of the room – 'Nice knowin' yer.'

In the doorway, Dora collided with the Colonel, coming in with a serious face.

'I'm calling a staff meeting,' he said. 'In my study at eleven o'clock. I want you all there.'

437

'I've got to go to town to get that part for the pump,' Steve said.

'It can wait. I want everybody there.'

'Can I miss school?' Callie looked up hopefully.

'I don't mean you, Cal.'

She kicked the table leg. 'I miss all the fun.'

'This isn't –' the Colonel looked at Anna and swallowed – 'exactly fun.'

It was not fun.

One by one, they came in to the Colonel's shabby, comfortable study, and settled themselves in various places.

The Colonel sat sideways at his littered desk, his long legs crossed, his unlit pipe in his mouth. He still coughed, even when it was not lit.

Slugger, who had worked at the Farm since the Colonel came here, sat in the chair by the fire, dwarfed by the high back and the deep seat, which left his boots dangling short of the floor. His woollen cap, which was like hair to him, was still on top of his balding head.

Dora sat on the floor hugging her knees, the Colonel's yellow dog leaning against her, one of the cats criss-crossing under her legs.

Steve was on the couch with a lapful of puppies. Ron lounged on the windowsill.

The Colonel cleared his throat, and looked round the room.

'I've called this meeting,' he said, 'to talk about money.'

Groans all round.

'I may as well leave right now.' Dora pushed away the cat and began to stand up, 'since that's a subject I don't understand.'

438

'Shut up and sit down.' Steve leaned forward and pulled her back to the floor.

'As you know,' the Colonel went on, not looking at anybody, 'it's costing more every year to keep horses. A lot of stables have had to close. People have had horses put down. Some of them have sent their horses here.'

'Or tried to.' Dora was still sulking about Ellis Elkins.

'Some we've been able to take. Some we can't, if they seem reasonably fit. Like that man's horse yesterday, Dora. He –'

'You should have taken it. I thought that was what Follyfoot was *for*!'

'When we can afford it.'

'We've always managed somehow. We will again.'

'Oh belt up, Dora.' Steve poked her with his foot. 'Don't preach.'

'But I don't understand,' Dora said. 'I thought the whole idea of Follyfoot was to save horses at whatever cost.'

'To hear her talk,' Ron said, 'you'd think she'd invented this place. I was here for years before you came. Remember the day she came, Col? Walked into the yard in those weird clothes and said, "Do you ever hire girls?" Didn't know the north end of a horse from the south.'

'Don't change the subject,' the Colonel said. 'I've called this meeting because –'

He was interrupted again by a banging and a kind of snuffling sound outside the French window. Steve opened it. Dottie the chocolate donkey was waiting outside. She expanded her nostrils to the smell of the fire, then ambled in on her neat feet, bent her legs and flopped down on the hearthrug, with her ears laid contentedly sideways.

Dora shifted her position so that she could use the solid shoulder of the donkey for a back rest.

'Because,' the Colonel went on patiently, 'the Trustees of

439

the Farm have been after me to cut down on expenses. Where do I start? We can't skimp on feed and hay. I suppose we could save on bedding by leaving more horses out at night, but it's getting too cold for a lot of the old ones.'

They waited. They knew all this.

'The Trustees have told me,' the Colonel went on, 'that if we can't cut down on the horses, we – we'll have to ...' He stopped, bit at a nail, scratched his head, rubbed his cold pipe along his cheek, cleared his throat, 'cut down on staff.'

He said it apologetically, like a question, but there was no answer. Everyone was all of a sudden very busy. Dora was carefully picking flaky bits of scurf out of Dotty's wispy mane. Steve was trying to make the largest puppy's ears stand up, as they were supposed to do, if his father really was an Alsatian. Ron had picked up an old tennis racket from the corner and was strumming it, with his eyes on the ceiling. Slugger, sitting back behind the high sides of the chair where he could not see the Colonel, was investigating his ear with a matchstick.

The Colonel cleared his throat again. 'Well – what do you think?'

He looked round the room. No one would help him out, so he had to add, 'It's either that, you see, or we may have to put down some of the old horses.'

The reaction was immediate and unanimous.

'You can't do that,' Steve said.

'No way, Col,' from Ron.

'Oh please – no,' Dora said.

Slugger shook his head and muttered, 'It's not right, Colonel. Be against everything that Follyfoot stands for.'

'Well then.' The Colonel sighed. 'We will have to agree with the Board of Trustees and cut down on staff. Someone will have to go.'

440

Dora said, 'We'll work for nothing. I will, at least. I've told you that a thousand times.'

'And I've told *you* a thousand times I can't let you do that,' the Colonel said. 'You'd –' he made a face, as if the words hurt him – 'you'd have to get yourself another job.'

'What as?'

'In another stable.'

'Who'd have me?'

'You've had a lot of experience here.'

'We don't do things like other people.'

'Are you telling me,' the Colonel lowered his brows at her, 'that I'm not a good horse keeper?'

'I'm telling you that I think you're a better horse keeper than most people who keep horses. I'm not leaving anyway.' She stuck out her lip.

'Steve? Strong boy . . . get something else . . .' The Colonel's words were spoken in a strangled way, as if they were forced out of him in pain.

'With my record?' Steve had been in a lot of trouble before he came to Follyfoot with the pony Cobbler's Dream. 'I'm not going, Colonel, and that's flat.'

'Well, Ron will have to go.'

'You can't sack me,' Ron said, ''cos me uncle's your grain merchant, innee? That's why you took me on.' He faked a little tune on the tennis racket:

> 'You can't sack me,
> Cos if you sack me,
> You won't get cheap oats
> From me uncle, see?'

'That's a point,' the Colonel said. 'Slugger?'

'Me!' Slugger sat up and peered round the edge of the chair

in outrage. 'I been here longer than anyone. Been with you right through the war, Colonel. Thick and thin. Pulled you out of that bomb shelter when the roof fell in. Nicked you a pair of boots that time yours rotted in the rain. Got you away from that blonde woman in Brussels . . .'

Ron let out a wolf whistle and the Colonel said, 'That's enough.'

Nothing was resolved. They looked at each other miserably. To their great relief, Anna knocked on the door.

'Sorry to interrupt the meeting.' She put her head round the door. 'Mrs Oldcastle just rang up. She says there's a horse in her vegetable garden and she's sure it's one of ours.'

Everyone jumped up.

'We haven't decided anything,' the Colonel said. 'Wait –' But they had all rushed out of the door.

6

THEY spread in different directions, to check on the horses in the various fields. They met again in the yard.

'It's not one of ours,' Dora said. 'We'd better go and find out whose it is.'

'Not our business,' Ron said.

'Any horse is our business, especially if it's loose in someone's vegetable garden.'

Dora wanted to take Robin out anyway. After the distressing scene in the Colonel's study, she was longing to get back to the realities of life, the simple joy of riding Robin. 'Coming, Steve?'

'All right.'

'Ron?'

'May as well. Nothing to do here but mucking out.'

They brought in Robin and Miss America and Hero, and put saddles and bridles on them without stopping to clean off the mud.

Slugger was mooching miserably about in the yard with his cap pulled over one eye.

'Come with us,' Dora said. 'You can ride Willy.'

'You must be barmy.'

'You used to ride in the Army, you know you did.'

'That was forty years ago,' Slugger said, 'when me legs was young. You won't catch me getting on a horse again.'

They clattered out of the yard, and rode without talking through the woods, across the main road, and down the narrow winding lane that led to the back entrance of Mrs Oldcastle's house.

It was a huge old house with turrets and many chimneys, and ivy crowding the walls as if it was trying to camouflage the house as part of the green landscape. Mrs Oldcastle's husband, who had died of big business, had left her plenty of money, but she lived alone in the rather creepy house, with priceless pictures and antiques, it was said, and a little dog and her old chestnut cob Harold for company.

Harold called from his ivy-hung stable as they came up the back drive from the lane. There was no sign of a loose horse.

'Hang on,' said Steve. 'Somebody had better get off and check for hoof prints before we make a lot more.'

He held Hero while Ron went to investigate.

'Tracks there all right,' Ron said coming back. 'They smashed the poor old lady's carrot tops and a row of brussels sprouts, which could be a good thing, according to taste.'

'Better go and ask her about the horse.'

In his cowboy hat and his pointed boots and decorated leather jacket, Ron went round the house to the front door. He wiped his boots on the scraper, rang the bell and heard no sound, and banged the big brass knocker.

Immediately there began a pulling of bolts and a turning of keys, as Mrs Oldcastle had been standing behind the door, peering through the stained glass lozenges of the side window. The heavy door opened. She was wearing an old green kimono, with her grey hair bundled into a sleeping net, but she received Ron as graciously as if she were fully dressed for dinner.

'I'm from Follyfoot.' Ron looked beyond her into the great shadowed hall, where a suit of armour stood like a metal butler, with a small silver tray held out in the fingers of its gauntlet.

'That's good,' said Mrs Oldcastle, in the breezy way which

matched her pink outdoor skin and cheerful blue eyes. 'Did you take your horse away?'

'It wasn't ours,' Ron said. 'None of ours is missing.'

'It's always one of yours,' Mrs Oldcastle said. 'They get out all the time.'

'No, lady, excuse *me*.' Ron's practised eye travelled round the hall, where dark portraits of the ancient dead looked down on carved chests and Chinese urns and porcelain figures and silver candlesticks. With all this stuff, she didn't need to be worrying about a few carrot tops and brussels sprouts. 'I detected hoofmarks there.' He gave her his sleuth look. 'But no horse.'

'But it's there. Among my sprouts. I saw it with my own eyes, a fleabitten grey, in a red webbing halter. Come and I'll show you.'

Ron followed the lumpy figure tied into the green kimono through the hall, down a panelled passage, through a pantry whose shelves were stacked with pieces of valuable china and blackened silver.

The kitchen beyond was cluttered with the debris of the old lady's random housekeeping. On the floor, a smug grey Persian cat lapped milk from a delicate flowered bowl.

'Go and look.' Mrs Oldcastle pointed at the window.

Ron looked out. He saw nothing except the vegetable garden, with Steve and Dora holding the horses off to one side.

'You see that grey horse? I know it's yours.'

She must be hallucinating. Ron said soothingly, 'Oh yes, I see it,' in case she was crazy and might attack him with a carving knife.

'Then you must be even more senile than me,' Mrs Oldcastle said tartly, joining him at the window, 'for now that I look again, it's gone. There's only that girl and whatsisname out there.'

Mrs Oldcastle waved to Steve and Dora, but they didn't see her, so she waved to Harold in his stable instead.

'Your grey may be anywhere by now. You'd better go after it.'

Ron said, 'All right,' which was easier than, 'We haven't got a fleabitten grey,' and accepted a rather stale chocolate cupcake, which she fished from a drawer full of string and rusted screws, tipped his ten gallon hat and followed her out through the pantry and the passage and the hall.

The sight of all the valuable stuff crammed into this house made Ron think about the unpleasant scene in the study, and the Colonel talking so unhappily about money. It didn't seem fair. As Mrs Oldcastle opened the front door, he managed to say, 'If you was ever thinking of making a donation to Folly-foot –'

'If you've come here to beg, young man,' she said ungratefully, since he had come here to help her, 'you've come to the wrong shop,' and Ron found himself out in the garden, with the heavy door swinging shut behind him with an aggressive, portcullis sound.

'Mean old devil.' He went back to the others, muttering, 'Wouldn't give you the dirt from under her nails. And she sees things too. Hallucinating.'

'But there are hoof tracks there,' Dora said. 'They go over the lawn to the front drive and then disappear.'

'You're hallucinating too.' Ron vaulted into Hero's saddle, which made the old horse stagger. 'Come on, I want me dinner.'

'We'd better look for the horse.' Dora walked Robin slowly down the drive, looking for tracks on either side.

'I'm going home.' Steve turned Miss America to follow Ron.

Normally he would have stayed with Dora, but he was

446

depressed by what the Colonel had said. He had meant it. Things were serious. As he jogged past Ron and trotted ahead, the Colonel's words kept going through his head.

Might have to cut down on staff . . .

And Steve knew who would have to go. The Colonel had taken him on as a favour, to keep him from trouble. Given him a home and a job. And a family. All right. So now it was over.

Ron kicked Hero in the ribs and galloped past Steve. He got home first, riding the horse too fast, and made it up by bringing him a feed of oats before he turned him out.

Life of Riley. Ron watched the horse grab at the feed, standing in deep straw in the comfortable loose box. Better off than some people Ron knew who lived in the bad areas of town, and down by the canal where Carter's coal yard was.

Ron grumbled about the work at Follyfoot, but at least he had a job, which was more than most of his mates had. If he lost this job, because of the money . . .

'Mean old devil.' He kicked the stable door, as if it were Mrs Oldcastle's portcullis. He was still angry with her.

7

Mrs Oldcastle's long front drive ran down to the road between tall pointed fir trees. Beyond them on either side was an expanse of good turf, where Mr Oldcastle had once kept prize cattle, but which was now grazed only by the ponderous cob Harold.

After Steve and Ron started for home, Dora went alone down the drive, looking right and left for the stray horse's tracks. She was tempted to look back to see if Steve had changed his mind and turned to follow her, but she humped her shoulders against the temptation, in case he was not following, but had turned to see whether she was looking to see if he was.

Rats, both of them, Steve and Ron. They were all supposed to be vigilantes for any horse in trouble, and a loose horse was always trouble, whoever it belonged to, with the main roads so busy, and drivers not caring.

Dora rode slowly, with the reins loose on Robin's neck. Steve going home was just one of the horrible things that seemed to be happening these days. She expected a few more before the week was out. If anyone had to be sacked, it was always the girl . . .

Halfway down the drive, she realized that there had been a trodden place between two fir trees, and turned Robin back to look. Large hoof marks – yes, going off into the thick turf. For a short while, she could see where the long wet grass had been brushed forward as the horse had moved in a rather wavering pattern – grazing perhaps – that soon became impossible to follow.

Dora pushed on Robin's neck to try to get him to put his head down.

'If you were a dog, you could track him.'

A bird flew suddenly up out of the grass. Robin jumped forward and set off in his beautiful smooth canter.

A shallow stream ran in a curly line half way across the meadow. If the horse had crossed it, it would be possible to trace him on the muddy banks. Dora started at the top end and followed its meandering course down towards the road. Robin jogged and fussed, wanting to canter again. When they found the trampled place where the horse had crossed, she jumped him over and let him go fast towards the hedge at the end of the grassland, which would be the next place where they could do any tracking.

The hedge ran from the road to the top of a slight hill. Even if the horse had jumped it clean, there would be hoof marks at the take-off. It was not until they were almost at the top of the slope that Dora saw broken branches where the hedge had been roughly pushed through by a cumbersome object that obviously didn't know much about jumping. A large lump of hedge had been pulled forward into the next field. A tuft of light hair and some grey tail hairs were clinging to a briar.

The next field was plough, so it was easy to tell where the horse had gone. Following the next furrow, Dora could see where the horse had walked, the fore and hind prints close together, and where he had trotted, with all four feet evenly spaced out.

At the end of the plough, a dry ditch led on to a road, and there she lost the tracks.

Down the road, a man was digging in a cottage garden.

Dora called to him, 'Did you see a loose horse go by here?'

'Fleabitten grey, kind of. Red halter. Chunky chap.'

'You couldn't catch him?'

'Going too fast. A car had hooted at him farther back and he was off at a kind of gallop. Sort of. I think he turned in that gravel pit down the road. He yours?'

'No, but I'm looking for him. Thanks.'

The gravel pit had steep, sandy sides. She could probably trap the horse there. Dora took off her belt to slip it through the halter, if she could get a hand on him.

The bottom of the gravel pit was overgrown thickly with bushes and brambles. Dora skirted round the edge and then she saw that the horse had gone out at the far end by floundering up a steep slope.

'Come on, Rob!'

Robin, like all good horses, responded to the challenge of a hill. He gathered his powerful quarters under him, and with an enormous bound, propelled himself to the top in a plunging gallop. Dora put her arms round his neck and hung on. She followed the horse's hoof prints along a path through a small beech wood and out on to another road, which ran along the back gardens of houses.

She had come out on the edge of a suburban development. She jogged round the streets for a while, followed by tots on tricycles and little girls running along the pavement crying, 'Can I pat him?'

Three of the girls ran with her for a long way, panting and puffing and gazing at Robin with adoring eyes. At the corner, Dora stopped and let them catch up to pat him. She could remember when she had been a little girl, running to the window any time a horse went past, cutting pictures out of magazines, in love with her uncle's carthorse, dreaming that one day she would live and work with horses.

'Did you see a loose horse?'

One of the girls nodded, stroking Robin's shoulder.

'Which way?'

450

'Down there.'

'No, down there, stupid!'

'You blind? It was that way.'

The girls began to fight and kick and pull at each other's clothes. Dora rode on, asking people she passed on their way home with shopping bags, 'Did a loose horse go by here?'

Most of them shook their heads and hurried on, but a woman hanging out laundry in her back garden turned and smiled.

'That big fat thing? It gets out once in a while. The fence isn't strong. Headed for home, it was. It always goes home after a bit.'

'Thanks. I won't worry then.'

The woman pegged down a flapping sheet and came over to the fence.

'You from that place,' she jerked her head, 'up in the hills, where they have all those horses?'

'Follyfoot Farm, yes.'

'My brother took some ponies there once. Two little Welsh.'

'Taffy and Coffee. Taffy is lame, but Coffee lives with a boy in the village.'

'Nice little chaps, they were. My brother was ever so pleased.'

The woman beamed, and invited Dora in for a cup of tea. 'And I've just taken some scones out of the oven.'

Dora's stomach responded instantly, reminding her that she had missed lunch. She took Robin into the garden, and hung the reins over his head to the ground. Because of his western training in America, he stood quietly, as if he was tied.

When she came out of the house and started for home, she realized how far the horse chase had taken her. She went home by the roads instead of cross country, so as not to get lost. Walking on hard surfaces, trotting on grass verges, it seemed for ever before she turned into the winding road that climbed the hill to Follyfoot.

Dusk had fallen out of a dull grey sky, much too early, a warning of short winter days, coming all too soon. Robin was not tired. He trotted up the last slope, anxious for his feed, but when Dora slid to the ground in the stable yard, her knees told her how long she had been in the saddle, and she almost sat down.

The horses that stayed in at night were already in their loose boxes, eating hay. Cobbler's Dream, who liked to supervise comings and goings, put his head over the half door and took a nip at Robin to hustle him into his box.

In the feed shed, there was a note in the oat scoop. *'Everybody fed. All gone to cinema.'*

They might have waited. Dora slammed open the feed bin. Here she was, out all day, doing their job for them, and they couldn't even wait for her. She had been right about nothing good happening.

She fed Robin and gave him a small amount of water and hay. She would come back later to turn him out after he had cooled off. She threw the feed bowl back into the bin, kicked the shed door shut behind her and dragged her tired legs into the house to take it out on Anna for letting the others go off without her.

Everybody was gone, even Anna and the Colonel. Another note on the stove said, 'Your lunch in warming oven. Late supper when we come back.'

Dora sat down to eat the plate of lunch, feeling very lonely and unwanted. This is how she would feel if she were sacked from Follyfoot. Perhaps they were trying to prepare her.

8

W𝐢𝐭𝐡 the coming of darkness, a breeze got up, and the door of the feed shed, which had not latched when Dora kicked it shut, blew open.

Cobbler's Dream observed this glimpse of the open door of heaven from across the yard, and began to work on the top bolt of his door.

He was the cleverest horse in the stable. With his muscular, rubbery lips, designed to work their way round a tuft of grass to prepare it for cropping by strong teeth, he could sometimes jiggle and fiddle the bolt and get his door open.

It so happened that Steve had oiled the bolts this week. Very obliging of him. The bolt slid back, and the Cobbler pushed the door open with his knee. He strolled across the yard, shouldered his way into the feed shed, and dragged down a hundredweight sack of horse nuts which was propped against the wall.

The sack was sewn across the top, but he tore a hole in it with his teeth, and with a contented sigh, began to eat.

Dora had gone to sleep in the bath. When her chin slid under water, she woke spluttering, got out, pulled on some clothes and went outside again to put Robin out for the night.

Half way down the buildings on one side of the yard, a bulk was sticking out of an open doorway. It was the back end of Cobbler's Dream. The front end was still eating.

He was going slow at this point, just messing the food about, pawing at the sack and spilling horse nuts over the floor.

Dora pulled him out by the tail, scolded him and shut the door. He was liable to bouts of colic, this pony, and although he seemed all right, Dora checked him for signs of trouble – distended stomach, tight skin, distressed eye.

She put a headcollar on him and walked him round the yard for a while before she put him in his box with a rug on him. When she came back after turning Robin out, Cobby seemed comfortable, but Dora stayed with him for a while to make sure he did not lie down and risk twisting intestines that might become filled with gas after over-eating.

Two hours later, when Dora was asleep in one corner of the straw and the chestnut pony was dozing in the other, resting a hind leg, lashes drooping over a bleary eye, the door opened and Callie came in.

'You missed a super film.'

She began to tell Dora the plot even before she came awake. 'It was about this man who had a thing for climbing up the outsides of skyscrapers, and there was this other man behind a window on the forty-eighth – no, the forty-seventh floor, and he was trapped there because he knew something about this other man – not the one who was climbing up the sky-scraper, but the one who'd killed the man who – what's the matter with Cobby? Is he all right?'

'Doesn't deserve to be.' Dora was awake blinking in the light from Callie's torch. 'He got into the feed shed.'

'How?'

'I left the door open.'

'Oh.' Callie switched off the torch. She knew how Dora would feel. There was no need to discuss that. 'Steve and Ron went to a dance place after the film,' she said. 'I came home with Mum and the Colonel.' Callie's mother was married to the

Colonel, which made him her stepfather, but she called him the Colonel, because everybody else did. 'You're to come in for supper.'

'I don't want any. I'll stay here for a while. Good night, Cal.'

'I haven't gone yet.'

Callie went over to put an arm round Cobby's neck, mingling her long brown hair with his chestnut mane.

'Dora,' she said, not looking at her, 'what was the meeting about this morning, with you and the others?'

'Oh – about money, of course. Everything horrid always is.'

'I'm sick of money. That's all we hear at school. All those rotten maths problems are about money. I'm fed up with it.'

'So am I,' said Dora, 'but it does buy oats and things, and pay the blacksmith. And us. Now there's not enough to pay us.'

'Why don't you work for nothing?'

'The Colonel won't let me. He's in a difficult mood. The Trustees have been bothering him. They told him one of us would have to go.'

'That's stupid.' Callie turned round and leaned against Cobby's shoulder. 'There's too much work as it is. Who'd go anyway?'

'Not me,' Dora said. 'I couldn't.'

'No,' Callie said, 'because then you'd have to grow up and be like other people.'

'Aren't I grown up?'

'Not really.'

'Good.' It was Dora's birthday tomorrow. No one had remembered, and she was not going to tell them.

'And Steve couldn't go,' Callie said. 'Who'd lift bales

455

and things, and drive the horse box? And Ron.' She gave a short laugh. 'Poor old Ron. Who else would have him? Slugger can't do much work, but the Colonel would never kick him out, any more than he'd kick out one of the old horses.'

9

In his cottage across the road, Slugger lay in the sagging brass bed with the patchwork quilt his wife had made before her fingers stiffened and her eyes grew weak.

Slugger had been on his own in the cottage for five years, since his wife died. The Colonel and Anna had wanted him to move across the road into the farm house, but the cottage was his shell, a container of the memories of all the years since he had been with the Colonel at Follyfoot.

Slugger's daughter had grown up and married from this cottage. All the things of his life were crammed into the tiny rooms with the low ceilings and sprigged wallpaper. The furniture he and Nellie had collected, the china souvenirs of their holidays, the pictures of Helen's wedding and the pictures of her sons and the pictures and pictures and pictures of all the horses Slugger had ever known.

He had gone to bed early, bumping his head six times on the pillow, which was safer and less aggravating than an alarm clock, and then thumping it once more for something very important he had to remember tomorrow.

He slept for what seemed like hours, then woke suddenly and put out an arm across the bed – stupid old fool, Nellie hadn't been there for five years. He tossed and muttered and counted herds of wild ponies, but he could not sleep again.

He got up to get his biscuit tin, and looked out of the window.

It was raining, a warm autumn drizzle that would keep the leaves from dying and falling too soon. Through a gap between buildings across the road, he saw a small light moving in the yard. Someone gone out to check the horses. Dora probably, good girl that she was. Or Steve. Slugger smiled when he thought of how much Steve had changed since he came, a prickly, silent boy, who had grown strong and dependable.

It was a good life here. How could Slugger bear to leave? He couldn't, of course, and the Colonel would never sack him. Hadn't they sworn, that night in the bomb shelter, to stick together, if they ever got out alive? But if someone had to go, Slugger was the obvious one, since he could no longer do his share of the work.

'But I'll not go,' he said to the invisible Nellie, with whom he still exchanged ideas.

You'll have to go, old man, she replied in her practical fashion, *if it's to help the Colonel.*

With his teeth out, Slugger mumbled on the softened biscuit. He wandered round the room, touching things and stumbling over the dog.

For pity's sake, Nellie admonished inside his head, *you've got something important to do in the morning. Get back into bed and go to sleep.*

'All right, all right.' Slugger climbed into the bed, turned over on his side away from the memory of Nellie, and was asleep.

When he woke promptly at six the next morning, he could not remember what he had thought about in the night, nor what it was he had to remember. Something only he knew about. Yes – that was it. He sat up and threw off the quilt. Dora's birthday. Nobody else had remembered, not even Dora. She blanked out birthdays, since she was dead set against growing up.

458

There was no telephone in Slugger's cottage. He had to wait until the farm house was empty, to make his important secret call.

Half way through the morning, Callie was at school, Dora and Steve and Ron out working, and Anna had taken the Colonel to the doctor.

Slugger went into the Colonel's study, and sat down at the desk, frowning at the telephone. He looked up the number of the cake shop, and cautiously dialled it with his shaky, knotted fingers.

It took him three tries before the call went through.

'Prudence's Cake Shop.' The woman sounded flustered and hot, as if she had just come from the ovens, and was getting flour all over the telephone.

'I want to order a birthday cake,' Slugger said, 'to pick up this afternoon.' He would make an excuse to take the truck and sneak into town, so he could surprise Dora and everyone with the cake at supper.

It took quite a time to settle on the size and colour and flavour, because Slugger kept changing his mind over such important decisions.

'Do you want somebody's name on it?' Prudence sounded impatient.

'I do.' Slugger had thought about that. He did not want an ordinary Happy Birthday message. 'I want "Horsey Birthday, Dora".'

'Happy Birthday, Nora. Got it.'

'No!' shouted Slugger. 'Dora. D as in dinner.'

'Happy Birthday, Dora.'

'Don't muck about. It's Horsey Birthday. Horsey, see?'

'Naughty?' You could hear the woman raising her floury eyebrows. 'Naughty Birthday? I don't believe that Prudence's Cake Shop – I mean, we do have a reputation to maintain.'

'Belt up, woman and listen.' Slugger was desperate. 'I'm paying for this cake, see, and I want Horsey Birthday, Dora and the picture of a horse's head on it – a thoroughbred, mind – in pink icing.'

He was so worn out by this tiresome conversation that he had to go and lie down for a while on the Colonel's lumpy, dog-haired couch.

IO

THE grey blur of rain had lifted. It was a glorious Indian summer day, the sky deep blue, the sun as strong as summer.

Something must be done to celebrate the season. An autumn ride would be the thing. They would invite all the local people with horses and ponies and take a long ride through the woods and stubble fields together, before the bad weather set in and it was too late.

Dora and Steve and Ron lay on their stomachs on the patch of grass by the barn, with an ordnance map spread out on the ground, planning the ride. Through the big wood and along the ridge, across the dip between Mark's Hill and the Bump down into the hollow by the dairy farm. They would have to make a detour here, as they could not cross the main road with a crowd of kids on ponies. Through Marston village with a stop for lunch on the common, and across the canal to the old tow path.

'We can't go across the road bridge, with all that traffic,' Steve said. 'We could sneak over the footbridge at the end of the valley, if we could go through Carter's coal yard. Would he let us?'

'He'd probably shoot us,' Dora said. 'Last time I tried to go through there, he set his dogs on me.'

'Yeah, he would.' Mr Carter was one of Ron's doubtful acquaintances, someone he kept on the right side of.

'Can you ask him, Ron, whether we can go through with a crowd of kids? He doesn't like horses, does he?'

'Or kids.'

Mr Carter did not like anything that had no profit for him.

'Are you scared to ask him?'

'Knock it off. Do anything for me, Mr Carter would. "Just name it, Ron," he says.'

'All right, name that we want him to let a funny looking crowd of people on unfit horses and hairy ponies through his coal yard and over the footbridge.'

'He'll let *me* through,' Ron said grandly. 'The hairy mob will follow. I better not get sacked before the ride.'

'What are you plotting?' The Colonel came out of the barn, where he had been looking over the winter's store of hay.

'An autumn ride,' Dora sat up. 'Going to come with us? Stroller's quite sound.' The Colonel sometimes rode the old brewery horse.

'How far are you going?'

'About ten miles.'

'Bit far for Stroller,' the Colonel said. But he really meant, *a bit far for me.*

'I say, Col.' As the Colonel turned to walk away, Ron rolled over and squinted up at him. 'You didn't really mean that, did you, what you said at the business meeting?'

The Colonel stopped and turned round. 'Yes,' he said, staring with no expression over the tops of the apple trees. 'Yes, I'm afraid I did.' He turned again and went towards the house.

As they got up from the grass, they saw Slugger, who had come across the road from his cottage and was climbing with some difficulty into the cab of the small truck.

'Where are you going?' Steve called. Slugger hardly ever drove.

'Into town.' Slugger stopped with one foot in the cab of the truck and one on the step. 'Got some things to get.'

'I'll drive you,' Dora said.

462

'That's all right.' Slugger seemed a bit flustered. 'I'll manage.'
He got in and shut the door.

'You look very suspicious.' Dora went up to the window.
'Have you got a date with a girl?'

'Course he has,' Ron said. 'Going to a tea dance, innee?'

'That's it,' Slugger grinned. 'That's why I got me teeth in.'

'Are you sure you need to go?' Steve asked. 'I've got to do
some shopping tomorrow. I could get your stuff.'

Slugger's driving was awful. They always tried to find
excuses not to let him use the truck.

'If it's all right with you, boss,' Slugger looked down at him,
'I'll go today.'

'I don't care. Just be sure and put some petrol in the truck.
It's almost empty.'

'I know that,' Slugger said, although he had actually forgotten
to look at the petrol gauge. 'I'm not blind.'

'Hang on a minute,' Dora said. 'I'll get Folly's headcollar. It's
got to be taken to the tack shop to be mended.'

Ron fished in his pocket and brought out a broken guitar
string. 'As long as you're going to the shops, you might go to
that music place, Sight and Sound, they call it, and get me
another one of these.'

Dora came back with the broken headcollar which had been
tied with string, and threw it on the seat of the truck. Slugger
started the engine on the fifth try, crashed into gear, moved
forward in a series of jerks, and almost ran into Anna, turning
into the gateway in her car.

She got out and came to the truck window. 'Where are you
going?'

'To the shops.' He clutched the wheel grimly. He'd never
get away.

'Oh good.' She took a ticket out of her coat pocket. 'You
can fetch my skirt at the cleaner's.'

As he took the ticket and the money she gave him, Slugger saw Callie walking from the bus stop with her school bag. Before she could burden him with another errand, he rolled up his window and made a fast getaway, kicking up the gravel and sounding his horn at a stone by the roadside that he thought was a cat.

11

Slugger negotiated the steep winding hill below Follyfoot with great care, as if he were coming down a mountain road in Switzerland. Once on to the straight road at the bottom, he settled down to his usual steady pace. At thirty-five miles an hour in the middle of the road, he drove serenely along, singing 'Born Free' in a cracked tenor, with four or five cars behind him, hooting and flashing their lights.

To their relief, he turned the truck into a side road, to take his favourite short cut into town. It was actually longer in distance and in time, but it got him away from traffic and into the country lanes he enjoyed.

He changed his song to one of the more solemn ones with which he expressed contentment. 'Abide with me' was quite nice to drive to. The autumn woods were changing to brown and red, with flares of yellow in the clear light. A whole population of migrating birds circled in a corner of the sky, forming up for their long journey.

This was a familiar road to Slugger. He checked off the landmarks as he came to them. The tree split by lightning. The hedge where he saw the two badgers. The church where his niece Ada had married that fellow nobody liked. The Bunkers' house where they had the fire in the stable and Jim's pony Barney had bitten off the tip of Mrs Bunker's finger, in the days before Dora made a Christian of him.

Mrs Bunker was out in the garden with a basket and a big hat with a scarf round it, cutting dahlias. Farther on, Slugger passed the field where Barney had been turned out to grass when Jim went away to school.

The bay pony was grazing near the gate. Slugger gave him a hoot and a friendly salute, in memory of the night when he had won the Moonlight Steeplechase against all those fancy ponies, and Slugger had nearly had a heart attack from excitement.

A little farther on, the truck began to falter and cough. Dratted thing. Slugger never could come to terms with engines. He pressed down on the accelerator, but nothing happened. The truck stopped. Failing to start it again, he switched off the engine, looked out of the window for two minutes, then tried to catch it by surprise. Nothing happened. He tried the starter a few more times, then got out to lift up the bonnet and peer underneath, as if he knew what he expected to find. Everything seemed to be there. He walked round the truck, kicking at the tyres, and even slapped it on the rump, as if it were a stubborn horse.

He got back into the cab, switched on the lights and the turning signals and pushed the heater lever back and forth, then sat back despondently. He looked down at the broken headcollar and the guitar string and Anna's cleaner's ticket – what did they think he was, a common carrier? It was a wonder Steve had not dumped something on him too.

But he had. What was it he had asked? Oh yes. 'Be sure and put some petrol in it.' Slugger had turned off on his favourite short cut before he got to the petrol station.

He switched on the engine and looked at the gauge. The needle did not flicker. Out of petrol.

Slugger got out of the truck and looked up and down the road. Not a soul in sight. The nearest house was the Bunkers.' He would have to walk back and telephone. It was almost a mile. Much too far for his old legs.

He looked at his watch. After four. He must get to the cake

466

shop in time, or there would be no birthday party for Dora this evening.

He looked again up and down the empty road. Barney had his large rather common head hung over the gate of the field, and was observing him mildly.

Slugger called to him, and the pony let out one of his deep, rumbling whinnies, with which he used to greet Slugger coming with food, when he was living at Follyfoot.

Slugger knew what he had to do. He took the headcollar off the seat, and found a length of frayed rope in the back of the truck.

He talked about his riding days in the Army, because the Colonel had been in the Cavalry, but in actual fact, he had hardly ridden at all. At Follyfoot, the Colonel and Steve and Dora and Callie and even Ron had tried to persuade him to ride, but although he was fond of the horses and enjoyed taking care of them, he remained firmly on the ground.

But this was an emergency. He opened the gate of the field and went inside. The pony came to him, and after some difficulty with the string, Slugger got the broken headcollar on and fixed the piece of rope to it.

He brought the pony out, climbed up two rails of the gate and put one leg over Barney's back. Thank God he was only a little 'un. There was a moment of suspense while Slugger hung between the pony and the gate. If the pony had moved, it would have been all up. The pony stood by the gate and Slugger managed to wriggle on board.

'Home, James!' Slugger hauled his head round and got him started down the road towards the house, hanging on to the mane and feeling very weak and insecure.

The pony was fat and slippery. When he jogged, Slugger flopped helplessly from side to side. If this was the riding the kids were so daft about, they could have it. Dora's birthday cake. He set his jaw and hung on.

It would have been all right, if a motorbike had not come down a track between the fields and suddenly shot out into the road right in front of Barney's nose.

The pony shied drastically away, and Slugger pitched forward over his head with his hands flung out to try and save himself.

A jar like the cracking of a fault in the earth's crust ran up one arm to his shoulder. Then his head hit the road and exploded in a white flash that carried with it all the photographs in his cottage of weddings and children and Nellie and horses and horses and horses, as he reeled out of the world.

12

MRS Bunker's dahlias had not done very well this year. There were not many flowers to cut. Most of the dahlias had been eaten away by bees, slugs, and the various unspeakable insects that seemed to wage a private war against Mrs Bunker's garden.

She had to content herself with cutting off dead and riddled dahlias and throwing them on the compost heap by the stable. She added a shovel of manure, as the gardening books told you to do. That was one thing, at least, she knew that horses were good for. She had not learned much else beyond the truth that they were dangerous at both ends and uncomfortable in the middle. She glanced at the tip of her shortened finger, as she always did when she thought about horses.

She was turning to go into the house to start preparing dinner for Mr Bunker, when she heard a wild clatter of hoofs in the road. Jim's pony dashed into the drive and came to a dead stop on the Bunkers' lawn, tearing at the short grass as if he had not eaten for months.

'Barney! You wicked thing. You're supposed to be in that lovely field down the road. Have you broken a fence again, you bad, bad creature?'

She shook her fist at him. Barney walked over the corner of the chrysanthemum bed to get to a patch of clover. There was no one to help her. Her husband would not be home for two hours.

Courage, Marion Bunker. She went into the tool shed where the oats were kept, put some in a bowl and walked cautiously over the lawn to shake it in front of the pony's nose, at arm's length, standing well away from him. As he reached for it, she retreated, trying to lure him towards the stable.

Walking backwards to keep an eye on him, she stumbled against the wheelbarrow, tore her nylons on a bush, and turned her ankle on a stone, but she managed to get him to follow her to the door of the loose box, where she shoved the bowl inside, and shut the door on him as he went in after the oats.

'You stay there, you wretched creature.' She wagged the mutilated finger at him. 'I'm going up to see where you got out, and if there's much damage done, you'll pay for it, you mark my words, when Mr Bunker gets home.'

In her red minibus, which had a plastic flower fixed to the top of the aerial, she drove down the road to the field. If the gate was open, she would know that it was those bad boys from the village, up to their tricks again. When she rounded the corner, she saw that the gate was shut. So it was not bad boys, but bad Barney, breaking fences again.

Near the gate, she saw what looked like a heap of clothes lying at the side of the road. What an extraordinary place –

She slowed, then stopped, and got out quickly. It was not a heap of clothes, it was a person. It was an unconscious person. It was that old man from Follyfoot Farm, lying on his side in a crumpled way, one arm flung out as if reaching for help, the other bent under him in an odd, unnatural way.

As Mrs Bunker stopped to lift him, the old man opened his eyes with a yell.

'What's happened?'

He groaned and shut his eyes again.

It had been a task for Mrs Bunker to get Barney into the stable, but that was nothing compared to getting the old man into the minibus.

'Come on, you can't lie here.'

She got her arm under what seemed to be his good shoulder and sat him up, leaning against her. She took the scarf from her hat and made a sling to support what was obviously a broken arm. When she managed to get the man on to his feet, he fainted, but she was able to prop him up, since he was very light. Half dragging, half carrying him, she got him into the bus. He lay back in the seat, pale as paper, and she was afraid that he would die before they got to the hospital, of old age, if nothing else.

13

WHEN Slugger was let out of the hospital, walking with a sideways tilt, partly because of the heavy plaster cast from wrist to shoulder, partly because he was still groggy, Anna would not let him stay alone in his cottage. She insisted that he sleep in the spare room at the Farm.

It was the best room in the house. Anna kept the door locked, so the cats could not go in and take over the bed, and people could not wander in to dump bits of the debris that silted up their own bedrooms.

Dora's room was an inferno of last winter's sweaters still waiting to be washed, horse pictures, plans for the new stable block they were going to build if they ever got the money, horse books and magazines, some ears of dried oats and bull-rushes sticking out of the tall silver cup she and Barney had won in the Moonlight Steeplechase.

Callie's room, you could not get into. Not because it was more untidy than Dora's, but because she had fixed a kind of gate across the door to make it into a stable. With more than twenty horses outside, she still spent a large part of her time being a horse herself.

No good redecorating those rooms, so Anna had let herself go in the spare room, with white paint, flower-splashed wallpaper, pink sheets and new chintz curtains and bedspread.

When Callie took in Slugger's breakfast, he was sitting up in the bed like a little old gnome in striped pyjamas, his weathered face and work-worn hands dark against the pink frilled pillowcase and sheets.

472

'You do look posh.' Callie put down the tray, and stroked the silky eiderdown.

'Don't I?' Slugger snuggled his head against the pillow. 'Worth breaking me arm any day of the week.'

Callie went to the window to draw the curtains, which filtered a pink light through the room, as if Slugger was living in a bowl of strawberry ice. Outside, a touch of night frost had left the lawn sparkling with a thousand crystals. Perfect day to ride. She began to invent possible excuses for not going to school.

Behind her, she heard the Colonel come into the room.

'Morning, Slugger.'

'Morning, Colonel.'

'Well then.'

'Well then.'

They knew each other so well, they communicated in a kind of shorthand.

'It looks as if your insurance is coming through,' the Colonel said. 'They'll give you a decent weekly amount until you can start work again.'

'Ah.'

'Yes,' said the Colonel, as if Slugger had spoken a whole sentence. 'That's what I was thinking.'

'Takes care of that then,' Slugger said.

'For a bit.'

'Takes care of what?' Callie turned round when the Colonel had gone.

'I'll get my sick pay, see, so he can tell the Trustees he's saving on one man's wages. Good joke, innit?'

'Not much of a joke,' Callie said, 'if a person has to break their arm to solve a stupid money problem.'

'That's the way it is though, girl.' Slugger shoved the tray

473

down to the bottom of the bed, and nestled down again into the pink sheets. A cat that had been under the eiderdown came out and began to clean off the plate. 'When you got an unsolvable problem, it takes some daft beggar like old Barney to find the answer.'

14

THE immediate danger was over. They could breathe again. They could enjoy the autumn ride without the unspoken threat: this might be the last ride for one of us – which one?

Everybody turned out for the Saturday morning ride. Everybody, that is, who had any kind of a horse or pony that could manage the ten mile distance.

Some of them could only manage it if they took it at their own pace. Dora and Robin spent part of the ride cantering up ahead to tell the competitive girls from the pony farm to slow down, it wasn't a race, and the rest cantering back to round up people like Johnnie Hatch on a low-slung ball of fur called Phoebe, who went all the way at an even jiggle, with no saddle on her broad back, and no bridle on her wooly head. There was no point in putting a bit in Phoebe's mouth. She just followed the other horses anyway.

It was a glorious day, with the ground neither too frozen nor too muddy, and the horses snorting briskly in the crisp air.

They trotted through Marston village, surprising Saturday shoppers, and came out on to the common on the other side to find Anna and some of the other mothers in the truck, with fried chicken and doughnuts and an urn of hot cocoa.

It was almost half an hour before everybody had collected together. The pony farm girls on their New Forests and Dartmoors, Ron on the mule, Toby on his welsh pony Coffee, Mrs Oldcastle on Harold, Callie on Hero, Steve on Cobbler's Dream, Jim Bunker, home for the weekend, on Barney, skinny Alice Hatch on her skinny pony, Dora, last to arrive, leading Phoebe by her halter, with Johnnie on the front of Robin's saddle. It was the only way to get them there before the others ate all the lunch.

When they were ready to start again, Johnnie Hatch was asleep on the seat of the truck. Steve and Ron picked up Phoebe and put her in the back of the truck with the cocoa urn, for Anna to take home.

Having been helped down from Harold to eat her chicken, Mrs Oldcastle needed help to get back on again. Ron gave her a leg-up and heaved so hard, she would have gone right over the other side, if Dora had not been hanging on to the stirrup, and could push her back into the saddle.

'That's better.' Mrs Oldcastle adjusted her hat and picked up her reins as if they were a conductor's baton. 'Thank you, young man.' She never knew anybody's name. 'I know you, don't I? You were in my house. I gave you a carroway cake.'

'Chocolate.' Ron looked up at her under the curled brim of his cowboy hat. 'And you threw me out.'

'Because you let your horse into my vegetable garden.'

'No, because I asked you for help, and you –'

'Well, there'll be no more stray horses in my carrots and sprouts, I can tell you that.' Mrs Oldcastle tapped him on the hat with her whip, like the Queen conferring a knighthood. 'I bought an airgun and pellets and I'm not afraid to use it, young man, remember that.'

Ron ducked as the whip lifted again, and she rode off calling, 'Come along, everybody I'm tired of waiting!' although everybody had been waiting for *her*.

They pounded off down the broad turfy stretch in the middle of the common, and all jumped together over the small ditch at the end.

Not all together. Dora turned and saw that two of the ponies had refused, Alice Hatch had fallen off and was looking for her glasses, and Willie the mule was on the wrong side of the

476

ditch, leaning back with heels dug in, while Ron had his heels dug in on the other side, tugging at the reins.

Dora jumped Robin back again, picked a stick, and shooed the refusing ponies over. Willie would not budge. Ron stepped back across the ditch, vaulted into the old Army saddle and said he was going home.

'We can't go through the coal yard without you.'

'You'll have to go by the road.'

'There's too much traffic. Ron, you must. Make him jump. Get up, you, Willie!'

She whacked at the mule's stringy grey quarters with the stick, and broke it. Ron sat there, kicking with his cowboy boots, and the mule sighed and put his head down to eat the coarse grass at the edge of the ditch.

'Come on!' Steve shouted. The others were tired of waiting. Mrs Oldcastle's nose was going blue. Alice Hatch's pony was out of control, because her glasses were broken and she could not see.

'I'll make him.' Dora got off Robin, pulled Ron off the mule and got on herself. She knew Willie of old. It was she who had taught him to jump, if you could call it jumping.

You had to take him by surprise. She walked him to the edge of the ditch, then turned him sideways, as if they were going to stay on this side. Then she suddenly tugged his head round and gave him a huge kick, and before he knew it, his front end was over, followed after a moment of standing spreadeagled over the ditch, by the unwilling back end.

'Ta.'

Ron stepped over the ditch, Robin hopped over by himself, and they cantered after the others.

The green common deteriorated into wasteland, with a dump of old cars on the edge of the run-down district by the canal.

They went in single file down the alley between the backs of the houses. At the gate of the coal yard, Mr Carter lumbered out of his office, a huge man, too fat to breathe. Ron spoke to him. Mr Carter nodded and wheezed and dropped his rolled chins into the rolled neck of his black sweater. He stood with hands in the pockets of trousers stretched wide over his belly, watching each person come through, as if he would want to know them next time he saw them.

As she rode past the window of a rusted iron shed, Dora thought she saw a face looking out through dirty yellow hair. A face with dark staring eyes that made Dora turn in her saddle to look again.

There was no face. But there was a space rubbed with a finger on the grimy window.

Across the footbridge, they turned thankfully on to the towpath on the other side of the canal where the land was green again, and the dingy neighbourhood soon left behind. Going from field to field through the narrow gates, they headed for the bottom of the hills, where the canal took a turn, and they could cross it by the humpback bridge and scramble up through the steep path slippery with wet leaves, big birds squalling up out of the trees ahead of them.

At the crossroads, they separated to go their various ways. Dora and Steve and Ron and Callie walked the last stretch of road that Dora loved, because it led to home, and went past one of their fields. Nigger and Frank and stiff old Ginger trotted up to the gate and called a welcome.

Through the lighted window of his study, she saw the Colonel stand up when he heard the hoofs in the road, and reach for his jacket on the back of the door. He was out in the yard with the dogs barking round him, as they rode in.

15

THE Colonel had been to the doctor for a medical examination before he went abroad. Since his lung trouble, he and Anna had to go away for a while every winter to give him a healing dose of sun.

Before they left, the Colonel held another staff meeting. Not solemn and frightening, like the one they had had in his study about cutting down staff, but casually, in the hay shed.

He found Steve and Dora bagging chaff, while Callie and Ron played cards on a bale of hay, and Slugger turned the creaking handle of the chaff-cutting machine with his one good arm.

'Well then.' The Colonel picked up a stalk of hay to chew. 'We're off in the morning. You'll be all right then?'

'Of course,' said Dora, 'if we're left alone.'

Once, he had moved in a dreadful woman called Phyllis Weatherby to take charge while he was away. They had got rid of her by fair means and foul. Mostly foul.

'Just remember then.' The Colonel put his hands in his pockets. 'No more horses till I get back.'

'We know that.' Dora thought about poor Ellis Elkins and his horse that was 'sort of a mottled colour', and was probably either dead by now, or going lame in the riding school.

'You've got a full stable,' the Colonel said. 'All you can manage.'

'We'll be all right,' Steve said.

'And so will the horses,' Ron added, 'in case no one's thought of them.'

'None of them is likely to conk out before I get back,' the

Colonel said, 'but you'll have to watch that leg of Ginger's, and if Cobby gets into trouble again, give him a drench without waiting to see how he feels. Dolly's feet are going to need trimming soon, and a few others, and if the Weaver doesn't stop coughing, you'd better isolate him in the foaling stable. Yes, I know.' He gave Dora a look. 'That would mean an empty loose box. Better let it stay empty. No more horses.'

'Does that include ponies?' Callie slapped down a card. 'Gotcher, Ron.'

'And donkeys,' the Colonel added, remembering the time when Dora's American friend Mr Blankenheimer had bought Dottie in the market and driven her here on the back seat of his car.

'So if,' Ron liked to give people a hard time, 'so if some horse come travelling up the road on three legs, waving the fourth and crying, "Save me, I'm dying," we just wave it on and say, "Keep travelling," right?'

'And so if,' said Callie, 'some poor old lady like Mrs Berry turns up at the gate with a home-made trailer and a horse that was doomed to be shipped abroad for slaughter, we're just to say, "Sorry, Mrs Berry, we don't take in horses that are doomed to be shipped for slaughter any more."'

'Stop trying to get my goat,' the Colonel said. 'I'm not talking about emergencies. You know what I mean. Do your jobs. I trust you. Any questions?'

'Just one,' Steve said innocently. 'Who's in charge this time?'

When the Colonel was away, Dora was apt to get a bit bossy.

'Yes,' said Dora. 'I'd like to know too.'

When the Colonel was away, Steve was inclined to get a bit bossy.

The Colonel looked at them both and smiled. 'Slugger's in charge. He can supervise.'

'Me?' Slugger patted the heavy cast on his arm. 'Can't even pick up a manure shovel.'

'The supervisor doesn't have to shovel,' the Colonel said. 'That's why you're in charge.'

Slugger shrugged his good shoulder. 'Always was, really.'

16

WHILE Anna was away, they shared her domestic jobs. Slugger could do most of the cooking, if someone helped him with things like peeling and chopping and opening tins, that needed two hands. Callie did the laundry by taking it into the bath with her, and sloshing it round in suds with her hands and feet before putting it through the wringer and hanging it on the line. It was everyone's job to do housework, which meant it was no one's. They would have a massive clean-up the day before Anna came back.

Dora did most of the food shopping. Coming out of the butcher's one day with a bag of sausages and stewing meat and some bones she had begged for the dogs, she almost bumped into a man in a raincoat, walking fast along the pavement with his shoulders hunched.

He side-stepped without raising his eyes and went on, and then he turned back just as Dora turned back and they both said, 'Hullo.'

Having said, 'Hullo', they each had no idea who the other one was.

'Excuse me,' the man said. 'I made a mistake.' He turned to walk on, and the droop of his shoulders reminded Dora.

'Mr Elkins.'

He turned back. 'Yes, and you're –'

'Dora. From Follyfoot Farm.'

'Oh yes.' He nodded curtly, and walked on.

Dora went after him. 'I felt terrible about – you know – not taking the horse.'

'It's all right.' He walked ahead without looking at her.

'What – I mean – what happened to him? Did you –'

'I don't want to talk about it.'

But there was traffic at the crossing, and he had to stop and wait for the lights to change.

'Please tell me.'

Dora had two heavy shopping bags, and although he did not really want to talk, Ellis Elkins was too polite not to take one from her.

'I've been worried about Kingfisher. Did you sell him to the riding school, or did you have to – have to – you know – have him – er, you know?'

Dora had lived with animals long enough to be able to talk sensibly about death, but with Elkins looking so dejected, she could not come out with it.

'I wasn't able to do either of those things.' He turned his creased face and bloodhound eyes to her. 'I'm leaving for South America tomorrow.'

'What are you going to do with him?'

'Nothing *to* do. I thought I'd just turn him loose to wander and fend for himself. It seems kinder. There's grass everywhere, and ponds and things . . .'

'You can't do that! Look – we'll have to take him.'

'But the man in charge at your farm said –'

'The Colonel isn't there at the moment,' Dora said. 'Actually.'

'Who's running it then?'

'I am. Actually. Please, please, *please*, don't turn Kingfisher loose.'

'Well, as a matter of fact,' Ellis Elkins looked at his shabby shoes, 'I did. The day after I came to your place. Actually.'

'Oh, you –' Dora could have slapped him. 'That's terribly dangerous. He could be hit by a car, or caught in wire – anything. You just don't leave horses on their own to wander about.'

'Well, I did.' Ellis Elkins looked at her apologetically. 'Before I shut up my house, I rode King a long way away, where we'd never been before. Then I got off and I put on his best red halter and led him on to some nice grass and said "Farewell".' He blinked. 'Then I threw the saddle and bridle over the wall of a churchyard – like burying your dreams – and got on a bus and went away. Goodbye.'

The lights had been green twice and were now red again, but he stepped off the kerb, and a bicyclist swerved and swore.

'My sausages!'

Dora grabbed her shopping bag, and Elkins weaved away through the traffic like a sleepwalker, and disappeared into the Saturday crowds.

Dora ran back to the car park with the shopping bags bumping against her legs. A fleabitten grey, Mrs Oldcastle had seen in her vegetable garden, and Ellis Elkins had said that Kingfisher was sort of 'mottled and freckled'. If the saddle and bridle were still in the nearby churchyard, then Dora would know for sure.

Reckless with anxiety, she drove the truck as fast as she dared. There was a church at the end of the village beyond the entrance to Mrs Oldcastle's house. Dora whizzed through the village, slowed, and pulled the truck off the road by the wall of the churchyard. She went through the gate and began to look among the graves near the wall.

'Are you looking for a dear departed one?'

A smiling lady in glinting glasses rose from a grave, where she was planting bulbs. 'I know just about everybody here,' she said sociably, as if she were offering to introduce guests at a party.

When Dora told her what she was looking for, the lady beamed.

'Quite a nice saddle it was,' she said. 'German made, but we

484

must face the fact that the British don't have a monopoly on leather goods. We sold it as treasure trove. Just in time to pay the electricity bill. "Saddles from heaven," I said to the vicar. "The Lord will provide."'

Dora hoped that the Lord would provide her with a sight of the fleabitten grey. It must have been Kingfisher she had chased across country that day. Red halter, the digging man had said, and the tea and scones woman had said that the horse was going home. That must be where Elkins used to live.

The tea and scones woman was glad to see her.

'I've just put the kettle on,' she said, 'and there's yesterday's buns.'

But Dora could only stay to find out on which road Ellis Elkins and the horse had lived.

The house was locked up tightly, with the blinds drawn, and a week's supply of wet newspapers rotting on the step. In the back garden, a makeshift stable and a patched up fence round a bare trodden patch looked like a hopeless place to keep a horse.

The window of the stable was boarded up, and a bar of wood nailed across the door. Outside, the ground was heavily trampled, as if the horse had come back and stamped about, trying to get in.

Poor old Kingfisher. Abandoned. Somehow getting himself home, and then finding it locked and barred against him. Dora could imagine him, with his new red halter on his mottled head, turning sadly away.

Where would he turn to?

She asked some of the neighbours, but nobody knew or cared. They had not liked the horse being there. Had complained to the Council many times about the smell. About the flies. Had not seen the horse come back. Did not know Mr

Elkins had gone for good. Close-mouthed, he was, not friendly, and they were not ones to poke their noses into other people's affairs, not they, although they could, if they chose, tell Dora a tale or two about bill collectors, empty gin bottles, runaway wives, etc. etc. etc.

It seemed hopeless. Dora drove round the suburban streets for a while, asking other people, but nobody had seen anything of Kingfisher.

She felt sad-hearted and heavy with failure as she drove home more slowly.

'I feel rotten.'

She found Steve doing accounts at the Colonel's desk, and flopped down on the hearthrug to tell him about it.

'I know.' Steve swivelled the chair round to look at her. 'The horse isn't your responsibility, *but –*'

'Nor is that stupid Elkins, *but –*'

'I know that feeling.' Steve looked down at her wisely, like the Colonel. 'You feel you've let them down.'

Dora nodded, picking at the fringe of the rug that the cats were fraying away, bit by bit, year by year.

'Let's hope he was caught and taken in somewhere. Have you rung up the Cruelty to Animals people?'

'Yes, and the police. No news. I told them we could take him here, if they –'

'The Colonel already told the man No.'

'But this is an emergency!' Dora sat up.

'Don't shout at me. Slugger's in charge.'

'Who takes my name in vain?' Slugger looked in from the passage.

'A person's horse is loose,' Dora said. 'He turned it loose, and then went away. If it's found, we have to take it in.'

'I don't think so.' Slugger shook his grey head.

486

'But it's an emergency.'
'Not yet. Not till they find him.'

Two days later, Dora got a telephone call from the police. A grey horse had been hit by a car at night, at a place where the road ran through open moorland. The driver broke two ribs on the steering wheel and cut his head on the rear view mirror.

'But the horse?' Dora's throat was tight. 'What happened to the horse?'

'Two legs broken. Had to be put down. I'm sorry, Miss. Was it yours?'

'Not exactly.'

But when she hung up the receiver, Dora felt just as bad as if he had been hers, this poor old horse she had never laid eyes on.

17

DORA went out through the kitchen. Slugger was kneading bread dough.

'Don't worry,' she said. 'That grey horse won't be coming.'

'Eh?' Slugger raised his head, the stubby fingers of his good hand pushing and pummelling at the rubbery dough.

Dora tugged open the back door and went out.

Before she talked to anybody, she had to go off on her own for a while to battle with her emotions. She did not want to weep when she talked about Kingfisher. Follyfoot was a place for courage, not sentiment.

Robin was out in the sun, thoughtfully eating bark off a young tree. Dora made a mental memo to tack wire netting round the tree trunk. She put on the saddle and bridle, which she had brought out so that no one would see her leave, and rode out of the hill pasture by the lower gate that led to the edge of the moor.

She rode for a long time, thinking about nothing, as you can when you are on a good horse and can abandon yourself to the pure pleasure of the rhythm and power, the shoulder muscles moving smoothly by your knee, hoofs reaching forward, pounding the turf, tucked up to reach strongly forward again, the finest view in the world the one framed by a pair of inward-curving ears.

But when she pulled Robin to a walk up a stony track, all the thoughts came back again. It wasn't the Colonel's fault. It was hers. If she had stayed to beg or insist, instead of going sulkily out of the tack room, he would have agreed to take the horse in. If she had not stopped for tea and scones with the

488

Welsh pony man's sister, if she had looked further round the streets, she might have found Kingfisher near his home. The horse was dead, from stupidity. She had been just as stupid as Ellis Elkins.

Grief is usually one quarter unselfish sorrow for the dead, and three quarters selfish regret. If only . . . if only . . .

Dora, who usually made Robin either walk, or trot out, let him jog restlessly along the edge of the sticky ploughland at the upper edge of the wood. His head was up, his ears tensely forward.

'What's the matter?' Dora put a hand on his neck. He whinnied, and lengthened the jog to a trot, and as they rounded a corner, there was a girl on a brown pony, riding bareback, with her shoulders hunched in a boy's duffle coat, and tangled yellow hair falling over her face.

The pony stopped and turned round. The girl flapped the reins on its neck, but it stood still. As Dora approached she saw that she did not know either the girl or the pony, which was odd, since she knew all the people who owned horses for miles round.

'Have you come a long way?'

The girl nodded, without raising her head, and muttered, 'I got lost.'

'Where are you headed for?'

'That place where they – I don't know – a farm, or something.' She spoke roughly, mumbling through her hair. 'Where they rescue horses.'

'Follyfoot?'

'Mm.' The girl looked sideways up at her, then down again. 'That's it. I been riding all day. I'm lost.'

'Not now. That's where I live. Come on, I'll take you there.'

The girl would not answer any questions. She trailed along behind Dora, flopping when the pony jogged, like a doll losing its stuffing. The only thing she said was an occasional, 'How much farther?' in an exhausted croak. When they finally came to the pasture gate, Dora got off to open it, because the latch was stiff. The girl swayed as the pony went through, and Dora grabbed her arm.

'Hang on,' she said. 'Almost there.'

In the yard, she got off Robin just in time to catch the girl as she slid off the pony, crumpled, and blacked out.

Dora shouted for help, but there was no one about. The pony and Robin, both loose, began to introduce themselves by squealing and striking out. Dora had to lay the girl down on the cobbles and grab them both. She put Robin in his box and tied the pony to a ring in the wall.

Although its rider looked so wretched and scruffy, it was rather a nice brown pony, well made with a small, intelligent head, trimmed and shod, as if it was well cared for.

As Dora turned back to the girl, she saw that her eyes were open.

'Are you all right?' she asked. 'Who are you? What's the matter?'

For answer, the girl closed her eyes again. She was quite small, not much bigger than Callie. She lay on the cobbles like a child asleep, head on one arm, her pale tousled hair covering her dirty face.

Dora was bending to pick her up, when she remembered you were not supposed to touch a body until you knew where it was hurt. She left her there and ran into the house.

Slugger was in the kitchen, ironing. He would not use Anna's electric iron, which gave off blue sparks when you dropped it. He preferred to heat the heavy doorstop flat iron on the stove, and bang away at tablecloths and pillowcases with his good arm, leaving rusty iron outlines when he banged too hard.

Dora gabbled her story. 'Come quick, she may be dying of an internal injury!'

The old man carefully set the iron on end at the back of the stove, folded the tablecloth up so the cats would not pull it down, and put on his woollen hat with maddening slowness.

'Quick, Slugger!'

'Can't go out without me shoes then, can I?'

He bent to look under the dresser, but Dora pulled him out of the door in his slippers and hustled him, complaining, out to the yard where the girl was still lying in the same position, like a limp doll flung down.

Slugger, who had some dim first aid memories from the war, poked her in different places, pulled back one eyelid, then stroked the tangled hair back from her bony little face.

'Don't seem nothing wrong,' he said. 'Exhausted, I daresay. How far have you come, girl?' He slapped her cheek gently and raised his voice. 'Who are you?'

She opened one eye and looked at him. The sun was low, and in the slanting light which sent a deep shadow across her face, she looked not like a child any more.

'Who are you?' Slugger asked again, and she groaned and said, 'Where am I?'

'At Follyfoot.' Dora was squatting on the other side of her. 'You wanted to come here, don't you remember?'

The girl shook her head, rolling it back and forth on the cobbles. 'Like a dream . . .'

'Dream or not,' Slugger said briskly, 'she can't lay here. Pick her up, Dora and bring her in the house, and I'll get some tea brewed. Never a dull moment . . .' He ambled towards the kitchen in his slippers to the tune of the automatic grumble with which he greeted any new situation. 'No peace for the wicked . . . something new every day . . .'

As Dora bent to try to pick up the small girl, who went very

491

limp and heavy and did not help, Steve and Callie came round the barn from the small field, leading the colt Folly in his lungeing tack of roller and side reins and mouthing bit.

'What on earth –' Steve ran forward.

'I found her by Badger's woods. She was coming here with that pony. She's ill or something.' Dora puffed, trying to pick up the inert body.

'Here, I'll take her.' Steve picked up the girl quite easily. She put her arms round his neck and he carried her into the house.

18

SLUGGER was back in his cottage now, so the girl was put to bed in the strawberry ice spare room where he had nursed his broken arm.

'Like a bloomin' hospital,' he said, stumping upstairs with a hot water bottle and an extra blanket.

The pony, who had a growing coat, as if he had been kept out, was turned into the small enclosure with the open shed where Specs and Folly, and later Dottie and her donkey foal, had been separated from the other horses.

Next day, when the girl woke and came down to be revived with sausage and egg and the bread which had turned out to be Slugger's best - light and crusty with big holes to fill with butter - she consented to talk a bit, in a rough accent, which was part cockney, part a sort of country dialect hard to recognize.

'Had to take the pony and split,' she said, looking round the table from under her hair in that trapped, suspicious way. 'Nothing for it.'

When someone asked, 'Why?' she said, 'I got to know. Will you take us in?'

'Strictly speaking,' sitting in the Colonel's place, Slugger put his fingertips together and tried to look In Charge, 'we ain't taking no more 'orses 'ere, nor 'umans neither.'

'It's life or death,' the girl said hoarsely. 'Will you take us or won't you?'

Slugger looked round at his troops.

'I say, no.' Ron had been quite nasty about both the girl and the pony when he turned up that morning. 'We need another horse like we need a hole in the head, let alone another human mouth to feed. I thought we was so poor.'

The girl slid him a look under her hair, and for an instant, Dora thought she had seen her before. Then the girl reached across the table for another slice of bread, tore off the good crisp crust and stuffed it into her mouth, and the illusion of having seen her before was gone.

'Of course they must stay,' she said. How could anyone think otherwise, after the terrible thing that had happened with Ellis Elkins and poor doomed Kingfisher?

'You said it,' Ron said. 'I didn't.'

'Steve?' Slugger pointed at him with the breadknife.

'She'll have to tell her story,' Steve said. 'She'll have to come clean.'

The girl said with her mouth full of bread, 'Not till I know I can trust you.'

It was strange. It seemed as if she was putting Follyfoot on trial, not the other way round.

'Tell us your name then.'

'Are you going to call the police?'

'What for?' Steve asked. 'Are you on the run?'

'No. Yes – no. Well, it's Yasmin.' It seemed a most unlikely name. She added quickly, 'But I don't use it. You can call me Yaz.'

'Yaz what?'

'Just Yaz.'

She was dressed in faded blue jeans, hacked off at the bottom and worn right through at the knees, a man's shirt, violent coloured socks, each one a different colour, and more hole than sock, and frayed grey sneakers. She was rather dirty. Her skin looked as if she had not washed for days. Her dry, straw-coloured hair was cut raggedly, as if she had chopped it herself with a pair of blunt scissors.

She pushed away her plate with a sigh, leaned back in her chair and asked Slugger for a cigarette.

'You're too young.'

'How old do you think I am?'

'Fourteen – fifteen?'

At times she looked even less than that. Sometimes she looked much older.

'I'm twenty.' Yaz clicked her fingers at Ron, who slid a packet of cigarettes across to her.

'All right then.' Slugger leaned forward, resting his plaster cast on the table. 'Let's have your story.'

Yaz lit a cigarette, narrowed her eyes, and looked round at them through the smoke.

'Where did you get the pony?' Steve asked.

'It's mine,' she said defensively.

Dora wanted to say, 'Don't call him it', but she said encouragingly, 'He's a nice pony. Got some New Forest in him, hasn't he?'

'I daresay.'

'Is something wrong with him? He looks fit enough.'

'Well, see, it's like – it's all messed up, you know?'

'No,' said Slugger patiently. 'We don't know. Not till you tell us.'

Yaz looked down at her grubby hands with the black, bitten nails. 'My mother's dead, for a start.' Her small face clouded over. 'I don't want to talk about that. I've been living with my father. He's an artist.'

She stopped. No one said anything. Dora cleared her throat and tried, 'That must be interesting.'

'It's hell.' The girl scowled at her. 'He's a drunk. We live miles away from anywhere, right off in the woods at the end of a muddy old road, with no electricity nor nothing. I do all the work. Look after the house, if you can call it a house.

495

Falling to bits, it is. Cold.' She wrapped her arms round her thin body and shivered. 'Cook for him. Grow the vegetables. Feed those rotten chickens. Clean up the mess when he goes into one of his drunken rages. He hits me sometimes.' She rolled up her sleeve and tilted her face up to the light. She had a bruise on her upper arm and on her right cheek.

'Why do you stay?' Steve asked.

'I promised my mother I'd always look after him.'

She paused. The room was very quiet.

'Why is everyone so quiet?' Callie came bursting in from the stables, mud and manure on her boots, strong wind in her unplaited hair, energy glowing in her face. 'Am I interrupting something?'

'Yaz is telling us her life story.'

'Who's Yaz?'

'This here is Yaz.' Slugger nodded at the girl. 'Take off them boots and shut up.'

'I've been making friends with your pony.' Callie slid into a chair, and grabbed for a piece of bread with one hand and the teapot with the other. 'What's his name?'

Yaz did not seem to hear. 'He's all I've got,' she said, talking as if to herself. 'My mother gave him to me before she died. I've had him for years.'

'He doesn't look all that old.' Callie poured tea and attacked the sugar bowl.

'He's my oldest friend. My only friend. Dad wants to take him away.'

'Why?'

'Because he reminds him of my mother. He wants to have him put down. He was going to send him away to sell him. But I said wherever he went, I'd follow, steal him back, so he said, "All right, I'll shoot him." He would too.'

'It's awful.' Callie was enthralled.

496

'Yesterday – day before – I dunno. What day is it anyway? He told me he'd asked the knacker to come and take away a horse he had to shoot. We had a fight. He hit me. Knocked me out, as a matter of fact.' She rubbed her jaw. 'When I came round, he was asleep. I took the pony and got out.'

'How far have you ridden?' Dora asked.

'What's the pony's name?' This was important to Callie.

'What are you going to do?' from Steve.

'You got any money?' Ron asked.

'Suppose he comes looking for you?' Slugger's eyes wandered to the antique musket that hung over the fireplace, as if he were considering a siege.

'I don't want to talk no more.' Yaz clamped her mouth shut in her aggressive way, and got up. She looked round the room defiantly and slouched towards the door.

'Where are you going?' Slugger was nervous.

'To take care of my pony.'

'I fed him ages ago,' Callie said, 'and groomed him too. He's got such good manners. What's his name?'

'He don't trust nobody but me,' Yaz said rudely, and went out.

19

THE pony's name was simply Pony. Dora thought that Yaz would move on with him if her father was after them. But that evening, when she came back from a long ride to negotiate with a farmer for a load of hay, Pony was still in the small paddock, and Yaz was in the kitchen smoking the cigarettes that Ron had given her, and playing draughts with Steve.

'Why are the curtains drawn?' They never drew the curtains at Follyfoot, because they were a long way away from any-body, and they liked to see the night, not shut it out.

'Yaz is scared,' Steve said.

'When is she leaving?' The sight of Steve playing draughts cosily with Yaz was extremely irritating to Dora.

'I don't know. She's got nowhere to go.'

'I thought she was on the run.'

'I am.' Yaz leaned back and put her dirty bare feet on the table.

The next day, she wore a sweater and slacks that belonged to Callie, and washed all her clothes and hung them on the trees at the back of the house, because the laundry line could be seen from the road.

'And the pony could be seen too,' she said. 'He's got to be shut away somewhere.'

'There isn't a spare box,' Dora said. 'Steve is creosoting the foaling stable.'

'He can go in that little fenced off bit down in the corner by the wood,' Callie said, 'where I hid Hero when I stole him from the circus. How long are you going to stay?' She was quite thrilled with Yaz, who had brought drama and danger to the quiet farm.

'Depends on what *they* say.' Yaz nodded at Dora, who was examining Pony carefully, looking at his teeth, feeling his clean legs, trying to decide how old he was.

'I'm sorry,' Dora said, with her head under his stomach. 'We can't –'

'I'll work for you,' Yaz said. 'I don't care what I do.'

'We can't afford to pay any more staff.' Dora stood upright and faced her.

'I'll work for my keep.'

'We can't afford to keep another person.' Dora did not know why she felt so antagonistic towards Yaz. She just did. 'Or a horse.'

The girl's eyes filled with tears. 'Come on, Pony.' She took the pony's halter rope, and jerked him rather roughly away.

Three days later, Yaz was still there. She was not much trouble, but she was not much help either.

'For someone who's had a pony for years,' Dora grumbled to Steve, 'she doesn't seem to know much about horses.'

She picked up a rake which Yaz had left lying with the prongs up, and added water to Ginger and Magic's buckets which Yaz had only half filled, since they were the farthest from the tap.

'She tries.' Steve was trimming hoofs, his job while the Colonel was away. He had Wonderboy's hind foot on the leather apron in his lap.

'When she's around. She's usually hiding in the house when there's work to do.'

'She's still afraid of her father. There's no way of knowing if he's hunting for her.' Steve dropped Wonderboy's hind foot and took his file and knife round to start on the other side. 'It's all a bit of a mystery.'

'Yeah,' Dora thought rather sourly, plodding back to the tap with a bucket, the age-old mystery of knowing how to get away with it. The kind of knowledge that Dora had never had.

Dora tackled Ron.

'She's got to go.'

'All right,' Ron said amiably.

'Get rid of her then.'

'Not me job.'

'Someone will have to.'

'What's the matter?' Ron grinned. 'You jealous?'

'She'll have to go,' Dora said to Slugger, who was making soup in the big iron cauldron in which he was stewing together meat, vegetables, potatoes, bread, the remains of the egg pie, to make Slugger soup, a weekly favourite.

'Bit awkward though,' Slugger said, stirring, ''cos she's got nowhere to go and no money.'

'Too bad.' Dora fished a piece of meat out of the soup and ate it.

Slugger slapped her hand, and splashed soup on his shirt. 'Tie the apron on me, there's a love. It's no joke being one-'anded.'

Dora went upstairs and knocked on the door of the spare room, where Yaz was playing the radio she had taken from Dora's room.

'Who's that?' Yaz had a cautious, breathy voice, sometimes hardly more than a whisper.

'Dora. Can I come in?'

'I don't care,' Yaz said uninvitingly.

She was lying on top of the flowered quilt with her shoes on, reading a magazine and eating chocolate.

'Got nothing to do?' Dora asked.

'No. Boring, ain't it?'

'You don't have to stay.' Dora stood in the doorway with her fists clenched.

'You didn't say that to Steve,' Yaz turned her head and looked at Dora shrewdly, 'when he came here with Cobbler's Dream. Wasn't even his pony, was it? He stole him. And he was let stay here.'

'How do you know?' Dora came into the room and shut the door.

'He told me.'

Dora felt pretty bad about that. Steve's past was his secret. She would never tell it to anybody. Why had he told Yaz?

'That was different,' she said. 'Cobby had been blinded in one eye. He was going to be put down.'

'Pony was going to shot. Don't you believe me?'

'I don't know.'

'Suit yourself.' Yaz put up the magazine and pretended to go on reading.

20

THE next day, a police car drove through the gate. A uniformed officer and a plain clothes man walked under the arch into the stable yard.

Dora and Yaz were up in the room over the tack room, putting clean sheets on Steve's bed. When the dogs began to bark, Yaz looked out of the window, then suddenly drew in her breath and shrank back against the far wall, as if an invisible hand had pushed her.

'What is it?' Dora stopped pummelling a large pillow into a small pillowcase.

'Police!' Yaz whispered. Her small face was like a hunted field creature. She looked so terrified that Dora forgot her dislike and doubt. Instinctively she wanted to protect her.

'Get under the bed,' she whispered. 'I'll go down.'

Yaz slid under the half-made bed. Dora went down the ladder to the tack room and out to the yard, trying not to look as nervous as she felt.

'Can I have a word with the Colonel?' The plain clothes man was casual and friendly, as if he had merely come to pay a neighbourly call.

'He's abroad. They won't be back till next month.'

'All right. Just making a – you know – a general survey, who's living where, how many staff you've got, that kind of thing.'

'Let's see, there's four of us working here, three living here, counting the Colonel's stepdaughter, and then there's all the horses. Robin, Cobby, Wonderboy, Hero, Magic, Nigger,

Fanny, Spot, Lancelot – he's the oldest horse in the world –
Ginger, Dolly –'

'All right, all right.' The man in uniform cut her off. 'We'll
take your word for it. No one new in the household then? No
extra stable workers?'

'No.' It was only partly a lie. You couldn't call Yaz part of
the household, and she certainly didn't work.

'Seen any strangers around?'

'No.' Yaz was not a stranger. Dora knew her pretty well
after four days. 'Are you looking for someone?'

'Not really.' The plain clothes man was still casual, bending
to pat an inquisitive dog, whistling at one of the donkeys, who
crossed a corner of the yard on the way to the water trough.
'Just a routine check.'

As they turned and went out to their car, Steve rode in on
Ron's motor bike, with a gallon milk jug swinging from the
handlebars. To save money, they had given up deliveries and
started to collect from the dairy themselves.

'What did they want?' Steve got off the bike.

'I don't know.' Dora had been breathing fast while she
talked to the policemen. Now she felt icy calm and clear-
headed. 'They were looking for someone. I think they were
looking for Yaz.'

'Where is she?'

'Under your bed.'

Dora went back up the ladder. Steve put the bike away and
followed her. Yaz came out from under the bed, coughing,
with fluff in her straw mop of hair.

'Could you hear?' Dora asked.

'Thanks for not telling.'

'Were they looking for you?' Dora asked. 'What is it, Yaz?
What have you done?'

503

Yaz looked from Dora to Steve. Then she sat on the bed and put her face in her hands. 'I can't tell you.'

'You'd better,' Steve said, quite roughly.

'All right, I'll tell you.' Yaz looked up and shook back her hair. 'I killed my father.'

Dora felt as if she had been punched in the stomach. She could not speak.

'Say that again,' Steve said grimly.

'It was like this, see.' Yaz did not look at either of them. 'Night before I came here, it was. He was drunk. Yelling and cursing, and hitting me every chance he got. I hid in my room, but he dragged me out of bed and made me cook a meal for him. It wasn't the way he liked it, so he threw it at me, plate and all. There was a fight then. He came at me with a chair. I ducked, and then he smashed the chair on the stone floor, and picked up the butcher knife. I got hold of a chair leg and I hit out – I didn't know what I was doing. I hit him at the back of the head, and he went down like a stone.

'I waited for a while to see if he'd move. Then I went and looked at him. His eyes were turned up and blood was coming out of his mouth. He didn't seem to be breathing. He was very cold. I couldn't find his pulse. I thought he was dead.'

'What did you do?' Dora whispered.

'Nothing for it but to run. I couldn't stay with – with that. I went and got the pony and got out as fast as I could. I rode and rode. I'd heard about this place – how you take in horses. It was my only hope.'

From the window of Steve's room, Dora watched Yaz leave the tack room, look furtively left and right as if she thought the police might still be about, and dart across the yard to the house.

504

'What are we going to do?' Dora turned to Steve.

'God knows. We can't turn her in. But harbouring a criminal, that's a crime too.'

'Can you be put in prison for that?'

'Probably.'

'We can't go to prison. We've got to run this place. What on earth shall we do? Tell Slugger?'

'He'd have a heart attack.'

'And I wouldn't trust Ron. He doesn't like Yaz anyway. If only the Colonel were here!'

'We could telephone him,' Steve suggested.

'It wouldn't be safe. Suppose the line is tapped? You can't tell a story like that over international telephone.'

'One of us could go out to him, if we had the money for a plane ticket. Do you think Mrs Oldcastle would lend it to us?' She was the only rich person they knew.

'I doubt it,' Dora said. 'She's turned mean. She was rude to Ron, remember, when he asked her for a donation to Follyfoot. Oh, I wish the Colonel was here!' she said again.

'Well, he's not.' Steve looked at her with his dark steady eyes. 'There's only you and me, Dora.'

When Callie came home from school, spinning her hat in one direction and her book bag in the other, she found Dora in Robin's stable, pulling his mane to thin it and make it lie down. She and Steve had decided that the best thing to do for the time being was to lie low and pretend that nothing had happened.

'What were the police doing here?' Callie demanded at once.

'What makes you think they were here?'

'When Laurie Drew's mother came to fetch her, she said she'd seen a police car in our gateway.'

505

'It was nothing.' Dora stayed on the other side of Robin, concentrating on back-combing and pulling his mane. 'You know there's been a lot of cars stolen. They thought one of them might have been dumped on our land.'

'How boring,' Callie said. 'All the way home on the bus, I hoped it was something exciting.'

21

THE police did not come back. Yaz calmed down, but Dora was nervous and on edge. Every time a car came down the road, she thought it was the police again. Every time the telephone rang, she jumped out of her skin.

For the umpteenth time, she said to Steve, 'She'll have to go,' and for the umpteenth time, Steve said, 'How can we turn her out?'

'But Steve –' Dora could not get out of her head the picture of Yaz with the chair leg in her small stubby hands, the man crashing to the floor. 'But Steve, she's a murderer.'

'Manslaughter,' Steve said. 'It was in self-defence.'

'Why doesn't she give herself up then?'

'She will,' Steve said, 'when she's ready. You can't make her.'

And for the umpteenth time, Dora wailed, 'I wish the Colonel was here!'

Yaz herself, the cause of all this agony, seemed to be more relaxed now that she had got it off her chest. On Sunday, she said that she was sick of staying in the house, and was going to take Pony out to the woods and look for some ferns.

'I'm interested in them too,' Callie said. 'Do you collect them?'

'I did. Nothing much else to do, living there with my father like that.'

'In the woods,' Callie said, 'if you go down on the north side, there's some quite rare ferns. Wait till I get Cobby ready, and I'll come with you and show you.'

507

'I'd rather be on my own,' Yaz said. 'I gotta think.'

'It's no fun on your own,' said friendly Callie.

'Pony doesn't like Cobbler's Dream.' Yaz was putting the bridle on the brown pony, fiddling and fussing with the buckles, because she was irritated.

'He does,' Callie protested. 'He likes everybody. You make him out to be so temperamental, but he's one of the easiest ponies we've ever had here, considering what ponies can be like. Look, you've got that curb chain twisted. Why do you ride him in a curb anyway? He doesn't need it.'

'How do you know?'

'I rode him when you were staying in your room.'

'You got no right!' Yaz spun round angrily.

'He needed the exercise. Look, Yaz, the curb's still twisted. You turn it like this, see, laying all the links flat –'

'Knock it off,' Yaz said, 'and give me a leg up.'

'If you can't mount bareback –'

'I gotta bad leg.'

'– how will you get on again after you get off to gather ferns?' Callie heaved her on to Pony's back. 'Better let me come with you, Yaz. You might get lost anyway.'

'Let her alone!' Ron shouted from half way up a ladder, where he was giving the weather end of the barn its yearly coat of paint before the winter. 'She's anti-social.'

As Yaz turned the pony to go out of the yeard, Callie put in a last word. 'Better take a halter if you're going to tie him up anywhere.'

'I'll tie him with the reins.'

'Oh Lord.' Callie swung her head and clucked her teeth like an old woman. 'Oh dear, oh dear, oh dear. Didn't anyone ever tell her?' She fussed and clucked, pushing the stiff broom across the yard, and Yaz gave the pony a slap on the ribs with the flat of her hand and trotted out of earshot.

'Why can't you leave people alone?' Ron hung his paint pot on a bent wire on the top rung and started to climb down the ladder. 'Everybody's got to do everything your way.'

'There's only one right way, with horses.'

'Horses, horses. What about the poor people? I think I'll take some time off on me own as well. I'm worn out.'

As his toe touched the ground, Slugger came out of the barn.

'Back up that ladder, young Ronald.'

'It's Sunday. It's not right to be working on a day of rest.'

'You know why you're working on a Sunday.' Slugger tipped his hat over his eye against the sun and squinted up at Ron sternly. 'To make up for all those mornings you been late to work. Now get on with that job. I want at least half that end done before supper.'

'The paint fumes make me dizzy.'

'I'll give you something that'll make you dizzy.' Slugger shook his fist at him, and Ron went slowly back up the ladder, dipped his brush in the paint and gave it a casual flick.

Slugger stepped back just in time. 'Watch what you're doing.'

'Stand out of the way then,' Ron said grandly. 'There's men working up here.'

But when Slugger had gone into the house for his afternoon nap, Ron came down the ladder again, stepped out of the painting overalls, stiff with years of different colour paint, and went to get his motor bike.

'Where are you going?' Steve asked.

'Just to get some fags. Yaz smoked me last packet.'

It took ten minutes to get to the village and back. When Ron had not returned in half an hour, Steve got out of the chair where he was reading the Sunday paper, climbed into the multi-coloured overalls, which told the story of every colour they had ever used at Follyfoot, and went up the ladder to finish the end of the barn.

Not to help Ron. To help Slugger. When the old man got angry with Ron, his eyes bulged and his face flushed the colour of a radish. He had trouble enough with his broken arm without getting apoplexy as well.

And although Steve did not admit this to Dora, he was dead scared about Yaz. Better to have some work to keep his mind off it.

While he was slapping away with the brush under the eaves of the barn, an extremely elegant woman whom he had never seen before rode into the yard on a tall chestnut horse with dazzling white stockings, impeccable tack, and no sign of the growth of a winter coat, which all the Follyfoot horses were showing.

The woman stopped in the middle of the yard, and looked round with her pointed nose in the air, as if Follyfoot were a sewage farm.

'Hal-loo there!' she called, in a high, clear voice. 'Anybody about?'

Steve came down the ladder and walked towards her in the baggy overalls, which had belonged to someone much bigger.

'Good afternoon.' The woman had difficulty in seeing him, since she kept her nose in the air and her chin tilted above her tattersall shirt. 'Do you have horses here?' she asked, although she could see for herself that there were about twenty loose-boxes, some with heads sticking out in innocent welcome for the grand chestnut horse, and old Flame was pottering about in a corner of the yard, snuffing up spilled chaff like a groggy vacuum cleaner.

510

'We do have one or two.' Steve grinned, taking in the sleek yellow breeches and boots he could see his face in.

The woman could, if she chose, also see for herself Slugger in his oldest, vilest pair of trousers tucked into muddy Wellingtons, creeping down one side of the yard, with one arm in a cast and sling, and the other pushing an extraordinary contraption made out of the body of a wooden wheelbarrow set on two bicycle wheels with a broom stick for a handle, which Ron had invented so that he did not have to do all Slugger's barrow work.

The woman in the boots looked once, winced, and averted her eyes.

'I'll tell you what it is,' she said. 'I've lost one of my horses. It's my daughter's, as a matter of fact, a bay pony –' she pronounced it poneh – 'common little thing, but she sets store by it. It was out to grass and it must have pushed through the hedge somehow. Ponies are more trouble than they're worth, don't you think?'

Steve grunted. No type of horse was more trouble than it was worth, because it was a horse.

'We've looked everywhere.' The woman looked down at him from her great height on the long-legged horse, raising her plucked eyebrows slightly at the clownish overalls and the paint in his black hair. 'I live a good way away, but I just thought, as a last resort, I'd see if it had wandered over here. It's stupid enough to do something like that.'

'Has he got out before?'

'Not till now, it's too maddening. My groom wants to bring him in to clip and get fit before my daughter comes home for the Christmas holidays.'

'Sorry,' Steve said. 'We've had no ponies wandering round here, but I'll keep my eyes open. A bay, you said?'

'Oh –' the woman clicked her fingers as if the pony were

511

hardly worth describing – 'sort of nondescript, I suppose you'd call it that. A very ordinary, common little thing. Not up to much, it never was, compared to the rest of the horses in my stable.'

'Mare or gelding?'

The woman laughed down her thin pointed nose. 'Absurd – I can't remember. My daughter calls it Scruffy. She can ride anything in the place – hunters, show horses – but it's a sort of pet to her. She'll give me hell when she comes home, if dear old Scruffy has disappeared, you know how it is.'

'Oh yes, I know,' Steve said, as if he had everyday dealings with girls who went to boarding school and gave hell to high-nosed mothers with tight canary yellow breeches and voices like a horse neighing for breakfast.

'I'll give you my card.' The woman produced a visiting card from the pocket of her tailored ratcatcher jacket. 'If you do hear anything about that rotten pony, I'll be obliged if you'd let me know.'

'All right.' Steve looked at the card. It said 'Lady Dillingham Joynes, High Pastures, Lesser Overton-by-Grymsdytch.'

'That's a good boy.' Lady D.J. turned the tall chestnut, striking sparks from the cobbles, and he clattered out under the archway, swishing his exquisite golden tail.

22

RON did not come back from the village. Steve had not thought he would. Ron had a lot of friends all over the towns and countryside, any amount of places where he could hole up for a chat and a smoke, and conveniently forget what time it was.

Steve had more than half the end of the barn done. Dora was up on the roof, clearing leaves and twigs out of the gutter before he got to the corner. Callie was sitting on the Weaver in the yard, trimming his mane with the hand clippers. He had a skin infection, which was easier to treat if his mane was hogged. Since a lifetime of weaving had left him unable to stop swinging his old head from side to side, rocking gently from one foot to the other, it was easier to trim if you were sitting on his back.

He raised his head, still swinging it, and gave out a cracked neigh.

Other horses took it up before anyone heard the sound of hoofs.

It was Pony, coming back sweaty and wild-eyed, with burrs in his mane and tail and his reins dangling broken round his legs.

'I knew it,' Callie slid off down the Weaver's shoulder to catch him. 'I knew what would happen if she tied him up by the reins. Some people have to learn the hard way. Poor Pony.' She patted him and put him into an empty loose box. 'What have you done with Yaz then?'

She took a bunch of hay and folded it into a figure-of-eight wisp to rub him down, hissing to him like the Colonel did.

513

'Do you suppose Yaz is in trouble?' Dora called from the roof.

'She's too stupid to get into trouble,' Callie grumbled.

Since she had discovered that Yaz was not only lazy and rude. but did not know enough about horses to deserve to own one, Callie was no longer quite so thrilled with her. 'She's only gone the other side of the little wood.' She looked over the door. 'She'll be back in an hour. Do her good to walk.'

Yaz was not back in an hour. Dora and Steve got in the truck to go and look for her.

'Why bother?' Callie said. 'She'll turn up for supper. That kind always do. Why are you looking so worried, Dora?' She stood on the step and peered into the cab. 'Something's up that I don't know about. Tell me. Nobody tells me anything.' Her constant complaint. 'There is some trouble, isn't there? Is her father after her? It's something to do with the police being here. Let me come with you.'

'It's all right, Cal,' Dora said. 'It's always worrying when a horse comes back without its person.'

'Ought we to tell her?' Dora asked Steve as they turned on to the road.

'Too young,' Steve said, and Callie's head, with the pigtails blowing in the wind, appeared at the open window from the back of the truck where she had hopped in when they said she could not come.

'Too young for what? I'm not half as young for my age as Yaz is,' she said. 'I'm twelve, but I behave like fourteen. Yaz is twenty, but she behaves like fourteen sometimes.' She had to shout against the wind as Steve picked up speed down the hill.

They turned down a rutted lane, and then bumped the truck into a field track at the edge of the little wood. When it

514

became too muddy, they got out and walked across the corner through the trees to the place where Callie had told Yaz she could find the special ferns.

The turf of the hillside sloped down to a marvellous view of the river and the rolling brown arable fields, patched here and there with the bright green of winter wheat, that climbed gently up the other side of the valley.

The autumn colour had faded from the thick trees that marked the river's winding course. Soon all the leaves would be gone, and the brown ploughland frozen into hard chunks, and the birds that were still making Sunday music among the trees would have gone wherever winter birds went when they were not hopping round the back door waiting for someone to shake out the breakfast tablecloth.

'Take a good look.' Callie felt cold in the strengthening wind, and wished she had brought a jacket. 'Next time we come up here, it may be snow.'

The view was fine. It always was. But there was no view of what they were looking for. No footmarks of either Yaz or her pony, no answering voice in answer to the calls they sent out.

'Ya-a-az!' It was a good name to yell. It came out like a shriek of agony. Callie stood and bellowed it out across the valley, and a sad bull bellowed back at her from one of the low-lying farms.

They drove the truck round the nearer lanes for a while, searching and calling, but there was no sign of her. When they got back to Follyfoot, Ron had come back on his bike, and was carrying away the ladder and paint pot, since it was getting too dark to paint.

'Where you all been?' he asked, 'walking out on an honest working man?'

'I did half your job.' Steve got out of the truck, still in overalls.

'Ta,' Ron said. 'So that's where me painting knickers was. I been looking everywhere so I could finish me work.'

'Do you know where Yaz is?' Dora asked.

'Gone botanical, hasn't she?'

'The pony came back without her.'

'Probably fell off. I daresay she's used to that. What's the matter?' Ron looked at Dora in the gathering dusk. 'Is something up?'

'No, I just thought she might be lost again.'

There had been times when Dora wished she could tell Ron, who skated round the edges of crime, and had friends who were always in trouble. He might know what to do about murder, or manslaughter. But he was too tricky to trust. Even when he was trying to help, he invented so many complications and secret schemes that you ended up in a bigger mess than you were in already.

Sure enough, just before supper time, Yaz walked in at the gate with a long grass in her mouth and a straggly bundle of leaves and roots in her hands.

'Where have you been?' Callie was going round with feeds. 'You weren't where I told you to go.'

'Did you go looking? Daft. I was all right.'

'Pony came back,' Callie said sarcastically, 'in case you were worried.'

'I guessed he would. Stupid thing broke his reins.'

'Stupid you to tie him up by them,' Callie seethed, but Yaz had walked on without hearing.

She had come back in rather a bad mood. She seemed quiet and depressed at supper, her small pale face sad and old. Callie, remembering about her dead mother and her brutal father, tried to make up for seething at her.

'Where did you go, Yaz?' she asked agreeably.

'Nowhere special.'

516

Callie had lost her father when she was younger. She could remember that she had wept and sulked and refused to eat or speak for days. It must be even worse to lose your mother. No wonder Yaz sat glumly with her elbows on the table, and a rough answer for everyone.

'What kind of ferns did you get?' She tried again. 'Where are they?'

'I left 'em outside.'

After supper, Callie went out to look. She would get out the Colonel's Encyclopedia of British Wild Flowers, and show Yaz how to identify the plants she had found. Callie did not stay angry with people for long. Knowing what it was to want people desperately to like you, she could usually find some way of trying to like even people she did not like.

The greenstuff that Yaz had gathered was thrown down under the tree with the thick horizontal branch where the swing hung.

There was nothing much. Some ordinary ferns. Maidenhair. Hart's tongue. Spleenwort. Nothing that you could not find in the hedgerows and copses round Follyfoot.

23

Ron did not turn up for work next day. Nor the next, nor the next.

Steve finished the end of the barn, and then he and Dora did the other end as well, since there was plenty of paint, and then Dora took Yaz across the road to paint the crooked shed in which Slugger kept the tools for his vegetable garden, which was threatening to supply turnip greens all winter.

'If Ron has gone for good this time,' Dora said when Slugger came out to supervise, 'that'll solve the staff problem when you go back on the payroll next month.'

'I wouldn't want nothing to happen while the Colonel's away,' Slugger said. 'Better give that door another coat, Yaz, my girl. It's warping. After all, I mean, good old Ron, he's a bad boy, any way you look at it. But he's got a good heart. He's been a bit sarky to you, Yaz, but that's only his idea of a joke.'

'It don't matter.' Yaz sloshed away, scattering paint on to herself and on to the turnip greens at the end of each stroke. She was in a funny mood today, vague and detached, as if she were not quite there.

Had she met anyone when she was off in the woods by herself? Dora and Steve had both questioned her, but she swore she had seen nobody. They had been watching the newspaper and listening to the radio news, dreading to hear about the discovery of a battered body, of fingerprints, of the obvious suspect wanted 'to help with enquiries'.

Nothing. It might be months before Yaz's father was found. She ought to pluck up courage and get away, far away, while she could.

That afternoon, she said she was going to go and look for more ferns.

'I hope you find better ones than last time,' Callie said.

'I was upset about losing the pony. And I had all that walk back. I didn't have time to look properly.'

'Sure you don't want me to come?'

'I told you,' Yaz said. 'No.' She kicked the pony forward.

'Take a headcollar!' Callie called after her.

Yaz turned and put a thumb to her nose. Callie stuck out her tongue, but Yaz had ambled away.

Dora took Robin out to the small field to school him over some jumps. They were going to have a Follyfoot hunter trials in the Christmas holidays, and there would be some pretty hot competition from the tough girls at the pony farm, who would tackle any jumps with their New Forests and Connemaras: over, under or through, whichever way they could get to the other side.

Robin was streets better, but he was still rushing his fences, so Dora was doing some slow work with him. She had set up several low fences, and was trotting him backwards and forwards to calm him down and make him use the muscles of his back.

At first he fussed and pulled, making a great production of a jump that was no more than a garden bench with the back broken off. After half an hour of patient work, he relaxed, and was hopping cleanly over every jump with a completely loose rein. Dora felt as though she was glued into the saddle. Robin always made you feel you rode better than you really did. He was the best horse she had ever had – well, he was the only horse she had ever owned – but he was the best she would ever have, if she lived to be a hundred and married a handsome millionnaire who did not expect her to cook or clean or wear skirts, or do anything but ride fabulous horses.

Perhaps she didn't need a millionaire, handsome or ugly. It was enough to have a friend like Earl Blankenheimer, who had given her this marvellous bay horse and still sent her cheques from America every few months to pay for Robin's keep.

Hop, he went over the low poles, hop over the little brush fence, trot a few yards, hop over the logs, turn, trot back, hop over the ditch, back over the rails again, at an angle this time, over the bench, the car tyres and the oil drums, and finally over the sheep hurdles, which were higher, and quite a stiff jump from a trot.

Perfect. Dora leaned forward to stroke his fine black mane down on his neck. He reached for a patch of clover and she nearly rolled off, but he threw her back in the saddle, as he suddenly flung up his head and pricked his ears.

A large brown car had stopped outside, and the heads of a man and a woman had appeared looking over the gate of the field that led to the road.

'Hullo! I say, hullo, there!' The man called out hesitantly.

Dora gathered up her reins and rode towards them.

'Do you live here?'

'Yes. This is Follyfoot Farm. Is there something –?'

The man and the woman looked at each other uncertainly and then the woman said, 'Yes, well, there might be something. May we come in?'

'Of course. Bring your car round into the yard. I'll go through the other way and join you.'

She rode back through the other gate, and put Robin into his loose box with his tack on.

The couple got out of the car. They seemed mild-mannered people, rather thickset and square, both with thin, greying hair and unremarkable faces, wearing the kind of brownish clothes you would not really notice.

'Did you come to see the old horses?' Dora asked.

Callie had been taking round the evening feeds. She always liked to show visitors round. In the fading light, she and Dora began the guided tour they never got sick of:

'This is Cobbler's Dream. He was a famous show jumper once, till he got blinded in one eye. This is Stroller, who used to pull a brewery dray. This old fellow is Hero, who came from a circus, where he was being mistreated. He was too stiff to dance or lie down, you see, but the woman had trained him by cruelty, and he was too scared not to try. This is Ginger, who used to be a milk horse, till some old ladies rescued him, because he was going to be shipped abroad for slaughter. This is Lancelot. Would you believe he is the oldest horse in the world?'

The square people followed them without comment.

'This is poor old Frank, who was found with a terrible dent in his nose where a tight headcollar –'

When they were about half way round, the woman cleared her throat and said, 'It's very nice, I'm sure, but it isn't exactly what we came for.'

'I'm sorry.' Dora shut the stable door on Frank and his famous dented nose. 'Most people like to see the old horses and hear how they came here.'

'Well, we would, of course, if we had more time, but it's just that this visit is for a different reason.'

'Oh.' Dora looked at them. They looked at each other, then down at their plain brown shoes. 'What is it?'

'Well, actually.' The man's Adam's apple took a plunge up and down his neck. 'We're looking for a missing person.'

Dora's heart stopped cold and was instantly frozen in ice. What if they were friends or relations of Yaz's father – somebody who was expecting him somewhere, and he had not turned up and they were looking for him? Why didn't they go to the house in the wood then! Perhaps they had, and found it all locked up as Yaz had left it, with the curtains drawn so no one could see in.

'What –' She leaned against Frank's door. She hardly dared say it. 'What kind of person?'

She held her breath to hear them say, 'An artist', but the man said, 'It's a child. A very beautiful girl with long brown hair.'

Thank God. Dora let out her breath. Yaz was safe for a while yet.

'How old?' Callie asked.

'Fourteen.'

'That's not a child,' Callie said, but the woman went on in a low voice, 'It's our daughter Joan. She's been gone for ages. We're worried sick.'

Dora and Callie looked at each other. First Yaz. Now this Joan. It seemed to be the season for runaways.

'Why did you think she might be here?' Dora asked. 'Is she interested in horses?'

'She always was, though she could never have one. We live in a flat in town. Near the University. My husband is a professor there.'

'I'm sorry,' Dora said.

'Thanks anyway.' The man sighed, his thin grey hair lifting in the breeze, his shadowed eyes showing how many night's sleep he had lost. 'We were just following a vague lead. The police did tell us that they had been here and found nothing, but we thought we'd stop and talk to you anyway.'

So the police had been looking for Joan, not Yaz. Thank God Dora and Steve had not telephoned the Colonel, or tried to borrow money to fly out to him. It was possible that nobody had found Yaz's father yet, lying dead in his own blood on the stone floor of the mysterious house in the wood.

Dora felt a hundred pounds lighter with relief. Then she

looked at the downcast couple, heavy with their own anxiety, and said with genuine sympathy, 'It must be awful not to know where she is.'

Dora had run away when she was thirteen. Although she had only stayed away one night, had her parents lost sleep over her? They had not said so. When she came back, exhausted, guilty, expecting them to fall on her neck with cries of joyous relief, her father had said, without looking up from his book, 'You're late for lunch,' and her mother had said, 'Wash your hands before you sit down.'

When she was older, she had run away again, to Follyfoot, and told the Colonel her parents would not care where she had gone. When he telephoned them, they had said, 'We've been so worried – how could Dora do this to us?', which was what they were supposed to have said the first time. Which proved you never knew where you were with parents.

This lot of parents looked very tired and dejected, so as they turned away from the stable where Frank was quietly chewing on the woodwork – a habit he had acquired when he was abandoned in the tight headcollar without food – she said impulsively, 'If you'd like to come into the house for some tea –?'

The weary faces loosened into smiles. 'It would be nice,' the woman said, 'to sit down for a while and get my thoughts together. We've been on the road since early morning.'

'Come on in.' Dora was glad she had thought of it. 'Slugger will brew you one of his special mugs of tea.'

24

CALLIE went to take off Robin's saddle and bridle and feed him. As Dora led Joan's tired parents up the path to the back of the house, Ron's motor bike came roaring up the hill, through the gate with a scream of tyres on gravel, and under the arch into the yard, where it stopped abruptly, like a bucking horse.

Ron switched off the engine and called to Dora. She took Joan's parents into the house, then ran back to the yard.

'Where's Yaz?' Ron was sitting on the bike, which was giving off a smell of heat and oil, his cowboy boots stretched out on either side.

'She's been gone all afternoon.'

'Where to?'

'Off in the woods somewhere.'

'Oh 'orror.' Ron groaned and put a hand to his forehead. 'This is the last time I'm ever going to get mixed up in any funny business. I mean that, Dora. Cut me throat, I swear it.' He swept a dirty finger nail across the crumpled orange scarf wound round his neck. 'I'm staying away from trouble, and you can have that in writing, *if* you like.'

'What are you talking about, Ron? I've got to go. There's some people in the house having tea.'

'People, what people? Get 'em out of here. We don't want no strangers nosing round.'

'What's going on?'

Normally Ron was cool and cocky, even when there was trouble. Dora had never seen him like this, jittery and scared, with his red hair on end, hanging on to the handlebars of his bike as if it were the only security in the world.

524

'I've got myself into a right old mess,' he said, 'and all because of you lot.'

'What are you *talking* about?'

'*I know where Yaz is.*'

And then suddenly Dora had a revelation. All the puzzling, mysterious things that had been going on – Yaz's fantastic murder story, her changeable moods, her funny accent, her weird behaviour, right back to the first meeting when she called her pony it instead of him – it was as if a dusky curtain had been pulled back in Dora's brain, and a scene of dazzling clarity revealed.

'Never mind *where* she is.' She hopped up and down with excitement. 'I think I know *who* she is.'

'What's that you say?'

'Some of what she's told us isn't true.'

'Ha!' It was not Ron's old jaunty laugh, but a bitter, jeering sound. 'You only just found that out? I was right then. You was born yesterday.'

'None of it is true, perhaps. She's not even twenty.'

'Ha! Fifteen, more like, if that.'

'Her father isn't mur- I mean, he's not even an alcoholic. Her mother's alive. She cut her hair and bleached it.'

'How do you know?'

'I'm guessing, but it all fits. Her name is Joan.'

'Tell me something I *don't* know.'

'All right, I will. Her parents are here.'

'Don't be daft.'

'Here, I tell you. They're in the kitchen at this very moment, being revived with Slugger's first aid mugs of tea.'

'That's torn it.' Ron beat his brow and left a greasy oil mark under his distraught red hair.

'Torn what?'

Ron glanced round, as if the horses were spies. He swung his leg over the back of the bike, and pulled Dora into the tack room.

Callie was in there with Robin's bridle on the cleaning hook that hung from the ceiling. She was going over the leather with neatsfoot oil.

'Out.' Ron jerked his thumb.

'Not on your life.' Callie stood her ground, with the oily rag in her hand. 'There's too many secrets going on, and I'm fed up with not knowing. Who are those people in the house?'

'Yaz's parents,' Dora said.

'Can t be. Her mother's dead and her father beats her. Oh.' Her mouth drooped. 'You mean it was all lies? She's Joan, not Yasmin? But they said "beautiful".'

'That's parents,' Ron said. 'Listen, I got this friend Mickey, see. Lives down by the canal, near Carter's coal yard.'

Dora had another revelation. In a flash, her mind went back to the first time she saw Yaz, and she thought that she had seen her somewhere before. It had been puzzling her ever since. Now she knew where she had seen that grubby little face.

'The ten mile ride!' she said.

'Ride, what do you mean, ride?' Ron grumbled irritably. 'Listen, Dora, this is serious stuff. We're not playing with gee-gees now.'

'The day of the ride,' Dora went on, 'when we rode through Carter's coal yard to get over the canal bridge, a girl looked out of one of the sheds. Her eyes looked sort of scared, as if she were shut in, or hiding.'

'Well, she was,' Ron said. 'That's what I'm trying to tell you, if you'll just shut up. My friend Mickey, he hangs out with that crowd down there, see. Big operators some of them are. Some are only into the little stuff, like stealing hubcaps and nicking fags. When old Yaz turned up –'

526

'Where from?' Callie was automatically rubbing the noseband over and over, staring at Ron.

'From where she lived. That part of it is true. She did run away from her Mum and Dad, who Dora says are in the kitchen, in peril of their lives from being poisoned with Slugger's tea. On the loose, she meets up with Mickey somewhere, see, and for various reasons, not unconnected with the kind if character she is, Mickey latches on to her to do a job for him.'

'Yaz never does any work,' Callie said.

'You've lived with me long enough to know what a job is,' Ron said sternly.

'A robbery?' Dora asked.

'That's about the size of it. Her parents were on the hunt for her, so she had to be hid. Old Carter, he owed Mickey a favour for some special stuff that Mickey had - well - found for him, so he agreed to hide her down the coal yard. The police came. They dragged the canal. Fished up a lot of old boots and a dead bicycle wheel. "What are you looking for, officer?" I happened to be down there that day, and got talking to one of the coppers in my pally way. "A young girl," he says. "There was a rumour she was seen down this way, and we don't want to leave no stone unturned, nor no ditch undredged."

'So after that, it wasn't safe for Yaz to hang about, with all them coppers buzzing round like wasps round the dregs of a glass of beer, so Mickey dreams up this fantastic solution. Hide her at Follyfoot.'

'You knew who she was,' Callie said. 'That's why you were so rotten to her.'

'Sharp girl. Of course I knew. And I knew one sure way to get her taken in here. With a sob story about a horse. So Mick finds her a bridle, and she borrows this pony –'

'Where from?' Callie asked.

'From a field, never mind. Everything was going lovely. Until today.'

'What's happened?'

'Well, old Mickey, he's a car fancier, see. Knows 'em all, including how to start 'em without a key. Detective Sergeant turns up and takes Mick down to the station. Wants to talk to him about some of these four-wheeled pets that have gone missing round the neighbourhood.'

'What's that got to do with Yaz?' Dora asked.

'Everything. Yesterday was the rehearsal. Today's the day of the job. Yaz is already in that house, waiting for Mick to come and give the special signal so she can let him in when the old lady's asleep.'

25

'*What old lady?*' A dreadful suspicion invaded Dora's mind.

'Well.' In the dim light from the tack room lantern, Ron shuffled his feet and looked uncomfortable. 'You know. Her what grows the brussels sprouts.'

'Mrs Oldcastle? But she's a friend!'

'As much as a rich person can be anybody's friend.' Ron had his own set of standards and morals. 'Mean old devil. She's got it to spare, you know. She's never going to miss it – some of that silver and stuff.'

'Well, I'm glad they took Mickey to the police station,' Callie said. 'Now Mrs Oldcastle is safe.'

'But Yaz ain't. Suppose Mickey talks about where she is? Turns informer to save his own neck. If they find Yaz, waiting in that house, she's had it. Not fair really. She's only a silly kid. Not much older than old Cal here.'

'I wouldn't get mixed up in a rotten mess like that.' Callie threw the oily rag in the box and hung up Robin's bridle.

'Yaz ain't had your advantages,' Ron said. 'Brought up too sheltered. She's wild for adventure.'

'It's crime.'

'It's a sort of game to her. She don't understand.'

'But you and Mickey do!' Dora flared. 'It's a filthy trick. We've got to get Yaz out.'

'That's the point,' Ron said. 'I don't know the signal.'

'One of us must get into the house, the same way Yaz did. How did she get in? Mrs Oldcastle keeps that place shut up like the Tower of London.'

'That's the other point,' said Ron. 'You know how tiny Yaz

529

is. The only way into that house is through a little dog hatch the old lady had made, with a flap that pushes back and forwards, so darling Pookie can go in and out at will. That's why Mickey picked Yaz, because she's got a lot of nerve, and she's narrow enough to get through that door. There's nobody else could do it.'

Callie came and stood in front of Ron with her fists clenched. 'There's me,' she said, and set her jaw.

'No, Callie –' Dora began.

'Why not? I'm no bigger than Yaz, and I've got just as much nerve.'

'You know the old lady's got a gun?' Ron said.

'Oh pooh, an air gun. I'm not scared,' Callie said, although she was.

'Good kid,' said Ron. 'But you've got to swear –'

'Let's get going.' Callie moved impatiently to the door.

'No, listen.' Ron shoved her up against the wall and pinned her there with a large hand across her throat. 'Swear,' he said, as Callie's eyes rolled at him above the dirty hand. 'Swear you'll never tell another soul the deeds of this night.'

Callie made some squeaky, choking noises. When Ron shifted his hand, she gasped, 'How can I swear when you're throttling me? Come on, you're wasting time – let's go!'

It was dark outside, and the wind was getting up. The big brown car had gone.

'Hurry, Ron!' Callie put a leg over the back of the motor bike.

'I dunno.' Ron hung back in the tack room doorway. 'Suppose something's gone wrong, and they've caught Yaz? I can't risk being seen round there.'

'To save Yaz?' In her anger with Ron, Callie had forgotten that Yaz was a cheat and a liar. The adventure was like a crusade.

'What's she to me? Save my skin, that's what I'm thinking about.'

'Get Steve,' Callie told Dora.

'Don't bring him in on this.' Ron grabbed Dora's arm.

She shook him off. 'Why not? *He's* not a coward.'

Steve had spent most of the afternoon trying to make the truck go. Seeing that there was a light in the cart shed, Dora went to find him. He had set the heavy duty torch on a beam, and was still working on the engine, wearing a pair of grimy white overalls that had once belonged to a racing driver he admired.

'Does it work?'

Bending over the engine, Steve jumped as Dora came into the circle of light. 'Hunk of junk. I'll never get it going.' Pieces of the engine were lying about on the ground. They did not look as if they would ever fit back in.

Dora groaned. 'Just when we need it.'

'Who needs it?' Steve stood upright and wiped his hands on one of Callie's old vests. 'We're not going anywhere, are we? Something good on at the cinema?'

'I wish it was the films, but it's real. Listen, Steve, I've got to tell you. Yaz is in bad trouble.'

'She can't be in any worse trouble than she is already.'

'It's all different. I can't explain everything now, but will you take Callie on the back of Ron's bike?'

'Where to?'

'Come on!' She took his hand and began to gabble some of the story at him as they ran across the yard in a spatter of blowing rain.

26

CALLIE loved to ride on the back of the motor bike. It was even better when Steve was up front. It was fun with Ron, but he took the corners so fast that you were never sure that he wouldn't skid on a sharp turn, and the whole bike fly out from under you, while you scraped the side of your face off on the road.

Steve rode just as fast, but he didn't swerve and skid so much, and his waist was more solid to cling to. The back of the racing driver's overalls, as Callie ducked her head to keep the wind out of her face, did not smell or feel as bad as the back of Ron's cracked leather jacket.

As she lifted her head to see where they were, the wind stung cold and raw against her face. Riding through the wood, where the trees leaned inwards to greet each other, the tops of the beeches were wildly agitated in the storm that was blowing up from the valley. As they roared out of the wood and turned the corner into the lane that led past the back of Mrs Oldcastle's house, a great barrage of rain came down in big drops like hail, and was all of a sudden a drenching torrent.

Steve turned into the back drive, and shut off the engine. No sign of a police car – yet. He pushed the bike under a spreading fir tree where it could not be seen.

At the side of the ivy-grown stable was a small fenced paddock in which Mrs Oldcastle put Harold out to graze, where she could see him from the house. The big lumbering cob was not there now, but tied up against the wall, with his head down and his tail tucked in against the rain, Callie and Steve could see the humped outline of Yaz's brown pony.

'She's here!'

There were no lights in the big gloomy house. Its creepered bulk loomed against the stormy sky, water streaming down the slate of the steep turret roofs, the line of chimneys ranged like a battlement.

The old lady must already be in bed. Asleep perhaps, with Yaz waiting somewhere in that darkened house for Mickey's signal to open the door and let him in.

Steve moved closer, crouching through the shrubbery in case there were eyes at any of the darkened windows, where the shades were all half way down, like lowered lids. Callie followed the white overalls, drenched by the wet bushes, one of her sodden pigtails in her mouth to stop herself squeaking when a branch cracked in the storm, or the sudden swaying of a loose creeper looked like someone moving by the house.

At the back of the house, near the kitchen door, was where Ron had told them to look for the dog door. Callie and Steve crept out of the shrubbery, stood upright to get their bearings and made a dash across the soaking lawn to crouch again among the dustbins, listening, waiting, holding their breath for movement inside the house.

Between the back doorstep and the kitchen window from which Mrs Oldcastle had seen poor Kingfisher desecrating her sprouts, they found the little dog door, a narrow flap on a hinge that looked much too small for anyone but a four-year-old to wriggle through.

'Go ahead,' Steve whispered.

'I can't.'

'Yaz did.'

Callie knelt to measure herself against the opening. 'It's too small.'

'Make yourself smaller.' Steve crouched beside her. 'Shrink into your bones. Suck in your breath.'

Kneeling among the eggshells and orange peel that some marauding dog had pulled out of an overturned dustbin, Callie leaned the top of her head against the flap and pushed. The worst part was sticking her head into an unknown room where anything might be lurking. She shut her eyes and pushed her head through, waiting for a blow, the lash of a cat's claws, the barking rush of a dog.

Silence. The ticking of a clock. Nothing else. She opened her eyes. In the faint glow from a pilot light on the gas stove, she saw the cluttered kitchen, dishes and packets of food and saucepans everywhere as she turned her head from side to side, a cheap alarm clock marking time among the shelves full of heavy china on the dresser.

Her head was in, but her shoulders were not. She knelt there like a sinner in the stocks, then pulled out her head.

'I can't get through.'

'Go sideways.'

The flap door was slightly longer than it was wide. By lying down on the wet garbage, Callie could just squeeze her shoulders into the opening. She stuck. For a moment of suffocating panic, she could not go backwards or forwards, then strong hands pushed against the bottom of her Wellingtons, and she was catapulted on to the kitchen linoleum with a dish of stale cat food at eye level, and the alarm clock counting her out.

When the motor bike swerved through the gate and roared off down the hill, Dora could not stand it. If there had been room for three, she would have gone with them. The waiting was going to be unbearable.

The yard was quiet, except for the soft hiss of the steady rain on the cobblestones, and the familiar stamp and blowing of horses busy with their hay. Now that Ron had gone into the

534

house, Dora realized that with all the panic about Yaz, they had forgotten poor Pony, so innocently involved, and perhaps tied up somewhere by his reins without shelter.

There was a way she could get into the drama. She could take Robin and go and look for the pony.

She took his tack out again and saddled him in the dark, adjusting girths and buckles quickly by feel, since she knew the feel of everything about him so well.

As she leaned over the half door to lift the latch, she saw that the back door of the house was open and a shaft of yellow light lit the rain slanting along the path. Slugger sloshed into the yard with a sack over his head, calling for her.

'In here!' Dora stood in front of Robin, so that Slugger would not see that he was bridled.

'What you doing, girl? You spend more time in that stable than you do in the house. Where is everyone? Ron gave me some garbled tale. He's in a state.'

'They went out for a bit.' Dora did not want to embroider a tale that might be different from Ron's.

'Where to? 'Ere.' The old man moved closer, lifting the sack to peer. 'What's that horse got a bridle on for?'

'I'm taking him out.'

'In the dark? It's pouring of rain.'

'Listen, Slugger. Something's up. I can't tell you now, but I promise I will later. Steve and Callie are out somewhere, and I've got to go too.'

'You've not then.'

He put his hand on the door, but Dora pushed it open, led Robin out and climbed quickly on to his back.

''Ere,' Slugger said, as she turned away. 'You can't do that. I'm in charge and I say you can't. 'Ere!' he wailed, as Robin slithered over the cobbles and clattered under the arch. 'I'm in cha-a-arge!'

27

CALLIE scrambled to her feet. Cautiously, feeling her way from chairback to table, along the edge of the cluttered table, and from chairback to counter to wall, she reached the doorway. On the other side, away from the faint glow of the pilot light, the passage was very dark.

She stood in the doorway, peering into what seemed to be a black tunnel, and whispered, 'Yaz?'

Ahead of her, the house settled into the night, with creaks and tiny tickings.

'Yaz?' She had no idea where Yaz would be. Very slowly, feeling her way in and out of the ridges of the wall panelling, she made her way down the black passage. On her right, a wide staircase rose. As her eyes grew more accustomed to the dark, she could dimly see carved bannisters, and ascending beyond them a series of portraits in heavy gilt frames.

She reached the bannister post and put her hand on its smooth acorn shape. Did she dare turn on a light? What was it like to get shot with an air gun? There were two wide doorways on her left, which probably meant switches between. Ahead of her, a high square hall stretched away on either side, a grandfather clock ticking, much too slow, vast shapes of heavy furniture looming, urns, great vases, candlesticks, obese lamps. It was like groping through a museum. Ahead of her was the double front door, with coloured glass on either side, but almost no light coming through on this wet black night, only a finger of ivy tapping. Outside, the wind made organ noises in the gutters, and the trees rushed with sound. By the wall, a man waited for her, with his arm outstretched.

Callie could not run. It was like a dream where you are rooted. When the waves of fear subsided, she saw that the man was rooted too. It was not a man. It was a suit of armour, one jointed steel arm held stiffly out with a silver tray wedged between the gauntlet fingers.

What other terrors lurked in wait for her in this ghastly mausoleum? Suddenly Callie could not bear the unknown darkness any longer. She stretched out her hand to the wall between the doorways, and as her fingers found the switch, a hand was clasped over hers, and her scream was stifled by another hand across her mouth.

It was Yaz's hand. It smelled of the pony. Yaz's voice breathed huskily, 'Shut up, or I'll kill you.'

She dragged Callie through one of the doorways and shut the door softly before she took her hand from Callie's face.

'Get out!' Callie whispered. 'They've got Mickey. You've got to get out of here.'

'Has he talked?'

'I don't know.'

Yaz breathed an oath that would horrify the parents of Joan. Moving like a silent cat, she opened the door again, stuck her head out into the passage, listened, then stepped out.

Callie was more clumsy. Following Yaz, she tripped over a stool, reached out to save herself, and pulled a picture off the wall.

The noise was deafening in the silent house. Yaz slid back into the room, grabbed Callie's wrist, and froze.

A distant yapping became louder, as a door opened upstairs, and the dog's nails rattled on the floor.

'Who's that?' The voice of Mrs Oldcastle, not old and trembly, but strong and unafraid. 'Who's there?'

The dog was barking itself into a frenzy at the top of the stairs.

'Shut up, you fool,' muttered Mrs Oldcastle. She evidently grabbed it by the collar, because it choked on a bark and began a strangled whine. 'Is there someone there? Well, *is* there?' she demanded impatiently, as if almost hoping that there was. 'Because if so, I have to warn you that I am armed.'

Yaz's nails dug into the flesh of Callie's wrist. They held their breath as the creak of a stair told them she was coming down. One creak. Two creaks. Three creaks. Very slowly. Not from fear. From rheumatism. Four creaks.

'Hullo there,' the old lady said in a conversational, matter-of-fact voice. They could hear her breathing, with little laboured whistles, somewhere in the darkness above their heads. 'Well then,' she said to the dog, or to herself, 'I was dreaming. *That's* all right then.'

She must have loosened her hold on the dog's collar, because it let out a sharp bark, muffled as she put a hand round its nose.

'Shut up, I told you. You're dreaming too. You're as big an old fool as I am.'

The stairs creaked again, more heavily, as she plodded back up to bed.

Yaz let go of Callie's wrist, but it felt as if her nails were still there. Without looking to see if Callie followed, she fled down the passage, Callie creeping behind in her Wellingtons, with her hand tracing the panelling.

In the kitchen, Yaz went on her knees, turned sideways and slipped easily through the flap of the dog door. Outside, she gave a little yelp of surprise, and Steve muttered something.

It was easier going out than coming in. Callie must have shrunk from fear. She fell on her face among the garbage, scrambled up and followed Steve and Yaz in a dash across the lawn to the shelter of the dripping shrubbery.

Steve gave Callie a nod as she joined them. He looked grim and rather angry, which meant he had been worried. Callie wanted someone to thank her, to say, 'Well done', or, 'Good old Cal', or something like that. But Yaz never would, even though Callie had saved her neck, and Steve did not look as though he felt like it.

Under the fir tree, Yaz swung a leg over the back of the motor bike, but Steve pulled her roughly off.

'You go back the way you came,' he said.

Steve lifted Callie on to the back seat. He wheeled the bike out on to the driveway, swung his leg over and started the engine. Callie put her arms round his waist, laid her head against his broad back and clung on exhaustedly, as he moved away fast.

28

WHEN Callie climbed off the motor bike at Follyfoot, she staggered, feeling as old as Mrs Oldcastle, and twice as feeble. She realized that she was shivering. Had been shivering for quite a long time, probably since that nightmare moment which she would never forget for the rest of her life, when she put out her hand for the light switch and another hand covered it.

Crossing the yard, she went automatically to Cobby's stable. His head with the bold white blaze was already over the door, his nose moving in a silent greeting, his rubbery lips searching her shaky hands for horse nuts.

'I was on a crusade, Cob.' She laid her tired head against his nose.

'Come on, Cal, into the house.' Steve took her hand. As she passed Robin's box, she noticed that the big bay horse was not there. Dora must have turned him out before she went to bed.

Dora was not in bed. She was not in the house at all. In the kitchen, Slugger was asleep in the rocking chair with his feet on the back of a snoring dog.

He opened his eyes when Steve and Callie came in, rubbed them, said 'Hullo' sleepily and smiled without his teeth, then remembered that he was angry with them.

'Pack of lunatics,' he fumed, looking along the mantelpiece for his teeth. 'Dashing off in the rain in the middle of the night like a bunch of wild apes . . .'

Callie went to kneel in front of the dying fire, holding out her stiff hands.

'Did Ron tell you anything?' Steve asked.

'Ron don't tell nobody nothing and I wouldn't believe it if he did. He rang up some pal of his who came to fetch him in a car that smelled of burning mattresses and sounded like the end of the world.'

'Where's Dora?'

'She took off too, the worst of the lot, taking that horse out in the pouring rain with his belly full of oats.'

'Where to?'

'Wherever you was, was all she would say, as she goes haring off and nearly knocks me down. I'm going to write to the Colonel. "It's not good enough," I'm going to say, "Colonel, it's not good enough the way they carry on like a crowd of murderous barbarians the moment your back is turned."'

'I'm hungry,' Callie said in a small voice, from where she crouched by the fire.

Slugger had been too busy raving to notice that she was on the edge of collapse.

'Ah, look at you.' He bent in a motherly way and put the wet straggles of hair back from her pale face. 'Your teeth are chattering. Here's a fine thing.'

He pulled the plaid rug from the back of the sofa and wrapped it round Callie and put her in the rocking chair.

'And what's this?' Rubbing her hands, he saw the red marks of Yaz's nails on Callie's wrists. She pulled them under the rug, and he said, 'Now you sit there, and old Slugger will get you a bowl of hot soup, then it's upstairs to a nice hot bath, and we'll tuck you up in bed and let you off school tomorrow.'

'It's a holiday,' Callie murmured, and fell asleep before he brought her the soup.

She woke as a rush of wind and rain came in at the back door with Dora.

'What a night!' Dora pulled off her soaked anorak and dropped it in a puddle on the floor. 'But Rob and I got Pony back all right. He leads like a dream.'

'Oh poor Yaz.' Steve laughed. 'How did you think she was going to get home?'

'I didn't,' Dora said. 'I was thinking about the pony.' She raised her head like a scenting dog. 'I smell soup.'

Slugger got between her and the stove. 'Not till you tell me what's been going on.'

'It's done with now,' Steve said. 'You'd better not know. You wouldn't like it, and you'd feel you had to tell the Colonel.'

'Because you're in charge,' Dora said sweetly. 'And the Colonel wouldn't like it either.'

Slugger sniffed. But he turned to the stove and ladled out a big bowl of soup for her.

'Come on, me old Cal.' He got Callie up, blanket and all, and helped her out, with his good arm round her. When they got to the door, he turned and said, 'And I suppose I'd better not ask where that Yaz is.'

'That's right,' Dora said. 'Better not.'

Yaz did not come back that night, nor the next day. They did not go to look for her. Ron turned up half way through the morning.

The farmer was delivering hay. Steve and Dora were helping to stack the bales in the high loft at the end of the barn.

'Get up here.' Steve looked down as Ron came into the barn. 'You're hours late.'

'Went to the village and got the letters for you.' Ron always had an excuse. 'Bills mostly.'

'Anything from the Colonel?'

'Dunno. There was an airmail letter, I think. I put it all in the house. Where's Yaz?'

'Disappeared.'

'What happened last night?'

'Everything's all right,' Steve said. 'No thanks to you. How on earth did you get mixed up in a mess like that, against someone like Mrs Oldcastle?' He glanced behind him, but the farmer was outside on top of the load.

'I told you,' Ron said. 'She's got it to give. She didn't want to give nothing, that time I asked her, did she? So it was doing her a favour, in a way, helping her to do us a good turn.'

'*Us?*' Dora's face appeared at the edge of the loft.

'Yeah – Follyfoot. All I been hearing since goodness knows how long is poor, poor, poor, can't pay the feed bills, can't take in no more horses, got to have Slugger put down. Mickey offered me a cut of the take see, if I'd help him by hiding Yaz. So as I knew how bad we needed the money –'

'But not stolen money,' Dora said quickly. 'Ron, how could you?'

'I thought you'd be proud of me.' Ron looked up at the surprised faces of Dora and Steve, hanging down above him from the floor of the loft. 'I did it for Follyfoot!'

29

Yaz did not come back.

'I'm glad,' Dora said, 'except for not knowing where she got Pony. It must be agony to lose a good pony like that. Well, any pony,' she corrected, so as not to insult the ancient shetland, who was browsing blindly about on the lawn, with his forelock half way down his nose, a legless mass of fur in his winter coat. 'But Pony has obviously been someone's friend. They must be going through hell.'

At the word 'hell' a memory surfaced in Steve's brain. *My daughter will give me hell, you know how it is.*

'Lady Dillingham Joynes,' he said aloud.

'What about her?'

'It's just possible. Nondescript, she said. Scruffy. But if she's got all those high class horses, her standards might be different. And if Yaz came up the valley from the canal through Locksley and round by Grymsdytch, she just might. . . .'

In the Colonel's study, the telephone was half smothered by a jumble of letters and bills and magazines and catalogues that had been dumped indiscriminately on his desk. He liked to sort them out himself when he came back, so that he did not have to read all his bills together, or all the pamphlets about hoof dressing and 'Revolutionary new intestinal agent for the early treatment of strongyles'.

Steve burrowed through the papers, sweeping some of them on the floor, and found the visiting card.

Her ladyship answered the telephone, 'High Pastures,' high in her high nose.

'Mrs – er, Lady Dillingham – er, Joynes?' Steve began, his voice rising to a croak.

'Ah-yaas?'

'That pony you were looking for.'

'Ah-yaas?'

'Are you still looking?'

'Who is that?' she asked suspiciously.

'This is Steve, at Follyfoot. You asked me to keep a look out.'

'Don't *tell* me there's any news!'

'That's why I'm ringing,' Steve said patiently. 'We've got – er, found a pony. He doesn't exactly match what you said. Brown or dark bay, he is, rather good looking. Two white socks and a small star. An old crescent scar on the off quarter.'

'Say no more. That's where it got kicked by one of my thoroughbreds. They absolutely can't stand ponies, you know what it is. Where did you find it?'

'Oh – wandering about.'

'It's been gone for ages. Must be in dreadful shape. My daughter will kill me.'

'He looks pretty good,' Steve said. 'He may have been taken in by someone who took care of him, and then got out again.'

'It's too sickening the way people simply *hijack* other people's livestock, and never dream of telling the police – not that *they're* any use. Please bring the pony over at once,' her ladyship said imperiously. 'Have you got a van?'

'Battery's dead,' Steve said. 'I'll lead him over.'

'And my van is gone for a few days collecting some yearlings. If you'll lead that little wretch over, I'll pay you for your time.'

'I don't want that,' Steve said, and quickly regretted his pride, looking at all the bills on the desk.

.   .   .   .   .   .

It took him about two hours, riding Cobby and leading the pony.

High Pastures was an impressive affair. A large brick Georgian house with a Jaguar and a Mercedes in the drive, white-fenced pastures, and long stable blocks of immaculate loose boxes on two sides of a yard that looked as if it must be swept every five minutes.

As Steve jogged in at the gate, clipped horses in green and yellow rugs challenged him and the ponies over the newly painted half doors. Pony said nothing. Cobby flung up his square head with its blind eye and gave back the challenge as proudly as if he were not wearing hairy heels and an untrimmed mane and tail.

A girl in a grooming smock came out of one of the boxes and said, 'My God, it's Scruffy. What have you been up to, you bad boy?'

'He's been all right,' Steve said.

'Of course he has, he's always all right.' The girl took the rope to pull the pony away from Cobby, whom he liked. 'Come on, the boss won't half play war with you.'

'Is that the boy with the poneh?' Lady Dillingham Joynes came through an evergreen arch from the garden in a tweed suit like a man's with trousers flaring over glove-tight boots. 'Funny thing,' you just "happened" to find him. I've heard some tales about that Collywobble place, or whatever you call it. The Colonel is mad as a hatter.'

'The Colonel's away,' Steve said, 'and the pony wandered on to our land.'

'I suppose that one just wandered in too.' She cast a globular eye over Cobbler's Dream, not looking his best, with his winter coat a bit sweated up, and his thick red mane lying on both sides of his muscular neck. She put out a hand to touch him on his blind side, and he jumped. 'Bit nervous, isn't he?'

546

'He's blind on that side.'

'Not a bad looking sort,' her Ladyship said, 'under all that wool.'

'He looks familiar,' the girl groom said. 'I've seen that pony before. I've seen him at shows.'

'Open pony jumping,' Steve said, 'before he got blinded. Nothing to touch him.'

'Cobbler's Dream!' Lady Dillingham Joynes exclaimed. 'He won the county championship, before those pushy people with that ham-fisted daughter bought him. I used to know them slightly. Not socially, you understand. There was an accident, wasn't there? And then some boy they'd tried to help stole the pony, and –' She looked up at Steve sharply. 'Was that you?'

'Me? Oh no.'

Steve put on his innocent look and lied, then wished he had not, when Lady D.J. said robustly, 'I was damn glad he did it. It was a good bit of work, getting this good pony away from that little monster.'

The girl put a rope round Pony's neck, and gave Steve back his headcollar.

'Thanks for bringing him over,' her Ladyship said breezily. 'I'm vastly relieved. So please don't be stuffy, dear boy.' She took a ten pound note out of the pocket of her tweeds, rolled it up and tucked it through the browband behind Cobby's ear. 'I *have* heard some tales about your place.' She smiled, and looked quite different. 'And I like what I hear.'

Yaz never did come back. She had disappeared for ever, as strangely as she had come.

Much later, long after the Colonel and Anna had come home, a letter came 'To all you lot', in a careless, scrawled handwriting, without a return address. Inside was a small passport-size photograph out of a machine, a child's narrow face, framed by long falling dark hair.

'This is what I used to look like. Will again, when my hair's grown out and the colour grown back in. I got a lift in a car that night. It was going towards where I live, so I thought I might as well go home, cuz I was hungry. I'm back at school now, what a drag. So wot else is new? I may stow away on a boat to Canada. I've got this friend, she knows a person who would give us jobs cooking in a lumber camp.

'Thanx for everything. Luv Yaz.'

30

THE storm that had blown so fiercely on the night of Callie's crusade, had not gone away. It was only going round in circles. Some time later, it came back with full force, and dumped four inches of snow on the hills.

When they were turned out in the morning, the horses went wild with joy. Even the very old ones bent their stiff knees and flopped down with a grunt to roll in the exhilarating whiteness, getting up with icing on them to lurch away with feeble bucks and squeals.

Robin, who had been used to deep snow in America every winter, rolled thoroughly, over and back and over, squeaking the snow beneath him, galloped in a trail of smoke down to the far fence, stopped, snorting, with his head and tail up like a stallion, then dropped his head and pawed at the snow in a businesslike way to get at the grass underneath.

The snow had been the storm's last message. The sun was out in a sparkling sky, and two days later, the snow had melted. It was almost like spring, although winter was only beginning. Dora grew restless. The routine of the work of the farm seemed dull after the excitement of the Yaz adventure.

'Let's do something,' she urged Steve. 'Let's go somewhere. Another big ride.'

'Not with all those kids and ponies,' Steve said.

'All right, just us. Let's go a long way. Somewhere we've never been.'

They decided to ride up into the hills towards the sea, stay the night with an uncle of Dora's who had a farm, and then back across the corner of the moors.

Slugger had been to the hospital to have his plaster cast off, and was able to use his two arms again. Callie recruited some horse-mad girls from school to help with the work. Ron swore on his life - 'for what that's worth' - to turn up on time, even on Sunday. Scared by the hazards of the Yaz affair, he also swore that he was going to stay away from Mickey and the coal yard gang. 'Better to die of boredom than be shot by Mrs Oldcastle.'

The long ride was lyrical and wonderful. Steve and Dora left very early in the morning, clattering through the village while everyone was still asleep. When little Toby at the pub heard the hoofs, he opened the window of his room under the roof, leaned out and shouted, 'Where you going?'

'A long way!'

'You coming back?' In Toby's insecure world, anything might happen. His father or his mother took off from time to time, after fights. He never knew when people might disappear.

'Back in two days!' Dora shouted.

The window below Toby's was flung open, and the furious red face of his father looked out with his hair and beard on end. 'Stop that row and let people get some sleep!'

'Good morning!' Dora waved happily, and they trotted on. Surely the whole world would not mind waking up if they could share in this happiness.

They rode all day, over the broad top of the hills, and down a long wooded slope, out to flatter land, where the wind had some salt in it, coming over the wide pastures from the sea.

The light was going from the sky and the warmth from the air, as they came to the farm where Dora's Uncle Fred had lived for years. He was her favourite uncle, the one her family did not think much of, because he had never achieved the kind of things they thought were important.

He was poor and shabby, barely scraping a living off the land he had bought long ago when he brought his new wife to live here. He had done quite well, but he only had a couple of shire horses now, and a few cows that he kept more because they were old friends than because they gave a lot of milk. By renting some of his grazing, and with his chickens and vegetables and big apple orchard, he just had enough to live on.

Since his wife died, Uncle Fred had slowed down, and was letting things go peacefully to pieces. He lived like a hermit in the kitchen, with the other rooms shut up. His bed was at one end of the low-beamed room, an ideal arrangement, since he could go to bed with the fire still burning.

After Uncle Fred's stew, which was full of onions and carrots and turnips and lumps of good fat bacon, they went out to look at the horses.

They had stabled Robin and Miss America in the huge barn, where Uncle Fred kept his cows and goats in deep litter. They found the horses standing close together at one end of the barn, as if this were their first day at school, watching the somnolent cows from a distance.

'Perhaps we should have some cows at Follyfoot.' Dora relished the milky, acid smell of the cows, who were lying down with their girlish lashes lowered.

'You can have those two old girls, if you like,' Uncle Fred said. 'The yellow ones. Neither one of them has been in milk for a long time. Too old to calve any more, they are.'

'Why do you keep them?'

'Because they've always been here, I suppose.'

Dora squatted down and lifted the cow's heavy head, with its square slobbering nose and dished-in face. Chewing cud, the cow opened big lustrous eyes and looked at her without the curiosity of a horse.

'Would they go in a horse box?' she asked

'Dora,' Steve warned.

'Why not? The Colonel said no more horses, but –'

'He didn't say no more cows. I know. But we don't need two more hay burners.'

Dora patted the knob of curls at the top of the cow's head. 'I wish . . .'

'I used to wish I had money,' Uncle Fred said sensibly, 'but I didn't get any, so I stopped wishing. That didn't get me any either, but it saved me a lot of energy.'

The horses went even better on the way home. Miss America flagged a bit on the last few miles, but Robin was stepping out as bold as ever, his ears keen, his large blue eye taking in every aspect of the scenery. On a ride, he did not behave as if it was just a job. He seemed to enjoy himself as much as Dora did.

It was dark when they got home, and there were lights in the stable.

Callie came running out, as if they had been gone for weeks, followed more slowly by Slugger. She looked over the horses critically, and led Robin to his loose box, where she had put down a deep, clean bed.

'How was your Uncle Fred?' she asked.

'He's nice,' Dora said. 'We slept in the kitchen on mattresses on the floor, because the rest of the house was so cold. He's got cows and chickens and goats and a pig and some pigeons and two dogs and a pack of mangy cats. He wants to give us two old cows. Do you think they would travel all right in the horse box?'

'Don't listen to her,' Slugger called from Miss America's box next door. 'There's not going to be one new animal at this farm when the Colonel gets home next week.'

'Well, that's a pity,' Callie said, going over Robin with a stable rubber, 'because there's a girl in my class, her mother's sending her away to school because she's unmanageable, and she asked me if we could take her pony.'

'No.'

'It's a show pony, and it'll get unmanageable too, if there's no one to ride it.'

'Forget it.' Slugger came into the doorway, carrying Steve's saddle. 'And you forget cows, Dora, and goats and pigs too, while you're at it. Please everybody, please do try not to take in anything, beast or human, before the Colonel gets back.'

31

WHEN the Colonel and Anna flew back, they were to stay one night with the Colonel's brother near the airport, where they had left the car.

That night, the telephone rang late.

'Colonel!' Dora said. 'Oh, it's good to hear your voice.'

The voice sounded rather nervous. 'Yes – hm – ha –' he always did badly on the telephone. 'And yours, my dear. I – er, look – listen, is Steve there?'

'He's in his room. Shall I get him?'

'Don't bother. Give him a message, will you? Ask him to – er, well, to – er –' He was doing even worse than usual '– to bring the horse box,' he ended in a rush.

'What for?'

'Oh, I – er, I've got some stuff to bring home.'

What on earth could it be? The Colonel did not normally go round Italy collecting antiques.

It couldn't be a horse.

It was. When Steve came home with the Colonel, Cobbler's Dream called out a greeting from the field. Something of the same species answered from inside the horse box.

Dora, Callie and Slugger started towards it from various corners of the farm.

The Colonel looked out of the window, with a cheerful grin on his tanned face.

'Colonel –' Slugger began.

'I know,' he said. 'I know. But yesterday when I was with my brother, he told me about this – er, this sort of pony he'd heard was being kept in a filthy shed near his house. Belonged to a junk dealer, but his legs have gone west. He can't be driven any more, but the junk man seemed to think he could. So, I – er, don't you see – bought him.'

'Quite right,' said Dora, and Callie said, 'Oh good,' and Slugger said, 'Of course you did.'

Callie opened the side door of the box and went in to untie the pony. Steve and Dora let down the ramp of the box, and a sorry specimen of junk dealer's pony tottered out backwards, with broken feet and swollen joints, pitifully gone over at the knees, with a ribby pot belly hanging like a hammock from his starved hip bones.

The Colonel dropped his arm across Slugger's shoulders, and they stood side by side and watched Callie lead the pony slowly across the yard, back legs wobbling like loose wheels, his long ears flicking bravely back and forward to the new sights and sounds.

Steve took Spot out of his box, and led him down to double up with his pal Hero, both veterans of the circus. Callie took the pony into Spot's box, where he staggered straight for the empty manger.

'Bran mash?' Dora asked the Colonel.

'With a bit of linseed and molasses – only a handful of oats for now. And you may as well start the vitamin extract right away.'

Slugger sighed under the Colonel's arm.

'It's just that we've been so careful,' he said. 'I was so proud of not having any new customers when you came home.'

'So you should be,' the Colonel said. 'More room for this poor fellow. Don't worry.'

'It'll be all right,' Dora said, going off to the feed shed. 'It always is.'

· · · · ·

When Dora took tea into the Colonel's study, she found him sorting through the mass of paper on his desk.

'Bills, bills, bills. It's hardly worth coming home.' Seeing Dora's face, he smiled quickly, and added, 'You know I don't mean that. It's marvellous to get home, even to all this mess. Looks as if one of the pups has been in here.' He bent to pick some envelopes off the floor. 'What's this? Here, it's for you. Haven't you seen it?'

The airmail letter Ron had brought the day after the Yaz adventure. By the time they had finished storing the hay, with scratched skin and dry, dusty throats, Dora had forgotten all about it.

It was from her friend Earl Blankenheimer in America. The regular amount he sent for Robin's keep. Regular amount! The figure on the cheque was much more than he usually sent. It had a comma and another nought tacked on.

'*Had a great bit of luck,*' his letter said. '*My firm got the contract to build the new country club, so I want Follyfoot to share in my good fortune.*'

'There you are, you see.' Dora handed the cheque to the Colonel. 'I told you it would be all right.'